STUCK IN Reverse

Bridge City Beats Book Two

STEPHANIE LOUISE

Contents

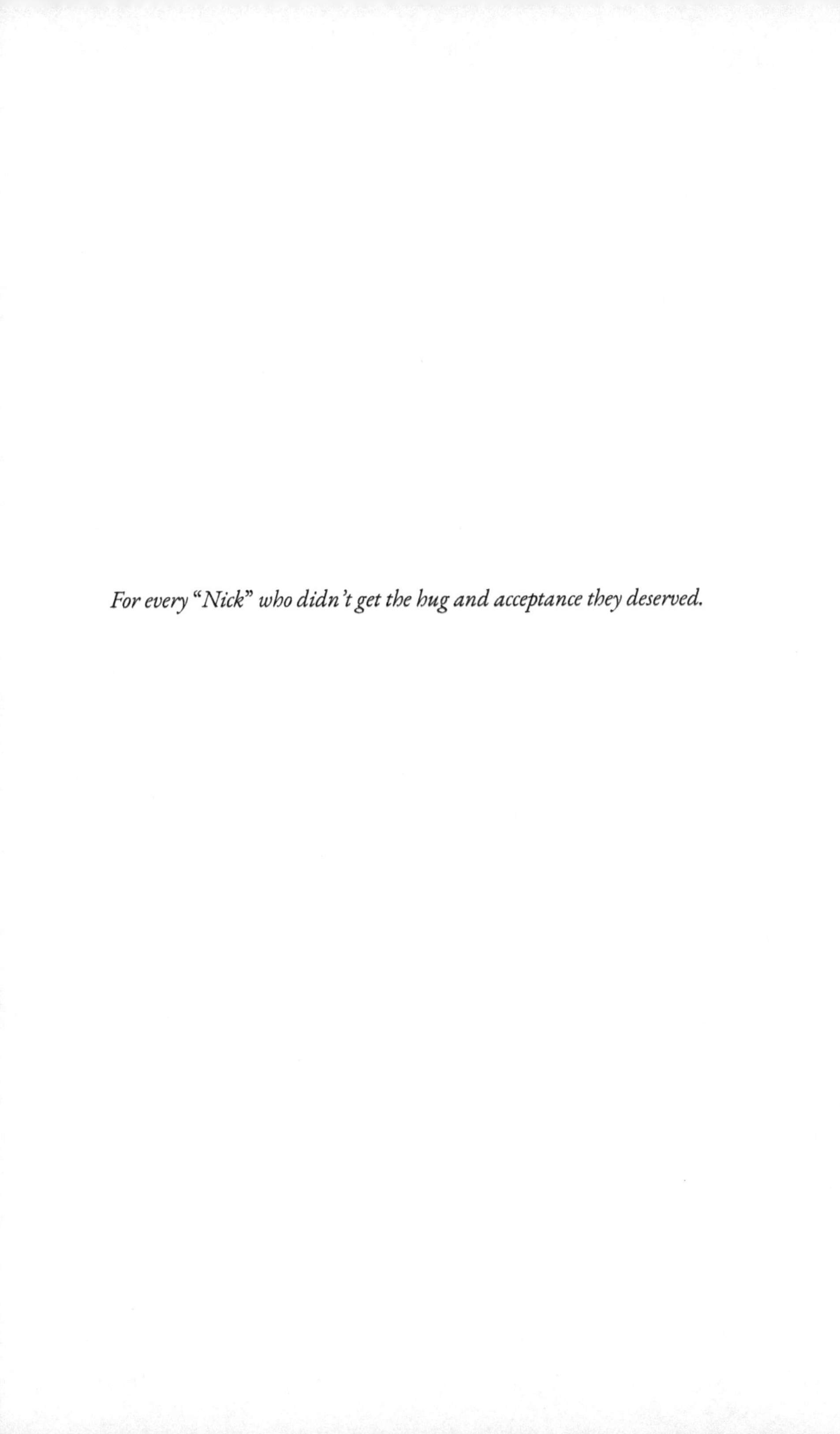

For every "Nick" who didn't get the hug and acceptance they deserved.

Content Warning

This book contains: profanity, explicit sex, threatened miscarriage (not graphic and off page), discussions of parent death (not graphic), physical and psychological abuse, slut shaming, a homophobic dickhead, a character coping with PTSD and depression, discussions of kidnapping, and substance abuse.

Author's Note

Two minor characters in *A Perfect Fit* have had their names changed in *Stuck in Reverse* to avoid confusion with similarly named characters. Trevor is now Luke, and Allison is now Jessica. They were never introduced on page, and only mentioned a couple of times, so it shouldn't be an issue. The current version of *A Perfect Fit* has been updated with the changes.

Hopefully my attempt to avoid confusion has not created any confusion. Thanks for reading.

Prologue

MATTHEW

August 1995

His psychiatrist's question hung in the air, menacing and heavy. Matthew shifted in his seat, the too-soft leather sofa squeaking with the movement.

"My last nightmare?" He swallowed the lump rising in his throat as memories flashed. "I was in the basement. My hands and feet were bound with duct tape. It was dark."

And cold. Really fucking cold.

"Who was with you this time?" Dr. Vega asked, her pen poised above her notebook.

Even after seven hour-long sessions, that book held few of his secrets. There was so much he couldn't bear to say to his brother or best friends, let alone a stranger.

Despite the sedative pumping through his bloodstream, his hands began to shake.

"Rafael."

Matthew tilted his head to his lap, his glasses slipping down his nose. He hated speaking his tormentor's name, as if saying it out loud would magically make the hulking wall of muscle with vacant, soulless eyes appear like Candyman or Bloody Mary.

"Only him this time?" she asked.

And Amy.

Always Amy.

He couldn't say *her* name at all.

Matthew gave a quick nod and glanced at the clock, willing the big hand to hurry the hell up on its climb to the twelve so this could be over.

"What was Rafael doing in the nightmare?"

Threatening me.

Taunting me.

Trying to kill me.

"I can't remember." Matthew sipped the chamomile tea she'd given him, his trembling fingers gripping the mug as the couch squeaked again. "It's fuzzy."

At the last appointment, he'd recounted the third day of being held captive. That same night, everything he described played out in his dreams. To avoid it happening again, that was all she was getting out of him today.

Dr. Vega made a *hmm* sound, and he could tell she wasn't buying it. He wouldn't have popped two Xanax an hour before if the memories weren't as vivid as when he woke up shaking and soaked with sweat.

"Is the medication helping?" She jotted something down even though he'd given her nothing. Maybe she worked on her grocery list when patients were being elusive pains in her ass.

Matthew thought about the question. The pills dulled his emotions, keeping him a few notches away from numb. Whether that was *helping*... That was questionable. But it beat what he felt before.

He nodded. "The panic attacks happen less."

Twelve weeks ago, he left the hospital thinking the worst was over. He'd almost died, but he was living, breathing, and grateful for the second chance. That first night home, the horrors he'd escaped from found him again in his sleep. He woke up gasping for air in the throes of a panic attack, certain he was dying.

"Good," she said, either taking more notes or adding butter and eggs to her list. "I'll approve another refill. I'd like you to keep a journal beside your bed to write down the details of your nightmares immediately after they happen. Before they go fuzzy."

No.

That wasn't going to happen.

Matthew's heart thumped against his ribcage, panic seeping through a tiny crack in the chemical-induced calm.

"And bring it to your next appointment so we can discuss the details," she added.

That wasn't happening either.

And he wasn't about to sit across from her one more goddamn time, explaining why he couldn't comply with her treatment plan while she stared and *hmm*'d at the pathetic, broken man he'd become.

"No problem," he said. A few warm drops of tea splashed over the mug's rim and onto his knee.

The next bottle of ninety pills would have to be enough.

Riding out the nightmares until they passed would have to be enough.

Because there was no way in hell he was ever doing this again.

I

Matthew

September 1995

"I'm going to be a fucking *uncle*?!" Matthew set down his vodka tonic and got to his feet.

Tyler and Charlotte shushed him in unison, their panicked eyes darting around the restaurant. Matthew used to think his rockstar brother was just paranoid about sneaky people gathering dirt on him wherever he went, but now, he knew better.

Feeling guilty for possibly spilling a secret that would make the tabloid rats cream their jeans, Matthew did his own visual sweep of the dim, candlelit room as he stood and made his way to the other side of the table. Fortunately, the nearest diners were at least twenty feet away, and no heads had turned.

"Congratulations," he whispered into Charlotte's ear, pulling her in for a bear hug.

When he drew back, he caught a flash of fear in her expression, but her wide, glowing smile meant she was more thrilled than anything. Of course, she was a little scared. Anyone would be at the thought of pushing an eight-pound, screaming red thing with a bowling ball head out of their body.

Matthew hugged his brother next while his date, Jessica, congratulated Charlotte and asked if she had names picked out. He'd expected a chill dinner spent catching up on the details of Tyler and Charlotte's recent tours. He wanted to tell them about the new merch he and his business partner designed for their brewery, and about the music space he wanted to create there to bring in more customers. And they finally had a chance to get to know his new girlfriend now that they were back in town.

Matthew finding out Tyler was going to be a father was a hell of a shock, but it was obvious he wasn't alone. It was written all over their faces that they hadn't seen it coming either.

Even though the baby wasn't planned, and the timing couldn't be worse for their careers, he knew what this meant to Tyler. Since ditching his psychotic ex-wife, he'd worked hard to leave his painful past behind, growing into a man who was ready to kick his next big dream—building a family—into high gear.

Matthew hugged tighter as a surge of conflicting emotions burned in his chest. While he was happy for them, he couldn't help feeling a sort of mourning over everything that would change. No more late nights spent backstage after shows, drinking beers and shooting the shit. Charlotte would stop coming over to share a pizza and laugh at stupid movies in their sweatpants.

Tears stung his eyes at the bittersweet realization that from that moment on, nothing in their tight little group would ever be the same.

"Aww…" Jessica put a hand to her chest. "Tears of joy. That's so sweet."

Matthew lifted his glasses and wiped his eyes before returning to his seat. He felt guilty for tainting the moment with selfish thoughts, but at least it didn't show on his face.

When he glanced across the table, Charlotte was looking at Tyler like their mother used to look at their dad. Matthew grinned, back to feeling nothing but happy for them.

He still couldn't believe that in three weeks, Charlotte, one of the best friends he'd ever had, was going to be his sister-in-law. And he was grateful that no matter how angry she got, she'd never attempt a triple homicide like his last one.

"It's early, so don't say anything to anyone," Tyler said. "Mom doesn't even know. We just couldn't wait to tell you."

"And Sandra and Amber," Charlotte added. "I told them this morning after the doctor's test confirmed it."

"Of course you did." Matthew laughed, not surprised her bandmates heard the news first. He could almost hear the chorus of excited shrieks that must've followed the announcement. "I'd say let's order champagne to celebrate, but you don't get to have any fun for a very long time."

Tyler looked at Charlotte, his eyebrow raising. "We're not lacking in the fun department, trust me."

"Amen to that." She pecked his cheek. "Also, don't be weird."

"Matthew told me your bands will be touring together in Europe next year." Jessica sipped her white wine. "How will that work with a baby?"

Charlotte exhaled a heavy sigh. "Well, since we've only known for a day, we're still figuring out the details. We'll probably hire a nanny at some point. Although, I predict my dad will beg for the job before we can even start looking."

"And I know bands that travel with kids." Tyler started tearing tiny pieces off his bar napkin and making a pile with the bits. "You can get a custom tour bus with a playroom, space for a crib, and everything else you'd need to keep everyone happy."

"Ty invited me to join them," Matthew said, "so I'm tagging along on the first leg."

"Oh." Jessica's eyebrows shot up. "That should be fun."

He stared at the shredded napkin. Was his brother nervous about the baby or something else? It must be overwhelming for him to know he'd soon be responsible for keeping a vulnerable little human alive who wanted to swallow Legos, hug strange dogs, and lick power outlets.

Fuck that noise.

Matthew thought about the two boxes of condoms in his apartment and made a mental note to restock.

He sat back in his chair. "You're going to be kickass fucking parents, guys."

It was a given. Tyler was only three and a half years older, but when their dad died, he took on that role. He made sure Matthew had clean clothes for school, checked his homework, and was always there to listen or offer advice while their mom was trapped in her grief. And there wasn't anyone as patient, kind, and fiercely protective as Charlotte. Their kid was lucky.

Tyler and Charlotte met each other's eyes, and their smiles grew. Her hand disappeared beneath the table, probably to rest on Tyler's leg. Since getting together four months before, they couldn't keep their hands off each other. The surprise Hall baby was proof of that.

Jessica nudged Matthew's elbow. "Don't forget to invite them to movie night at your new place."

He'd wanted to be the one to tell them that news, but it was fine. She was even more excited about the move than he was, so it wasn't surprising she'd beaten him to it.

"New place?" Charlotte swallowed the sip of water she'd taken, her eyebrows furrowed. "What did I miss?"

A lot had happened in the two months while she and Tyler were away on their respective tours—good and bad. As always, it was lonely when both bands toured at the same time, leaving Matthew back home without his brother and three of his best friends. With the trauma from the attack so fresh, this separation was the toughest yet. But regardless of how he felt, he always tried to keep their phone conversations light and neutral, knowing they needed to focus on their gigs, not stress about his stupid issues.

"I bought a condo in NoPo." Matthew cut into his steak and speared the piece with his fork. North Portland was his favorite neighborhood—full of smoky dive bars, vibrant street art, and used record stores. "Right off Mississippi, and close to work. I've only moved a few things in so far, but I'm doing movie night on Wednesday if you guys are free."

Now that his friends were all back in town, he was looking forward to the return of their group's longstanding weekly meetup for junk food and vegging out in front of the TV. Plus, it would be a chance for them to get to know Jessica better and for him to see how well she fit into that part of his world.

"Wow." Tyler's eyes popped wide, probably surprised Matthew hadn't mentioned it during any of their calls while Tyler was away. They'd talked a few times a week, but Matthew preferred to discuss major life events in person, mainly to see his brother's reaction. Tyler's face gave away more about his opinions than his words ever did, which was saying something. "Mom will be stoked. Owning your own place at twenty-four is fucking awesome. But you loved that apartment. What made you decide to do that?"

Matthew opened his mouth, but Jessica jumped in before he could speak.

"His brewery's doing better than ever," she said. "Time for him to move up in the world. He can't play video games on that stinky couch the rest of his life." She laughed, but everyone else stayed quiet.

The mood shifted in a way that made Matthew uneasy. He could sense the confusion and maybe even judgment about Jessica's bluntness coming from the other side of the table. While her phrasing wasn't always ideal, her intentions were good. She wanted him to reach his full potential, not be bogged down by old habits. He was sure they'd see it once they got to know her better.

Charlotte's salad-covered fork stopped halfway to her mouth. "Matty, you love video games. And that stinky couch. Are you sure?"

He took another bite of steak, chewing slowly. "After the attack, I felt stuck. Trapped. Like my apartment was my only safe place to hide." In those first weeks, he spent endless hours on his couch, stoned and staring at nothing. He'd found that the surest way to avoid waking up the terrible memories was to hide and stay as numb as possible. With all his closest friends hundreds of miles away, it was easy to sink into that pit without anyone noticing.

But Jessica took care of him in the hospital and knew what he'd been through. He tried keeping his damage from her while leaning into the pleasant distractions of a new relationship, but as they grew closer, she saw the truth. She did all she could to guide him out of the darkness, making him want to feel alive again.

"It's time to let that go and move forward," he said.

Jessica set her wine on the table and squeezed his hand. "I'm proud of you."

Matthew turned to her, grazing the soft skin of her jawline with his knuckle. "New woman, new place, new start." Her moss green irises slid to his face, the flecks of hazel at the edges sparkling as she smiled. She often said she saw potential in him that he didn't, and he was grateful she cared enough to nudge him in a positive direction.

"And new couch." Jessica laughed, her nose wrinkling. "The next one won't reek of pot."

Tyler and Charlotte exchanged a quick, odd look before returning to their dinners. Later, he'd ask them what it meant. For now, he was enjoying finally sitting down with three of his favorite people.

Now that his napkin was reduced to confetti, Tyler tapped an erratic beat on his water glass.

"You okay, bro?" Matthew asked. "You seem nervous tonight."

Tyler's fingers stilled. "I quit smoking. I feel like my fucking skin's crawling, and I can't stop fidgeting with shit."

Now, it all made sense. Tyler smoked at least a pack a day, so the withdrawals must be horrendous. Matthew wasn't looking forward to a few weeks of his brother being a grumpy asshole, but at least he'd be a healthier grumpy asshole.

"You made him quit!" Jessica raised her wine glass to Charlotte. "Good for you."

Charlotte shook her head. "It was his decision. I don't make him do anything but smile." She looked at Tyler, proving her claim.

"I'm proud to say I got Matthew to quit smoking pot." Jessica rolled her eyes. "Most people stop after college. It was time."

He caught Tyler and Charlotte flashing each other another look, but this one was easier to read. It had *is this bitch serious* written all over it.

They didn't have to understand the changes he was making or why. Jessica cared enough to encourage him to grow past comforting vices, and he was willing to try anything to become an even better version of himself than before the attack.

"I guess a lot has changed since we left." Charlotte swirled spaghetti around her fork. "I'm not sure if we can make movie night, but we'd love to check out your new place and say goodbye to your couch. You're not the only one with fond memories of it." She winked at Tyler.

Matthew's face scrunched. "What the hell did you freaks do on my couch?"

"Not *that*." Tyler smirked. "The night the brick was thrown at my car window, and I slept on your floor..." He wiped his mouth on his napkin and set it on the table. "Charlotte held my hand in the dark. And I kissed it." He took her hand and did exactly that. The diamonds on her finger caught the light from the chandelier above their heads. "I was finally starting to acknowledge my feelings for her, but I wasn't ready to take that leap."

"And I wasn't ready to be leaped on." Charlotte took another bite of spaghetti. "Not until I knew you were officially done with what's-her-face."

Jessica shook her head and frowned. "Ugh, Amy Carey."

Just hearing the name made Matthew's fists clench.

Amy Fucking Carey—former queen of Portland's underground music scene, Charlotte's ex-bandmate, Tyler's ex-wife, and co-star of Matthew's nightmares.

"When Matthew first came to the ER," Jessica continued, "I heard snippets of what happened, but I read all the details in the papers over the next few days. You're all lucky to be alive."

Usually, anxiety took hold whenever someone mentioned *that night*, but the good company, the vodka, and the two Xanax he'd taken that afternoon mostly kept it at bay. Instead of a full-blown attack, there was only a faint, manageable, yet annoying hum in the background.

"We have Warrior Woman to thank for that." Matthew grinned, his eyes drifting to the friend who saved his life. "I was too out of it to see what happened, but picturing Charlotte popping off three rounds into those assholes makes me want to buy her a fucking pony."

Matthew didn't see the shooting, but he was still conscious enough to hear it. The three loud bangs often appeared at the end of his nightmares, like a sudden, violent ellipsis on the last page of a horror story. But like an ellipsis, it was more of a *to be continued* than an ending, and there was always more where that came from.

Matthew drained the rest of his vodka tonic as his pulse kicked up.

"Roxy gives us all the shit and fur we can handle right now, but thanks." Charlotte shook red pepper over her plate. "And I'd happily shoot any other assholes who fuck with my family."

That widened Matthew's grin despite the anxiety creeping in. They were a family. His DNA was linked to the tiny creature growing in her belly, but even if it weren't, it would still be true.

Jessica dabbed the corner of her mouth with her napkin and set it in her lap. "As someone who helps save lives every day, I don't think I could ever take one."

Charlotte's slightly narrowed gaze flickered to Jessica's face and back to her pasta.

"No one really knows what they're capable of until someone they love is at risk." Charlotte pushed away her plate. "I hope you never have to find out."

There was a sudden tension between the women Matthew didn't fully understand. Hell, there was a lot about women he didn't understand. But he knew Charlotte well enough to recognize that she wasn't sold on his girlfriend. Jessica hadn't meant to offend anyone with that comment; she'd just spoken without thinking it through. A lousy first impression wasn't ideal, but if things progressed, there was plenty of time for the women to find common ground and learn to appreciate each other's quirks.

For now, it was better to move on.

Matthew grabbed a menu, scanning the back. "Anyone getting dessert?"

"Only if sugar cures nic fits." Tyler ran his hands through his dark hair, tugging at the roots.

"I know it's hard," Charlotte said with a sympathetic pout, "but you'll get through it. We'll grab some nicotine patches and gum on the way home."

"Good idea, baby." Tyler leaned over and kissed her forehead. "Hopefully, they'll make me less of a pain in your ass."

Charlotte grinned. "Fingers crossed."

It was impossible not to envy their connection. Matthew had been in plenty of intense, passionate relationships, but he'd never been in love. Around the five-week mark, things became too complicated, and he was ready to return to carefree bachelorhood with no one to answer to. But watching from the sidelines as Tyler and Charlotte fell in love made him realize what he was missing.

While it looked like a hell of a lot of work and came with the risk of having your heart shredded to bits like Tyler's napkin, he hoped to find it someday.

Two months in, it was too soon to know if things would go that way with Jessica, but it was possible. She was kind, hard-working, and ambitious as hell, so he'd be stupid to let her go. He didn't feel the intense spark Tyler and Charlotte felt for each other, but maybe it would take time to ignite.

"Are you from Oregon?" Tyler asked her.

Jessica shook her head. "I grew up in Florida. I'm still not used to the rain and the dark winters here, but I wanted to go to OSU, so here I am."

She was a registered nurse but starting medical school in the spring to become a surgeon. The fact made her seem way out of Matthew's league but also motivated him to grow up a bit. It was nice being with someone who challenged him to be a better version of himself instead of someone who wanted to use him for free concert tickets or to bum some weed.

"Rain's a little less dangerous than alligators." Matthew took her hand, entwining their fingers. "I'm glad you're here."

"I hope this isn't a rude question," Charlotte said, "but is Matthew the first patient you've dated?"

Jessica laughed while Matthew choked on the bite of steak he'd just taken. At least she knew the Heimlich maneuver if it came to that. "Yes, the first and only. I've been asked out a lot, but something sweet and genuine about him made me say yes. When he was in the hospital after the attack, we'd play Uno or chat during my breaks. He always apologized if he winced during an injection or spilled something. And he sent me flowers and a thank you card after he was discharged."

Charlotte smiled. "Nice work, Matty."

"Maybe I'm finally learning from my steaming pile of failed relationships." He hoped so. Jessica deserved a lot better than the guy who didn't always communicate well with the women he dated, made stupid decisions, or got bored and stopped calling.

The double doors to the kitchen burst open, and a breeze of oregano and garlic wafted to their table. The conversation stopped as the waiter refilled their waters. "Another vodka tonic, sir?" He picked up Matthew's empty glass.

"We're good, thanks." Jessica shook her head at the waiter, and his gaze swung awkwardly to Matthew before he walked away with the empty glass.

Matthew was stunned that she'd spoken for him, and when he glanced at Tyler and Charlotte through the curtain of his dark blond hair, he knew he wasn't the only one.

Jessica leaned close to his ear. "Not with your meds. One was pushing it."

Knowing what was coming next made him want that drink even more.

"Meds?" Tyler lowered his voice. "I thought you were off the anti-anxiety stuff. Is it something new?"

Matthew shrunk back in his seat under the weight of the scrutinizing eyes across the table. He'd told Tyler he stopped taking them so Tyler wouldn't worry while he was working. Medication meant Matthew was still struggling, and his selfless, protective big brother probably would've canceled his tour until he knew everything was okay. "Same stuff. I still need them sometimes. Don't make a big thing of it."

"Sorry." Jessica frowned. "I didn't mean to upset anyone. A nurse is never truly off duty, and I wouldn't want you to have any ill effects from mixing the two."

"Why would you take it today?" Charlotte's tone was soft. "Were you worried about something?"

"It's not like that." This wasn't how he wanted this dinner to go. One minute, they were asking questions to get to know Jessica better, and the next, the conversation took a sharp left into a muddy ditch. "I had a nightmare last night, and it makes the day easier if I take the edge off. I won't need them forever."

"You still have nightmares?" Tyler asked quietly, but Matthew still searched the room to make sure no one had heard.

"Sometimes." Blood rushed to his face, his pulse thudding in his neck. He felt guilty for downplaying it, but they had more important things to think about, especially now that they were going to be parents.

"It's only been three months since the attack," Jessica said. "Trauma that severe can take a considerable amount of time to heal."

"But you said things were getting better." Charlotte's eyes stayed on Matthew. "We wouldn't have left you if we'd known that wasn't true."

Matthew pinched the bridge of his nose, trying to tamp down his frustration. "I wasn't going to have you put your lives and careers on hold to babysit me, Charlotte. I'm fine." The lie burned on his tongue. "I'll be fine," he corrected.

"How often do you see Dr. Vega?"

Fuck.

He knew Charlotte would ask the question eventually, and she wouldn't like the answer. She recommended Dr. Vega because she'd helped Charlotte cope when Rafael was leaving threatening notes that nearly turned her into a hermit.

"She helped for a while." He averted his eyes, staring at a trail of breadcrumbs dotting the blood-red tablecloth. "But I stopped going two weeks ago."

"What?" Tyler stilled.

The edges of Charlotte's mouth tipped down. "Matthew, you need to be in therapy."

"We can talk about this another time." He picked up the menu, pretending to read the desserts while considering a trip to the bathroom to swallow another Xanax or two without anyone knowing.

"Matty..."

He slapped the menu onto the table. "It was making it worse, Charlotte. I'm glad she helped you, but spilling my guts to a stranger isn't what I need."

Charlotte shook her head. "How do you even know what you need?"

"Because it's not the first time I've had to deal with hard things. And like all the other bullshit I've struggled with, it'll get a little easier every day until it's finally behind me."

His resilience had been tested plenty. At six years old, he lost his father in a motorcycle accident. Then, he grew up with his mom's parade of losers disrupting their lives before ditching out. Three years ago, he found Tyler unresponsive on the floor from a heroin overdose. He thought his brother was dead, and that image still haunted him.

Add in a few handfuls of ugly break-ups and random disappointments, and he was left with the knowledge that time doesn't heal all wounds, but it always closes them enough to make them bearable.

"You have PTSD, not a head cold," Charlotte snapped back.

"Shh…" Tyler touched her arm. "We can talk about this later."

Matthew was too frustrated with Charlotte's response to let it go. "You know damn well that's not what I—"

"Hey." Jessica took his hand, the touch helping to cool his temper. "I understand your concerns, but you guys don't need to worry about him anymore. I've been here to support him on the bad days, and I'm sure better ones are ahead."

With their disapproving grimaces, neither seemed convinced, but he hoped they'd let the subject drop.

"Sorry, Matty," Charlotte said. "I worry about you. We both do."

He nodded, taking a few deep breaths. "And I love you both, even when you're being massive pains in my ass."

They laughed, the tense mood finally lifting. He savored it while it lasted because there was no way Charlotte or Tyler would let the subject drop for good.

The waiter came with the check, and Matthew grabbed it before his brother could.

"Come on, I got it." Tyler reached across the table.

"Not this time." The dinner was Matthew's idea, and just because his brother was loaded didn't mean he had to pay every time they went out. He slid his credit card into the sleeve, and the waiter took it and walked off. "I'm glad you guys finally got to meet Jessica. She's already bought a killer dress for the wedding."

It was silky, black, and fell to her knees.

The first time she put it on, he nearly fell to his.

She smiled. "I hope I don't twist an ankle in the stilettos I got to match."

"My girl won't have that problem." Tyler aimed a crooked grin at Charlotte. "She's wearing Docs under her dress."

Jessica's eyebrows shot up. "Boots with a wedding dress?"

Matthew's head tipped back as he laughed. "That's easily the most Charlotte thing I've ever fucking heard."

Even in a fancy white dress, she couldn't resist adding a touch of punk rock.

The conversation stayed light as they said their goodbyes and walked to their cars, but Matthew couldn't shake the lingering anxiety from the tense conversation. He still had no interest in returning to therapy, but he hated disappointing his brother and Charlotte and making them worry.

He had to believe the day would come when he wouldn't need the pills anymore. Days and weeks would pass with no nightmares and the raw memories of the attack would fade into the background of his life as he moved forward.

Maybe healing would be easier now that they were back home. With familiar friends and family around, things might start feeling normal again. Maybe it would help him remember who he used to be because some days, he didn't even recognize himself.

In the meantime, Tyler and Charlotte needed to focus on the family they were building. They'd always been there for him, but he didn't want to be a burden that tainted the happiest time in their lives.

So, Matthew would work harder to hide his damage until there was nothing left to hide.

2

Amber

Amber's face had gone numb. "Europe. Co-headlining with Tomorrow Mourning. For six weeks." Was this what a stroke felt like? She didn't smell burning toast, so that was a plus. "Are you fucking with me?"

Sandra laughed as she thumbed through Amber's records, making her think her suspicion was correct. Her friend was about to get her curly red hair pulled if that was the case because it would be a pretty fucked-up joke, even for her.

"Nope." Sandra slid a Runaways album out of the crate and set it on the dresser. She wanted to borrow a few records to show her girlfriend the bands that influenced Killing Daisies. It was adorable that Sandra wanted to share that major part of herself and said a lot about how close they'd become. "Eliza told me this morning. She called your ass too, but Beth told her you were out getting your hair bleached."

Amber grumbled. *Thanks, Beth.* She'd give her sister hell later for not telling her about the call. They had lunch together after she returned from the salon, so it's not like there wasn't an opportunity to tell Amber to call her manager back to get the biggest news of her career.

"Holy. Fucking. Shitballs." She grabbed Sandra by the shoulders as reality sunk in deeper. "We're really doing this?"

"We're really doing this."

Amber screamed, and Sandra covered her ears, laughing.

"That's what I said! My bedroom window was open, and my neighbor thought I was being stabbed. Pretty sure he shit himself."

Excitement sparked from Amber's head to her Converse-covered toes. "Do you have any *idea* what this means?" *Bigger venues, better record deals, my wildest, most impossible dreams coming true...*

"Yeah, duh." Sandra shrugged her tiny shoulders. "It means a lot more people will be staring at us while we play—most of them dudes."

Amber's jaw hit the floor.

"Kidding!" Sandra laughed at her expression. "It's the big time, baby! We'll grow our fanbase. It'll be an instant boost to the stratosphere."

That was putting it mildly. Their first album got the tiniest blip of attention. Their second reached gold and earned them a sold-out Canadian and East Coast tour. The article from *Spin* framed on her bedroom wall predicted their third would go platinum. This tour with one of the biggest rock bands on the planet would basically ensure it.

If that happened, the life goal at the very top of her list would be achieved. A platinum record meant one million copies of their album were spinning in record players, CD boomboxes, and cassette decks all around the world. Nothing said *you've made it* quite like that.

The fact that it would be the ultimate middle finger to her father was a sweet bonus.

"I'm so fucking ready," Amber said. "For all of it."

She knew from being in Tyler's orbit that a surge in success would bring plenty of negatives too—the critics and haters would multiply, nosy paparazzi would come sniffing around their private lives, and the pressure to create and perform would intensify—but it would all be worth it.

Sandra went back to flipping through the records. "You should've been there when the guys invited Char and me onstage when we surprised them in L.A. Hearing a crowd that size go nuts for us was un-*fucking*-believable. I'm getting chills just thinking about it." She pushed up the sleeve of her purple cardigan and pointed at the goosebumps on her arms.

Amber was having too much fun exploring New York City to join her band-mates for the night in L.A. Later, she regretted missing out on an opportunity to perform with Tomorrow Mourning in front of tens of thousands. But in a few months, the dream first sparked when she was thirteen years old would finally come true.

A memory flashed of her younger self, closing her eyes as she practiced, imagining the roar of a crowd that paid to see her play. It took devoting half her life to her instrument, including three years of struggle and sweat with her band, to make it a reality.

"I still can't believe the guys are good with it." Amber collected the gum wrappers, lipstick-stained tissues, and phone numbers scribbled on bar napkins from the top of her desk and tossed them into the trash. "Why not pick a band closer to their level like usual?"

"Our Charlotte has a magical vagina," Sandra said, adding a Pretenders record to her pile. "And we're really fucking talented and earned it. Mostly the latter."

"Whatever the reason is, I'll take it." Amber screamed again as the excitement surged, clapping her hands and jumping on the balls of her feet. "We get to go to Italy! And France! And smoke hash in Amsterdam!"

Sandra cupped Amber's face. "Take a chill pill, Jill. We have an album release and all the hoopla that comes with it to handle first. Then, we'll have *a lot* of rehearsing before we hit the road. Our set has to be tighter than your mama's tooter, and we have ten months to make it happen. Plus, we have setlists to create and new equipment to buy, and we have to make sure Luke has all the old and new songs down. His basslines on a few of the new tracks have been a little shaky."

Their bassist joined the band only three months ago, but Luke had more talent in his pinkie nail than all his predecessors put together. There was no doubt he'd master those tracks long before the tour started in July, but Sandra was an expert at finding shit to worry about.

Amber's eyes rolled at the sudden buzzkill. "Can't you be screamy and excited with me for a damn minute before you start planning and organizing and all the other boring shit?"

Sandra's lips smashed together before a scream burst out of her. She wrapped her arms around Amber as they jumped up and down, laughing their asses off. The whole thing felt surreal. She wanted to pinch herself, but if she was dreaming, she sure as shit didn't want to wake up.

"That's more like it," Amber said, brushing a few blonde strands from her eyes.

Sandra turned back to the records, and her gaze caught on something beside the crate. "What's this?" She picked up the unopened letter that'd been sitting on Amber's dresser for two days, inspecting the front.

"Nothing." Amber snatched it and shoved it inside her top drawer, slamming it shut. In hindsight, she should've hidden it so her sisters wouldn't see it, but after reading the sender's name, she threw it like it'd burned her. Hell, she probably should've burned *it*.

"The postmark said Chicago," Sandra said. "Isn't that where—"

"Yup." Amber clenched and unclenched her fists. Anger threatened to trample her joy, but she refused to let it. He'd taken enough from her already. "I'm way too happy to talk about that right now. Drop it, or I'll drop you." She put her fists up, play-punching Sandra while they laughed.

Sandra gave her a light shove. "You don't scare me, Little Drummer Girl."

Amber scoffed. She was five foot eight and toned but curvy. She'd been called many things in her life—slut, cock tease, bitch—but never "little."

"Oh! And Matthew's joining us for a few cities." Sandra punched the air. "How fucking cool will it be to have the whole crew traveling together?"

Amber smiled. The backstage vibe was always better when Matthew came to their shows. And he was fun to sneak off and share a joint with. "I know he's always wanted to do a pub tour in London to sample their stouts."

"Fuck, beer's gross." Sandra shuddered. She pushed Amber's laundry pile aside and sat on the bed. "Especially when it comes with hints of coffee and chocolate or whatever."

"More for the rest of us. Speaking of which..." Amber beckoned Sandra to follow as she walked into the kitchen and grabbed a beer and a Zima from her fridge. "I swear, you and my sister Beth are the only ones who like these things." She handed Sandra the Zima.

"It tastes like lemonade and battery acid." Sandra popped her cap and took a swig. "What's not to like?"

"And *that* is why I'm handling the booze for Charlotte's bachelorette party."

Since finding out Charlotte was pregnant, they'd had to tweak the party plans. Drinking games were out. There'd be no riding the mechanical bull at the bar they were considering for the venue. But no matter what, they'd ensure their friend had a wild night of laughter, sexy gifts that made her blush, and a delicious array of mocktails.

Sandra held a finger in the air. "As long as I get to pick the strippers. We'll have one of each since Char's bi."

Amber laughed. "The stripper picking's all you, maid of honor."

"Ugh." She stuck a finger in her throat, pretending to gag. "Why does that title have to sound so antiquated and dull?"

"Would you prefer Queen of Bitches?" Amber laughed at Sandra's raised middle finger. "That's what we all call you behind your back." A selfish thought struck, and she took a long swig of beer before perching on a barstool at the kitchen counter. "Not to sound like an asshole, but won't a baby screw up the tour? Charlotte will be sleep-deprived, the kid will be screaming on the bus. She won't have time to hang backstage after shows."

Sandra pressed her lips together with a nod. "Some of it will suck, no doubt. The first time I see a shitty diaper on our bus, I'll be the one screaming. But Char wants this, and we're all family, so we'll make it work."

Before Amber could respond, her sisters, Beth and Kate, came through the front door, their arms loaded with grocery bags. They made it to the kitchen and plopped the bags on the counter.

"Hey, Sandra." Kate swept her strawberry blonde bangs out of her eyes. "What's shakin'?"

"1962 called," Amber deadpanned. "They want their lame-ass phrase back."

Kate scowled at Amber before digging into the grocery bags and putting away the eggs, bread, and milk.

"What's up with you girls?" Beth swiped Amber's beer and took a sip before handing it back. "Band shit or friend shit?"

Amber made a show of wiping the mouth of her bottle on her shirt. "Both. We just found out we're touring with Tomorrow Mourning next year."

Beth dropped a carton of strawberries, and they scattered across the kitchen floor like they'd sprouted tiny legs. "Are you *kidding*?"

"Oh, god." Sandra covered her ears. "I know what's coming."

Beth shrieked at a much higher pitch than Amber was capable of. Beth had been a massive fan of Tomorrow Mourning since their first album came out. She had every cassette, CD, and vinyl they'd ever released, along with various posters, patches, and T-shirts. Nothing was weirder than seeing your friend's face emblazoned across your sister's chest.

"You'll be trapped on a bus with Tyler Hall?" Beth fanned herself with a pack of corn tortillas. "You lucky bitches."

"Be jealous of Charlotte, not us." Sandra scoffed. "We'll be sleeping on cold bunks with headphones on while they're in the back, humping like bunnies."

Beth slapped the tortillas onto the counter. "That lucky bitch."

Kate picked up the package and inspected it. "You broke three of them, genius. No tacos for you tonight."

"Where's the tour?" Beth asked as she went back to putting away groceries.

"Europe." A wide grin ate up Amber's face as the last threads of disbelief vanished and the incredible, thrilling, gold-dipped and sprinkled-with-glitter reality fully sunk in.

Beth's head tipped back, and she groaned. "I click away on a keyboard all day, and you get to go to Europe with Mr. Sexy Rock God? Life is so fucking unfair."

Clicking away on a keyboard? Hardly. Beth was a regional manager for a multinational bank and was set to make six figures before she turned thirty next year. Kate was a family law attorney. Amber grew up in that house with four beautiful, overachieving sisters who each earned college degrees, went on to excel at their careers, and stayed out of trouble. Amber was a C student in high school because she only cared about two things—drums and boys. After graduation, she was too busy chasing a music career to consider college and too determined to make it to bother formulating a Plan B. With this upcoming album and tour, she finally felt like she wasn't choking on her sisters' dust as they raced far ahead.

Amber's nose wrinkled. "Please don't call him that. He's like our brother."

"If that's the case," Beth said with a smirk, "bring on the incest."

"You are truly disgusting." Amber grabbed a few groceries and put them away. "Please tell me you remembered my chunky peanut butter."

Kate put away the lettuce and shut the refrigerator door with her hip. "Gross. Everyone likes creamy except you, so you'll have to deal."

Amber's eyes rolled. *Fucking great.* Peanut butter seemed like such a minor thing, but she was tired of someone taking the last of the chips, sipping from her beer without asking, or using up her favorite shampoo without replacing it. And she wanted to have the things she liked always available—like chunky fucking peanut butter. With the fluorescent lighting, weird smells, and obnoxious Kenny G music, grocery stores were her own personal hell, otherwise, she'd just go herself.

Fortunately, the positives of living with her four sisters outweighed any negatives. There was always a shoulder to cry on and someone to ask for advice or a ride home. The comfort and familiarity of the house was a welcome refuge whenever the outside world kicked her square in the ass. Plus, the house was paid off, and all their names were on the deed, so she didn't pay rent. Between that, her band cash, and the drumming lessons she gave on the side, Amber had a very healthy savings account.

"I wonder if Matthew will bring his new girlfriend." Sandra took a long drink of her nasty clear liquor.

"I'm sure Amber would love that," Beth mumbled.

Amber jabbed an elbow into her sister's ribs. "Don't start."

Her sisters got off on teasing her about the guys in her life, no matter how platonic the relationships were—one of the delightful "perks" of being the baby of the family. The year before, after a round of shots with Kate, she made the mistake of admitting to having a crush on Matthew. Ever since, her sisters poked her with it like it was their favorite new hobby.

"It's not a secret you have a thing for Matty." Sandra sat at the kitchen table. "If I were straight, I'd climb him like a fucking maple tree. He's awesome."

"Yeah, he's awesome. And now he's with Jessica and says he's happy with her." Amber sipped her beer. It tasted like an ale Matthew made every spring. Something about hops ripening in March. His shop talk was usually over her head, but she liked it when he shared things he was passionate about. He was her only friend who wasn't a musician, and it was interesting to hear about a different world for a change. "Besides, I still have a life that makes a relationship impossible for the foreseeable future, so I'm happy for him."

Her band's success was her primary focus, so casual hook-ups free of strings and complications were enough. The upcoming tour cemented it further. She didn't have the time or headspace for relationship drama.

She also had her mother's words of warning in her head any time she started liking someone: *Never let a man have your heart because he'll take it with him when he leaves.* It was always *when*, not *if*, like it was a foregone conclusion men aren't to be trusted because no matter how great they seem at first, they'll always disappear.

So far, no one had proven otherwise.

"Whatever." Sandra raised her eyebrow in a way that said they'd be revisiting the topic someday. "Maybe when we're in Paris, you'll fall in love with a dude named Pierre, and you'll feed each other croissants off his ripped abs."

Amber laughed. "Guys who eat croissants probably don't have ripped abs, but I appreciate the mental image."

"You can borrow my guidebooks from when I backpacked in Europe after college." A corner of Kate's mouth tipped up, and the look of pride on her face made Amber smile back. At thirty-five, Kate looked more like their mother every day. After moving to Alaska twelve years before, their mom didn't visit much. She had reasons no one could argue with, but Amber still missed her so much it hurt. They were close before her dad left and still talked every Sunday night, but weekly phone calls weren't enough to fill the double crater left in their lives.

But it was nice being reminded of her smile in the form of her oldest daughter. "I'm happy for you, kid."

"Thanks." Amber appreciated the sweet sentiment, and Kate was the only sister who could call her *kid* without getting an eye roll or arm smack. When their mom moved to Alaska, Kate became Amber and Beth's legal guardian, so she was like a second mother to them. That earned her extra privileges and a hell of a lot of respect. "I've always wanted to go to Paris. And Rome. And Barcelona."

"Well, we're doing it, bitch!" Sandra polished off the rest of her Zima and tossed the bottle in the trash. "Pierre better buckle the fuck up."

3

Matthew

"*Drink the fucking water.*"

The mouth of the plastic bottle pressed harder. Matthew's teeth cut into his bottom lip so deeply he tasted blood.

"*Unless you want me to go say hi to your pretty friend.*"

The thought of Rafael hurting Charlotte made him open wide, and the bitter, metallic-tasting liquid flooded his throat until he choked. It was hard to swallow after days of being starved and left to breathe the cold, stale air that reeked of mildew and rot.

Matthew got a few gulps down before the bottle was empty.

His filthy clothes were wet from the overflow, making him shiver. He was already freezing in this dark pit of a basement, and now, it would be even harder to sleep.

How can I fight if I can't sleep?

"*Tomorrow's the big day.*" *Rafael squeezed the sides of Matthew's face before releasing him and slapping his cheek, the sound cracking in the still, dank air.*

"*Wha...*" *As the drugs took hold, Matthew couldn't form words. Not that his questions would be answered anyway.*

Why am I here?

What are you and Amy planning to do to us?

Am I going to die?

A sharp pinch in the crook of his arm.

Then... darkness.

Charlotte screaming.

The sounds of Tyler sobbing, pleading.

Three loud bangs.

Sirens.

The darkness is pulling him under, clawing at his skin like demons dragging him to hell.

Matthew shot upright in bed, grasping at the invisible hands wrapped around his neck. He gasped and choked as his lungs burned, fighting like hell to fill with air.

His wide eyes skittered around the space, searching for danger that wasn't there.

You're safe. It was only a dream.

A nightlight illuminated his bedroom enough so every detail was clear. He felt stupid for needing it, but along with the nightmares, the attack left him with a paralyzing fear of the dark. Apparently, being bound and locked inside a trunk and then a pitch-black basement for three days, wondering if you were about to take a bullet to the head will do that to you.

Sweat dripped into his eyes, and he rubbed his arms as his limbs shook from the powerful adrenaline rush. Once the fight or flight kicked in, turning it off wasn't easy.

You're safe. It was only a dream.

Matthew slipped on his glasses and focused on a small crack in the wall, repeating the mantra like Dr. Vega taught him to do. At least he got some use out of the long, invasive therapy sessions.

Next came deep breathing.

Breathe in, two, three, four.

And out, two, three, four.

The ritual made him feel more than a little crazy, but after a few rounds, it helped.

Still in an anxious, wrung-out haze, Matthew reflexively slid his hand to the other side of the bed. Of course, Jessica wasn't there. She'd only slept at his apartment once, afterward insisting they stayed at her place on her nights off. Her upscale townhouse was much nicer than his bachelor pad, so he understood. Mostly, he liked living alone, but on nights like this, he would've given anything for a soft, warm body beside him to drag against his chest and hold until he fell back asleep.

A glance at the clock said it was just past five. It was useless to stare at the ceiling for four hours before he had to get ready for work, so he got up, stretched out his tight muscles, and hit the bathroom.

After a long, hot shower, Matthew shuffled to the kitchen, the cold tile floor on his bare feet sending a chill through his bones. He set up the coffee maker for a full pot and slipped a slice of sourdough bread into the toaster. Jessica was on twelve-hour shifts, so she'd be up and getting ready for work. He grabbed the cordless phone off the wall and dialed her number.

"Nightmare?" she asked after the second ring. The caller ID and ungodly hour always gave him away.

"Yeah." He rubbed his exhausted eyes as the toast popped up. "I was in the basement this time."

That's where most of the nightmares took place, but sometimes, he was back on the floor of Charlotte's bedroom staring at the gun pointed at his brother's head.

He'd take the basement over that any day.

"If my shift didn't start at six thirty, I'd be right over."

"I know." He set the toast on a paper plate and grabbed the peanut butter from the fridge. "I need to be able to handle them on my own. I just wanted to hear your voice."

When they started dating two weeks after the attack, he'd fooled himself into believing he could shove his issues far enough aside to try a relationship with the cute nurse with the kind smile who brought him magazines and extra dessert. Then, on their third date, a waitress dropped a tray of dishes, and the sound of shattering glass made his lungs seize and his vision blur.

With her medical training, Jessica recognized his panic attack. After paying the check, they got to his car, and she talked him down from the certainty he was dying. He hated feeling so weak in front of her, but she never seemed to think less of him for it. In fact, she seemed happy to help. It was nice not having to suffer through it alone or to feel guilty for worrying Tyler and their friends when they had their own lives to lead.

On days when Matthew was too afraid to leave his house, she'd bring him food. She drove him to work a few times when the thought of driving past the brewery parking lot where he was abducted made him shake so violently that he couldn't grip the steering wheel. Now, he parked two blocks away to avoid it.

"Even though she was a bit harsh," Jessica said, "I agree with what Charlotte said last night. You should give therapy another shot. I think it might help."

He set the jar of peanut butter on the counter with a sigh. "I can't, Jess." He appreciated her advice and had taken it in other areas of his life, but there wasn't a one-size-fits-all cure for what happened to him. He'd reached a point in therapy where it was just too fucking hard to dig deeper. "I need to look forward, not keep my brain stuck in the past."

She was quiet for a moment. "Okay. Feel free to stop in later. I'll take lunch around one. It's nacho day in the cafeteria."

He smiled. When he was in the hospital, she'd snuck him an extra helping of chips covered in delicious orange goo along with the hot sauce packets he liked. "Wouldn't miss it. Have a good day, Jess."

"You too." She made a kissing sound before hanging up.

Matthew spread peanut butter on his toast, filled a mug with coffee, and sat on a barstool at his kitchen counter. A notebook full of to-do lists, notes for the brewery music space, and random things he needed to remember sat beside the sugar bowl. He slid it in front of him along with a pen and flipped to the page where he'd written his best man duties. Most items were already crossed out, like *order tuxedos and hire strippers for the bachelor party*. The only things left to do were to write a speech for his toast at the reception and buy a wedding gift.

There were three and a half hours to kill before work, so he might as well start on the one thing he could do from his kitchen. He took a bite of toast, chased it with a sip of coffee, and picked up the pen.

~~I'm honored to be my brother's best man.~~

~~Let's raise a glass to the beautiful couple!~~

~~Weddings are crazy, right?~~

Matthew groaned, setting down the pen and sipping his coffee. His brother had a talent for putting words together in a way that moved people. Matthew failed any school assignment involving poetry because he didn't see the point in all that flowery bullshit.

Cut out the cheesy metaphors about stars and just say what you mean, Walt Whitman.

He internally kicked himself for leaving the speech until now, but he'd hoped to feel a surprise burst of inspiration that would magically make the task effortless. He also hoped the thought of speaking in front of that many people would stop making him nauseous.

So far, no luck on either front.

He finished his toast and coffee, abandoning the speech for now. Needing to stay busy, he grabbed a thick roll of tape from the junk drawer and packed the contents of the hall closet into boxes. His bedroom stuff was ready to go to the new place, and all that was left to box up in his bathroom were a few towels and basic things he needed to get ready for work and bed.

All his band posters and technicolor tapestries had already come down, leaving behind brownish rectangular outlines and tiny pushpin holes on the walls. It was strange to see his beloved apartment, full of color and character only a few days before, looking so empty and plain. For six years, it'd been his favorite place on earth—safe, comfortable, and familiar.

A wave of sadness rolled in. It felt like he was saying goodbye to an old friend who'd been there for some of his best and worst times. All the movie nights, laughter, and drinking games. Parties and late-night talks that drifted into morning. Now, he'd be starting over in a place with no memories—good or bad. He couldn't decide if that made the whole thing an exciting new adventure or really fucking depressing.

Finding out Tyler and Charlotte were going to be parents made the emotions of the move hit even harder. Too many things were changing at once. The attack left him craving security and stability, and the sources he'd always relied on weren't so reliable anymore.

There were two weeks left on his lease, but the fact that Jessica wouldn't sleep over made him want to speed up the transition. The disapproval was written all over her face the first time she walked in. He was embarrassed to look around and imagine what someone like her must've thought of his blacklight posters, two-foot bong, and massive horror movie collection. Before her visit, he'd cleaned for two days and stocked the fridge and cupboards with things she liked. It hurt to feel like it still wasn't good enough. That nothing he could do to that place ever would be. It made him see his apartment and, really, his life through a different lens.

Why did he still dress like a sixteen-year-old skater in hoodies, faded band T-shirts, and jeans? Why would a grown man read X-Men comics before bed? Was it pathetic to spend his days off smoking pot with his friends, zoning out with video games, or staying out all night at a dive bar?

Though he hadn't met them yet, he knew Jessica's friends spent their free time at museums, tasting wine, or walking through botanic gardens. His friends cursed, wore leather jackets, and drank beer at rock shows, often their own. He couldn't imagine the two groups mingling, but it was bound to happen if things progressed. And he'd make sure it happened with plenty of alcohol.

After Jessica's first visit, he'd wake up at her place to find circled listings for condos and townhomes on her kitchen table. While it was a strange thing to do so early in a relationship, she meant well. Considering all she'd done to help him cope with his PTSD, he took it as more not-so-subtle encouragement to help him be the best version of himself he could be. She said holding onto old habits and comforts was holding him back, and moving on would make him stronger.

That was all it took to wake him up and motivate him to change. He'd felt so powerless and weak after the attack, and nothing he tried seemed to do much good. So, he trusted her advice because, more than anything, he wanted to feel strong again.

Even if it meant saying goodbye to some things he loved, he was willing to do whatever it took to get there.

4

Amber

With The Gits blasting on her stereo, Amber checked her makeup in the mirror, dabbing her crimson lipstick with a tissue. The dark lines around her eyes came to a sharp point in the outer corners, and she'd added an extra layer of smoky gray to her lids.

Damn, I look hot.

Like any woman, she had days of feeling like a bloated, oily-faced cow, but now, she was confident she looked fabulous. She adjusted her boobs in the black push-up bra before sliding on a black tank top that ended above her pierced navel and dipped at the top to showcase her ample cleavage. Topping it all off was her signature don't-fuck-with-me black leather jacket.

If shy, awkward middle school Amber could see her now, she'd have a coronary.

"Turn it down!" her sister Denise yelled through the bedroom door before banging on it three times.

Denise wasn't home much because she practically lived with her car salesman boyfriend, Roger. The sisters never had relationships that lasted more than a few months, so even Denise was surprised by how well it was going.

Amber grumbled and turned down the volume. Three much kinder knocks followed. When she touched the knob to unlock it, her eyes darted to the opened top dresser drawer. The envelope from Chicago still sat on top of her socks, flipped upside down. She'd almost thrown it away several times, but something always held her back—the chance it held answers to questions she couldn't let go of. She slid the drawer shut.

Amber opened her door to find Denise with keys in her hand. "I'm heading to Roger's."

"Shocker."

Denise's eyes rolled as she pushed her way inside the room. "What time will you be home?"

Amber resisted the urge to roll her eyes right back. Her sister's overprotectiveness was sweet but annoying since Amber was almost twenty-six. "Late. The band goes on at nine, and Sandra scored us all-access passes, so we'll hang backstage until closing. Maybe grab a bite after." She was meeting Sandra at the Marquis to check out a new riot grrl band from Olympia that was getting a lot of buzz, which likely meant coming home after sunrise.

"Sounds fun." Denise grabbed the stack of plates and coffee mugs on Amber's desk, balancing them in the crook of her arm. "Not having mice or ants in the house is also fun."

That time, Amber didn't resist rolling her eyes at her neat freak sister. "We've never had either, and I plan to clean up tomorrow."

"Mmhm." Denise assessed Amber's outfit with a disapproving scowl. She reached out and tugged the front of her top further north. "They're going to bounce right out of your damn shirt. Please cover up a little."

Amber slapped her hand away, laughing. "Don't be jealous because you're not as blessed."

There hadn't been an actual parent in the house since Amber was fourteen, but she'd been surrounded by nosy but well-meaning mother figures who always thought they knew best. Sometimes, it was sweet and appreciated; others, it was obnoxious and exhausting.

Denise groaned. "Whatever. Just be careful." Her gaze slid to the wall above Amber's bed, and her scowl deepened. "Ugh, I don't know how you can stand to look at his stupid fucking face every day."

Amber didn't need to look to know what photo she was referring to. It was the only one left of their father in the house—all three thousand square feet wiped clean of any other proof of his existence aside from the five daughters who'd all inherited his deep blue, almond-shaped eyes, and the ability to pretend everything was fine when it wasn't.

For Amber, there were enough good memories to hold onto at least one piece of him.

"Call me at Roger's when you're home safe." Denise leaned forward and kissed Amber's cheek, the plates and ceramic mugs on her arm clattering together.

"You got it. Have fun, D."

Amber shut her door and tugged her top back where she wanted it. She hadn't always appreciated her body, and it felt like she was making up for lost time.

She was one of the "lucky" girls who developed early. By seventh grade, she was in a C cup and had gently curving hips emerging below her waistline. Amber felt like a freak. She hated her body and would've given anything to hide in a cave until all the other girls at school caught up. She still wanted to play with Barbies, for fuck's sake, not look like one.

And there was the teasing. Girls who still had flat chests and baby hair on their legs were calling her a slut long before she'd even held a boy's hand. Her sister Kate had to explain what the word even meant. The boys at school would snap her bra at recess and dare each other to touch her breasts when the teacher wasn't looking. Amber's face would turn lobster red, her skin flaming with her first introduction to the searing heat of shame.

The sound of elastic snapping against skin still made her shudder.

Amber slipped her favorite black boots over the fishnet stockings covering her long, pale legs. When the laces were tied, her eyes drifted to the photo of her father. He was grinning like a carefree fool behind a gold and white drum kit at a club in downtown Portland, wearing sunglasses and a loosened necktie while he played make-believe rockstar.

Like the kids at school, he'd made her feel ashamed for not fitting into a neat little box constructed of impossible standards and unfair expectations.

Bastard.

Begging him to teach her to play drums was a way to pull him closer, but even that didn't last. On the bright side, that attempt to connect sparked her passion for playing music, which led to the career she loved. Still, she would've given anything to keep her family whole.

But even though his leaving was partly her fault, it was never up to her.

Amber's bedroom phone rang, thankfully pulling her out of her spiraling thoughts. She turned down the music before snatching it off the cradle. "Hello?"

"Is it cool if Christa tags along?" Sandra chewed something crunchy while she talked, poking at one of Amber's few pet peeves.

"Only if you stop chewing in my ear. Are you eating rocks?"

"Close. Fruity Pebbles."

Amber laughed. "Don't sneak off to feel each other up or whatever. If this band sounds as good live as they do on their album, maybe we can talk Eliza into booking them to open for us after Europe."

Killing Daisies' first headlining gig was nearly five months ago, and it was still surreal to see their band's name on the tops of fliers and marquees. She was looking forward to using their new position to help boost other talented bands.

"Wow. After we blow up, I guess it'll be our turn to help the little fish. Good thinking." Sandra crunched her cereal again. "We won't ditch you, I swear. And don't you dare ditch us for some random dude with stupid hair."

While getting railed until Amber forgot her name sounded pretty nice, a night with the girls and a mosh pit sounded better.

"Deal. See you in thirty."

At the entrance to the Marquis, Amber, Sandra, and Christa held up their IDs and the bouncer pressed bright blue stamps onto their wrists—a devil holding a martini glass. Next, he handed them all-access lanyards that they slipped around their necks.

Inside the club, frenzied beats and angry guitars blared through the speakers as a tiny chick with cropped blonde hair growled into the microphone. It was only eight fifteen, and the club was already packed with sweaty bodies clad in leather jackets, flannel shirts, and babydoll dresses. The vinyl floor was sticky beneath Amber's boots, and the air was grey and reeked of cigarette smoke, fried food, and stale beer—a scent combination that made her grin as she was struck by endless memories of shows she'd seen and played. With Sandra and Christa trailing behind, she waded through the crowd, nudging elbows and mumbling "excuse me" to part the sea of half-drunk patrons.

"Drinks," Sandra shouted, pointing toward the bar. "Then dancing." She hooked her arm around Christa's waist and guided her toward the nearest bartender, a brutally hot twenty-something guy with ink-black hair and a pierced lip. Amber almost regretted promising Sandra she wouldn't bail later with a random dude. Since this guy's hair was far from stupid, maybe there was a loophole to work with.

"First round's on me." Christa pulled a few bills from the back pocket of her skin-tight grey jeans. Her long blonde hair was pulled back in a ponytail that swished against the center of her back as she studied the liquor shelves. When the bartender glanced over, she held the cash in the air. "Dirty Shirley, Bacardi and Coke, and an IPA."

He plucked the bills from her hand and worked quickly, setting the drinks on the bar before moving on to the next cluster of thirsty punks.

"Thanks, Christa." Amber raised her beer bottle. "I got round two."

They carried their drinks toward the stage, the volume rising with every step.

As always, an unseen magnetic force drew Amber toward the music—a beckoning, irresistible siren song. Every beat, chord, and shouted lyric called to something inside her, promising to clear her mind of clutter and heal every crack in her heart. As the feeling took hold, a broad smile bloomed on her face. Her head bobbed along with the relentless beat, her hips swaying and popping to the rhythm as she slipped through the crowd with her friends.

Halfway between the bar and the stage, they stopped. It was Amber's favorite spot to camp out at a show—close enough to feel the vibrating hum of the bass in her chest but a safe distance from the elbows and knees in the mosh pit so she could enjoy her drink instead of wearing it. Later, when her hands were free, and she was buzzed enough to ignore the groping dickheads that were an inevitable part of the otherwise blissful pit experience, she'd dive in.

When the song ended and the next one kicked off, she glanced back at her friends. Sandra's arm was slung over Christa's shoulder and the way they smiled at each other—like the rest of the room had fallen away—made something ache in Amber's chest. No one had *ever* looked at her like that. She was more accustomed to judgmental stares, flirty glances, and creepy eye-fondling than anything remotely resembling the unmistakable love in their eyes.

No boy will ever love or respect you if you look and act like a slut.

The memory made her wince. Both of her parents had branded words of wisdom on her brain regarding the opposite sex. Even thirteen years later, her dad's still felt like a slap.

But he wasn't wrong. It only took a couple of heartbreaks for Amber to give up on ever receiving love or respect from the guys she hooked up with. Now, she didn't let herself get attached. Since her look wasn't one most guys would want to take home to their mother, no one got attached to her either. It was safe and easy that way. Lonely, but safe and easy. And since she'd never change to make herself more palatable, it would likely stay that way.

While it would be nice to have someone look at her like these lesbian lovebirds looked at each other, she'd continue settling for the occasional warm body to make her feel wanted and less alone for a while. Anything else required a level of trust no one had proven worthy of.

When the final chords faded in the speakers, and the opening band left the stage, Amber's ears were ringing.

"They were fucking badass," Sandra said with a wide grin. Her cheeks were flushed pink, and sweat glistened at her temples. She set her empty glass on a vacant table and turned to Amber. "We'll find a booth if you grab the next drinks."

Amber saluted before heading for the bar. The line was long, and after a few minutes, she scanned the booths for her friends to see where they ended up. She spotted Sandra's red curls in the far corner, and she was making out with Christa like one of them was leaving for war.

Again, Amber felt a pang of envy for their passion and easy affection. And felt like a ditched third wheel. That happened whenever she went out with

Charlotte and Tyler, too, and now even fellow chronically single Matthew had a girlfriend, so going out with him would also be different.

That one stung.

Amber had never told anyone, but she'd always thought she and Matthew would end up together someday. In a few years, her life might be less chaotic, and her old wounds might be far enough behind her to stop holding her back. She figured they'd watch everyone around them partner up and then finally have the balls to give it a shot. Neither had made any serious moves in that direction, but their relationship had always been platonic with a subtle dash of something more. They exchanged mixtapes and laughed at inside jokes, and he didn't mind when she hung on him like a floppy monkey when she was drunk.

Most of all, she trusted him. She'd shared her dreams, fears, and other pieces of her life with him that she didn't give away easily.

Matthew Hall was a fucking catch, so it was only a matter of time before someone snatched him up. Now, there was a very real possibility that someday, everyone in their circle would be paired up except her. They'd all be happy and in love while Amber was a pathetic, lonely spinster with a hoard of shelter cats and daddy issues.

Along with her next beer, she ordered a shot of whiskey, which she tossed back before tucking the beer into the crook of her arm and grabbing her friend's cocktails. They were still kissing, of course, and Amber set their drinks on the table. She chugged her beer and set down the empty bottle.

"When you guys are done sucking face," Amber said with a small burp, "I'll see you out there."

She didn't wait for a response and pushed her way through the crowd. Though she'd been looking forward to enjoying the band with her friends, it wouldn't be the first or last time she'd hit the pit solo.

When the headliner took the stage, screams and cheers erupted, bodies crashing together. As the first song began, the pit became a swirling tornado of flailing limbs and nodding heads. Adrenaline spread through her veins as her heart rate spiked. Amber joined the circle, kicking up her feet and punching the air. The band was an all-female trio and punk as fuck, loud and intense in a way that instantly shifted the vibe in the room to something dangerous but divine.

All the self-pity from moments before melted away. Nothing beat the high she got from music, and at her lowest moments, it tempered the pain, making it easier to bear.

Where would I be without music?

A few months after her dad left, Amber was fiddling with the radio late at night and stumbled upon a local college station. The music was melodic and fierce, the lyrics dripping with angst and loud, urgent calls for riot and rebellion.

Amber had discovered punk rock.

From that day on, she lived in her headphones where angry voices screamed about struggles she knew well—being picked on, overlooked, and unappreciated. Those angry voices on the radio taught her that people will inevitably judge you but fuck them all. Shitty opinions from shitty people don't matter.

And it helped her to accept her dad wasn't coming back. So, fuck him too.

Those voices of rebellion made her no longer want to hide. She'd let the bastards make her hate her own body long enough and wasn't about to let them win one more goddamn second. To make her outside match the changes inside, she cut the sleeves off her T-shirts and wore short skirts dotted with safety pins. Her nails were painted black or violent shades of purple and red. Eyeliner became her best friend. Judgmental stares were met with a swift middle finger.

There was power in not giving a fuck.

She was a stifled wildflower finally figuring out how to bloom, and she had Johnny Rotten, Johnny Ramone, and Joan Jett to thank for it.

Six songs in, Amber was panting, sweat dripping into her eyes and over the smile plastered to her face. *Fuck, I needed that.* Another beer sounded like heaven, so she pushed her way out of the pit and hit the bar.

"IPA and a shot of Jack," she called out over the noise.

When the shot was filled, she poured it down her throat and chased the burn with a long, cool sip of beer.

"Amber?"

Her head swiveled toward the deep male voice as the alcohol loosened her muscles. The voice belonged to someone very cute—dark brown hair to his chin, hazel eyes, sexy scruff of a beard.

"Amber Jamison?" he asked.

"Yeah," she said, her tone wary. "Do I know you?"

He looked familiar, and she searched her brain for why. A one-night stand? Or someone from one of her shows?

"Your dad threatened to kill me," he offered with a smirk. "Does that help?"

With that, it hit her. "Derek Russell?"

The first lips she'd ever kissed curved into a sexy grin as he nodded. *Damn.* The thirteen-year-old kid with shaggy hair and braces grew into a hot-ass man.

"Bingo," he said, moving closer. "I love your music. These girls are great, but your band's fucking killer."

"Thanks." Amber took out cash for her drinks, but he waved her off and tossed a twenty onto the bar. She clinked her bottle against his glass of dark liquor. "Thanks again."

Derek ran a hand through his hair as he checked her out from head to toe and back again. "Flying solo tonight?"

She shook her head, leaning in as the volume rose. He smelled like clove cigarettes and Cool Water cologne—a strangely alluring combo that made her thighs squeeze together. "My friends ditched me to make out." Amber tipped the neck of her bottle toward the booth where Sandra was sucking Christa's neck like a horny vampire.

His eyebrows shot up. "Damn. Wasn't expecting a free show."

Amber's nose crinkled like a dead possum was just dropped between them, her lady boner officially killed.

Strike one.

"Don't be an asshole."

Derek winced. "Sorry. That wasn't cool. I promise to refrain from gawking at your friends."

With the deal she'd struck with Sandra about not ditching each other clearly voided, the thought of ending the night with someone who kissed well and smelled nice was very tempting. Aside from his shitty comment, Derek was a decent candidate.

"You're fucking sexy all grown up." His eyes trailed down her body again, detouring at her tits before returning to her face. He wet his lips, moving close enough for the sharp, smoky scent of whiskey to reach her nose.

Derek was clearly good to go. He checked all her usual boxes—cute, clean, confident, tipsy but not drunk. And even as an awkward teenager, the guy had skills. Her first kiss was epic. When Derek's lips pressed to hers, she felt the electric charge to her toes.

Then, her front door swung open, and her dad threatened to bury the poor kid in the backyard. He ran home, and after that, they avoided each other at school.

"So how many of your boyfriends did your dad end up murdering over the years?" he asked with a chuckle.

"Six." Amber sipped her beer. "Maybe seven, but I have a feeling that last one's hiding in Cuba."

In reality, her father never had the chance to chase off any other boyfriends let alone kill them. Four days after she was caught kissing Derek, her dad moved to Chicago to start a new life with his knocked-up side chick and never looked back. It was a shock to everyone, especially her mother, who was clueless about the affair until his bags were packed. A few months later, Amber's grandmother reported that he got the son he'd always wanted—a final bonus stab in the heart to her mother, who'd given him five daughters.

Since he left, there were no birthday cards, no calls, nothing. The silence was painful but probably a blessing considering how he made her feel about herself before he left.

He hadn't reached out, but for some reason she wasn't ready to learn, the envelope in her dresser came from his house. Thinking about it poked at the questions burning in her brain since it arrived.

Does Dad know about the letter?

Is he happier in his new life?

Is he better to his new family than he was to mine?

Derek didn't need to know any of that. Sometimes, alcohol made her more open than she'd like, but she wasn't about to spill her drama to an old crush in the middle of a rock club.

"I hope those poor bastards at least got more than a kiss before they bit the bullet." The corners of Derek's mouth curled up.

"Oh, yeah." Amber nodded as she brought the bottle to her lips. "They died happy."

Derek laughed, his perfect teeth gleaming in the club lights. "I bet." He reached out, boldly tracing the collar of her leather jacket with the tip of his finger. "I'm glad I ran into you, Amber."

"Me too," she said. He was fun to flirt with, and the nostalgia was strangely soothing. The alcohol helped too.

"Want to come back to my place and finish what we started when we were thirteen?"

Was she in the mood to revisit Derek's lips? Clearly, the rest of him was on offer too. While she pondered that, the song changed to something with a fast, furious tempo that ignited the mosh pit into a churning sea of bouncing, flailing bodies. The pull to join them was strong. And the headliner just started. She'd planned to watch their whole set to see if they'd work as openers for Killing Daisies after Europe. And she wanted to meet them backstage and give them props after the show.

"Not tonight." Sex sounded great, but it would break her number one rule: music always comes before guys. This band was incredible, and she wasn't going to miss it for a couple of hours of naked fun. "The pit's calling, but it was nice seeing you again."

As she turned, Derek grabbed her wrist. She looked at his hand and blinked, giving him the benefit of the doubt, but also considering breaking his fingers. She pulled her hand back, and he released her.

Strike two.

"Come on," he said. "I bought you a beer. You owe me."

Strike. Fucking. Three.

He winked like he was trying to frame what he said as cute, but even a few beers in, she saw right through him. Her pulse ticked in her neck, and alarms blared in her brain. No one was more punch-worthy and dangerous than a guy who didn't take no for an answer.

And no one was more vulnerable than a woman who appeared weak.

Amber tipped her wrist, pouring the rest of her beer onto Derek's sneakers.

"What the fuck?" he shouted, jumping back. "You crazy bitch!"

She scoffed even as her pulse raced, setting the empty bottle on the bar. "Real original insult, dickbag. I hope you and your right hand have a nice night."

Instead of hitting the pit, Amber rushed to the bathroom, panting like she'd jogged a mile. Tears stung her eyes, and the alcohol sloshed in her stomach, threatening to make a reappearance. She ducked into the first empty stall, locking it behind her with trembling hands.

With her back pressed to the door, she sucked in a few deep breaths. Guys needed to see her as tough so they wouldn't fuck with her, but it didn't make confrontations like that any less scary.

After a few minutes of calming herself, she made a beeline for Sandra and Christa. Derek wasn't wearing a lanyard, so he wouldn't be backstage. Once they met the headliner and started swapping band stories and taking shots, all would be right with her world.

Music and great friends were all she needed. Men brought complications. They could be a fun distraction, but they couldn't be trusted.

That was the last, most indelible lesson her father ever taught her.

5

Matthew

Matthew walked the brew room with a pen and clipboard in hand. "Did the Mosaic hops get ordered? I'm only seeing Cascade and Chinook here." The data on the inventory sheet wasn't adding up. Maybe the figures were wrong, or maybe he was too goddamn exhausted to make sense of things. Waking up from a nightmare at five was a hell of a way to start the week—as if Mondays needed help being shitty.

"Coming Thursday." His business partner, Evan, dragged a box of drink coasters along the concrete floor, stopping beside a lager tank. He was wearing one of the new High Notes T-shirts they'd designed together, and the patterns on the sleeves seemed to merge with the various tattoos covering his arms. A new one—a black and red skull—peeked out from the left sleeve, covered in a shiny layer of ointment. "Why do you look like an extra from *Day of the Dead*? Jessica keep you up late?"

Matthew rubbed his forehead, the numbers on the inventory sheet mashing together until they went from making little sense to none at all. "Bad dream. Couldn't get back to sleep."

Evan sighed heavily. "I told you to call out whenever you need to. When you aren't here, I've got shit handled. And I can blast the hip-hop that gets on your nerves."

"I'm good." Matthew scratched his eyebrow with the pen before looking up at his friend. People warned them that going into business together could harm their friendship, but the opposite proved true. All the hours spent talking about everything and nothing while working on a new batch and brainstorming ideas on getting more drinkers in the door cemented their bond more than anything else in the six years since they met in a college biology class. "But thanks, man."

Although Evan didn't seem to mind picking up his slack, Matthew felt guilty for not pulling his weight since the attack. He took three weeks off after leaving the hospital. Since then, he'd called out a handful of times when something triggered a panic attack that made him afraid to leave his apartment. And Evan sent him home once or twice a week because he hadn't slept.

When Matthew felt more stable, he planned to give Evan some long overdue time off. Since they opened the brewery two and a half years ago, he hadn't taken more than a handful of days off in a row. While Matthew appreciated his work ethic, everyone needed a break.

"We got another order from O'Brady's," Evan said. "We'll end September three thousand above what we expected."

"Fuck yeah." After making the down payment on his condo, the extra money couldn't come at a better time. Matthew's old apartment was dirt cheap, and his living expenses were low, so fortunately, he still had a fat nest egg. But it wouldn't last forever if his income didn't increase. "Makes up for last month, but profits are still flat for the year."

"Yeah, but we'll turn it around." Evan shrugged. "The new merch isn't giving us the boost I'd hoped for. And Carmine's Pub and Shiner's closing down didn't help. They were two of our biggest customers. We'll just keep hustling to get our product out there."

Evan was better at the business side of things, while Matthew handled making contacts with local bars and restaurants, ordering supplies, and advertising. The actual beer-making was their favorite part of the job. What started as a fun weekend hobby in college turned into something they both excelled at, so they split those tasks down the middle.

It was nice not having anyone to answer to except each other. Matthew flipped burgers in high school, and his manager was a raging asshole. That experience made him determined to reach the day when he'd never have a boss again. Now that it was a reality, he planned to keep it that way.

Matthew turned to the boxes stacked in the corner by the wide windows. It was wasted space, and the idea that'd been scratching at his brain since they opened was becoming more urgent as profits leveled out.

"Ready to talk about using that corner for more than storage?" He pointed at the area with the tip of his pen. "Or do you want to look at the books again and cry a little first?"

As Matthew stared at the space, he could see the boxes disappear, a small stage erected in their place. It was the perfect size for open mics and local bands to play while people sipped beer and took a break from their stresses. He grew up watching Tyler practice guitar, and when he started playing shows, Matthew would tag along. He fell in love with live music and its ability to make a room full of strangers come together, sharing a powerful experience before parting with blissed-out smiles on their faces.

The space wasn't massive, but they could fit at least fifty seats on show nights. Local talent could get exposure and build a fanbase. The extra money in Matthew and Evan's pockets would be nice too.

The biggest reason he was tired of putting it off was that the project would be the perfect distraction from his stupid problems. Plus, he'd have something positive to look forward to—a place filled with happy music lovers sipping beer and enjoying a break from their own stupid problems.

"The business is fine." Evan grabbed a box cutter and slashed the top of the box of coasters. "Why rock the boat and risk our savings?"

"Why settle for fine?" They'd had this conversation before, but this time, Matthew wouldn't back down. He needed this. "We could potentially double or triple profits with the crowd we could pull in. This city fucking thrives on live music. Plus, people will keep coming back after finding out we make the best goddamn beer on the West Coast."

Evan grinned, offering a fist bump. "Hell yeah, we do, brother." Matthew knew that would rouse his interest. They both took great pride in their product and loved seeing people smile after taking their first sip. "Unless we get an investor, it seems reckless. You really want to shell out a big chunk of cash after buying a new place?"

Matthew didn't want the complication of adding an investor into the mix. Tyler helped get the business off the ground with a generous loan that covered half their start-up costs—a loan they'd tried to pay back over time, but Tyler's stubborn, generous ass refused to cash the checks. If the live music venture flopped, Matthew didn't want anyone to pay the price but him.

"If you don't want to throw in," Matthew said, "I've got it. Either way, I'll do all the work because I think a new project's just what I need."

Evan closed the box cutter and tucked it into his pocket. "No way, partner. If you're in, I'm in. Just be sure to get your brother and all your rockstar friends to pop in once in a while to help create buzz."

Matthew laughed. "Will do." They all came in already to drink and bullshit, so that would be easy. "Are you serious? We're really doing this?"

Evan dug into the box and pulled out two shrink-wrapped stacks of drink coasters, setting them on the shelves beneath the register. "Yup. Give me a number, and it's on. We already have the perfect name."

He was right. They'd thought up "High Notes" one night in college. They were brainstorming business names while stoned out of their minds listening to *Dark Side of the Moon*. The name combined two of their favorite things—music and marijuana. Since there are also tasting notes with beer—pine, citrus, floral—it seemed perfect.

Matthew let the positivity soak into his tired bones. He already had a notebook full of measurements and ideas, and he'd finally get to put them into action. It would be a huge risk; there was no denying that. If Matthew lost his investment and business didn't pick up, he'd have to sell the condo and return to renting a smaller place. It would be a major setback that would take years to correct. But *what ifs* weren't going to stop him. He was too busy being grateful for something to focus on instead of the past.

"Aside from the nightmare last night, you doing okay?" Evan kept his eyes on his work. He knew Matthew well enough to know he didn't like being stared at when he might share something personal.

"Yeah. Better." Maybe if he said it enough, it would start to feel true. The uncomfortable tightness in his chest said he was ready for the conversation to change. "Jess and I had dinner with Ty and Charlotte last night." It was hard not to spill Charlotte's pregnancy news, but he'd promised to keep it on the down low.

Evan loaded a keg onto a dolly and rolled it to the tasting area. "How'd that go?"

"Kind of weird. Like they didn't know what to think about her. I know she can come off as a little blunt and assertive, but it's her personality." Matthew crossed his arms, hugging the clipboard. It wasn't his favorite quality because sometimes her words stung, but no one was perfect. At least she was honest. "She's a lot different than the people we usually hang with—more proper and straight-edge—so maybe that's part of it, too."

"Maybe." Evan hooked the keg to a tap beneath the tasting counter, his expression tight. "If *I* can be blunt, they know what a fucking disaster most of your relationships have been, so they're probably reserving judgment until they know if this one'll stick. They want what's best for you."

Matthew nodded, mostly agreeing with his assessment. He didn't have the best taste in women before meeting Jessica, so it made sense that everyone would assume she'd be as temporary as the rest. Growing up with a massively talented older brother whose face made women weep left Matthew grateful for any female attention he received. Over the years, he'd had plenty of action, but it was always shallow, purely physical. There was no spark, lying in bed talking until dawn or imagining a future together. He hoped once his brain wasn't so muddled by the trauma, he could have that with Jessica.

"You like her, right?" Matthew asked.

Evan's eyes didn't waver from the tap he was connecting. "I like how much she's helped you. I don't know where you'd be right now if she weren't there to talk you down from your panic attacks when they were happening daily."

He was about to point out that Evan didn't really answer the question when the bell above the door jingled. Their heads turned. Jessica walked into the taproom wearing her nurse's scrubs, her eyes roaming the space.

"Hey! You finally made it in." Matthew rushed over, kissing her with his arm around her waist. "You on a break?"

Her eyebrows pinched together as she studied his face. "You don't know?"

"Know what?"

"Hey, Jessica." Evan wiped the sweat off his forehead with the back of his wrist. "Got any cute nurse friends into guys with more tattoos than sense? If so, hook it up."

She ignored him. "Charlotte's in the hospital."

"*What*?" The clipboard slipped from Matthew's grip and landed on the concrete with a sharp crash. "What happened?"

"I overheard a few candy stripers squealing about seeing Tyler in the E.R., so I went to check it out. I saw Charlotte through the window of her room. She was in bed crying, and he was holding her hand. I didn't want to disturb them. I thought you might be too upset to drive, so I took an early break and headed over."

Matthew turned to Evan.

"Go, man. I got this."

The first thought that struck as he buckled into Jessica's passenger seat was that the baby was gone. Charlotte's fear of losing the ones she loved most would be coming true. He knew what that would do to her.

Jessica turned right and headed toward Legacy Emanuel Medical Center. The same place an ambulance brought Matthew after a forced heroin overdose nearly killed him. The place where his attacker, Rafael, took his last breaths, and Amy recovered from a bullet to the gut. His stomach churned as the memories threatened to invade, but he fought it. He needed to be strong for Tyler and Charlotte; falling apart wasn't an option.

Their tight-knit group had dealt with more than enough trauma, and the threat of one more made him wish he hadn't left his bottle of Xanax in his jacket at work.

Jessica led the way as they quickly navigated the long hallways, rushing past nurses' stations and various beeps and alarms of hospital equipment. She stopped in front of a door with a tiny rectangular window. He took a deep breath and peeked into Charlotte's hospital room. Even in the dimmed lights, he saw the tears in her eyes as she clutched tissues in her fist. His heart sank at the sight of her in pain. His brother didn't look any better. Tyler's jaw was tensed, and his hair was mussed like he'd been running his hands through it. Matthew took another deep breath and turned the knob before walking in on slow, quiet feet.

"Hey, Butt Face." Matthew forced a grin as he approached Charlotte.

Her eyes widened a bit, then relaxed. "Hey, Turd Boy." Her lips twitched, but it was miles away from an actual smile.

Matthew hugged her gently, his eyes drifting to Tyler over her shoulder. He looked broken. Judging by their faces, the tiny person they'd wanted more than anything was gone.

Jessica touched his arm. He'd almost forgotten she was there.

"I have to get back to work," she said, "but I'll find you on my next break."

Matthew let go of Charlotte and gave Jessica a weak smile before she walked out and silently shut the door behind her.

"What happened?" Matthew struggled to keep his voice steady. It was so unfair. Grief and pain should be behind her now. She'd earned it.

"There was blood." Charlotte's voice cracked, and her eyes flooded with tears. He took her hand and held on tight. "And cramps. But the doctor said the baby's okay. For now."

Matthew let out a sigh of relief. "Really? Shit, you scared me." He looked at Tyler. "Why do you guys look so sad? You got good news."

Charlotte swiped her wad of tissues beneath her eyes. "It was really fucking scary. And they said it could happen again. This could be a sign something is wrong and—" Her low, heart-crushing sob cut her off.

"Shh…" Tyler leaned over and pressed a kiss to the top of her head. "Let's not go there right now—Matthew's right. We got good news. Whatever the future throws at us, we'll survive it."

Charlotte's fingers slipped from Matthew's, and she covered her face and wept. Tyler wrapped both arms around her, whispering sweet, calming words, but Matthew could hear everything.

I love you so much.

You're strong, and so is our baby.

We'll all be okay no matter what happens.

For the first time, Matthew felt like a third wheel. Like he didn't belong so close to their intimate, private bubble of love and shared pain. It hurt to feel excluded, but he was grateful they had each other to lean on.

"I'm going to grab a coffee." He aimed his thumb toward the door. "You guys want anything?"

Tyler slowly lifted his head and shook it.

Halfway to the door, Matthew turned back. "Want me to call Sandra?"

"Already did," Tyler said. "She wasn't home, but Amber's on her way."

"You didn't need to call them, Ty." Charlotte blew her nose and tossed the tissues into the trashcan beside her bed. "I'll be discharged soon anyway."

"Your friends love you." Tyler swept his thumbs over her damp cheeks as more tears spilled. "I love you. We're going to be here for whatever you need."

"Why didn't you call me?" Matthew asked, trying not to sound hurt that they'd reached out to everyone but him.

Tyler shook his head. "I couldn't ask you to come back to this place. And the last thing you need is something else to stress about."

He was right, as usual. Matthew hated being back in the hospital for another fucked-up reason, but he'd never failed Charlotte when she needed help. He wouldn't start now just because the location sucked.

When Matthew opened the door, Charlotte's voice stopped him. "Hey, Matty?"

"Yeah?"

"Can you get me some chocolate?"

The guys laughed, and she got close herself, her chest jumping and the corners of her lips tipping up so slightly it would be easy to miss if you blinked.

"Lady, I'll buy you *all* the fucking chocolate." In three broad steps, he was back at her bedside. He kissed her forehead, hot tears pricking his eyes. "Hang in there, Warrior Woman."

When he was at his lowest, drugged and dying on the floor of her old bedroom, she was the voice in his ear telling him to hold on, promising everything would be okay. Even with a gun to her head, she was comforting him. There was *nothing* he wouldn't do for her.

When Matthew closed the door behind him, a few tears broke loose, sliding to his chin. The baby was okay. If they were this distraught over the *threat* of losing it, what would they do if it happened?

Hell, he was getting excited about the little rugrat too. He never wanted kids because they required a level of patience and self-sacrifice he'd never be capable of. His dad died when he was six, so he wouldn't know how to do the job well even if he had those qualities. But he loved the idea of a little partner-in-crime to help him prank Tyler with whoopie cushions. Someone to thrill with an underdog on a swing like Tyler always did for him. Someone to teach how to make beer. When it was age-appropriate, of course. He was even looking forward to buying brightly colored, noisy ass toys that would randomly go off in the middle of the night and drive his brother crazy.

And he really liked the sound of "Uncle Matty."

Now, with this fear of loss over her head, Charlotte needed to hear only positive things. She needed her people to lift her up. When Rafael began terrorizing her with threatening notes two years ago, making her afraid to leave her house, it was Matthew's usual teasing, crass jokes, and pointing out the positives that eventually crowded out the negatives looping through her head. His vow to rip the nuts off anyone who tried to hurt her helped, too.

Normalcy, even when faked, and unwavering support got her to take those first steps. This wouldn't be any different. Except this time, she also had Tyler. If things went south with this baby, Matthew knew his brother could help her through it in a way Matthew or even Sandra couldn't. And he was nothing but thankful.

He took the elevator to the second floor and wandered the small gift shop filled with colorful flowers and Mylar balloons, all printed with increasingly cheesy variations of "Get Well Soon." On impulse, he grabbed a green stuffed bear the size of a Buick and tucked it under his arm. It was Charlotte's favorite color, and the scrunched-up, threaded face was so butt ugly he might even get a smile out of her.

Next, he raided the candy. He grabbed Snickers bars, Reese's cups, and seven bags of peanut M&M's—another one of her favorite things. The next aisle was greeting cards, magazines, and newspapers. When he spotted his brother's face, along with his bandmates, Zack and Adam, on the cover of the latest issue of *Spin*, he grabbed that too. He had a box at home of magazines and newspaper articles chronicling the rise of Tomorrow Mourning, so he'd add it to the collection.

At first, he was jealous of Tyler's money and fame, but the ugly downsides made Matthew grateful to have a face that could walk into Target without causing a stampede.

He got a small taste of it after the attack when reporters shoved microphones in his face as he left the hospital, rattling off inane questions like "How does it feel to be alive?" The details of the attempted triple murder and what led to it—complete with sex, drugs, and rock n' roll—made headlines around the world. Matthew was harassed for weeks by reporters begging for a juicy sound-bite from the kidnap victim of the infamous Amy Carey. After a few weeks, the attention died down. He couldn't imagine hiding from the paparazzi every day or dealing with his personal life being splashed all over the front page for everyone to see.

Tyler had earned every good thing in his life and had grown strong enough to handle the bad that came with it.

And Matthew was proud of the lucky bastard.

He paid for the items and walked out, clutching the hideous bear in one hand and the bag of candy in the other. When he was back in the hallway leading to Charlotte's room, he spotted Amber sitting on a chair outside the door. Her arms were wrapped around the same ugly green bear as the one he'd bought. They must've just missed each other on the elevators. Her pale blonde hair fell back when she looked up, and tears lined her eyes.

"Hey." Matthew crouched in front of her, touching a knuckle to her chin. "Is the baby still okay?"

"I—I think so. I haven't gone in yet." She sniffed and wiped the corners of her eyes with the back of her hand. "I peeked through the window, and Charlotte looked so scared. I don't want to go in upset and make it worse."

He understood. The last thing he wanted was to do or say something that would make this harder on Charlotte. It wasn't easy tamping down his emotions when she and Tyler were so distressed.

"She'll be glad to see you," he said. "Just take a few deep breaths."

She pulled in a long inhale and let it out in a loud rush. "Sandra's better at this emotional stuff, but she went to Seattle with her girlfriend, and Charlotte made me promise not to disrupt her trip." She bit her bottom lip, and he could tell she was trying hard to keep it together. Her skin was flushed, her mascara smeared, and her eyes tinged pink, but she was one of those girls who was so naturally beautiful it was hard not to stare like a creep.

"Can I get you anything?" he asked. "Coffee, coconut rum?"

She chuckled softly. "How about both mixed together?"

He patted his pockets. "Shit. Must've left them in my other pants."

She laughed again, finishing it off with a snort that obviously caught her off guard. She covered her mouth. "Pretend you didn't hear that."

He smiled. The sound was adorable, and coming from the always cool and put-together Amber made it even more endearing. "Hear what?"

The corners of her lips curled up as she pulled a small mirror from her pocket and took a quick glance at herself. She slapped her free hand over her face. "Fucking hell, I'm a mess. My eyes are all puffy and ugly, and I probably have snot dripping from my nose."

"Come on now." He took her mirror and tucked it back into the pocket of her black leather jacket. Her makeup was a mess, and a longer inspection would only make her feel worse. "You couldn't be ugly if half your head fell off. As for the snot... I don't have a tissue, but you can use my sleeve." He grinned at the muffled laughter behind her fingers. "I'm sure I have grosser things on it than that."

Amber's hands slipped from her face. "She'll be okay, right?" She touched her chest, fresh tears brimming in her eyes. "Even if..."

Obviously, they both knew how that sentence ended, but neither wanted to hear it out loud.

"Hey, our girl's tough. She can get through anything." He rose to stand in front of her chair, opening his arms. Amber was tough, too, and it was hard seeing her so upset. Like he'd done for Charlotte so many times, he wanted to take away some of her pain and make her smile again. "I'm shit at a lot of things, but my hugs are legendary."

She blew out a heavy sigh, pushing off her chair to stand. Matthew's bag crinkled as he hugged her. Gradually, he felt her body relax. Her chin rested on his shoulder, and her gentle sigh ruffled the hair at his neck.

In the three years since they met, he'd discovered Amber was full of contradictions. She hammered away at the drums harder than any man he'd ever seen and cursed like a drunken pirate, but there was something soft and vulnerable about her offstage if you looked a little closer. As if the dark makeup and signature snarl she wore in Killing Daisies promo photos were just a façade to hide behind. It challenged you to either take it at face value and fuck off or try to earn an invite to the genuine layers beneath. Now, even in her black boots and leather jacket, she smelled like peaches and flowers.

He felt lucky to be one of the few she felt comfortable enough with to let her guard down. That level of trust didn't come easy or quick, but she was so sweet and fun to be around that it was worth the wait. He couldn't count how many times they'd snuck off after a show to share a joint and talk for hours. She often dropped by the brewery to try their latest batch and chat with him and Evan as they worked.

There was even a time they'd almost kissed that he hadn't been able to shake. Sometimes, he wondered if Amber thought about it too, but never had the balls to ask. If only he'd had the balls to move a few inches closer and erase the *almost*.

"Thanks, Matty." Her arms slid higher up on his back, and she squeezed him tighter. Despite the sad circumstances, being so close to her felt nice. "After all she's been through, this is fucking bullshit."

"It really is. But she'll be okay." They stayed like that for a while, maybe because they were afraid to go into the room looking upset or because it felt good, and the rest of the day had been so awful. Who doesn't love a good hug?

"Oh. Hello."

Matthew pulled away to find Jessica frowning, her arms crossed over her chest. She gave Amber a once-over, her gaze settling on Amber's lower half—a black miniskirt that stopped mid-thigh and fishnet stockings, which led to a pair of black boots. After a head tilt, Jessica's eyes went to the cleavage poking out of the shredded L7 tank top that ended right above Amber's belly button. It was her usual attire for a night out, but standing close to Jessica in her scrubs, they couldn't look more different. But Amber was a drummer in a punk band. It would be weird to see her in a sundress or turtleneck. He liked the way she dressed and appreciated how comfortable she always seemed in her skin.

Matthew stepped closer to his girlfriend. "Jessica, this is Amber, one of Charlotte's best friends. And her drummer." He gestured at her clothes. "Obviously, she just got out of church."

Amber smacked his arm before wiping her eyes again. "Hi, Jessica. I've heard lots of great things about you."

"This is the first I've heard about you, but it's nice to meet you." Jessica's eyebrow rose. "Sorry if I'm staring, but that's not an outfit I see every day. Your style is so... unique."

Amber smiled, but her eyes narrowed a bit. "Coming from someone wearing pink scrubs with tiny butterflies on them, I'll take it as a compliment." Her smile grew. "Kidding. I went out with Sandra last night and haven't had a chance to get home and change. But in our circle, leather jackets and fishnets are practically a uniform. If you're around our crazy friends long enough, you'll get used to it."

Jessica let out a small, halfhearted laugh. "I'm not planning on going anywhere, so we'll see. Anyway, I'm glad you can be here for your friend." She touched Matthew's chest. "Dr. Berlinger will be taking care of Charlotte, so she's in good hands."

"Good to know." He gestured to the door, eager to see how Charlotte was and to end this suddenly awkward exchange. "We should..."

When they walked inside Charlotte's room, Tyler looked at both bears and laughed. "Was there a buy one get one free sale on ugly shit?"

"Yeah, that's why they had a magazine with your face on it." Matthew threw the bear at Tyler, who caught it and set it on the foot of the bed.

Amber put her bear beside it before hugging Charlotte. "How are you doing, sweetie?"

"Okay, I guess. They said I can go home if the last blood test turns out okay. I forget what they're looking for, but fingers crossed."

"They're most likely checking your hCG levels," Jessica said. "It's not a foolproof indicator of viable pregnancy, but typically, if the level rises, your chances of carrying to term increase. If it drops, the pregnancy is likely not viable."

Matthew's stomach sank at her words. Charlotte had finally calmed, and her eyes were getting shiny again.

Tyler took her hand and kissed it before holding it to his chest. "We'll see what the doctor says."

Matthew turned to Jessica. "The news has been good so far. Let's focus on that." He dug into his bag, pulled out the candy, and set it on Charlotte's lap. "And we'll celebrate that good news with sugar, red dye number forty, and delicious ingredients no one can pronounce."

Tyler grabbed a bag of M&M's, tore it open, and passed it to Charlotte. She managed a tiny smile and dumped a colorful handful into her palm. She ate two and held the rest out to Tyler. He took a few and settled back beside her. Their silent communication said everything about what they meant to each other.

"It's nice to stay positive," Jessica said, "but they should also be realistic and prepared for the worst-case scenario. Statistically, about twenty-five percent of pregnancies end in miscarriage. Most happen before the woman even knows she's pregnant, which obviously would make it easier than this."

Charlotte's lip quivered, and she drew in a jagged breath.

Amber's head whipped toward Jessica. "What the fuck did you just say to her?"

Tyler frowned, his brows pinching together. "Jessica, stop talking like that. Please."

"Hey." Matthew touched her arm, hoping to snag her attention before she said something else. He understood her job relied more on facts than feelings, but what she said was making everyone feel worse. Including him. "Like I said, let's keep it light."

Jessica's eyes bounced between Charlotte and Tyler. The pain on their faces was impossible to miss, so he hoped now, she would watch her words. "Sorry, but this job teaches you that the human body can be unpredictable. On the bright side, at least you know you *can* get pregnant. My sister's been trying for years. Even if you lose it, you can just try again."

Charlotte covered her face and bent forward, her shoulders quaking.

"What kind of shit is that to say?" The volume of Amber's voice rose. She touched Charlotte's back, rubbing it with slow circles. "Can't you see she's scared?"

"You need to leave," Tyler snapped, his glare aimed at Jessica's confused expression. "*Now.*"

Matthew's palms started sweating as Tyler's anger was directed at his girlfriend. As Jessica's words replayed in his head, he knew it was justified. Still, she often spoke her mind without considering how it might come across. That didn't excuse it, but it didn't mean she deserved to be attacked over a misunderstanding.

His brain scrambled for words to set things right again, coming up empty.

Jessica released a loud, exasperated sigh. "Fine. Sorry if I upset you. Good luck." She turned to Matthew. "I'll see you in the hall." A whoosh of cold air entered the room when she opened the door and walked out.

When Matthew looked at Amber, she was staring at him, slack-jawed, seemingly waiting for something. He still had no words, his brain a foggy, muddled mess.

Before the attack, he had an answer for everything. And there was never any confusion or hesitation holding him back from doing the right thing, especially when it came to his friends. Even stoned, he could navigate his way through almost any tough situation.

Now, he wasn't even sure what the right thing was. The frustrating brain fog was another shitty side effect of the trauma and always hit right before a panic attack. He took a few calming breaths to hopefully prevent things from tipping in that direction. All their attention and support needed to remain on Charlotte, not get diverted to Matthew because he couldn't keep his shit together.

After a few moments of tense silence, Amber's jaw snapped shut.

"I'll be right back, Char." She jabbed a finger at Matthew. "Let's talk outside."

Now, anger was directed at him, and he didn't understand why. Anxiety flared in his chest as it tightened, every shallow breath a struggle. He tucked his shaking hands into his pockets, hoping no one could see how close he was to falling apart.

When they returned to the hallway, Jessica stood beside the chairs outside the room.

"I didn't do anything wrong," she said. "I simply pointed out that if she loses the pregnancy, she isn't alone. It happens all the time. And that she's better off than a lot of people. Those are facts."

Matthew rubbed the back of his neck, still searching for the right words. If only she'd done the same a few minutes ago. "Your intentions were good, but I know Charlotte. She needs positive thoughts right now. This is her worst nightmare, and she needs our comfort and support, not statistics that make it seem like the odds are stacked against her."

"It's part of life, Matthew."

Amber scoffed. "Yeah, so are pets getting ripped apart by coyotes, but you don't tell someone that when their cat is missing."

"Why are you attacking me?" Jessica's features twisted into a scowl as the two women locked eyes. He'd never seen her upset before, making him feel even worse. "I just met you."

"Because instead of offering my terrified friend comforting words, you basically told her things were hopeless." Amber's fists curled at her sides like she wanted to hit someone. "How do you keep your job when you suck so hard at reading people?"

While Amber was overreacting a bit, he understood where she was coming from. She was being protective of her friend. He didn't want Charlotte hurt, either. But he also didn't want them to view Jessica as the enemy, especially when their relationship was beginning, and he wanted them all to get along.

"Hey, let's calm down." He touched Jessica's back, and she tore her gaze from Amber to turn to him. "It was a misunderstanding, and your heart was in the right place."

"Thank you." Jessica pecked his cheek. "I'm glad someone sees it. See you after work, babe." Without a word to Amber, she walked to the elevator. The doors opened, and she entered, disappearing as they closed again.

Amber's fingers poked the center of his chest, startling him.

"No, it fucking *wasn't* a misunderstanding," she gritted out. "We all told her to stop saying that heartless shit, and she didn't. If anyone else upset Charlotte like she did, you would've had their head on a spike. Where's your loyalty all of a sudden?"

"My *loyalty*?" Matthew's cheeks heated. His anxiety had mostly receded, but now his pulse thudded in his neck for a different reason—he was pissed. "What the fuck, Amber? How can you say that after everything I've done for Charlotte? To keep her safe. To make sure she's happy. I offered Amy and Rafael my *life* in exchange for hers." He threw his arms up, frustration buzzing under his skin. "Jessica sees people going through hard things every day in this place. She helped me a lot when I was here. And she tried to help Charlotte in her own way; you just don't know her well enough to see it."

A puff of air escaped her lips. "Maybe I don't know *you* as well as I thought." Her voice cracked with emotion, her eyes glossing with tears. She'd gone from angry to hurt so fast he couldn't keep up.

Before he could say another word, she returned to Charlotte's room.

Matthew stood in the hallway, feeling like he'd been punched in the face.

Was Jessica as out of line as everyone else seemed to think? Or was she simply operating on logic instead of emotions like her job trained her to? Did loyalty mean choosing one side while turning his back on the other?

Matthew had only been in a few relationships lasting longer than a month, and they'd all crashed and burned. He'd started to suspect one reason was how much time and energy he devoted to his friends and Tyler. Maybe he needed to pull back and focus on building a life with Jessica.

If he wanted things to work out, he'd have to make her the priority she deserved to be.

6

Amber

Sandra stirred chopped carrots and celery into the pot of vegetable soup on her stove. "Are we talking about the same Matthew Hall? The one who literally gave me the shirt off his back when that freak outside Satyricon threw a beer at me?"

When the soup was finished, they'd take it over to Charlotte's along with the lemon muffins they bought from her favorite café and the dozen chocolate chip cookies they'd baked. There wasn't a lot they could do to make her feel better about the scare she'd had the day before, but at least they could add some comfort food to her fridge while she healed up.

"I know it's hard to believe, but it's true. I was shocked he just stood there." Amber added salt and pepper while Sandra stirred. Neither was skilled in the kitchen, but they could follow recipes well enough. "Like he was in shock."

"It was a shocking situation, I get it." Sandra rubbed her chin, going quiet for a moment. "But Matty wouldn't choose some girl he's been seeing for two months over Charlotte. You sure you didn't get all hotheaded and misread the situation?"

Amber groaned. It was getting harder to keep her irritation at bay, but Sandra wasn't getting it. "You weren't there. You would've had the bitch's blood under your fingernails if you were. Jessica was way out of line, and Matthew defended her. Those are facts regardless of how hotheaded I can be."

Amber dug through Sandra's cabinets and found a large Tupperware container and lid.

"Okay, here's the deal." Sandra set the spoon on the counter and turned to Amber. "I'm not saying I don't believe you."

Amber scoffed. "Always a great opener."

"Hear me out." Sandra pushed a few rogue curls out of her eyes. "You, like my fabulous self, have a flair for the dramatic. And, sometimes, you jump to conclusions, and your blood starts boiling before your brain fully grasps all the details and nuances of what's happening."

Amber's eyes rolled. "Sandra..."

She held up a hand as if to say *hold on.* "Remember the time you swore that chick backstage called you a blonde skank? You flipped the fuck out until she whipped out an autographed photo of Tom Hanks. You were going to shred the bitch's face off for talking about Forrest fucking Gump!"

"Jessica told her if she loses the baby, she can just try again." Amber threw up her hands, nearly knocking over the saltshaker on the counter. "Like it's no big deal."

Sandra's eyebrow cocked, unconvinced. "Do you honestly think a super logical, twenty-four-year-old half-stoned dude's going to understand how that can be a shitty thing to say to a woman?"

"Tyler understood. And Matthew wasn't half-stoned because she made him quit pot. Charlotte told me."

Sandra blinked rapidly like her brain was on the fritz. "For real?"

"And he's moving to the other side of the city because of her. He *loves* that apartment. But Jessica's going to be a big fancy doctor, and god forbid her boyfriend would be below her status." Amber grabbed the spoon and stirred as the soup came to a simmer. "Hopefully, med school will teach her how to remove that giant stick up her ass."

"Is this just about what she said to Charlotte? You and this girl seem to have more beef than Burger King. And some of it stinks." She chuckled. "Stinky beef."

Amber exhaled loudly, frustrated for a whole new reason. "She's trying to change him, Sandra. And the worst part is, he's letting her! I don't want him to change. He's incredible. He's funny and generous, and he gives the best goddamn hugs in the world. He chases away backstage creeps that get too close to me. He randomly buys me stickers of bands I like and always saves me a growler when he brews my favorite beer."

"And you like him."

"Yeah." Amber frowned, too exhausted to bother trying to deny it. "And I like him. And if I wasn't such an idiot, I would've told him before he met that judgmental bitch."

Her feelings for Matthew started shifting from platonic to more at a Killing Daisies show almost two years ago. It was the night she saw a guy in the audience that looked like her dad. When the show ended, Amber foolishly chased after the man only to confirm it wasn't him. She ducked into an empty dressing room before the first tears fell. A few minutes later, Matthew found her and held her while she cried, whispering reassuring words as she let her armor fall and came apart in his arms. He listened to her talk about the pain of feeling abandoned. How even though she wanted to give her dad a black eye for running out on her family, a part of her still missed him. And hoped he was proud of her.

Matthew wiped her tears and wrapped his favorite black and grey flannel around her shoulders before driving her home. He never asked for it back, and she still wore it sometimes when she felt low. The scent of hops, weed, and aftershave had faded, but the soft fabric and memories it held were comforting against her skin.

Sandra leaned her hip against the counter. "So, the reasons you haven't told him have magically disappeared?"

"Nope." Amber set down the spoon. "I'll still be away for weeks on end when we tour. I still go out all night and sleep all day. I still lock myself in the garage with my drums for hours. And the list is only going to get longer after Europe. If we blow up, it'll mean more travel, photo shoots, interviews, and studio sessions. I have time for my friends and my drums. Even my sisters bitch that I don't see them enough, and I fucking live with them!"

Sandra's head tilted to the side, a curl falling onto her forehead. "A boyfriend who loves to travel and is used to musician bullshit wouldn't fit in there?"

"Nope." Amber grabbed a kitchen knife and chopped the chives and rosemary on the cutting board before adding them to the soup. "Remember Marco? That sexy-as-hell Spanish guitarist I was dating when I joined the band?"

Sandra nodded.

"We were solid for four months. Couldn't keep our paws off each other." Amber set the knife in the sink and wiped her hands on a kitchen towel. "I almost said the L-word, which would've been a major first for me. But he dumped me three weeks into working on our first album and playing club shows every weekend to get our name out there. Said he felt like he'd dropped to last on my list." Her stomach sank at the memory of his hurt expression as he ended things. "And he was right! He had. How can my priorities not be my band, friends, and family? Whatever guy I'm with is competing with everything else. That's not fair."

The breakup poked at old feelings of rejection from her dad leaving. Another important man in her life bailed when things got tough. She assured Marco they could figure out a compromise, but in the end, it became clear she wasn't worth fighting for. Amber was determined never to let someone make her feel like that again, so it was her first and last serious relationship.

Losing Marco was bad enough. If she took a chance with Matthew and things went the same way, she'd lose a good friend. The close group they treasured would implode. Of course, there was no guarantee they'd even get that far. If he wasn't interested, he'd reject her, and things would be awkward. She valued his friendship too much to risk it.

"Is it fair to you to accept being lonely?" Sandra asked. "If Marco ditched you that easily, he wasn't right for you, so good riddance. If he didn't see you're worth the effort and compromise, it's his fuck-up, not yours. And just because you weren't worth the trouble in his sexy, dumbass eyes doesn't mean you won't be to someone else. Like someone you already know would walk through a river of lava for the people he loves."

"You mean the someone who didn't stand up for one of his best friends and is changing himself to please an uptight bitch who doesn't deserve him?"

Sandra frowned. "Okay, fine. Not Matthew, then. But find some other guy who appreciates you and will stick around when things get hard. I didn't realize what I was missing until Christa came along. It's nice to have someone to hold you at the end of a long day." She tapped Amber's ankle with the tip of her shoe. "You must be getting sick of the casual hook-ups by now."

Amber gave a weak shrug, exhausted by the conversation. "It would be nice to have someone. But it's not just lying in bed holding each other. It's arguments, obligations, and complications. I need to focus on preparing for the tour, and I need relationship drama like I need a third boob."

Another life lesson her mother hammered into her daughters' heads was to always be self-sufficient. Achieve your own success, and never let a man derail it. Again, she was right. After the breakup with Marco, Amber missed a few band practices because she was too busy crying and cramming Snickers bars into her face. No relationship was worth risking her career over, especially when it was about to take off into the clouds.

"You know," Sandra said with a hand on her hip, "for someone who has no problem fighting for what she wants in every other part of her life, you sure sound ready to accept your fate when it comes to this."

Amber turned off the burner and moved the soup off the stove to cool. Sandra was right—Amber was a fighter. She'd fought her way past old wounds and lived a dream life she'd built through sweat and dedication. It would be amazing to fit a loving partner into that picture, but how was that possible without someone ending up feeling rejected or inadequate? She didn't want that for herself, and she sure as hell didn't want it for someone she cared about.

"I'm glad you and Christa and Tyler and Charlotte have figured out how to balance things, but mentally, I'm just not there." Amber hopped up to sit on the counter between the cutting board and seasonings. "Maybe after the album release and the European tour, I'll feel ready to pursue something more serious than a one or two-night stand."

It was hard to accept a certain degree of loneliness as her fate, even temporarily. It would be nice to have someone to kiss goodnight and wake up to every morning. But for now, at least she had the love of her amazing friends and family, which a lot of people didn't.

Still, the conversation left her longing for something she'd never had—someone who understood how challenging life with her would be and dove in head-first anyway. Then, stuck around when things got hard and complicated. But how could she believe it was possible when even her own parents had bailed on her?

"Back to what Matthew did or didn't say at the hospital." Sandra hopped up to sit on the counter beside Amber. "Do you honestly think he was being an asshole? Or was he stuck between his friends and the woman he cares about and did the best he could?" She put up a hand before Amber could respond. "Keep in mind that even though he's made some progress, his trauma still affects the way he handles stressful shit."

Amber couldn't believe she hadn't considered that. He'd been through a lot in the last few months, so judging his reactions based on who he was before the attack was unfair. Maybe some of the questionable choices he'd made lately—like sticking with his controlling girlfriend, moving out of his beloved apartment, and quitting pot even though he loved it—were because he still wasn't back to normal.

"Shit." Amber's eyes shut, and her shoulders slumped as the realization hit. "I'm the asshole. I should've considered what he's gone through and cut him some slack."

"That's my smart girl." Sandra grinned, clearly pleased with herself for finally getting the message through Amber's thick, stubborn skull. "So, how are you going to fix it?"

Matthew had an apology coming his way. For the sake of keeping the peace, Jessica did, too. That one was harder to swallow. What she said to Charlotte was wrong, and it was hard for Amber to let go of her anger when someone hurt her friends or family.

But she would do it for him.

Amber rubbed her temples, the depths of her assholery sinking in further. "I'll go the brewery tomorrow to make things right." Before Sandra could jump in, she added, "And I'll try harder to think before I go all aggro on someone."

"Fuck, man." Sandra's mouth tipped up in another self-satisfied grin. "I love it when I'm right."

7

Matthew

When Matthew walked into High Notes, he was surprised to find Amber sitting at the tasting counter with a half-full pint glass in front of her. A blue version of the hideous stuffed bear they bought Charlotte sat on the stool beside her. It was his favorite color, so maybe that was a good sign. They hadn't spoken since the confrontation at the hospital two days ago, and he hoped they weren't about to have another.

Their friendship was too valuable to risk with another fight. They were the only ones in their group who appreciated long hikes in the rain, rollercoasters, and making fun of terrible slasher films. She always intently listened when he talked and gave honest opinions when she tried new beers he made. He'd been on edge since their fight, and they had to fix this.

"Who's your friend?" he asked, standing beside her and pocketing his keys. "Can I see his ID?"

"He's not drinking." She spun around to face him. "He's just here in case you need something to throw at me because I was such an asshole."

Her admission caught him off guard. "No, you weren't."

The more he'd thought about it, the more he realized she wasn't in the wrong. Neither was Jessica, really. It was one of those unfortunate situations where misunderstandings led to hurt feelings, and things got out of hand. He needed some distance from the heated moment and impending panic attack to see it.

"Yeah, I was. I shouldn't have questioned your loyalty, of all things. The curly-headed voice of reason explained that maybe guys don't understand how the stuff Jessica said could be so hurtful to a woman." She held up a hand. "Not that it gives you a pass not to consider someone's feelings, but ignorance doesn't make you disloyal."

"So, I'm ignorant, huh?" He started to relax, tightening his lips to hold back a smile. "Because I own a pair of testicles?"

"In this case, yes." She shrugged, finishing off her beer. "The situation also touched a nerve because… One of my sisters lost a pregnancy a few years ago. I saw how it tore her apart. And her dumbass boyfriend said the same sort of stuff Jessica did—'we can just try again' and 'it happens all the time.' Those things didn't make it easier. She already knew all of that. She needed us to hug her, bring her soup, and do her chores until her grief was bearable. That's what Charlotte needed. Not hearing someone say the terrible things already running wild in her head."

Her anger at the hospital made more sense, and he felt terrible for her sister. "Is your sister okay now?"

A corner of her mouth rose like she appreciated the question. "Yeah. She's good."

Evan walked in from the back office. "Another round, Amber?"

"My friend here's driving, so why not?" She aimed a thumb at the bear before turning back to Matthew. "I still don't like what she said, but I should've handled it better for your sake. We're like family, and it wasn't cool of me to attack your girlfriend like that."

Evan picked up her empty glass, refilled it under one of the seven taps behind the counter, and set it on a fresh coaster. "Ooh, did I miss a catfight?"

"Don't you have beer to make?" She tossed a coaster at him like a frisbee.

Evan dodged it and started wiping the counter with a white dishrag, a broad grin on his face.

"And don't think I'm leaving here without one of those T-shirts," she said. "That new logo's badass." Amber swiveled in her stool, her gaze landing on the empty corner where Matthew had removed the stacked boxes and swept the floor. "Tidying up, huh?"

"Our boy's got big plans," Evan said.

Amber turned to Matthew, her head tilting to the side. "Ooh, do tell."

Matthew took the stool beside hers. He hadn't told anyone but Evan about his idea, but he knew she'd appreciate it. "I'm turning that area into a stage for open mics and small bands to perform. We'll add some seating, maybe introduce some new bar snacks."

Amber's face lit up with a wide smile. "Badass! I can totally picture it." She sipped her beer and licked foam from her lip. "It's hard finding venues to play when you're starting out. A chill, cozy place like this would be perfect for giving new artists a taste of performing."

"And all the shops around us close early," Evan added, "so the noise wouldn't be an issue."

Amber grabbed Matthew's wrist, shaking it. "We can pass out fliers at our shows!" The excitement radiating off her and the unexpected contact made him grin. "Have you looked at equipment?"

Matthew shook his head. "I have research to do. And I was going to ask Ty for advice."

She took another sip and set her glass on the counter. "I'd be happy to help. I even have a connection at Music Planet who gives me a discount. But I'll only let you use it on one condition. Well, two."

Things were moving quickly all of a sudden, but Matthew appreciated her enthusiasm.

"Name them." Evan leaned across the counter on his elbows.

"My drumming students get to play here once in a while. And at least one night a month's devoted to female-fronted bands. It's hard to get exposure when you're an unknown without a dick between your legs."

Evan waggled his eyebrows. "Keep talking dirty, baby."

Since Evan wasn't in striking distance, Matthew shot him a scowl that hopefully conveyed the message: *shut the fuck up*. Amber caught the look and laughed as Evan put his hands up in surrender and poured himself half a pint of al-most-black stout.

"Amber, my friend," Matthew said, holding out his hand, "you've got your-self a deal."

"Awesome." She shook his hand. Her skin was cold from the condensation on her glass, but it was soft, and her grip was gentle. "So, the shitty things I said to you in the hospital the other day are officially forgiven?"

Matthew nodded as she pulled her hand back. "Of course."

He appreciated that she'd taken time out of her day to come and make things right. Her questioning of his loyalty stung, and he was relieved to put that issue to rest. And it was generous to offer to help get the music space equipped and off the ground. She seemed as thrilled as he was by the project, and having a rising star in the music industry attached to it in any way could only help.

While he was happy to put their disagreement behind them, he couldn't let go of how poorly everyone seemed to think of Jessica. It was hard seeing the people he cared about most not embracing his new girlfriend like he'd hoped. "Other than the shit she said... What do you think of Jessica?"

Amber chuffed, exchanging a look with Evan.

Why do people keep fucking doing that?

"I'm not touching that one," she said.

"No, really. Your opinion matters to me. Do you think she's good for me?"

What if she said no? What if none of the people he loved ever accepted Jessica? Could he be with someone who didn't fit in with their group? They weren't easy questions to answer, and he hoped he wouldn't have to. Like so much in his life lately, he'd take it one day at a time.

Amber stared at her drink, tapping the side of her glass with her short, silver fingernail. "You need to answer that yourself, but I'll say this." She exhaled, swiveling to face him. "I think you're amazing the way you are. So do Tyler and all your other friends. She nudged his knee with hers. "What about her? If you didn't move to a 'nicer' place, would she want to go over for dinner or watch a movie on your couch? Would she stay the night? If so many things are conditional, what does that say about her feelings for you?"

Someone in their group had a big fucking mouth. Who told her Jessica hated his place so much and refused to stay over? Before he could ask, the bells above the door jingled.

"Matthew Hall?"

"Yeah?" Matthew turned around.

All the air was ripped from his lungs as a hot, dizzying shot of adrenaline raced through his blood. The room tilted as panic set fire to his system, every cell in his body screaming *RUN*.

Rafael.

The same cold, black eyes that feasted on his suffering stared from ten feet away.

It's impossible.

He's fucking dead!

Those facts were useless as Matthew's vision tunneled, fuzzy blackness encroaching on the edges while one thing remained in focus—the face that had come straight from his nightmares, darkening the doorway of one of the few places Matthew felt safe.

8

Amber

In her periphery, Amber watched as Evan walked behind the counter and grabbed something from a low shelf. She couldn't take her eyes off the stranger's face. His resemblance to Rafael instantly put her on edge, but she was more worried about Matthew.

With a quick glance, she noticed his hands were balled into tight fists and shaking. His eyes were wild with panic, like a rabbit that just realized a wolf was closing in and ready to pounce. She could hear his shallow, panted breaths beside her and worried he might pass out. He needed help for his panic attack, but first, they needed to deal with the stranger causing it.

Amber got to her feet and stood between Matthew and the man in the doorway. "Who the fuck are you, and why do you look like a dead man?"

The man flinched like she'd kicked him—she would if she didn't like his answer. "Rafael was my brother. I'm not here to cause trouble. I just want to talk."

She'd never seen Rafael outside of newspapers and TV news, but his face was branded in her memory. He was Tyler's ex-wife Amy's bodyguard, and when Tyler walked in on them doing the nasty in his living room, it set off the series of events leading to Matthew being kidnapped. They'd planned to frame him for murdering Tyler and Charlotte before killing him, too—all for revenge, fame, and a huge payday. Fortunately, Charlotte got the upper hand, killing Rafael and wounding Amy, who's spending the next decade and a half in prison.

Footsteps on Amber's left turned her head for a quick look.

Evan gripped a baseball bat like he was about to hit a homer. Or crush a skull. "We don't care what you want. Turn back around and leave him the fuck alone."

Matthew pushed off his chair to stand but staggered back, grasping the countertop behind him with both hands for support. He looked seconds away from toppling over and hurting himself. With an arm behind his shoulders, Amber pulled him to stand, guiding him behind the counter with Evan. Matthew slid to the floor with his back against the cabinets, his limbs shaking as he fought for air.

The man stepped closer. "Is he okay?"

Amber scowled at the nerve of this fucker. "Not after the shit your brother put him through."

"Look," he said with raised arms, "my mom's been trying to contact Charlotte through her management company with no luck."

"You won't have any luck here either." Evan aimed the bat's tip at the door. "Walk."

"Like I said, I'm not looking for trouble." The man's arms were still raised in surrender, but he stepped closer. "She lost her oldest son. She wants to know his last words."

"We'll find out your last words if you don't get the fuck out of my place," Evan snapped.

Matthew's trembling hands covered his face, and Amber could hear him counting in a whisper.

Breathe in two, three, four.

Out two, three, four.

"Go in the office and lock the door." Evan dropped keys between Matthew's feet, but he didn't react. He just kept reminding himself to breathe. As she listened, her heart squeezed in her chest.

"Fine." Fists curled at the man's sides. "I didn't mean to scare anyone. We'll try again another time."

"The fuck you will," Amber shouted, her cheeks flaming. "No one has any-thing to say to you about your psycho brother. He almost killed three of my friends, and he deserves the grave he's rotting in. *Go!*"

The man's jaw ticked, and he shifted his stance as if he were going to take another step forward but hesitated. "This isn't over." The ice in his tone made Amber shiver.

The bells above the door clanged and rattled as he shoved it open. A few moments later, a black car peeled out of the parking lot.

Amber knelt in front of Matthew, pulling his hands away from his face. "It's okay. Just keep breathing." She pressed her forehead to his, matching his long inhales and releasing the air along with him.

There was a metallic rattling of keys on the other side of the room, followed by a loud click as Evan locked the door.

Matthew's eyes slammed shut, and a lone tear broke free, sliding to his chin.

She wished Charlotte or Sandra were there—they'd known how to calm him. Even Jessica, who took care of people for a living, would be better at it despite her shitty personality. But Amber was all he had aside from Evan, so she'd try her best.

"Matty," she said, cradling his face, "look at me."

His wide eyes were glossed with tears as they slowly opened to connect with hers.

"He's gone," she said in a tone she hoped was soothing. "You're okay. We're all okay."

Matthew dug into his pocket, pulling out an orange prescription bottle.

"What's that?" When he didn't answer, she looked at Evan.

"Xanax," Evan said. "For panic attacks." He disappeared in the back, re-turning with a bottle of water that he opened and set on the floor in front of Matthew.

Matthew's hands shook so violently that he struggled to open the pill bottle. Amber took it from him, dumped a tiny white tablet into her palm, and held it out.

"Two," he said, his voice shaky and small.

He looked like he wanted to crawl out of his skin. Tears pricked her eyes to see him in so much pain. She felt like the worst friend on earth for not knowing he was still so deeply affected by the attack. Of course, she'd been on tour for two months, and since she got back, he'd spent most of his free time with Jessica. The times Amber saw him before the tour, they were at parties or shows where he was stoned and smiling, seemingly back to his old self. Either he was great at faking it, or she'd missed the signs something was wrong.

She added another pill to her hand. He pinched them between two fingers and tossed them to the back of his tongue. He frowned at the water bottle before swallowing them dry.

Amber wanted to ask why he did that but didn't want to risk making things worse. She sat beside him, wrapping an arm around his shoulders. "How often does this happen?"

Matthew pulled in a stuttered breath and slowly let it out. "Not as much as it did right after…" He stared blankly at the water bottle on the ground. "His face. Just like my fucking nightmares."

Evan sat on Matthew's other side. "It wasn't him. It wasn't Rafael. That motherfucker's in the ground. I saw his grave for myself when I pissed on it."

"Wow, Evan." Amber huffed a stunted laugh, some of the tension unfurling in her chest. "You're a really good friend."

Evan slid his arm around Matthew's shoulders, stacked on Amber's. "Don't let your brain fool you into thinking he's still out there, waiting to snatch you out of the goddamn parking lot. That's over now."

"What if his family wants revenge?" Matthew's hands shook harder, and he dragged them through his hair. "What if they go after Charlotte?"

Amber set a comforting hand on his knee. "They lost someone they loved. Just because he was a violent freak doesn't mean anyone else in his family is. Maybe they do only want to know his last words. For closure."

When Matthew turned to her, his eyes were still glassy, blown pupils crowding out the blue. "Don't tell Tyler and Charlotte."

Amber shook her head. "I won't tell Charlotte. She has enough to worry about. But Tyler should know they're trying to talk to her."

"I'm with her," Evan said. "He can even get a restraining order to try to keep them away from his family." He nudged Matthew's elbow. "You can, too, if it'll make you feel safer."

"A piece of paper won't do anything." Matthew barked out a humorless laugh, his chest jumping. "Tyler had one against Amy, and she still almost fucking killed us."

Amber searched her brain for what to say or do to help the situation. There was no guarantee Rafael's family wouldn't seek revenge, so empty platitudes wouldn't bring comfort. She'd never had a panic attack but helped Charlotte through a few of them when she started getting threatening notes. That shithead Rafael was to blame for that, too.

Charlotte seemed to appreciate hugs and reassuring words as she rode it out, so Amber would do the same for Matthew.

He opened and closed his fists before wiggling his fingers.

"That was a bad one," Evan said. "Fingers still numb?"

Matthew nodded slowly.

"Remember Charlotte's panic attacks when the notes first started?" Amber asked.

He nodded again. "She always thought she was about to faint, and her fingers went cold. During the worst ones, she'd swear she was dying. You don't really understand until you're in the same fucking boat."

It was a good sign he was talking. His hands weren't as shaky, and his breathing was almost back to normal. Had the pills kicked in, or had enough time passed since the peak to be able to calm himself?

Evan got to his feet. "Want a fresh beer?"

"No, thanks." She wasn't about to leave Matthew's side and wanted her hands free and head clear in case he needed something. "You guys closed for the day?"

Evan flipped his wrist, checking his watch. "Might as well. I think we could all use a break after that."

She wrapped her other arm around Matthew and squeezed. "I'm sorry that happened to you. Is there anything I can do?"

His chin slowly lifted, and their eyes met. Something about the way he looked at her made fresh tears sting her eyes. There was a raw vulnerability there she'd never seen before.

As their gaze held, the energy between them shifted. Like they'd grown closer without moving an inch. A crease appeared in the space between his brows, disappearing as quickly as it came.

"Thank you." He'd said it so quietly she almost missed it. It wasn't an answer to her question, but somehow, it said everything.

Maybe she wasn't so bad at taking care of people after all.

Amber cupped the side of his face in her palm. The stubble on his cheek was rough on her skin, and he smelled like fresh hops and aftershave. They were so close she felt the warmth of his slow, steady exhales on her cheeks. It reminded her of the time last year when they'd almost kissed. They'd been just as close, his eyes roaming her face, seemingly searching for clues about what'd changed between them.

"Anytime." A soft smile touched her lips.

"You going to movie night at Matthew's new place?" Evan's voice beside them broke the spell.

"Wouldn't miss it." Amber turned back to Matthew. "Unless you want to cancel."

He shook his head. "It's still on."

"Wish I could make it," Evan said, "but my cousin set me up on a blind date." He tapped Matthew's ankle with the tip of his sneaker. "Do yourself a favor. Make it a comedy and smoke some weed."

"I quit."

Evan held out his hand, and Matthew took it, standing on wobbly knees. "Sure, you did."

"I didn't quit," Amber said, pushing off the floor to stand, "so feel free to walk through my cloud later for a contact high." She ran a hand down Matthew's back before hugging his side. It was tough seeing her usually fun-loving friend so miserable. "It's probably better for you than those pills."

"Not if you ask his nurse girlfriend," Evan muttered. Matthew shot him an annoyed look. "Sorry, bro."

"I haven't needed them in a couple of days. That was just…" He gestured at the door. "*Fucked.*"

"Sure was." Evan clapped Matthew's shoulder. "But it's over now."

"And we have a fun night ahead of us." Amber grabbed the ugly bear and tucked it under Matthew's arm. "Don't forget your new friend."

It almost got him to smile, but not quite. It would take a lot more than a stupid bear to cheer him up this time.

She'd make it her mission to ensure movie night was as stress-free and chill as always. After what Charlotte and Tyler just went through, they could use it too. So, Amber would set aside her hatred of grocery shopping to load up on everyone's favorite snacks. And she'd kick the first person who brought up anything heavy.

Everyone was going to have fun whether they liked it or not.

9

Matthew

The rough gray fabric of the new couch made Matthew's skin itch, and if he sat on the middle cushion, a metal spring pushed against his ass cheek. The couch looked and smelled brand new, but it was stiff and lacked personality. He was tempted to punch the cushions and spill something so it wouldn't look like it'd just left the showroom or the set of some shitty sitcom.

It was delivered a few hours earlier, and the only other things in the condo were a sleeping bag, his TV, the blue bear Amber gave him, a few groceries, and a new DVD player to replace the one he'd spilled a beer on. The place came with a microwave, so at least he could make popcorn for the movie.

He'd planned to keep sleeping at his old place until moving in the rest of his stuff, but after the confrontation with Rafael's brother that afternoon, being at an address easily found by thumbing through the white pages was out of the question.

Since leaving work, he'd almost canceled movie night a dozen times. The bone-deep exhaustion that always followed a panic attack made him feel drained and ready for bed. And he didn't want concerning looks if he wasn't smiling or laughing as much as everyone thought he should.

But those objections were overshadowed by the fact that Matthew couldn't stand being alone in this strange, spotless place. It didn't feel like home yet, and he didn't belong in his old place anymore. It wasn't a feeling he was used to, and he couldn't wait for it to pass.

Hopefully, the normal, no-stress night with his friends would be good for him. So, for his sake and theirs, he was determined to make the most of it.

People would arrive any minute, so Matthew dug into one of the grocery bags on his couch and pulled out candy, chips, and a box of microwave popcorn. At the bottom were DVDs of *Clerks* and *Tommy Boy*. He'd wandered the aisles of Blockbuster Video for twenty minutes before taking Evan's advice and grabbing comedies.

Jessica was coming after work, and he hoped she'd like the movies. Her sense of humor differed from what he was used to with his friends. She laughed at crazy patient stories her co-workers shared and PG-13 rom-coms. Once, she stopped by his apartment and found him watching *Beavis and Butthead*. Her face crumpled like she was about to hurl on his carpet.

They had enough things in common that he tried not to focus too much on their differences. They both valued honesty and loyalty. They liked suspense novels, Thai food, and the Rolling Stones. He figured things are often awkward in that early phase of a relationship when you're still discovering each other's quirks, so maybe she'd loosen up once they got more used to each other's worlds.

The doorbell rang, and Matthew set down a bag of Reese's Pieces to answer it.

Through the peephole, Amber held a grocery bag and, fortunately, not another hideous bear. Her lips were pressed in a tight line, her eyebrows slightly pinched. She was probably still worried about him from earlier. It was embarrassing to break down in front of her, but it couldn't be helped.

He'd never forget how distressed she looked when he needed to take pills to breathe again. Despite that, Amber instinctively knew what he needed, calming him with her reassuring words and touch. That was no easy feat when he was spinning out, and he was grateful she'd been there.

Matthew unlocked the deadbolt and turned the knob.

"Hey, Rockstar," he said, taking the bag from her hands and stepping back to give her room. "Welcome to my new digs."

"Thanks, I can't wait to see it." She walked inside, her head turning in every direction as she took in the space. "Wow. This is a huge step up."

With an extra eight hundred square feet and a second bedroom, it was a huge step up from his tiny apartment. He even had a small back porch where he could host barbecues and a skylight above the couch to watch the stars at night.

He set her bag on the kitchen counter. "Yeah, it's time to let some other sad bachelor have that old place."

She kept looking around, nodding slowly. "I never pegged you for a white walls and granite countertops kind of dude, but whatever makes you happy. It all looks really nice."

The walls of his old place were painted a soft yellow that brightened up the rooms, and his countertops were cheap Formica but unique—a grass green base with pale blue swirls that looked like tiny tornadoes. He still wasn't sure if white walls and granite countertops would make him happy, but he was giving it a shot.

The way she emphasized the word *looks* was very telling. He hoped once his familiar things were unpacked, it would *feel* nice, too.

Amber pulled a massive bag of peanut M&Ms from her grocery bag. "In case Charlotte decides to come."

"I just talked to Tyler. They're staying in to catch up on lost sleep."

"Damn." She plopped the candy on the counter. "I was hoping to get that girl laughing and loaded up on sugar."

"Me too, but she needs rest." Matthew opened the popcorn box and stuck one of the bags in the microwave. "It'll be us, Sandra, and Jessica tonight. And a shitload of junk food."

"Sandra isn't coming." Amber gnawed her bottom lip. "Christa surprised her with Babes in Toyland tickets. No way we could compete with that."

Shit.

"So, it's just us and Jessica, then?" An unexpected burst of anxiety tingled in his chest. "Cool."

The last time the two women saw each other was during the heated confrontation at the hospital. But this could be a good thing. He could help them talk it out and get on a better track. It would be awful if two people he cared about couldn't get along.

"I guess I should apologize for jumping down her throat. My sister Beth says I need anger management classes." She scoffed. "I still say Jessica was out of line, but I need to learn to shut up and think before I go off, especially since she's important to you."

Amber was important to him, too, and he was relieved she wanted to make amends. "You didn't need a class to figure that out. Take that, Beth."

Amber laughed as she ripped open the bag of candy and popped one into her mouth. "How are you feeling about what happened earlier?" she asked, touching his wrist. "It's okay if you don't want to talk about it."

He'd talked to her about personal things before. They'd both lost their fathers, though for different reasons, and they'd talked about how those losses affected them. She knew about his complicated relationship with his mother. He even told her about feeling inferior in the shadow of his famous older brother, something he didn't often share. Between Amber's tour and hectic schedule afterward, he hadn't opened up much to her about the attack's lingering effects. After their shared experience that afternoon and considering how great she was at listening without judgment, he felt comfortable being honest.

"It's frustrating that I can't assess a situation, see there's no danger, and shrug it off. The guy didn't have a visible weapon and didn't threaten us. But I know why it affected me like that." Matthew moved to the couch, taking the center cushion so she could be comfortable. She took the end that wasn't covered in bagged junk food. "One thing that sticks with me from Rafael's attack is the surprise of it—being grabbed from behind without knowing what's going on. The tape slapped over my mouth so I couldn't scream. I'm strong... or at least, I was then, but he was stronger. I couldn't fight."

"How often do you have nightmares?" Her features were soft with empathy, making it easy to keep talking.

"At least a couple times a week. It's like I can *feel* that needle stab through my skin. I can hear Charlotte screaming and Tyler begging them to stop. Then, I wake up sweating and shaking, and it takes a while to convince myself it isn't real."

Amber took his hand and gave it a reassuring squeeze. The gentle contact felt so good he felt a little guilty for not pulling back. He had a girlfriend, after all—one who'd probably be hurt if she saw them touching. "I'm so sorry you're going through that, Matty. I can't imagine how hard it must be."

He glanced at their joined hands. Something like regret flashed in her expression, and she pulled away. He kicked himself for making her feel awkward, but if Jessica used the key he'd given her and walked in, she would've had the wrong idea. Still, the comfort was nice when his thoughts had gone so dark.

Suddenly restless, he fiddled with the strings on his gray hooded sweatshirt. "I like being with Jessica because I want things to be calm, stable, and predictable. I want to come home to a quiet place and zone out in front of the TV or with a game or a book. I want to feel... normal, I guess."

Before the attack, he was adventurous, spontaneous, and fearless. He loved meeting new people and exploring new places. Now, anything outside his shrinking comfort zone felt too overwhelming. There was no telling where danger lurked and triggers for his panic were everywhere—the water bottles at work, duct tape at the hardware store, and even the smell of mildew would remind him of the basement and set him off. Hard to escape that smell in a state as damp as Oregon.

"Wow. You sound super old for twenty-four." She chuckled and seemed pleased when he did, too. "I wish I could handle normal and quiet. When I play or watch shows, my nights are full of action, lights, and noise. It's like a high that takes forever to come down from. But when I do come down, I feel... sad, I guess. Like nothing else can ever feel as good, so most everyday shit feels dull and pointless. It'd be nice to appreciate slow, peaceful moments."

He never would've guessed that. Amber always seemed so upbeat and carefree, even off the stage. "Nothing else has ever made you feel like that?"

"Nope." She shook her head slowly. "Not booze or sex or roller coasters. Music's my favorite drug, and the withdrawals suck hard."

"You should put that in a song."

She laughed. "Sandra and Charlotte have the words covered. I just beat the hell out of my drums to back them up."

He was surprised she was downplaying her role. Amber always seemed so confident in her skills and place in the band. "I think what you do is amazing."

"Really?" Her brows drew together. "Why?"

Matthew slipped off his shoes and moved to sit cross-legged, getting comfortable. "Everyone pays attention to the players out front, right? Especially the lead singer. But it's what you do that shakes the floor. People feel that kick drum in their chest. Your beats are what make heads bob and toes tap. Without you, the heart of the songs would be gone."

She grinned, her eyes sparkling in a way that made him glad he'd said it. "That might be the nicest thing anyone's ever said to me."

He smiled back before clearing his throat and checking the clock on the DVD player. "Jessica must've changed her mind. Should we start the movie?"

"Sure, I'll hit the lights."

"I'll get it," he said too quickly. Her brows furrowed for a second, but she let it go.

He turned off the lights in the living room but left on the ones in the hallway and kitchen.

"If she's not coming..." Amber pulled a cigarette case from her pocket and slid out a joint. "Can I be a terrible influence?"

Matthew couldn't think of anything he'd rather end the day with than a soothing head change. "Hell. Yes." He pulled a lighter from the pocket of his jeans, sparking it. "So, what's your vote? *Clerks* or *Tommy Boy*?"

Amber put the joint to her lips and slowly inhaled as he held the flame to the tip. When she pulled back, she held the smoke in her lungs for a few seconds before blowing out a dense white cloud between them. "My answer will always be Chris Farley."

"*Tommy Boy* it is." He savored the skunky, piney scent filling the space. Sitting with her like this, with that scent in the air, felt so familiar that it made the new place feel more like home. He took the joint. She'd left a pink lipstick print behind, and he swallowed hard before taking a hit and passing it back. "You have excellent taste in movies, my friend." The pot warmed his skin, his muscles relaxing more thoroughly than they had in weeks. Like there'd been a knot inside him, pulled tighter every day, and it finally unfurled. "And fucking great taste in weed."

Her lips curled up as she took another hit. "You can thank Molly."

He nodded, unsurprised. Of course, it was Molly's. She was the guitar tech for Killing Daisies and had a greenhouse in her backyard where she grew several strains of potent marijuana. The side business kept Portland's music community stoned and happy while keeping her from having to grind away at a nine-to-five.

"I'll grab the popcorn while you start it up." Amber left the couch, and he set up the DVD, grabbed the remote, and sat back down. She shook the bag of popcorn and plopped beside him, taking a handful before passing him the bag. She slipped off her shoes when he pressed play, tucking her feet beneath her.

"Are you cold?" he asked.

She wore a tight black tank top and jeans with tattered knees. The room wasn't freezing, but there was a chill. He couldn't seem to find the thermostat's sweet spot.

"Kind of." She hit the joint and passed it back to Matthew.

"I only have my sleeping bag and a few hoodies. Everything else is at the apartment."

"A hoodie would be perfect. Thanks."

He handed her the one draped over the back of the couch he'd worn the day before. It was clean, and he'd put it on right after a shower, but it smelled like the hops he was working with at the brewery. Knowing Amber, she'd probably like that.

She slipped it over her head, her arms swimming in black fabric. Her hands looked tiny as they popped out of the sleeves to take the joint.

He was really glad she came. Now that Charlotte and Tyler were always together in their love bubble, Evan was out with his brothers most nights picking up girls, and Sandra was off with Christa all the time, he missed hanging out with someone familiar and without expectations—someone who let him be himself and let his guard down. With all the changes going on, he was afraid moments like this were over.

Matthew enjoyed being with Jessica but could never fully relax around her like this. He was always worried he was slouching or had food in his teeth. Amber didn't care about that shit. She'd even held his hair back once while he puked after too many beers. Instead of judging him as some women would have, she sat on the floor beside him and told him about all the times she'd been in the same position to make him feel better. She even put a cool washcloth on the back of his neck and brought him ginger ale.

"Do you like living alone?"

The question disrupted his thoughts. "Mostly. It's nice not having anyone to complain about my dumb habits or having to tiptoe around when I can't sleep."

She exhaled and passed him the joint. "Sounds amazing. It can be a drag living with my four crazy sisters. There are major reasons, like lack of privacy, and small ones, like I can't even have chunky fucking peanut butter because everyone else likes creamy. I hate grocery shopping, so I just deal." She tucked her arms behind her head, leaning back against the corner of the sofa. "Mostly, I'm tired of the constant drama, and someone's always up in my business. And accusing me of stealing their shit."

He inhaled a deep hit, the smoke slowly drifting from his lips. "Do you?"

She smirked, her eyes half-closed and rimmed with pink. "Lip gloss. And Beth and I have the same shoe size, so I take her heels on the rare occasions I need heels. And Kate has these cute babydoll dresses I tend to snatch. I give them back. Usually. Often with a red wine stain or a burn mark from a fallen cherry, but I give them back. Speaking of which..."

He looked at the joint in his hand and tapped the hot ash over an empty beer bottle. She laughed at something Chris Farley said on the screen before her gaze drifted around the room again.

"This place is really nice, Matty. And a smart investment. My sister Tara sells real estate, and she's hammered that into my head for years."

"Tyler too. I guess we're both stuck with siblings who always know better than we do." He laughed and sank further into the couch, barely noticing the metal spring underneath him. Feeling sufficiently stoned, he wet his fingers and pinched the joint's tip to extinguish it before setting it on the table. Abstaining for a few weeks made him a lightweight. "Why haven't you moved out?"

She hugged her knees to her chest, her cheek resting on the back of the couch. "I'm too comfortable, I guess. When my mom moved to Alaska a few months after my dad left, we all came to rely on each other for different things to fill that gap. Beth makes sure the fridge and pantry stay stocked, Kate gets off the earliest, so she cooks for everyone, Tara takes everyone's share of the bills and pays them, and Denise is obsessed with keeping everything spotless."

"And you?"

Amber shrugged. "I'm the youngest, so no one expects much from me. I pitch in a lot, don't get me wrong, but they're used to me being gone, hiding out in the garage with my drums, or crashing out in my room all day, recovering from shows." She ran her fingers through her pale blonde hair, a few rogue strands drifting over her forehead. His fingers twitched with an unexpected urge to brush them back. "I guess my main contribution is testing their patience with my noise."

He chuckled, the strong weed making his head warm and floaty. He'd really missed that feeling. "So if you don't want to be too comfortable anymore, what do you want?"

She brushed the hair off her face and tucked it behind her ear. "I think I'm so used to people taking care of me that I want to prove to myself I can stand on my own. Right now, my list of life skills is pathetically short."

"I wouldn't say that. You've always been a great listener. In a world where people just want to hear themselves talk, that's one of the most useful life skills there is. And you give great advice. I bet you've helped your sisters through some jams with that over the years."

She shrugged a shoulder. "I've given them plenty of relationship advice, although I'm pretty fucking clueless on the subject." She chuckled, the sound low and gravelly from the smoke. "It's such a kick in the nuts how much easier it is to figure out other people's problems than your own."

He nodded in agreement. "True that."

Their heads tipped up in unison as rain pelted the skylight. The rhythmic tapping was soothing, and they listened in comfortable silence for a while.

Matthew's thoughts drifted back to that afternoon. Without hesitating, Amber stood between him and potential danger while he fell apart. Her reaction made him feel something he hadn't felt in a long time—safe.

Even when Jessica talked him through panic attacks, he didn't feel safe again when they passed. Nothing Dr. Vega ever said had achieved it either. But when Amber got beside him on the floor, he focused on the warmth of her arms as they wrapped around him and her gentle, calming words, drawing him out of his panic. Knowing he could trust her completely made him comfortable enough to fully let go. While it was embarrassing to be so weak in front of her, he was glad she'd been there.

"You took great care of me earlier." Matthew turned to her, his eyelids heavy. "When my brain short-circuits like that, it's scary. I appreciate having people around who can make me feel safe."

The tiny dimple in her left cheek showed itself when she smiled. It was one of the cutest damn things he'd ever seen, and he savored every time it made an appearance.

"Glad I could help." Amber's eyes stayed connected with his until she blinked hard and pulled her knees closer to her chest. "Honestly, I wasn't sure what to do at first. The only things I've ever taken care of were a goldfish when I was eleven that I forgot to feed and an orchid that turned brown and crispy from lack of water."

Again, she seemed to downplay how capable she was. What or who made her feel like she was anything less than incredible?

Knowing what her father did to their family made him the most likely culprit. And like she said, with her sisters taking care of her she'd never had the chance to prove to herself what she could handle. Hopefully, someday, she'd see her worth more clearly.

As their attention returned to the rain tapping at the skylight, a deep sense of calm washed over him. It wasn't just the killer weed she brought. It was her.

It was so easy being in her company that all the day's problems faded into the background. Matthew reveled in the all-too-rare break from his stresses.

"I know I said I don't like slow, peaceful moments…" Amber sighed heavily beside him. "But this is nice."

He turned his head. Amber looked so fucking pretty with the soft glow of the TV on her skin and her hair pushed away from her face. It was too dark to see the color of her eyes, but he knew the deep, intense shade of blue by heart. Like the Northwest skies after a storm has passed.

It was absurd that she didn't have a boyfriend. He'd always thought that. She was so cool, talented, and ridiculously beautiful. Since that dickhead Marco ditched her shortly after Killing Daisies formed, she hadn't been serious with anyone. Why had she been single for so long?

Amber would be an incredible girlfriend—the kind who took you as you were and never tried to impress you or ask you to change.

"Do all the units have skylights?" she asked.

He shouldn't be looking forward to wearing his black sweatshirt tomorrow because it would smell like her. He shouldn't want to move a few inches closer, hoping to wake up the undeniable sparks he felt between them when their faces were inches apart that afternoon.

Maybe he was making a mistake being with someone who made him feel ashamed of where he lived and made judgmental faces at the shows he watched. Was he settling for a relationship without sparks because Jessica looked so good on paper? Did the bond they'd formed when she took care of him in the hospital make it easy to overlook or accept her faults?

If Matthew had been brave enough to tell Amber how he felt ages ago and by some miracle she felt the same, she'd be tucked against his side as the movie played. He would know what it was like to kiss her. And he'd never let her doubt what she was worth.

Of course, there was no telling what the future held.

"I'm not sure," he said. "But it's possible."

Her big blue eyes stayed on his face as a slow grin curved her lips.

"It's weird that you don't have a boyfriend." He hadn't meant to say it out loud, but there it was. *Damn weed.*

"Wow." She pushed his leg with her toes. "Thanks, *friend.*"

"No, I'm not being a dick. I just mean... Look at you." Was it an inappropriate observation to make when he had a girlfriend? Probably. But he was so at ease that it was impossible to be anything but real with her. "I've seen lots of guys at your shows throw themselves at you, but aside from that fuckwad Marco, you never go out on more than a few dates. Is commitment not your thing?"

He'd always hated seeing her walk off with random guys after shows—guys many notches hotter and cooler than Matthew would ever be. He told himself it wasn't jealousy, but what else would make him fantasize about strangling the unworthy jackholes with the backstage lanyards swinging around their necks?

"You could say that." She shrugged. "But it's not like I'm celibate. I get plenty of company."

He could've done without hearing that.

She continued, "I don't have space in my head or heart for what a relationship requires. Aside from Tara, who bats for Sandra's team, I've watched my sisters go through dozens of boyfriends. It's a lot of work to end up hurt when it ends."

"Not every relationship ends."

"From what I've seen, they do. Usually when things aren't so easy and fun anymore. That's why my dad left. And that fuckwad, Marco. I'm afraid if I open my heart to someone else, they'll just break it and leave too." Amber slipped her hands into the pockets of the hoodie. "Tyler and Charlotte give me hope, but what they have is rare. Most people never find love like that."

Matthew could've done without hearing that, too. He didn't need a reminder that he may never know what it felt like to love and be loved so intensely. And it was a damn shame that Amber's fears might keep her from experiencing it someday.

"The handful of dudes I have brought home were subjected to my sisters' relentless interrogation about their job and past dating history, and Kate even had the nerve to ask one guy when his last STD test was and what the results were."

"Shit."

"She asked him for a copy."

"Double shit."

"Yeah. That doesn't keep butts in the seats." Her hand left her pocket to sweep her hair over one shoulder. "Plus, I'm judged a lot by how I look. Guys think I'm either easy or scary. Not many have bothered to actually get to know me." Sadness settled into her expression, but it disappeared as quickly as it came. "Besides, my career's my boyfriend, and I'm good with that."

"Don't you get lonely?" Matthew did, especially now that his mind was poisoned with memories too dark and awful to talk about. It was a very personal question, but he wanted to know. Amber didn't deserve to be lonely.

"Sometimes. But it's a sacrifice I'm willing to make for the life I have. Hopefully, if the right guy comes along someday, I'll be ready to make space for him."

The doorknob jiggled, and Matthew's spine stiffened.

Fuck.

He hadn't done anything wrong, but the first slithering tendrils of anxiety crept into his chest.

Jessica walked in, stopping in her tracks when she saw them on the couch.

Matthew got up quickly and kissed her on the cheek. "Hey, Jess. I was worried you'd changed your mind about coming over."

"I grabbed a bite and went home to get out of my scrubs." She looked Amber up and down like she'd done at the hospital, giving him a frown when she was through. She sniffed. "Were you smoking pot?"

Double fuck.

A knot of tension formed in his gut at her tone and look of disapproval. It felt like he'd been busted by his mom, not his girlfriend.

"Yeah." Matthew raked a hand through his hair, frustrated with being made to feel guilty for something that wasn't a big deal. "We had a pretty big scare this afternoon and—"

"I thought you quit."

"I should go." Amber stood, slipping into her shoes. "I'll call for a ride since I smoked and get my car in the morning." She walked to the kitchen and used the phone while Jessica stayed silent, staring at the carpet.

Everything was going wrong. He didn't want Amber to leave. He wanted the women to shake hands and try to be friends, even if only for his sake.

Amber hung up the phone and took off his sweatshirt.

"You don't have to go." He glanced at Jessica, hoping she'd jump in and back him up, but she stayed quiet. As the silence stretched on, Amber looked even more uncomfortable, her gaze dropping to her shifting feet.

"No, really." She set the sweatshirt on the couch and walked around them to the door. "Beth's waiting up for me. Thanks for the Farley fix." She gave an awkward wave. "See you guys around."

The door shut behind her, and Jessica stared at it for a few moments before speaking. "Is something going on between you two?"

"No. We're just friends. I'm sorry about the weed, but—"

"Why is that girl always half-dressed around you? And wearing your sweatshirt?" She picked it up, shaking it between them. "What the fuck, Matthew?"

"Please don't make a big deal out of it. I'm glad you're here. Want me to restart the movie so we can watch it together?" He slid his hand around her waist, but she pulled away. "We have enough snacks to eat for a week."

She looked at the screen, the corners of her mouth downturned as Chris Farley sang "Fat Guy in a Little Coat."

"What is this? It looks stupid."

A shot of clarity broke through the marijuana haze, and anger bubbled in his chest. From the moment Jessica walked in, he'd been unfairly accused of infidelity and looked down on for smoking weed, even though he did it when they met. She'd judged Amber for what she wore and showed no concern whatsoever for what frightened him earlier that day.

Calling a hilarious Chris Farley movie stupid was the last straw.

"Jessica..." He grabbed the remote and turned off the TV. "We need to talk."

10

Matthew

From his seat at her kitchen table, Matthew watched Charlotte scrub the same part of her stove for the third time. The scent of lemon cleanser was thick in the air. The dark circles under her eyes said she still hadn't caught up on sleep, and her face was pale. Her hair looked like she hadn't brushed it in a while, and it was pulled back in a gray scarf with black polka dots.

She'd already declined his offer of help and yanked the sponge from his hand when he didn't take no for an answer. When Charlotte was stressed, a project distracted her, so he let her do her thing. He could relate.

"So, I have some news." Maybe she could use another distraction: his personal problems. "I broke up with Jessica last night."

The relief he felt when she left his condo surprised him. It didn't feel like his heart was broken, and he had no regrets about how things played out. He'd never be who she wanted him to be, and he realized she wasn't what he wanted either.

Matthew wanted what Tyler and Charlotte had—passion, love, and an intense connection that was impossible to deny. It wasn't there with Jessica, and he'd rather be alone than settle for anything less.

Charlotte's head turned, and her gaze skittered across his face before she set the scrubber in the sink, washed her hands, and sat across from him at the table. She was probably grateful for a distraction that wouldn't dry out her skin. "Lay it on me. What happened?"

"She saw me and Amber alone, sitting on my couch and—"

"Hold up." Charlotte raised a hand in the air. "Why were you and Amber sitting alone on your couch?"

"Sandra and Evan had dates, and you guys crashed out here, so she was the only one who showed up for movie night. Until Jessica came after work. She saw us and asked what was going on. She looked at Amber's ripped jeans, and when Amber took off my sweatshirt—"

"Amber was in your clothes?" Her eyebrows shot up. "Please get to the part where I'm on your side, not Jessica's."

That surprised him, especially coming from Charlotte. "What do you mean?"

"How have you not learned more about women after being around me and Sandra all these years?" Her head tilted to the side, and her expression said she thought he was special, but not in the nice way. "You knew what a big deal it was when Ty let me wear your dad's jacket. And if I were only dating a guy a short time and walked in on him, alone in his house with a girl as hot as Amber, I wouldn't be happy either. They only met once, and it didn't go well. How would Jessica know she isn't trying to put the moves on you?"

Knowing his intentions were good didn't change how it appeared to Jessica. But there was another thing he couldn't shake. Something he couldn't tell Charlotte. He'd said he had a big scare, and Jessica didn't seem concerned about what'd happened. He brought it up during the argument that led to the breakup, but she claimed she hadn't heard him say it. That felt like a lie, but maybe it wasn't. Maybe she didn't hear it because her fears about what might be happening with him and Amber were louder.

"Maybe," he said, his shoulders slumping, "I fucked up." Roxy's tiny beagle feet tapped their way to the kitchen, and she set her front paws on Matthew's leg. "What's up, dog?"

Charlotte laughed. "It'll never not be funny when you ask her that." She got up, grabbed two pink lemonade Snapples from the fridge, and set one in front of Matthew before sitting back down. "Maybe you didn't fuck up. I didn't like how proud Jessica seemed that she *made you* quit pot. And I got the impression that you wouldn't be moving without her pressuring you. If she doesn't think you're good enough as is, she's wrong. And you dodged a bullet." She popped the cap off her bottle.

"You're probably right." Matthew scratched Roxy's ears and chin. Her tongue lolled out of her mouth in gratitude. "I appreciated that she wanted me to grow and level up, but her judgmental bullshit was really getting to me." Especially when it extended to his friends. He hated seeing that judgment aimed at Amber the night before. She didn't deserve that.

"In some ways, sure, you need to grow and change. But you have to do it for yourself. And don't just focus on faults; keep your best qualities in mind too. You're already killing it. You own your own business, you're an amazing brother and friend, you pay your bills on time, and you've never been a liar or a cheater. Does she appreciate those qualities or just focus on what she doesn't like?" Charlotte reached across the table, touching the back of his hand. "Are there some rough edges that need smoothing? Sure. She has them, too. We all do. Don't feel like you have to change to be good enough for her or anyone else because you're already completely fucking awesome."

"Thanks, Charlotte." He rolled his bottle cap in his fingers. "It's just... I never connected with someone like her before. She's successful, smart, and has all these amazing goals for her life. If I kept living like I was, I'd keep attracting the same kind of women as before. Potheads with minimum wage McJobs who bum money off me to pay their rent. Girls I have to pick up from clubs at two in the morning so they don't get a DUI. Or ones who lose interest in me once they find out who my brother is. Girls who key my car or dump bleach in my bushes when we break up."

Charlotte helped him through several of those breakups, so she was the first person he wanted to talk to about his latest one. She was a great listener, always had helpful advice even if he was too boneheaded to take it, and she was never afraid to call him out on his bullshit.

"Yes, you've dated some god-awful women who didn't deserve you." She patted his wrist. "But that has nothing to do with your address, my friend. It has to do with your sense of self-worth. You deserve a high-quality girlfriend, but that doesn't necessarily mean someone with a fancy career, a fat 401k, and sky-high expectations. It means someone who appreciates who you are at your core and recognizes your worth without wanting to mold you into someone you're not."

"I've looked for her, Charlotte. Either she doesn't exist, or she lives on a houseboat in Iceland or some shit."

She pulled her hand back, the beginnings of a smile making her lips twitch. "Or she's closer than you think, and you're as blind as your brother was before he realized he still had feelings for me. Maybe it's genetic."

"Charlotte..." He sipped his Snapple. "I know what you're getting at."

"Maybe Jessica noticed something you and Amber have been trying to pretend isn't there. You sure as hell aren't fooling any of your friends."

Of course, he had feelings for Amber. He was caught off guard by how strong the pull was to be closer to her when they sat on his couch the night before. How good it felt when she held his hand—not just comforting, but exciting too. It made him crave more of that feeling, that connection.

There had been other moments between him and Amber where there was *something* buried in a look or touch that felt deeper than friendship. Like when she gently brushed ashes off his knee at a party at Sandra's and when they waded through a crowded club in Seattle, and she grabbed his hand to stay together. Both times, their eyes met after the contact, and they shared a grin that said maybe she felt it too. Whatever "it" was.

But every time, he ended the night convinced it was wishful thinking. And he reminded himself she was so far out of his league, it was ridiculous. Amber was a ten, and he was maybe a six on his best days. She could have any man she wanted. Why would she settle for a guy who needed pills to calm down and slept with a nightlight?

Women like her belonged with guys like Tyler—ridiculously handsome, charming, and capable of giving them anything they ever wanted.

Jessica was out of his league, too, but there was one key difference—his life would eventually return to normal after things didn't work out with her. If things went south with Amber, it would ruin their friendship, and the close circle they'd all built over the years would fracture. It would probably keep him from going to their shows and joining them on tour. There were enough changes going on, and he couldn't lose her.

Matthew scrubbed his face with his hands, shoving those thoughts away. He couldn't stomach an extended lecture about his low self-esteem if he shared any of that with Charlotte. "Amber told me last night that the band is her boyfriend, and that's how it has to be. She doesn't have space in her head or heart for a relationship."

"An excuse easily be squashed if the right guy was willing to deal with her schedule and lifestyle." She screwed the cap back onto her bottle and pushed it aside. "Would you be okay with her coming home at four in the morning? Could you handle not seeing her for weeks at a time when we're touring? Lots of people in our industry make it work, and plenty of others give up because it gets hard to sleep alone and worry about all the temptations your partner has around them."

His knee bounced beneath the table. "Does she even like me like that?" Charlotte wouldn't spill a friend's secrets, but he hoped she'd give him something. To confirm he wasn't imagining things, if nothing else.

She cocked an eyebrow. "I accused *you* of being blind, but I'm not. She's never told me outright, but I see how you look at each other."

Interesting. His suspicions that the attraction was mutual were always easy to shrug off as wishful thinking, but if Charlotte caught it, maybe it was real.

"Great." He gave Roxy another scratch behind the ears before she took off toward the living room. "Now I'm more confused than when I got here." He groaned at the whole mess. "What if you're wrong? Should I risk rejection from Amber? And possibly risk our friendship? Or should I be alone while I get my shit together?"

Maybe it would be wise to wait to pursue another relationship until the nightmares and panic attacks were behind him. Amber caught a brief glimpse of his damage, but far from the worst of it. What if she saw how deep it went, and it scared her off? It was a huge gamble.

Of course, maybe being with someone he trusted, who was supportive and understanding, could help him get past his trauma more quickly than stumbling through it alone.

Charlotte looked at him with pity in her eyes. "You know I can't answer that for you."

The front door opened, and Roxy barked her head off.

Tyler walked in, crouching to pet her. "Hey, Rox." She calmed for a few seconds before zooming down the hallway.

Tyler made a beeline for the kitchen with an arm behind his back. He kissed the top of Charlotte's head before setting a bouquet of purple and red tulips on the table in front of her.

She grinned, raising her chin. "Thanks, Ty."

"I missed you." He planted a line of kisses on her neck, and her smile grew.

"What's up with you?" he asked Matthew. "Why are you all frowny and shit?"

"I broke up with Jessica. Not sure whether to be alone or move to Iceland to hunt down my dream girl in a houseboat."

"And he has a thing for Amber," Charlotte added, helpful as always.

Tyler's dark eyebrows jumped toward his hairline. "So, you're confused as fuck and hoping Charlotte can tell you what to do?"

She laughed, making Tyler grin. Both men were pleased she seemed in better spirits. "Basically." She picked up the flowers and pulled a vase from the top of the fridge before filling it with water.

I should be alone for a while. Digesting Charlotte's advice and reflecting on the past few months with Jessica made Matthew realize he'd made a mistake by jumping into a relationship so soon after the attack. The break-up was proof. His judgment was off, and he'd clung to the comforting distraction instead of focusing on getting his life back in order.

Now that Tyler was there, Matthew needed to shift gears to something even more upsetting than his fucked-up love life.

While Charlotte arranged the flowers, he stood and leaned close to Tyler's ear.

"Can we talk alone?" he whispered.

Tyler gave a barely perceptible nod. "Baby, we'll be in the music room. I want to show him my new Epiphone."

She didn't respond. The joy on her face had disappeared. When she finished with the flowers, she picked up the sponge and returned to scrubbing the spotless stove. Tyler frowned, worry darkening his eyes. He wrapped an arm around her and planted a gentle kiss behind her ear before whispering something Matthew couldn't hear.

Tyler gestured to the hallway, and Matthew followed him to the massive music room.

A wall of soundproof glass split the space down the middle, and a door allowed people to move between the two sides. On the right was a studio filled with various instruments and shiny recording equipment that probably cost a small fortune. None of the stuff in there made much sense to Matthew, but it was Tyler and Charlotte's happy place.

The left side was a lounging area with a huge black sectional couch, three comfy recliners, a few tables, and a refrigerator. There was also a large mixing board, headphones, and four swiveling high-backed stools. They had the room built so both of their bands could work any time of the day or night, making it easier for everyone to hang out and stay close. He'd spent many nights there drinking beer and watching the bands rehearse and record, marveling at their talent.

The walls were soundproof, which is probably why Tyler chose it as the place to talk. He closed the door behind them.

"I know this is a stupid question, but..." Matthew headed for the lounge side of the space, settling on the corner of the couch. "Is she okay?"

"You already know the answer to that." Tyler grabbed two beers from the fridge and passed one to Matthew. "But she will be. We see her doctor tomorrow for another ultrasound and blood test, so hopefully, it goes well. What do you need to talk about?"

Matthew's pulse kicked up in anticipation of reliving yesterday's panic attack. He also wasn't thrilled about adding more stress to his brother's already rough week. "Rafael's brother came to High Notes."

Tyler's bottle was almost to his lips before he set it on the table with a thud. "He *what*? What the fuck did he want?" Foam climbed up the neck of his bottle and slipped over his fingers, but he didn't seem to notice.

"He's been trying to talk to Charlotte. Said his mom contacted the band's management to connect them."

Tyler's face reddened, and Matthew could tell he was trying hard to hold it together. "What do they want from her?"

"Closure, I guess. His mom wants to know Rafael's last words. That's all I know."

Tyler let out a dark, humorless laugh. "That won't bring her closure. It'll retraumatize Charlotte." He swigged his beer and set it back down. "And you. Are you okay?"

Matthew drained half his bottle in four deep swallows. "It set off a panic attack. Amber was there to apologize for our argument at the hospital. She helped me through it. And Evan."

"I'm glad they were there. If his mom called Charlotte's management, Eliza might have more details. And contact info for the family. I'll see what I can find out."

"Ty... What were his last words?" Matthew was too far gone from the heroin to have heard it himself.

Tyler leaned forward in his seat, and their eyes locked. "It was about you. The last thing that sick motherfucker said was, 'He's breathing, but out cold.' Right after sticking the goddamn needle in your arm. Right before Charlotte put two bullets in him. Would it really do his mother good to hear that? Or his brother? They need to grieve on their own and leave our family the hell out of it."

Anxiety burned in the pit of Matthew's stomach as he was shot back in time to the horrors they'd faced in Charlotte's bedroom. His hand mindlessly rubbed at the spot on his arm where the needle went in and delivered an almost fatal dose of a drug he never would've touched willingly. A drug that nearly killed his brother and took Charlotte's mother from her when she was twelve.

Burning alongside the anxiety was anger. How could the family of the man who tried to kill them have the audacity to think his victims owed them something?

"Tell me what Eliza says." Matthew tossed back the rest of his beer and wiped his mouth with the back of his hand. "And if you call the mother, tell her whatever she wants to hear so we can be done with this. Ignoring them might make them more persistent, and that's the last thing we need."

Tyler finished his beer and picked at the label. "I agree."

Matthew watched his brother's eyes slide to where he rubbed the crook of his arm. He cleared his throat, his hands wrapping around his empty bottle. "How's the not smoking going?"

Tyler scoffed. "I want to rip out all my hair and scream into a fucking pillow. The patches help a little. It's not like I can be a moody shit around Charlotte with what she's dealing with, so I try to take a walk or grab my guitar when I feel irritable."

"I'm proud of you, Ty." He nudged his brother's knee as it bounced, his foot making a rhythmic tapping sound on the floor. "You're like an actual grownup and shit."

Tyler smiled, but it was shaky at the edges after their tough conversation. "I guess now it's your turn. When do I get to see your new pad?"

"At your bachelor party."

Tyler's smile dropped. "Nope. Not happening."

"Ty..."

"We did that my first time around. And it's stupid to celebrate my last days of being single when I'm so ready to call that woman my wife, I'd marry her tomorrow if I could."

He was such a romantic, it was nauseating. No one Matthew dated had ever made him want to declare his love from a rooftop or go ring shopping. Maybe he wasn't the type to get carried away like that.

"It'll just be us and the guys," Matthew said, "drinking beer and shooting the shit. Nothing crazy."

Tyler went quiet, but his foot kept tapping. He was probably trying to figure out a valid reason why having a bachelor party was a terrible idea, but his taking so long to come up with one was a good sign.

Finally, his eyes narrowed, and his index finger jabbed toward Matthew. "No strippers."

Matthew grinned at the victory that was imminent. They both could use a night of beer and laughing with the guys. No heavy conversations or worries, and the biggest decision they'd make was what toppings to get on the pizzas. "No strippers. I promise."

A heavy sigh of resignation made Tyler's shoulders drop. "Fine."

Matthew's smile grew, satisfied by the win. "Hell yeah."

On the way out to his car, Matthew made a mental note to get his dining chairs and massive beanbags to the condo so everyone had a place to sit.

And to cancel the strippers.

II

Amber

"**L**uke, if you kick one of my guitars again, I swear to Christ, I'll punch you in the balls." Sandra gave him the stink-eye as she moved her precious guitars and their stands to the other side of Amber's garage. All of Amber's sisters were working, so there was no one to complain about the noise. They were used to her drumming, but that was nothing compared to the volume of the band.

They were running through the setlist for their third album's release party, ensuring the songs sounded perfect. They had a week to nail it. The lead-up to major events was always stressful, so Charlotte's bachelorette party less than twenty-four hours away was excellent timing. Luke was going to Tyler's bachelor party at the same time, so they'd all have an opportunity to let loose before the chaos.

"Sorry, but you know I can't stand in one place." Luke slung his bass behind him, the black strap stretching across his chest. "I need space to roam, or I get twitchy."

He was their first bassist who'd come with high-end equipment and a resume that was impressive as hell. His previous band, Black River, had three hit albums under their belt before personality clashes ended things. Fortunately, his laidback style and sick sense of humor fit right in with Killing Daisies, and his signature sound and ample experience elevated their rhythm section in a way his predecessors couldn't.

And Sandra wasn't complaining about the surge in gorgeous female fans wandering around backstage all hot and bothered. With Luke's dark cropped hair, tattoos, and head-to-toe black clothes, he had that sexy bad boy thing going on that made heads turn. Including Amber's, if she was honest. But she'd never complicate things by getting involved with him. She always found *Don't shit where you eat* to be a revolting phrase, but the meaning rang true. If they hooked up and things soured, he might quit. After years of having trouble holding onto a bassist, the last thing they needed was some awkward Fleetwood Mac-style relationship drama spoiling the band's dynamic.

"Well, twitch your ass closer to the drums where you belong." Sandra was extra bossy today and kept getting into petty little disagreements with Luke. Maybe it was the pressure of nailing the set or because Charlotte was so quiet that it made the vibe in the space feel even more tense.

Charlotte re-tuned her strings for the fifth time. "We can work in our home studio next time. Zack and Adam just got back from Mexico, so they went to my place to record. The guys have a deadline, and we don't need the recording equipment, so they got first dibs."

"Why were they in Mexico?" Amber asked.

"To blow off steam after the tour by doing body shots off of girls in bikinis." Charlotte swept her hair up into a messy bun.

"Why don't we do that?" Luke asked with a devilish smirk.

"I'm with him." Sandra hiked her thumb in his direction.

"Finally, you guys can agree on something!" Amber's head fell back with the shout.

"Are we done?" Charlotte moved her guitar to her back, touching her stomach.

Sandra's forehead creased with worry. "You okay, babe?"

"Just a little nauseous."

"That's a good sign, right?" Amber remembered that from when her sister was pregnant. When the morning sickness stopped, things went downhill.

"I guess." Charlotte sipped the ginger ale she'd been nursing all practice. "Sorry, but my head's not into it today, you guys."

Amber set her drumsticks on her snare and stood. "My arms are pretty spent anyway." It was a lie, but she hoped it'd make Charlotte feel better about packing it in early. "At least we got a few good hours in."

"Works for me, ladies." Luke unplugged his bass. "Gives me time to work on my bike before dark."

"Does it have a cute little basket in front like Dorothy's in the Wizard of Oz?" Sandra looped cords around her elbow and hand.

"No, but it has enough horsepower to drag a house off a witch." Luke put his bass in its velvet-lined case and snapped it shut.

"I can't believe your bachelorette party's tomorrow, Char!" Amber gushed, hoping to get Charlotte to smile. It didn't work. "We promise not to let things get too crazy."

Charlotte took another sip of ginger ale. "Would you kill me if I wanted to cancel?"

"No," Sandra said, "but we'd at least give you a good maiming."

"Is that a real word?" Luke asked.

"If not, it is now." Sandra faced Charlotte, touching her cheeks. "We'll keep it low-key, I promise."

"Tell that to the strippers," Amber mumbled.

"*Strippers*?!" Charlotte's eyes rounded, then narrowed in a glare. "No fucking way am I having half-naked people grind their crotches against me when it takes all my energy not to puke and cry."

"Oh, babe." Sandra's bottom lip puffed out, and she pulled Charlotte in for a hug. "We won't do anything you're not comfortable with. It's your special night."

"Yeah, we can just have a slumber party with junk food, facials, and dumb movies like the good ol' days," Amber said, joining the hug.

The women laughed when Luke's arms wrapped around all three of them. "You had me at facials."

Amber shoved him, laughing hysterically. "You're disgusting."

"What?" He raised his hands, feigning innocence. "My T-zone gets dry." He traced a line from his forehead to his cheeks.

Sandra laughed and shoved him, too. "Judging by Amber's face, you're about to get kicked in the D-zone. Better run home to your broken bike, Lukey."

"Yeah, I should go before my junk's threatened again." He picked up his equipment. "Later, ladies."

"Bye, Luke." Charlotte touched his shoulder as he passed. When he shut the garage door behind him, she grinned. "I'm so glad we found him."

"Did you hear that bassline he wrote for 'Confronted'?" Amber touched her chest. "I felt that shit in my throat."

Sandra nodded. "He's got mad skills, and he better not bail like the others. We need him for Europe and everything after."

"I'm heading out," Charlotte said, her frown returning. "I have a doctor's appointment in two hours, and we're supposed to meet with the wedding planner after dinner. Maybe I can get a few hours of sleep in between." The worry and exhaustion came off her in waves, and Amber felt bad that she had to stand in the stuffy garage for a few hours.

"Let us know how the appointment goes," Sandra said.

Amber hoped Charlotte would have good news to share, but they'd be ready to support her if she didn't. "Get some rest and let us know if we can help with any wedding shit."

"Thanks, honey, but none of us are the picking out centerpieces and bouquet flowers type. That's why we're paying someone to do all that frou-frou shit." She tightened the bun on her head. "Oh! In case he hasn't told you, Matty broke up with Jessica."

Amber's head jerked back. "Really? Why?"

Did it have anything to do with Jessica finding them alone in his new place? The look on her face said Matthew was getting an earful of bullshit when Amber closed that door. Regardless of the reason, this was great news.

"Not my story to tell," Charlotte said. "Honestly, I think he's better off. Between the out-of-line shit she said to me in the hospital and the way she was trying to run his life, she's a walking red flag." She put her hands on her hips. "He was even considering getting contacts because she said some doctor at work looked better after swapping glasses for them. I don't know what kind of weird hold she had over him, but I've *never* seen Matty try to change for someone like that. It was disturbing. That bitch could start a cult."

"I didn't like her either," Amber said. "She made a shitty comment about my clothes and acted all possessive when she saw us hanging out together at his new place. He has friends with tits, lady. Get over it or get over him."

Now, Jessica had no choice but to do the latter.

Sandra's nose wrinkled. "I'm glad I never got the chance to meet her. Good riddance."

A tingling rush of nerves swirled in Amber's belly. Matthew was single again. Did it make a difference? None of her barriers to a relationship had changed, and his wanting something stable and predictable left her out.

But seeing him so vulnerable when Rafael's brother confronted him made something shift in her. Like instincts she didn't know she had were woken up by his need to be taken care of. It meant a lot that he trusted her enough to let her take the lead and be there for him.

And when Amber was too upset to go into Charlotte's hospital room, she let herself be vulnerable with him. She'd never let her tough act drop with a guy before. They had to know she wasn't someone to toy with or take advantage of. But she didn't need that armor with Matthew. She never had. And he was right—one of his legendary hugs was exactly what she needed.

But while she'd love to give a relationship with him a shot, Amber still couldn't give him what he wanted and deserved from a partner. She didn't know what to do with those conflicting facts.

If he wanted a woman who dressed and acted like Jessica, Amber never stood a chance. She'd never change to please someone, and it still bothered her that Matthew was willing to bend over backward for anyone, let alone a stuffy, judgmental bore. It would never work out if he couldn't be happy being himself.

A painful realization made tears of disappointment sting her eyes.

Maybe they weren't as compatible as she once thought.

12

Matthew

After opening all the folding chairs, Matthew scattered a few large bean-bags around his living room. Evan would bring the keg soon, and Tyler's bandmates, Zack and Adam, were heading over with plastic cups, ice, and, knowing them, enough hard liquor to pickle every liver in the room.

Luke was still pretty new to the group, so it didn't feel right to ask him to pitch in, but his sister ran an erotic bakery, and he offered to bring a cake shaped like a naked woman. Who could say no to that?

It would be the tamest bachelor party Matthew had been to, but he wasn't about to make his brother uncomfortable on a day he needed to kick back and forget the negative shit weighing on him for a while. And Matthew felt more anxious than usual since seeing Rafael's brother at work. He could also use a night of tequila, junk food, and not thinking.

The doorbell rang, and Matthew kicked a purple beanbag out of the way to answer it. Someone's finger blocked the peephole. There were only two people who'd do that.

He opened the door to find Adam with a bottle of tequila in one hand and a bottle of whisky in the other. Zack stood beside him with a package of plastic cups and two bags of ice.

"The party's here, motherfucker!" Adam pushed his way inside, heading for the kitchen. "We've got backup booze in the trunk, so no one has to do a run later."

Zack followed, shoving the ice into Matthew's freezer and tossing the cups on the counter beside the chips. "It's feeling like a shots kinda night, my dudes. We need to get our boy Ty nice and toasty. Been too long."

"Poor Charlotte's stuck sipping on fruit juice." Matthew tore open the package of cups, setting them up on the counter beside the booze. "That girl used to drink me under the table."

Before Charlotte hooked up with Tyler, she and Matthew often hung backstage after her shows or went to parties together, often with Sandra and Amber in tow. Charlotte wasn't the type of wild party girl to whip off her shirt and dance on tables, but she loved throwing back a few drinks, smoking some weed, and laughing at stupid jokes until the sun came up. He missed those days.

"Once that kid's out and off the tit, she'll do it again." Adam poured a healthy slosh of tequila into a cup and tossed it back.

"I wouldn't bet on it." Matthew sliced a few limes and grabbed his saltshaker. "They're both ready for a different life when they're not on a stage, and I'm so fucking happy for them."

"Not a life I'd want." Zack refilled Adam's cup and poured tequila into two more cups before passing one to Matthew. "But since Ty got with Charlotte, he's happier than I've ever seen him, so cheers to that."

They all licked their wrists, and Matthew sprinkled salt on the damp spots. After throwing back their shots, they each sucked on a lime wedge.

"Just like being back in Mexico." Zack grinned, a chunk of lime pulp stuck between his front teeth.

There was a knock at the door, and Matthew opened it to find Luke holding a large pink box.

"Did someone order vanilla tits?" He handed the box to Matthew.

"Zack's mom is here?" Adam's head raised from his drink.

Zack kicked his shin and refilled their empty cups. "Down for a tequila shot, Luke?"

"Just one?" Luke joined them at the counter, taking the red plastic cup Zack held out. "Where's the lucky bachelor?"

Matthew licked his wrist and sprinkled salt on everyone who held out their hands. "He'll be here any minute."

They licked their salted wrists, drained their cups, and sucked on the last of the sliced limes.

"Are we seriously not having strippers?" Adam frowned. "What kind of bachelor party is this?"

"Remember Ty's first one?" Zack laughed, brushing salt off the front of his shirt. "Three strippers, two kegs, an ounce of weed—"

"And a partridge in a fucking pear tree." Matthew grabbed his paring knife and cut more lime wedges. "Enjoy the memory because our boy's never having a stranger's tits jiggle in his face again."

"If I had a woman like Charlotte," Adam said, "I wouldn't need that shit either."

"I'll drink to that." Zack raised his glass and took another shot.

"You'll drink to the fucking weather forecast." Adam refilled everyone's cups.

They were all a few shots deep, and the guest of honor hadn't even shown up. Matthew could see this going downhill fast if he didn't reign things in before they got out of control.

"Let's pace ourselves, gentlemen. We've got all night."

The doorbell rang.

"Come in!" Matthew left it unlocked so guests could come and go.

Tyler walked in, and the room exploded with whoops and cheers.

"Get the fuck over here and take a shot, brother." Adam handed him a cup.

Tyler swallowed it in one gulp, his face scrunching up. "Fuck, tequila's gross." He held out his cup. "Hit me again."

Matthew clapped him on the back. "We're all three shots in, so catch up. Evan's bringing a keg in a few."

Zack refilled Tyler's cup, and he tossed it back. Then, he did another.

"You sure you're ready to walk the plank again, man?" Luke dunked a tortilla chip in the bowl of salsa on the counter. "Marriage seems like a huge fucking drag."

Matthew would've agreed if he hadn't witnessed his parents' connection. They were always kissing and staring at each other with love in their eyes. He couldn't remember a single time when they argued. Tyler and Charlotte weren't married yet, but it was clear they'd be just as happy.

If Matthew could find a connection like that, he'd do anything to hold onto it, including putting on a tux and eating stupidly expensive cake.

Tyler grinned, the liquor making his eyelids droop a little. "The first time was a plank. This couldn't be more different. I'd toss Charlotte over my shoulder and carry her to the courthouse right now if she'd let me." He took another shot. "But she deserves the white dress, flowers, and anything else she wants as long as when it's over, she's all mine."

Luke nodded slowly. "Maybe I just haven't met the right chick. I've never wanted to stay past breakfast, let alone every goddamn day."

"Same here, man." Adam raised his cup. "Soak up the freedom while we're young. Maybe someday, shackles won't seem so bad."

Matthew couldn't imagine Adam or Zack ever settling down. Although, Zack gave it a shot once. He fell hard for a woman in Denver named Mandy last December. He tried making it work despite the distance, but it wasn't enough for her. When she broke it off, Zack returned to his old ways. He and Adam seemed happy living the bachelor life, but as Matthew knew all too well, life was unpredictable. Maybe someday they'd find women who could see past their crass jokes and nonstop partying and appreciate the generous, fiercely loyal men they were.

It made him think of what Amber said about guys judging her as easy or scary by her looks. It was a crime so many amazing things about her had gone unnoticed and unappreciated by a bunch of blind, foolish dickheads. She was funny, considerate, and the first to defend anyone who needed defending. She wouldn't hesitate to drop everything for a friend. She was an incredible listener who never made him feel judged or uncomfortable. And she was trustworthy and honest—two traits as precious as they are rare.

"Can I say something that stays in this room?" Luke asked.

"Of course, man." Tyler bit a lime and wiped his mouth on his sleeve.

"I'm thinking about asking Amber out."

As Matthew reached into the bowl of potato chips, he froze. The words caught him off guard, and the alcohol buzz made it hard to keep a neutral expression.

"Bad idea," Tyler said, his eyes darting to Matthew and back to Luke. "Trust me."

"Why?" Luke's dark eyebrows pinched together. "She seeing somebody?"

The tequila churned like acid in Matthew's stomach when the realization hit. Luke would be perfect for Amber.

Her reservations about dividing her time between her band, family, and a boyfriend wouldn't be an issue. She'd see him at practices and sleep on the same tour buses. They could explore new places between gigs and write songs together. Plus, he had a look that made women in the audience drop their panties and toss them at his feet. How could Matthew compete with any of that?

"No, but you're in a band together." Tyler set his cup on the counter. "If shit doesn't work out, it would be awkward as hell, and you'd probably quit. You're a great fit for them, so it'd be shitty all around."

"Fuck." Luke ran a hand over his dark hair with a nod. "Maybe you're right."

Tyler glanced at Matthew, raising his cup with a reassuring smile. Matthew tapped his cup against his brother's, more grateful than ever that he always had his back.

Hopefully, Luke wasn't already too far gone to remember the conversation the next day.

"Is that a fucking phone?" Adam tapped the bulky black device peeking out of Tyler's pocket.

"Yeah, I got it in case Charlotte needs to reach me. Hopefully, she has a fun, stress-free night with her friends. She really needs it." Tyler grinned over the rim of his cup. "Hell, I wouldn't be mad if they had strippers as long as my girl had a smile on her face."

"You hit the jackpot with her," Zack said, a hint of somberness in his tone. "The girls I hook up with *are* the strippers."

Tyler looked around the condo, nodding his head. "This is a really nice place, Matty. You even have a skylight."

Matthew smiled, remembering listening to the rain with Amber. "Yeah, it was hard giving up my old place, but it's great having a working dishwasher and electrical outlets that don't blow if I run the TV and microwave at the same time."

"No offense, but it's kinda beige," Adam said, crunching on a chip.

"What are you talking about?" Matthew shook his head. "Nothing in here is fucking beige."

"Not the color. The vibe." Adam gestured at the white walls, cream-colored carpet, and granite countertops. "It's so normal and dull. You're not a beige dude."

"Is that some sort of fucked-up compliment?" Matthew poured another shot into his cup.

"Hell yeah, it is." Zack nodded, grabbing a handful of salted peanuts. "Your old place had personality. You had those cool blacklight posters and tie-dyed blankets and shit. There's no *you* in here yet."

"Maybe that's not me anymore." Matthew shrugged, not sure exactly who he was these days. He didn't feel like the same man who bought brightly colored decorations at flea markets, sang along to Nirvana while he did housework, and used a rainbow bong as a centerpiece on his coffee table. That guy wasn't perfect, but he wasn't broken. He didn't wake up screaming or jump at loud noises.

Matthew often wondered if he'd ever resemble his former self again or if he'd just have to forge a new version with the pieces that were left.

"I like this opportunity to start from scratch. To figure out what I still want and what I don't." It wasn't exactly the truth, but it was an easier response to give in a room full of guys who all had their lives figured out.

"What if it did work out?" Luke asked, turning everyone's head.

"Huh?" Adam squinted, looking as baffled as everyone else.

"With Amber," Luke explained. "What if I ask her out, we hit it off, and we become this awesome musical power couple?"

Tyler scoffed. "Been there, done that. Trust me, you don't want it."

While Matthew appreciated Tyler's attempt at a cautionary tale, it wasn't a good one. Anyone could've predicted his marriage to the infamous Amy Carey would go tits-up. Matthew certainly did, endlessly begging his brother not to marry her. He hoped everyone was too drunk to point out the most obvious exception to the rule that was staring them all in the face.

"What about you and Charlotte?" Luke asked.

Motherfucking fuck.

Tyler shrugged and wobbled a bit, obviously feeling his tequila. "Touche."

"I like Amber, okay?" Matthew slammed his cup on the counter. "Don't ask her out because I really fucking like her, and as soon as I have the balls, I'm going to tell her." He poured another shot while everyone stared, as surprised by the confession as he was.

Matthew knew he should probably be alone for a while to reassess his life after the breakup with Jessica, but the thought of Amber with Luke or any other guy sealed it. If he waited until the perfect time, it may never come, and she could end up falling for someone who didn't deserve her.

If she was willing to take him as he was—and that was a big *if*—Matthew would do his best to ensure she didn't regret it.

"Damn, dude." Luke tapped his cup against Matthew's. "I didn't know. She's all yours."

"Not quite." Matthew swallowed his shot, the room going hazy at the edges. "But thanks."

"Why are we standing around talking about chicks and shit?" Zack asked. "We're here to fucking party!"

As if on cue, Evan walked in, pushing a dolly with squeaky wheels. "Where do you want the keg?"

13

Amber

Amber sat on her living room couch watching Charlotte open very naughty bachelorette gifts beside her. Most of the guests lounged on a pile of blankets and fluffy pillows on the floor. Everyone was in pajamas, and the coffee table was littered with glasses of various colorful cocktails with names like Tangerine Clit, Slutty Sinner, and Virgin Blood. Sandra brought over the recipes on a sheet of notebook paper, and Amber suspected she'd made up the names herself to hear people ask for them all night long.

Each glass had a flesh-colored penis straw poking out of it, which Kate and Beth used for a sword fight earlier in the night. It made Charlotte laugh so hard she nearly peed in her pj's.

"Shit!" Christa yelped as her cup of Virgin Blood slipped from her hands, falling onto the hardwood floor under her feet. "I'm so sorry!"

"Don't sweat it, babe." Sandra bolted for the kitchen and returned with a roll of paper towels. Together, they blotted up the mess.

"Can you imagine if Denise saw that?" Tara laughed.

It was a good thing Denise was at work because their clean freak sister would've flipped the fuck out. She was stressed about the mess she'd come home to after having this many people in the house, but she understood. Their five-bedroom, two-story Craftsman was a lot bigger than Sandra's apartment, and they didn't want to make a mess at Charlotte's, so it was the perfect location for a slumber party with eight wild women. Amber fully intended to make the place spotless when everyone left.

Charlotte lifted an obscenely endowed purple dildo out of a box to a chorus of shrieks, arching an eyebrow at Molly.

"For when Ty's working late," Molly said with a saucy wink.

Beth's cheeks flushed pink at the sight of the dildo. Probably because she had an identical one in her nightstand drawer. Amber accidentally found it while looking for a book her sister borrowed and was still scarred by the memory.

Christa was on the couch beside Sandra in blue and white cloud pajamas. "I feel like a bore for getting her candles."

"Candles can be as naughty as dildos." Sandra grinned, her hand moving to Christa's knee. "Remember your birthday?"

Christa bit her bottom lip as she smiled. "Point well made, sweetheart."

The phone rang, but they all ignored it, letting the machine pick up while Charlotte opened a box filled with skimpy black lingerie. It wasn't nearly as wild as her bachelorette party would've been if she wasn't knocked up, but under the circumstances, it was perfect. She seemed to be having fun, and that's what mattered most.

Beth grabbed a penis-shaped finger sandwich and bit it in half. "I bet Tyler's the type to appreciate nice lingerie."

Amber shot her sister a look of warning. "You promised you wouldn't be weird."

Charlotte laughed. "It's fine. And yes, he does. I apologize for taking him off the market before you could take a crack at him."

Beth choked on the other half of her penis sandwich. Hopefully, it would keep her big, dumb mouth busy for a while.

The "Pin the Dick on the Man" game was still taped to the wall, and it was a big hit when the ladies first arrived. The phallic theme wasn't original for a bachelorette party, but thanks to aisle five of the local adult shop, it was an easy one to stick with. They hadn't had a chance to dig into the package of chocolate cock cookies sitting on the kitchen table, but Kate had been eying them all night. Either she had a sweet tooth, or she really needed a boyfriend.

"Who called?" Tara asked. "Can you make sure it wasn't Denise? Her car keeps crapping out, and she might need a ride home."

"Her boyfriend sells cars," Sandra pointed out. "Why doesn't she buy a better one from him?"

Beth rolled her eyes. "She refuses to give up the old Mustang she's had since college."

"I'll check the message." Amber pressed play on the answering machine and turned up the volume.

"Amber, you're pretty."

"Is that... Matthew?" Molly asked.

Everyone shushed her, and the room fell silent.

"Like soooo fucking pretty iss not fair."

A few of the women said *aww*, but Amber was too shocked to react. She'd seen and heard Matthew drunk before, but he sounded beyond trashed. He was slurring his words like he'd guzzled a dozen beers.

"And iss not fair you smell like peaches if I can't taste the peaches."

Amber gasped and lunged for the machine to stop the message from playing.

"Don't you dare!" Beth yanked her back, slapping her hand away. "This is too good to miss."

"And iss no fair I like you. You don't like me." There was a pause, and the phone crackled like he'd exhaled into it. "I haddalotta beer."

There was a muffled clatter as he hung up, and the line went dead.

"Oh. My. God." Sandra slapped a hand to her mouth, looking almost as stunned as Amber felt.

Amber wiggled out of Beth's hold.

I like you.

She couldn't believe he'd said the words and was more than a little embarrassed everyone in the room heard them, too.

"That thing about the peaches was sweet." Beth's lips smashed together as she held back a smile.

"Shut up, Beth. He was fucking wasted." Amber glared at her sister and tossed a pillow at her head. She'd get teased for this for weeks. "He didn't know what he was saying."

Charlotte touched her knee. "Alcohol's a truth serum, sweetie. It doesn't make people talk out of their ass."

"Do I call him back?" Amber felt out of her depth. She'd never been drunk-dialed before. Would he remember if she called him back? Would he even remember what he said the next day when the hangover kicked in?

"Bad idea," Kate said. "He's probably got his head in a toilet right now. I say you play it off like it never happened."

"No fucking way!" Sandra clutched her Tangerine Clit with both hands. "She likes him too. When he sobers up, she needs to tell him."

Charlotte lifted a pair of handcuffs and a blindfold off her lap—a gift from Kate—and set them on the coffee table. "I'm with her. A guy like Matthew doesn't come around every day. When he wants to taste your peaches, you let him."

Amber groaned and tossed a pair of edible underwear at Charlotte while she laughed. "My band is my boyfriend."

"For the love of god, Amber, stop saying that!" The volume of Tara's voice rose with every word. "If you want it to work, you'll find a way."

"Close your eyes and imagine kissing him," Molly said, swirling the Slutty Sinner in her glass.

Amber stared at her and blinked. "What?"

"It's like, a test." She took a quick sip through her penis straw. "I read about it in Cosmo. Just do it."

What was it about the combination of alcohol and pajamas that made full-grown women regress to silly, boy-crazy twelve-year-olds?

Amber sighed. "Fine. But if Beth tries to sprinkle penis confetti in my hair again while my eyes are closed, someone needs to smack her for me."

Amber hugged a couch pillow to her chest and closed her eyes, the room spinning a little from the four Virgin Bloods she'd tossed back. She pictured Matthew sitting in front of her, his sweet, familiar grin putting her at ease. He leaned in slowly, and so did she, their lips gently brushing before they both really went for it. A wide smile spread across her face, a swarm of butterflies fluttering low in her belly.

"Test over." Molly clapped her hands, and the rest of the women joined in. "Did you all see that smile?"

"Amber and Matthew sittin' in a tree," Sandra sang. "F-u-c—"

The singing stopped when Amber's pillow nailed her in the face. She threw it back, laughing her curly-headed ass off.

"Ugh. Fine." Amber slapped her hands over her face to hide the grin that showed no signs of subsiding. "Tomorrow, I'll bring him coffee and a couple of Advil and tell him how I feel."

Drunken, high-pitched cheers filled the room, and Charlotte circled the air above her head with the purple dildo like it was a victory flag. In a weird way, that was fitting. Charlotte had always rooted for love, even when it scared her. She took a massive risk by falling in love with Tyler, and things turned out great for her.

Maybe Amber would have the same luck with Matthew.

Maybe the usual doubts holding her back from love could be overcome. She knew him well enough to know he wasn't the type of man to quit on someone he cared about or leave when things got tough.

And maybe she could even help him heal and get his mojo back in the process.

The thought of taking that step made her stomach flip, but not in a bad way. More like the butterflies she felt when she imagined kissing him had woken back up, ready to party like the crazy, wonderful women in her living room sipping alcohol through plastic penises and twirling purple dildos in the air.

14

Amber

Amber's living room looked like a pink and black battlefield as the morning sun seeped through the cracks between the curtains. Six women lay sprawled out on the floor, half-covered in blankets. Kate had retreated to her comfortable bed, but everyone else crashed together sometime around three in the morning. Someone was snoring. If it was Beth, Amber would mock her for the next month as payback for stopping her from silencing Matthew's message on the answering machine. After tiptoeing further into the room, she learned the snorer was Tara, her second least annoying sister. She'd let it slide.

Amber kept tiptoeing toward the kitchen and set up the coffeemaker to brew a twelve-cup pot. While she waited, she dug through the cup cabinet and found a massive travel mug and lid. She'd stopped after five weak cocktails, so she didn't have even a whiff of a hangover. Judging by how he sounded, Matthew would be waking up with a throbbing headache and a very fuzzy memory on the other side of town. The guys must've hit the hooch hard. Knowing Zack and Adam were in attendance, it wasn't surprising. They could talk the pope into joining them for a round of shots.

She would've preferred for Matthew to be sober when confessing his feelings, but she knew how easy it was to talk yourself out of chasing what you want. Alcohol had a way of erasing that filter, for better or worse.

When the coffee was brewed, Amber filled the mug and a smaller one for herself to sip while she got ready. What do you wear to tell a guy you've been friends with for almost three years how you really feel about him? It was crazy to think the kiss she imagined last night could be a reality soon.

What would things be like if they progressed even further? Was he the gentle type? That's what she suspected, given his considerate, respectful nature. The kind of guy to take his time and whisper sweet words in your ear. She didn't have much experience with gentle and sweet, but enough to know she liked it. Or he could surprise her. Maybe he preferred to take charge, pin a girl down by her wrists, and give it to her hard. Both styles were nice, but Amber was a huge fan of the latter.

After washing her face and brushing her teeth, she slipped on jeans, a black t-shirt, and Matthew's black and grey flannel. She ran a brush through her hair and tied it back in a ponytail.

Amber looked in the mirror at her face without the usual mask of thick eyeliner and dark lipstick. Her clothes were simple and comfortable, and she found herself smiling at her reflection.

She only needed to be herself with Matthew.

And she'd never ask him to be anything but the incredible man he already was.

She rifled through the medicine cabinet and stuffed a jar of Advil into her pocket. After one last look in the mirror, she tiptoed to the front door to avoid waking any of the sleeping beauties in her living room. As she made her way around the blankets, someone's fingers tapped her ankle. She looked down to find Charlotte smiling. Her top half was out of the blankets, and the dark circles beneath her eyes were gone. After the break from her stresses, she'd finally caught some decent sleep.

"Good luck," she whispered.

"Thanks, babe," Amber whispered back.

She unlocked the door as quietly as possible and walked out, locking up behind her. On the drive to Matthew's, her heart thumped wildly in her chest. Was it naïve to think this could work? Probably. But the best things in her life came from taking risks, and she wasn't about to back out now, forced to wonder what might've been if only she'd jumped instead of staying in the safety of the friend zone.

Her hands shook as she pulled up to the front of his complex.

There's nothing to be afraid of.

He likes you, too.

You can make this work.

After the internal pep talk and willing her hands to stop shaking, she grabbed the travel mug. With the bottle of Advil rattling in her pocket, she marched up to his front door.

She knocked softly, not wanting to wake any bachelor party stragglers who might still be passed out on his couch or floor. After another soft knock, Matthew opened the door in a pair of plaid lounge pants and nothing else.

Amber swallowed hard, her courage dipping with the unexpected distraction. She'd never seen him without a shirt and wasn't surprised when her palms started sweating. He was lean but strong, and he'd been hiding some actual muscles under his baggy clothes. There was a tattoo on his chest of a mountain she immediately recognized as Mount Hood, her favorite. It was surrounded by trees and ferns etched in black ink.

"Amber." His arms crossed over his bare chest. "Hey."

"Hey."

His dark blond hair was a tangled mess, and his eyelids drooped over puffy, bloodshot eyes, but she couldn't keep her gaze from moving to his lips. Would they feel as good pressed to hers as they did in her mind?

His brows pinched for a second before his eyes rounded, and he stepped onto the porch, carefully shutting the door behind him. "What are you doing here?"

"I brought you this." She held out the mug, and he hesitated for a beat before taking it. She fished the pills out of her pocket and pressed them into his other palm. "And these."

"Thanks, but..." He scratched the stubble darkening his chin and cheeks. "Why?"

"I figured after last night, you could use them. You sounded—"

The door cracked open behind him.

"Matthew?" The female voice made Amber's stomach drop. "Who is it?"

Jessica poked her head out, scowling when she saw Amber standing on the porch like the dumbass she was.

"Give us a minute, Jess."

Fuck.

Tears stung Amber's eyes. Embarrassment made her want to hide in his bushes and pretend none of this ever happened.

Jessica was in his house at nine in the morning.

He used a nickname.

They were back together.

Jessica closed the door, and when Matthew turned back around, Amber caught the struggle playing out behind his eyes. She was too shocked, hurt, and desperate to flee to ponder what it meant.

"I'm sorry." She blinked back tears, hoping he hadn't noticed them. "I didn't know. I—" She turned around, ready to bolt for her car parked a few houses away.

"Wait."

She stopped and slowly turned back to him, her stupid pounding heart as confused as she was. Wouldn't he want to get back to Jessica before she accused him again of cheating?

"What were you going to say before she came out?" His gaze swept over her face, searching for the answer she could no longer give him.

For fuck's sake, don't let him see you cry.

Amber squared her shoulders, her familiar armor sliding into place. "It doesn't matter. I hope you guys are happy together. Really." She took a few steps toward her car before turning around for one last look. "See you later, Matthew."

He stepped off the small porch and looked poised to protest, so she walked faster. Luckily, she made it to her car and shut the door before the first tears broke loose and trailed her cheeks.

I'm so stupid.

A trapped sob burned in her chest. All the excitement she'd felt earlier had turned into a big, stinking heap of disappointment. And embarrassment. She'd let herself get carried away over a drunken answering machine message, and now she'd have to explain to everyone back at her house why she was coming home a sad loser.

A knock at the window beside her head made her jump.

Tyler stood outside with a puzzled look on his face and a smoldering cigarette in his hand. He gestured for her to roll down the window.

"Amber? You okay?"

She wiped her cheeks on the sleeve of the flannel. "Yeah, I just love sitting in my car feeling like a massive idiot."

"Want some company from another massive idiot?" He held up his cigarette before taking a long drag and blowing it out toward the sky.

She chuckled and unlocked the passenger door. "Get in here, bozo."

He stomped his cigarette out in the street and sat beside her. "Since you're outside my brother's place crying in your car, I'm guessing he did something stupid?"

"I'm the stupid one." She sniffed, the sting of rejection making it hard to keep more tears from spilling. "He left me a message last night. About liking me and wanting to taste my peaches or some crazy shit."

Tyler stared at her blankly. "Okay. Peaches. Got it."

"He was obviously drunk off his ass, but it happened."

"Oh, he was definitely drunk off his ass. He woke up fully clothed in his bathtub, hugging the telephone and an ugly blue stuffed bear."

She almost laughed at the mental image, but knowing he was holding the bear she bought him made the pain worse. What happened between that phone call and this morning to make him change his mind about her?

"So," she said, "I came here with coffee and fucking Advil to ease his hangover and talk. Well, maybe more than talk."

"Oh. Wow."

"Yeah, wow." She exhaled loudly. "But Jessica popped her happy little head out, so I guess they're back together."

Tyler shrugged. "Honestly, I have no idea. I snuck out to smoke right when she got here. Not her biggest fan."

That wasn't surprising considering his reaction to what Jessica said to Charlotte in the hospital. If none of Matthew's friends liked this girl, why did he? If it was because she was stable, predictable, and had a respectable career, Amber never stood a chance whether they'd made up or not.

"What does he see in her, Ty? I don't get it."

Tyler was quiet for a moment, his fingertips tugging at a loose thread on his jeans. "I think he feels like he owes her. A month after the attack, the people he was closest to left on tour. He swore things were getting better, but I should've known he wasn't okay. It's one of my biggest fucking regrets, but that's beside the point." He sighed. "Anyway, she was there when he was falling apart. He trusted her because since he was in the hospital, she took care of him. I can see how that would create a bond, especially for Matty."

She nodded along, listening. "Why especially for him?"

He plucked the thread loose and started fidgeting with another. "After our dad died, our mom was awful at taking care of us. Matty got used to leaning on me or hiding and dealing with shit on his own. Having someone hold his hand and listen to his fears must've felt amazing. Someone to talk him down when his mind had him reliving the hell Rafael and Amy put him through. He got it worse than any of us." Tyler's eyes went distant, his throat jumping as he swallowed. After a moment, he seemed to shake it off and continued. "I feel guilty I was so far away when he needed support, but I'm grateful she was there."

"So, he won't let her go despite her treatment of him and his friends because he feels indebted to her?" Amber frowned. "That's not healthy."

Tyler shrugged again, pulling a cigarette from his pack. "Charlotte's my first healthy relationship, so I can't throw stones. But my brother's smart. If he didn't shoot her down this morning, it won't be long before he realizes she's wrong for him and moves on."

Amber's gaze fell to her lap, digesting his words.

Tyler poked her knee with the unlit tip of his cigarette. "Is he worth waiting for?"

Could she stand watching him and Jessica together? After the high she felt that morning over the possibility of being with him, it wouldn't be easy to return to just being friends. The thought of him out of her life was even worse.

Maybe Tyler was right, and Matthew would get tired of Jessica's bullshit again and break it off for good. But then what? Did Amber really want to be his rebound after he ran back to someone like Jessica so quickly?

"In the words of the great Etta James," she said, "'only time will tell.'"

He chuckled. "I knew you listened to more than punk."

She smiled, grateful for the insight and hope Tyler had given her. "I know I'm asking you to break bro code, but please don't tell him we talked. If someday, he wants me sober as much as he wanted me drunk, he has to make it clear on his own."

Tyler nodded, his expression warm with sympathy and maybe a dash of pity. "I hope he does."

He tucked the pack of smokes back into his pocket and touched the door handle. "You good? Because I have to go apologize to my pregnant fiancée for fucking up and smoking a cigarette. Or three." He smacked the side of his head on the window.

"So you and your brother both need to learn when to let something go?" She cocked an eyebrow.

"Yup." He snapped his unlit cigarette in half, rolled down the window a few inches, and tossed the pieces into the gutter. "Now it's his turn. Good luck, Amber." With one of his signature crooked grins that made Charlotte, Beth, and millions of female fans sweat, he was out the door.

Instead of going home and having to explain what happened to her house full of nosy women, Amber drove around the city without a destination. Wispy gray clouds stretched across the late morning sky, small patches of vibrant blue fighting to break through.

She turned on the radio and found her favorite local rock station, bobbing her head along with the upbeat rhythms of Pavement and Veruca Salt. Two songs later, Charlotte and Sandra's dueling guitar riffs filled the car, and Amber smiled. Her thumbs tapped the steering wheel in time to her drumbeats, grateful for something to focus on besides her disappointment. There was a time when she would've sold her soul to get on the radio, and here it was. She'd never take that for granted.

Was this the universe's way of reminding her that as long as she had her band, she'd be okay?

On the Fremont Bridge, traffic was at a standstill. When she reached the center, Amber turned her head to the east, soaking in the magnificent views of snowcapped Mount Hood, the glimmering windows of downtown skyscrapers as the sun peeked through the clouds, and the colorful sailboats dotting the Willamette River. She loved her hometown and was always a little sad when she had to leave it to go on tour. If she had a relationship with someone she could truly fall for, leaving them would be a thousand times harder. Did she want that?

If it meant coming home to Matthew, yes, she did. It would've been nice if she'd realized it before he met someone else, but there was no changing the past. She hoped Tyler was right, and Matthew would recognize Jessica wasn't good for him and let her go. Feeling indebted to someone who helped you while at your most vulnerable isn't a reason to stay in a relationship, but Tyler's explanation made sense. Instead of thinking Matthew was stupid for getting back with a controlling bitch, she understood that his trauma affected his ability to make wise decisions.

If he stayed with Jessica, Amber would have to accept it. And hopefully, someday, that imaginary kiss would stop replaying every time she closed her eyes.

I5

Matthew

As soon as all the passed-out partiers cleared out, Matthew was driving to Target for blackout curtains. The sunlight creeping in between the miniblinds fried his retinas and made the pounding in his head feel like someone had worked him over with a sledgehammer.

He was relieved he didn't have a nightmare while everyone was over. If the alcohol kept it away, he'd rather not know. The last thing he needed while trying to put himself back together was to turn into a drunk.

Matthew picked a corner off one of the pastries Jessica brought over, and it tasted like sugary ashes on his tongue. He couldn't remember ever having cottonmouth this bad.

It was worse than regular cottonmouth because it tasted like beer, stomach acid, and sour tequila. Matthew walked to the sink and stuck his mouth under the tap, guzzling water before swishing and spitting out a mouthful.

The coffee Amber brought was on his counter and he picked it up and took a sip. It was still hot and made exactly how he liked—with just enough sugar to kill the bitterness. It was incredibly thoughtful but confusing as hell. Why was she on his porch at nine in the morning? She showed up in normal, casual clothes with no makeup and her hair pulled back, but she still managed to be breathtakingly fucking gorgeous.

What was she going to say before Jessica interrupted them? Did she start to say *he sounded*? What did that even mean?

He grabbed a fork from the counter and stabbed it into the left tit of the cake Luke brought. Most of the guys wanted a piece of the crotch, complete with shaved chocolate pubes, but Matthew had always been and would always be a boob guy. The nipple was made of gel frosting that tasted like strawberries, overpowering the nasty taste in his mouth.

If the worst hangover of his life hadn't muddled Matthew's brain, he would've insisted Amber wait so they could talk. Jessica left for work a few minutes later, so they would've been alone.

When Jessica came over, bubbly and smiling, with a boxful of pastries, he fought to keep his expression from looking as irritated as he felt. He didn't appreciate the unannounced visit, especially while he still had guests, but he didn't want to be rude, so he let her in. The hollow apologies that followed and the look of disgust when she saw the men scattered around his living room, sleeping off their wild night, only reinforced it was over.

Matthew didn't need anyone in his life who judged him or his friends for how they chose to live. And he was done trying to be someone he wasn't to please her. There were plenty of incredible people who appreciated him as he was. Like the woman who'd been thoughtful enough to bring coffee and Advil, knowing he'd need them.

But what was she about to say? The question was driving him crazy.

Tyler walked in the front door and looked around. "She gone?"

"Jessica? Yeah." He passed his brother a fork and held out the cake. "We're still over."

"Good." Tyler grinned, digging into the chocolate sprinkle hair. "I'm sure you'll have better luck with the next one."

Matthew set the cake on the counter and took another sip of the coffee Amber brought. He stared at the mug in his hand, a flash of memory from the night before jabbing at his brain. He turned to his brother. "Did I call anyone last night?"

Tyler's lips pressed into a straight line, and he shrugged. "No idea. Hey, I'm kinda hungry." He walked further into the kitchen and dug around in the fridge. "Got any peaches?"

The mug slipped from Matthew's hands as another flash of memory hit. He was holding a phone in the bathtub.

What the fuck did I do?

Coffee trickled out of the spout, and he quickly picked up the mug. He tore off a wad of paper towels and wiped up the mess as his mind raced, grasping for more details. He did call someone. He remembered stabbing at the fuzzy numbers on his cordless phone.

Then it hit him.

"Amber!" he shouted at his brother. "I fucking called Amber!"

A few groans and grumbles came from the bodies in the living room.

"Shut the fuck up, dude!" Zack glanced at his watch and covered his face with his blanket. "It's not even noon."

"Sorry." Matthew stared at Tyler, searching for information in his suspiciously blank expression. "Why did you say peaches? Did you hear something?"

Tyler held his hands up. "I don't know shit. I was pretty drunk my damn self." He grabbed a paper towel off the roll and wrapped it around two pastries. "Thanks for throwing me a kickass party, brother." The men bumped fists. "I've got to get home. You good?"

Matthew rubbed his temples as his headache returned with a vengeance. "Yeah, go. I hope Charlotte kicks your ass for smoking."

"That reminds me." Tyler took a pack of cigarettes from his pocket and tossed them into the trash. "It's important to know when to let things go."

With a wave, he was out the door.

Tyler's words echoed in Matthew's mind. Jessica was out of the picture, but there was still a lot he needed to let go of—the fear he'd never feel strong again, the weight of other people's opinions, and the doubts that kept him from telling Amber how he felt about her. Needing a quiet place to think, he walked to his bedroom, sitting on the only piece of furniture in the room aside from the air mattress—a massive blue beanbag.

He couldn't let go of two unknowns: why Amber had come over and what he'd said to her on that call. They had to be related, but how?

The twisting in his gut told him it was probably something embarrassing. She didn't seem upset or offended when she showed up on his porch, so that was a good sign. He replayed their interaction in his head, trying to figure out if her body language and words offered clues he'd missed.

When Matthew opened the door, Amber was smiling.

She was wearing the flannel he put on her shoulders once when she was upset about her dad, and he was comforting her.

She'd cared enough to bring him hangover cures.

Would she have been so thoughtful if he'd made a fool of himself?

Then, Jessica came out, and Amber's demeanor changed completely. She looked... disappointed. Deflated might be a better word for it. Like she came in riding on a bubble of air, and Jessica held out a needle.

He could only think of one reason seeing his ex-girlfriend would make Amber look like that.

She has feelings for me.

He'd held back all these years, searching for signs the attraction wasn't one-sided. Once last year, he swore he caught a flicker of interest and almost kissed her. They were hiding in a janitor's closet at a club in Phoenix because Amber was overwhelmed after a long, loud day. Killing Daisies was part of a punk festival raising money for homeless teenagers, and he'd flown down for the weekend. They sat on upturned buckets and had just finished sharing a joint. Amber rested her head on his shoulder. He asked why she chose the drums, and she started talking about her dad. She was grateful he'd helped her find her passion for music but didn't understand how someone could show so much love one day and turn their back the next, like flipping a switch.

Her head lifted, and she gazed into Matthew's eyes in a way she hadn't before. It was deeper somehow, seeing past his stupid hair that never fell right and the glasses that never stayed put. Past the sense of humor he used to cover up the holes in his heart from losing his father, having an absent mother, and feeling inferior to his brother.

She saw him.

Something sparked and flared in his chest, an invisible thread tugging him closer to the lips he'd stolen so many glances of since they met, he could draw them from memory.

But a highlight reel of failed relationships played in his head, and he knew he'd fuck it up like he fucked-up every relationship he'd ever had. He would forget to call her back, say something stupid that hurt her feelings, or something else from his pile of inadequacies would smother the undeniable sparks between them. He couldn't risk losing her friendship, so he left the janitor's closet and hit the bar. He ended the night fucking some pink-haired twenty-something chick in the backseat of her Jeep.

Matthew didn't want to be that guy anymore.

He was far from perfect, but he had to admit, he'd grown up a lot in the past year. The attack set back his progress, but as he worked to get past that trauma, he could make Amber happy. It wasn't a foregone conclusion his relationships would fail, and he would do all he could to prevent it by learning from his mistakes and avoiding new ones.

This was his chance to get it right. The nerves in his stomach became sparks of anticipation as the realization took hold. His drunk ass must've admitted he liked her, and instead of coming over to reject him, she'd come to say she had feelings for him too. Right before Jessica gave her the wrong idea and chased her off.

His head lolled back, and he groaned. If he was right, Amber must've felt like a fool. She'd come all that way, finally ready to give a relationship a shot despite all her reservations, only to be disappointed.

He had to set things right.

Matthew took a quick shower to scrub away the lingering stench of beer and tequila, shaved, brushed his teeth, and threw on clean clothes. He grabbed the mug of coffee on his way out the door. Evan had keys to his place, so he could lock up if everyone woke from their alcohol comas and bailed.

When Matthew got in his car, he felt more hopeful and like himself than he had since the attack. Finally getting to tell Amber how he felt without the fear of rejection cemented a grin on his face. Well, there was still *some* fear of rejection, but he had to try.

He was certain no one else would ever accept all his broken pieces. But he'd fallen apart in front of Amber, and she'd still shown up on his porch that morning with her heart in her hand.

When he got to her house, and she answered the door...

Matthew would offer his in return.

16

Amber

By the time Amber got home from Matthew's, the bachelorette party guests had all cleared out. In the living room, Beth tossed dirty paper plates and napkins into a trash bag while Denise gathered bottles and cans. When the door shut, they turned to her.

"So?" Beth smiled, obviously eager to hear the good news Amber couldn't give.

"So, nothing." Amber tossed her purse and keys on the coffee table and flopped onto the couch. "I think he's back with Jessica."

Denise gasped. "No! That's so fucked-up!"

Amber threw up her hands. She was proud of herself for trying but frustrated as hell by the outcome. "I'm telling you, I'm destined to be single. When I retire, I'll start collecting cats, so I'll have someone to talk to."

She pushed off the couch and grabbed a trash bag to help with the post-party cleanup. As she shoved torn wrapping paper into the bag, the doorbell rang.

"Probably Charlotte." Denise held up a pair of edible underwear. "I'm sure she's sad she forgot these."

Amber set her bag down to answer the door. Looking through the peephole, her eyes bugged out when she found Matthew standing on her porch. He was holding a plastic grocery bag.

She turned to her sisters. "It's *him*!" she whisper-screamed.

"Matthew?" Beth's eyebrows shot up.

Denise rushed over and looked through the peephole. "Damn, girl, he's cute!" she whispered. "Like River Phoenix with a dash of Kurt."

"Let him in!" Beth did not bother to whisper, earning her a death glare from Amber.

This was seriously confusing. If he was back with Jessica, why was he here?

It was tempting to hope Amber had misread things. And that he was here to repeat the words he said in the message, only with complete sentences and a lot less slurring. But hope often led to disappointment, and she'd had enough for one day.

Amber flapped her hands at her sisters to return to what they were doing, and after a steadying breath, she opened the door.

"Hey," he said with an amused grin. "Which sister shouted at you to let me in?"

"That would be Beth."

"And who whispered that I'm cute?"

She laughed. "Denise."

"Hi, Matthew," her sisters sang it in unison, and Amber gave them the finger.

"Ignore them. So, what's up?" There was no way in hell she'd say more and risk feeling like an idiot again. The ball was in his court. She crossed her arms over her chest to conceal her shaky hands as she waited for answers about why he'd come.

"Bringing me coffee was really nice, and I didn't want to come empty-handed." He reached into the bag and pulled out a jar of chunky peanut butter. "I got you this. Same one I have at home."

Matthew held it out, and she blinked at the jar before taking it. Now, she was even more confused but also touched by his thoughtfulness. She was holding proof he'd been listening on movie night when she shared her frustrations about living with her sisters.

"Look, Amber..." He rubbed the back of his neck, clearly nervous. "I don't remember exactly what I said when I called you last night. I'm sure I sounded like a drunken asshole."

She shook her head. "You didn't sound like an asshole. Drunk, absolutely. But not an asshole."

"Invite him in, dummy!" Beth shouted from the living room.

Amber's eyes rolled. "Want to come in and meet two of my obnoxious sisters?"

A corner of his mouth lifted. "I'd like that."

Amber shot the women a look of warning as he came in and closed the door behind him.

"Matthew, this is Denise." She gestured toward her dark-haired sister with a smirk on her face as she shamelessly sized him up. "And this is Beth. I apologize in advance for her behavior."

Beth lightly smacked Amber's arm before taking his hand and shaking it. "Don't listen to her. I'm delightful."

Denise scoffed before shaking his hand. "More like demented. Nice to finally meet you, Matthew."

"Nice to meet you, too." His gaze drifted to the "Pin the Dick on the Man" game still taped to the wall. His eyebrows jumped. "Looks like you ladies had fun. Nice dick-orations."

Beth laughed and picked up a discarded penis straw from the arm of the couch. "Imagine the look on the garbageman's face when he sees a bag full of these babies at the curb." She waggled the straw in the air.

"Just looking at that thing makes me nauseous." Denise touched her stomach. "This girl sucked way too many Tangerine Clits through her penis."

"*Excuse me?*" Matthew's eyes bulged out of their sockets as he busted up laughing.

Denise explained to him about Sandra's uniquely named cocktails, and Beth told him all about the cock cookies Kate couldn't get enough of. Watching him laugh with her sisters was nice. He'd been there five minutes, and she could tell they already liked him. They could be a pretty tough crowd, but with Matthew, it was an easy thing to do.

He turned to Amber. "Any chance you have more of that coffee? It was a hell of a night for the guys, too."

"Sounded like it," Beth muttered.

"Huh?" His eyebrows furrowed.

"I warned you, Matthew." Amber glared at Beth before leading him to the kitchen by his elbow. "She comes off all friendly and innocent, but she's a fucking menace."

Amber set the peanut butter on the counter before filling two mugs with coffee and stirring in some sugar. "Let's go out back," she said, handing Matthew a mug. "Away from prying ears."

"You'd better give us details later, sis," Denise shouted before making kissing noises and giggling with Beth like a couple of middle schoolers.

Amber rolled her eyes with a groan. "I love them to death, but fucking hell." She opened the sliding glass door, and Matthew followed her outside.

He sat on the wrought iron bench by the door, and she settled beside him. When he shifted in his seat, the scents of laundry detergent and mint toothpaste wafted over. He looked a lot more awake and put together than earlier. Obviously, he'd taken the time to shower, shave, and, unfortunately, put on a shirt.

"So..." Amber's heart thudded against her ribs with an unsteady beat, as uncertain as her mind was about how to feel about all this. "What did you come over to talk about?" There was a chill in the morning air, and she sipped her coffee, wrapping her hands around the mug for warmth.

Matthew angled his body to face her, and their knees bumped. Her gaze fell to the spot, her pulse doubling in speed at the unexpected contact. She was even further gone than she thought.

"Amber, I like you." His shoulders sank with a deep exhale. Like he'd been carrying the weight of those words and could finally relax now that they were out. "As a friend, but also so much more. I still can't remember exactly what I said to you last night, but I have a feeling I said that."

She nodded in confirmation but stayed quiet, wanting him to continue.

"And I don't want you to think I only felt that way because I was wasted."

It was something she'd considered, so it was nice to put that worry to rest. She stared at the steam rising from her mug as she processed his words, and her hair fell from behind her ear, tickling her cheek. Without a word, he brushed it back with a slow, gentle graze of his fingers.

Her breath caught, and her eyes lifted to meet his.

"I said it because it's true." He took her hand, intertwining their fingers.

Tingling heat gathered low in her belly, and she forgot how to speak.

"After drinking my weight in liquid courage," he said, "I was finally brave enough to let it out."

Something had to be settled before things went any further. "Why was Jessica at your house this morning?"

"I didn't invite her and told her to leave right after you did. She showed up with pastries and empty apologies, and I told her we're never getting back together."

That was a relief. Amber would never want a guy still hung up on an ex.

"Why were you afraid to tell me how you felt?" She shivered from the cold as she studied his expression.

He released her hand, unzipped the front of his hooded sweatshirt, and wrapped it around her shoulders. "I'd think of all the reasons you'd reject me. All the ways you're so far out of my league, it's ridiculous to even think I have a shot."

"Stop. I could easily say the same thing. You own a business and your own home, and you have a college degree. I'm a straight C student who plays with sticks for a living."

His mouth fell open. "*You* stop. You know damn well you're the shit."

Amber shrugged. "I am. But so are you, so no more of this 'out of your league' business." She pulled the front of his sweatshirt closed over her chest. "Continue. Why else haven't you told me how you felt?"

"I didn't want to risk losing you as a friend if it didn't work out."

"And now?"

"I'm still afraid of that." He slipped his hand back into hers. "But I'm tired of letting fear run my life. I won't let it stop me from going after something that could be incredible for both of us."

It was hard to convince herself this was happening. With Matthew's sweatshirt on her shoulders, his warmth and scent were on her skin. The hand holding hers was strong and steady, grounding her as her mind and heart raced.

A hot drop of coffee spilled onto Amber's knee, startling her. She'd been so focused on his words she forgot she was holding the mug. She set it on the patio table in front of them. He did the same before his warm hand drifted to her face and cupped her cheek.

The touch was so gentle, his eyes so sincere that she had to say the words that would change everything between them.

"I like you too." It was barely above a whisper, but the grin spreading across his face said he'd heard it just fine. "You understand our relationship won't be anything like the one with Jessica, right? I don't sleep normal hours. I'm messy and moody, and I can't cook for shit."

His thumb glided over her cheek in a way that was so tender she closed her eyes to savor the feeling. Guys were rarely sweet and gentle with her. She assumed her punk looks and tough attitude made them think she didn't want that, but she did. Matthew was different in all the ways that would make him better for her than anyone she'd been with. He would compromise before giving up. He would really listen to her and respect her point of view. With him, she could drop the tough façade and feel safe enough to be open and trusting.

"All that might be true," he said, "but you're also kind and funny and an amazing friend. You appreciate chunky peanut butter, good weed, and Chris Farley. You've never tried to change me or anyone else because you understand the value of being yourself and letting others do the same. Not to mention, you're so fucking beautiful my hand is shaking from finally getting to be close to you."

"I noticed." Her smile grew. "I appreciate that my looks weren't the first or only thing on the list." It would be nice to be done with guys who only wanted her because of her big boobs and short skirts.

He shook his head with a look of disbelief. "I don't know how anyone could fail to see there's so much more to you than a pretty face."

Unexpected tears welled in her eyes.

That was easily the sweetest thing she'd ever heard.

Someone knocked on the glass door behind them, breaking the spell—someone about to be stabbed in the face for disturbing the moment.

Amber turned to see Kate smiling at them and waving.

Amber groaned. "Want to meet another sister, or was two more than enough?"

"Yes, and yes."

They laughed and got to their feet. At least Kate was the mature one in the family and wouldn't embarrass her like her other sisters loved to. Probably. Amber crossed her fingers, and they went back inside.

"Hi, I'm Kate." She held out her hand.

"I'm Matthew, but you already know that." He shook her hand before retaking Amber's.

Kate's gaze slid to their contact, and her grin widened. "You guys got any plans today?"

"I'm stopping by Charlotte's later to work on a few new songs she wrote," Amber said, "but the rest of the day's wide open."

Matthew squeezed her hand, and the warm, delicious tingles in her belly rushed back. "I was going to hang with Ty later, so we can go together if you want."

"I'd like that." Amber turned to her sisters. "Now, if you nosy witches don't mind, I'm going to show him my room." She led him by the hand toward the hallway before turning back around. "If anyone knocks on my door, they're getting shanked."

Kate put her hands up in surrender. "Go. Be safe, young people."

Halfway down the hall, Matthew stopped walking and started laughing. "*Seriously?*" He pointed at something inside Beth's open bedroom.

Amber followed his line of sight to the Tomorrow Mourning poster on her wall and burst out laughing. Not what you'd typically find in a twenty-nine-year-old woman's bedroom, but Beth was far from typical. "Yeah, she's had a major crush on your brother for years. When Charlotte first told him, he brought Beth some old demos and band T-shirts. I didn't warn her he was coming. I thought she'd faint when she saw him through the peephole."

Matthew shook his head, his eyes still on the poster. "Yeah, he's got that bad boy thing going on chicks go nuts for."

Amber shrugged. "I don't know. I've always preferred guys who are cute in a more subtle way. A way that makes you want to corrupt them a little while running your fingers through their hair." She raked her fingers through his dark blond locks and moved close enough to feel his breath on her lips.

His pupils widened like her words and touch caught him off guard.

She liked that look and fully intended to see it again, preferably when she could reach down and unbuckle his belt.

Beth came up behind them. "Why are you guys standing outside my room?"

Amber cleared her throat, shaking off the pent-up lust that nearly made her pounce on him in the hallway. "We're making fun of your crush on his brother."

"Bite me." Beth turned to Matthew. "What was he like in high school? I bet he brought tons of girls home."

"Actually, no. He was a band geek who spent most of his free time in an old dude's apartment."

Her sister's face crumpled like someone had tossed a stink bomb into the hallway.

He laughed. "Not like *that*. Jim was his guitar mentor. Ty gave up any hope of a social life in high school to learn from him. Made up for it plenty when fame first hit, though. I'd hear him banging girls in closets, in dressing rooms—"

Beth covered her ears. "Enough! I'd like to hold onto the illusion he's saving himself for me. In my dreams, at least. Don't want stupid reality ruining it."

Matthew nodded, an adorable, patronizing smile on his face. "You got it."

Beth jabbed a thumb toward him. "I like this one. And he can get me VIP tickets to Tomorrow Mourning shows, so don't fuck it up."

"Goodbye, Beth." Amber pushed past her sister, grabbing Matthew's wrist and guiding him toward her room. "Sorry about her. She's the worst one, I promise."

He shrugged. "I like her. She's real and doesn't hold anything back. In a world full of fake-ass people, I respect that."

"Let's see how you feel after she harasses you for concert tickets and a clipping of your brother's hair."

17

Matthew

Amber's bedroom wasn't what Matthew had imagined. The scents of leather, peaches, and weed smoke surrounded him, and everything was decorated with shades of purple, black, and gray—those details didn't surprise him. Neither did the pile of unfolded laundry and nearly overflowing garbage can. She'd said she was messy, after all. But there weren't any band posters, only framed photographs and colorful show flyers. While there was an unsurprisingly massive collection of CDs, cassettes, and vinyl on a shelf above her dresser, an even bigger collection of books lined two floor-to-ceiling bookcases in the far corner of the room. Most of the spines were pink or red, but he couldn't read any titles from that distance.

"I'll put some music on," she said.

He explored a bit while she flipped through a crate of CDs.

On the wall above her bed was a photo of a slightly younger Amber beside a middle-aged woman with light brown hair and a few silver streaks at the roots. Underneath it was a shot of a man wearing sunglasses and a necktie while seated at a drum kit. It looked like it was taken inside a club somewhere.

"Your parents?" He pointed to the frames.

"Yep. The one of my mom was from my last visit to Alaska and my dad's was at an old blues club downtown. Guess no one gave him the memo that sporting sunglasses indoors is more douchey than hip." She gave a wry smile.

Beside those photos was one of Amber and her sisters wearing backpacks on a forested trail.

She turned her head, following his line of sight. "We hiked ten miles on the PCT last summer. Beth swore she heard a cougar in the woods and ended up dousing a poor guy taking a shit behind a bush with bear spray. Good times."

Matthew laughed. "Note to self—don't go hiking with Beth."

On her bed, a fuzzy black comforter looked soft and inviting. A few candles were arranged beside it, along with a lighter that, knowing Amber, she probably used for more than candles.

On another wall was a colorful row of framed Killing Daisies show flyers. He had a collection of them too. He'd saved the fliers from every show he'd been to as a reminder of how far his talented friends had come. He admired how they chased their dreams and worked their asses off until they came true. When he was a kid, he wanted to be a forest ranger, but a nasty run-in with mosquitos and poison ivy on a hike was all it took to give it up.

Beneath the flyers was a shot of Amber with Charlotte, Sandra, and Luke, their arms slung around each other's shoulders. They all wore the signature look of sweaty, post-show bliss on their faces.

Music started playing on the stereo, and he recognized it immediately—Nirvana's *Bleach* album. It was a shame the popularity of *Nevermind* and *In Utero* overshadowed the album that, in many ways, he thought was their best. Amber knew it was one of his favorites, and he appreciated the gesture.

"I remember this." Matthew pointed at a photo of him and Amber taken after Killing Daisies' first sold-out gig. She tried to wrestle her drumsticks out of his hands while he held them out of her reach. He had at least six inches of height on her, so it was easy. They both wore wide grins, and he remembered how hard they laughed. He could almost hear it as he stared at the picture. "Who took it?"

Amber came up beside him, her eyes on the photo. "The photographer Eliza hired to take candids for promos. He knew you weren't in the band, but he said we were having so much fun, he couldn't resist taking it." She smiled, the tiny dimple in her cheek making an appearance. "He asked if you were my boyfriend."

Matthew's head tipped to the side as he studied her face. "What did you say?"

"I said no." She took his hand, her thumb gliding over the pulse point in his wrist. "But maybe someday."

Matthew released her hand and cradled her face in his palms.

He didn't want one more second to pass without knowing what it felt like to kiss her.

Her warm exhales fanned across his cheeks, and he moved in closer. She dragged her tongue along her bottom lip and wet it, his eyes tracking the movement. He'd been the king of self-doubt lately, but Amber wasn't pulling back, and her hooded eyes looked as hungry for this as he was.

Finally, Matthew closed the space between them, and their lips crushed together.

He slipped his fingers into her hair, and a low, sexy hum rumbled in her throat. The sound embedded itself in his mind, and he was desperate to earn another. Her tongue parted his lips as her soft fingertips drifted under the back of his T-shirt, ghosting up the ridges of his spine inch by inch. His chest rose and fell with quick, shallow breaths at the sensation, the delicate tease stoking his hunger.

When her touch reached his shoulders, her nails bit into his skin. He groaned into her mouth, but the sound was buried in the frenzied guitar chords and drumbeats filling the room.

Amber broke the kiss but stayed close. "Did that just happen?" A wicked grin curved her mouth, the tips of their noses touching.

"Yes." Matthew gripped the hair above her nape, and her breath hitched. "And it's about to happen again."

Her smile grew as he pressed his lips to hers. She melted against his chest, and he angled his face, deepening the kiss. She tasted like mint, and there was a hint of the sweetened coffee they had on the porch—fitting because the kiss made him feel more awake and alive than he'd felt in a very long time.

Craving more of her skin, he released her hair and his hands slipped to her waist, pulling her closer. Another hum of pleasure vibrated across his lips when the hardness in his jeans pressed between her legs. As consumed as he was in the moment, the worry someone would hear them scratched at the back of his brain. He was used to living alone and not worrying about moans or squeaky mattress springs. It felt weird to make out with Amber while her sisters were home, especially since he'd just met them.

"You're making it hard to be quiet." He pulled back to catch his breath. She was making it hard, period. "Do you think your sisters are listening with a glass to the door?"

Amber chuckled against his lips. "They're nosy, not creepy. But just in case…" She went to her stereo and turned up the volume.

When she returned, his fingers slid back into the hair at her nape, and he used the grip to tilt her head back. He planted slow kisses along the side of her neck, grazing the skin with his teeth. Her fingernails dragged down his back, tempting him to lay her on the bed a few feet away and plant slow kisses somewhere a lot more fun. But again, the awareness of people in the other room crushed that thought.

"We need to stop," he whispered.

She pulled back, her eyes still hooded and hazy. "Why?"

"Your sisters are in the other room." His hands slipped into the back pockets of her jeans, the curves of her ass filling his palms. "As much as I'd love to throw you on that bed and wrap your legs around my head, we should stop."

Her pupils blew wide. "What if I kill them? Then, can we do that?"

He grinned and kissed her again, his tongue sliding against hers. Each kiss was deeper, more urgent. It felt surreal that after three years of admiring the girl in his arms, he could finally touch and taste her.

The day they met, she was wearing a Bikini Kill T-shirt, leather jacket, and combat boots, and it was the closest thing to love at first sight he'd ever experienced. She was stand-offish and intimidating at first, but slowly warmed up and let him in. That's why now, he was glad he didn't have the balls to ask her out back then. They needed the three years of friendship to develop the trust and connection that brought them to this moment.

She broke the kiss with a frustrated growl, their foreheads touching. "We do need to stop. Or at least, take this back to your place?"

An enthusiastic "Yes!" burned on his tongue. He wanted nothing more than to break in his new place by fucking her on every surface of every room, but that was part of the problem—the surfaces were limited. His new bed wouldn't arrive for three more days. There was his couch, but he wasn't about to spoil their first time with a metal spring jabbing into his back or anywhere else. A narrow air mattress with a slow leak wasn't any better.

"If I had a bed and we weren't expected at Ty and Charlotte's, we'd be halfway to my place already."

"Right." She exhaled through her nose. "When will you have a bed?"

"Thursday."

Something changed in her eyes before they darted around like she was working a problem out in her head. "Fuck. Let's put a pin in this. The wedding's in thirteen days, and we have best man and bridesmaid duties. I'm giving three drumming lessons this week. Plus, I have five days to prepare for the record release, and there are interviews, signings, meetings—"

"Hey." Matthew pinched her chin between his fingers. "Don't worry about making time for me right now. I know how the game's played. Do whatever you have to do, and we'll have plenty of time after the release events settle down." He kissed her softly, her eyes fluttering shut. "I'm not going anywhere."

When her eyes opened again, she held his gaze. "Will you be my date to the release party? Obviously, you're going anyway, but—"

"I'd love to. Especially if you'll be my date to the wedding." A grin tugged at his lips. "Obviously, you're going anyway, but—"

"I'd love to." Her dimple popped as she smiled.

It was ridiculous how perfect she was. Everything that made Amber a fun, loyal friend was still there; only now, he could kiss her and feel her skin against his. That major shift would take some getting used to, but unlike many recent changes in his life, he welcomed it.

"Can I take you to lunch before we go to Ty's?" he asked.

"After the party clean-up, you're on. We can talk about the music equipment for the brewery while we eat." She grabbed a blue notebook from the top of her dresser. "I took some notes."

He appreciated that she was so invested in helping with the project, even though she was short on free time. She would know the right equipment to buy and bands to invite, and he could plan out the seating areas, food, and of course, drinks. Utilizing both of their strengths could make the project a huge success.

"Let's do it." Matthew turned for the door, but something on her nightstand caught his eye. He picked up the well-worn paperback with a shirtless man on the cover. "*You* read romance?"

She rolled her eyes, grabbed the book, and tossed it onto her bed. "Don't stereotype. They're not just for bored, lonely housewives or whatever. I haven't had much actual romance in my life, so it's fun to live vicariously through the women in books. Most of these were my mom's." She gestured at the bookshelves. "I'd swipe them from her room when I was way too young to read smut and got hooked."

"What does Fabio do in that one that's so great?"

She laughed, her nose wrinkling. "That's not Fabio, but I'm sure I stole a few from my mom with him on the cover. In that one, the guy's a poor deckhand in love with a duchess. He thinks he's not good enough for her, so he dumps her and works his way up to captain of a trading ship. When he returns to show her he's successful and ready to give her everything she needs, she's engaged to someone else. So, he murders that guy and feeds him to his dogs."

Matthew's eyes popped wide. "*What*?"

She laughed. "Kidding! Just wanted to see if you were paying attention. And to see that face if you were."

He poked her shoulder. "What really happens?"

"When she's visiting her parents in London, he breaks in and leaves roses all over the house. She retires to her room for the night, and he's beside her bed, waiting. He rattles off all the reasons he loves her. He realizes how stupid he was for leaving her and begs for forgiveness. The dude even bows at her feet and kisses them. Nasty, considering she'd been walking around the city all day, but it's still sweet."

The phone rang, but she ignored it.

"Amber!" One of her sisters shouted from the other room. "Phone!"

She grabbed the cordless handset by her bed. "Got it!"

"Hello?" Amber grinned at the caller. "Hey, sweetie. How are you feeling?"

He guessed from Amber's tone and the *sweetie* it was Charlotte or Sandra, but he didn't want to interrupt.

Amber's face lit up, and she grabbed Matthew's arm, shaking it. "That's fucking awesome! I'm so happy for you guys." She went quiet for a minute, listening. "Yeah, I'm coming over with Matty in a few."

Her eyes connected with his, and a pale pink blush painted her cheeks.

Possibilities he hadn't considered struck as the connection held. They could go on double dates with Tyler and Charlotte. Triple dates if Sandra and Christa joined them. If his finances allowed, he could join them on tour whenever possible to share amazing new adventures between shows.

And once everyone in their group found solid, healthy relationships, their big, happy family would be happier than ever.

"Okay, you too," Amber said to the caller. "See you later, babe." She hung up, a broad grin eating up her face.

"Charlotte talked to her doctor, and her hcg levels... Or is it hgc? Whatever. The level that says whether the baby's still growing or not keeps doubling, so it looks like everything will be okay." Amber held a hand over her heart. "She sounded so relieved."

Tears of joy and relief welled in Matthew's eyes. He knew what this meant to his brother and Charlotte. Maybe now they could relax and enjoy the rest of her pregnancy without the constant dread sucking the joy out of it.

"Your eyes are watering." Amber touched his face. "It's sweet how much they mean to you."

Matthew blinked back tears. "It was hard seeing them so sad when it should be one of the happiest times of their lives. And I can't wait to meet that little rugrat."

"Me too," she said, sitting on the edge of her bed. "But it's going to be weird touring with a kid. We're used to being loud and crazy on our bus, not worrying about letting a cranky baby take a nap. It'll be a big adjustment."

Matthew sat beside her, their shoulders touching. "Do you like kids?"

"Sure. Mostly. I don't want any myself because I love my freedom too much to sacrifice it, but I'm all for people choosing what's right for them. Even though their baby wasn't planned, I know how much they want to be parents." Amber tucked a foot underneath her and leaned into his side. "I'm happy for them but can't help worrying about what will change."

He knew *exactly* what she meant—all of it. It felt good to finally be on the same page with a woman he wanted to be with. "Not trying to assume anything about the future based on a few epic kisses, but for the record... I don't want kids either."

Amber studied his face for a second, a corner of her mouth curling up. "Good to know."

Matthew stood and held out his hand. She took it, and they returned to the living room to find all the penis decorations, blankets, and other evidence of the party gone. Her sisters sat at the kitchen table, talking and eating tiny sandwiches that looked like rocket ships.

"Okay then." Amber waved at her sisters. "Thanks for finishing the clean-up. We're out of here."

Beth waved back. "Nice meeting you, Matthew. Tell your brother I said hi."

18

Amber

In between bites of turkey club, Amber went over the notes she'd made with ideas for the brewery music space. Matthew's smile never wavered, making his appreciation clear that she was excited by the project.

"I'd love to have it ready by Halloween, if possible," he said. "It would be an awesome day to break it in with a party."

Four weeks. Amber skimmed her notes for any details that might make the timeline impossible. The only variable would be the time it took for equipment to be delivered and set up, but four weeks should be plenty.

"Using your measurements," she said, "we can get quotes from carpenters to construct the stage. I'm no expert, but I doubt it'd take more than a few days to construct. An electrician should be able to wire everything pretty quickly. I think four weeks will work for the rest, too. And I fucking *love* Halloween. It would make opening day extra fun to throw some spiders and skeletons into the mix."

She visualized the space done up with spiderwebs, witches, and ghosts. They could put pumpkins on the stage and tasting counter. It wasn't her place to dictate those details, but it would be a hell of a lot of fun to help decorate if he and Evan were game.

"Perfect." Matthew took a bite of his Reuben and licked mustard from the corner of his mouth. Knowing what his lips felt like made it easy to be distracted by them. "Please tell me you still have that sexy pirate costume from last year."

She laughed, remembering the wild party at Molly's that raged until dawn. Amber knew she wasn't imagining his stolen glances at her ass in the tight black skirt she wore. "Got a thing for pirates, eh? I caught you appreciating my generous booty a few times." She sipped her pink lemonade, grinning around the straw.

His head cocked to the side. "I've got a thing for *you*, with or without an eyepatch."

Amber licked a sweet, tangy drop of lemonade from her lip, his gaze flickering to the movement before he shifted in his chair. She hadn't meant for it to be sexy, but clearly, they both possessed a new power over each other to stir up desire. Maybe it'd always been there, kept on low like a pot of water beginning to simmer. Since admitting their feelings a couple of hours before, there were moments when the heat was cranked, the energy between them bubbling like mad. During their first kiss, it nearly boiled over. If her sisters weren't home and she didn't have practice, it would have.

Amber cleared her throat, shifting back to the topic at hand before getting carried away. "I've been meaning to swing by Music Planet for a few things. Want to go after this and look at equipment? It's right up the street."

His eyebrow lifted. "You don't waste any time, do you?"

If only that were true with everything in her life. "With some things, I do."

She regretted not making her feelings for him known sooner. It would've spared them both a lot of awful hook-ups, and she could've been the person he leaned on after the attack. She would've seen him struggling and dragged him along on tour. He would've been far from the triggers back home and surrounded by people who loved him.

And she wouldn't have let him quit therapy. If he tried, she would've pushed him back into it or offered to go with him and hold his hand. If he asked, she would've stayed with him every night in the apartment Jessica hated. He might've been further healed if someone had cared enough to be beside him while he fought demons in his sleep.

"If you mean us," he said, "I'm glad we waited. Now, we're starting on a foundation of friendship and trust. If we'd jumped in before that was fully built,

I don't know if we would've made it." He squeezed a lemon wedge over his iced tea, the sharp, citrus scent tickling her nose. "Not that it guarantees we'll make it now, but I think we have a better shot."

Amber nodded and bit into a fry. "You're probably right." Still, she couldn't shake the feeling he'd be stronger if he'd had a partner who wasn't so fixated on things that didn't matter and focused more on helping him heal. She didn't want to bring it up and spoil their first real date, and it wasn't healthy or productive to dwell on what should've been. She could only control the kind of partner she'd be now.

"I'd love to look at equipment with you after this." Matthew wiped his mouth with his napkin. "Thanks for helping. Evan's not into that stuff, and it's nice to not have to pester Ty with my questions about what microphones to buy and how to get the sound right when he's got the baby stuff to worry about."

"Happy to help." She pushed her plate away. "Let's do it."

At Music Planet, Amber took Matthew's hand and led him to the microphone aisle. She was suggesting a few when a salesman with an orange mullet approached.

"Can I help you find something?" Mullet asked.

"She has the finding covered," Matthew said, "I'll take the ones she's holding and anything else she suggests."

Amber smiled as warmth flooded her cheeks. She appreciated that he valued her opinion so highly. Mullet took the microphones from her hands. She rattled off the models of speakers and amps that wouldn't blow Matthew's budget, and Mullet pulled a small notepad from his pocket and jotted them down. A few aisles over, she found a mixer and basic lighting setup and Mullet added them to the order. After all the equipment was selected, Matthew whipped out his credit card and wrote down the brewery's address for the delivery.

"That should cover it." She turned to Mullet. "Carson gives me a fifteen percent discount, so please apply it to all this stuff."

Mullet's eyes rose from the order form to look at her. "I'll have to check with him. One sec." He left the desk.

Shit. Carson usually worked the late shift, so she was hoping he wasn't there. They'd hooked up twice last year. He wanted more, but he was so ridiculously selfish in bed, she shot him down. He offered the discount anyway, and she accepted, thinking of it as weird compensation for failing to care about giving her orgasms. Hey, fifteen percent was fifteen percent.

"Amber," the low male voice behind her purred. "Been too long, babe."

A cold, clammy hand on her shoulder made her shudder. She brushed it off and caught the narrowed glare Matthew was burning into the side of Carson's skull.

"Hey, Carson. The discount's still good, right?"

"Of course." Carson shot a quick glance at Matthew like he was sizing him up. "Who's your friend?"

Matthew's glare intensified as he slid an arm over her shoulders. "Boyfriend, actually."

Okaaay.

Amber wasn't sure how to react. Was he staking his claim or something? His possessiveness and use of the word *boyfriend* was surprising. And… surprisingly hot.

She arched a questioning brow at him before turning back to Carson. "Yeah, this is my boyfriend, Matthew. He's setting up a space for open mics in his brewery."

"Cool." Carson punched a few keys on the register. "Feel free to post fliers on the board. Local players are always looking for a mic to stand behind."

Carson himself was a local player, but not the kind who needed an instrument. It didn't surprise her that he wasn't fazed by her relationship. He had plenty of numbers lined up for a booty call.

"Forget the discount," Matthew said as Carson picked up his credit card. "I'll pay full price."

"What?" Amber's gaze snapped to him. "Why? That's like a thousand bucks."

Carson's head jerked back. "Seriously, dude?" He scoffed, punching a few more register keys. "Whatever. Give us a week for delivery."

Matthew's eyes stayed on Carson. "Perfect."

"Good luck, man." Carson handed Matthew the receipt before winking at Amber. "Nice seeing you, Amber."

Matthew pocketed the receipt and turned toward the exit with her still under his arm.

"What the fuck just happened?" she asked, trying to keep up with his quick pace.

He stayed quiet. They left the store, got into his car, and as she reached for the buckle of the passenger seat, he touched her hand, stopping her.

"Why did you bring me here?" His tone was flat, his expression unreadable.

"I'm so fucking confused right now. You needed equipment, you got it. Why did you drop an extra grand instead of taking the disc—"

"Because he obviously gave it to you to get in your pants. Unless..."

She crossed her arms over her chest, raising her armor against whatever he was about to say. "Unless *what*, Matthew? Spit it out."

"Did you sleep with him?"

Amber's eyes narrowed, heat flaring in her chest. She knew him well enough to know he wasn't suggesting she whored herself out to save a few bucks, but men had surprised and disappointed her plenty so that had to be settled. "Yes, I did. Twice. Both times were terrible and meant nothing. Are you asking if I fucked someone to save some money?"

His shoulders stiffened. "Jesus, Amber! Of fucking course not. But I was really goddamn uncomfortable standing there while he checked you out, touched your shoulder, and fucking *winked* at you."

So that was it—Matthew was jealous. That, she'd let slide. And she had to admit, the staking his claim arm-over-the-shoulders bit was pretty fucking cute. The fire in his eyes and all the cursing meant he was angry that she'd even suggested something so offensive.

A slow smile lifted the edges of her mouth. "Wanna know what you have that Carson doesn't?"

Matthew's gaze skittered across her features. "What?"

She leaned across the center console, closing the space between them until their faces were a breath apart.

Amber brushed her lips against his. "Me."

His hands shot up from his sides, fisting her hair and slanting his mouth over hers. His tongue pushed past her lips, and as the kiss grew hungrier, a low moan hummed in her throat. She gripped the front of his shirt, wishing she could rip it from his body to kick off an exploration of every last inch of his skin. But in a parking lot, his mouth had to be enough.

Her tongue swept over his, and he tasted like citrus and bitter tea. The scent of his sexy aftershave was heavy in the closed space, and she prayed it would transfer onto her clothes so she could breathe him in during practice.

Matthew abruptly broke the kiss, his eyes glazed with lust. "Sorry I got all Neanderthal on you back there. It was stupid and immature."

She grinned and shook her head, their noses bumping. "I liked it. I was waiting for you to start grunting and pounding your chest like a pissed-off gorilla."

"If he tried touching you again, I would've pounded the stupid fucking smirk off his face."

His thumb glided over her cheek as her smile grew. It was nice to catch a glimpse of the old Matthew, fiercely protective and unafraid. He'd been in a handful of fights, and in all of them, he'd defended someone who needed it—a scrawny guy at a bar being bullied by testosterone monsters, an elderly woman being harassed on a sidewalk, and a few times, women touched without their consent. After seeing how helpless he was when faced with Rafael's brother, she didn't think he could handle a fight so easily now. Still, she felt safe with him, certain if someone tried to hurt her, he'd find his courage and stop them.

He brushed loose strands of hair off her forehead. "I'm also sorry I said I was your boyfriend. Our first kiss was like two hours ago, so I don't really think—"

"Matty..." She touched a fingertip to his lips. "I liked that too."

Did she want a boyfriend? A week ago, she would've said no. It didn't make sense with her priorities and lifestyle. She couldn't see how it was possible to trust a man not to leave with a piece of her heart. But as they grew closer in this new way, a boyfriend was exactly what she wanted—as long as that boyfriend was Matthew Hall.

They smiled together as their lips met again. This kiss was slower but still held plenty of heat. And it was a million times better than what Carson or any other guy she'd been with was capable of. Matthew had skills, but it was also the feelings it stirred—desire, connection, even hope.

Maybe she wasn't cursed to be a cat-hoarding spinster after all.

He pulled back. "Thanks for helping me shop. I've been thinking about transforming that sad little corner of the brewery since we opened, and I can't believe how quickly things are coming together. I couldn't have done it without you."

Amber shook her head, pinning him with her gaze. "Matty, you can do *anything* if you want it badly enough." She hoped her words fully sunk in. They were true, and he needed to believe them for a lot more than the music space.

A loud knock at Amber's window made Matthew gasp and jump a foot off his seat. She turned to find Carson waving at her before getting in his car and driving off.

When she turned back to Matthew, he was white-knuckling the steering wheel. His chest jumped with heavy breaths, and the muscles in his jaw ticked. It was startling how quickly he went from relaxed to panicked when surprised.

"Hey," she gently touched his shoulder. "You okay?"

He nodded, his eyes closing as he a took long, slow inhale. "Just surprised me. I'm fine."

No, he wasn't. And she didn't like him saying it if it wasn't true. Maybe it wasn't the right time, but there was a nagging thought she was tired of holding in. "Would you consider going back to therapy?"

Matthew sank back further in his seat, and his eyes opened, his gaze on the windshield. "I appreciate your concern, but I can't. Seeing Rafael's brother the other day just has me on edge. It'll pass."

Amber didn't believe that for a second. Ignoring problems and hoping they went away never worked. They always came back to bite you eventually, usually with sharper teeth.

She slid her hand from his shoulder to his chest, rubbing the space over his heart. It thudded like a kick drum at first but gradually started to slow. "I think you should get a cat."

Matthew barked out a laugh, the distraction working. "What? Why?"

"So you have someone to keep you company at home. Someone to curl up next to you at night."

"Someone to terrify when I wake up screaming." He pinched the bridge of his nose and shut his eyes. After another breath, they opened. "Maybe someday. I don't really want to mess with a litterbox or worry about getting home in time to feed anyone but myself." He took her hand into his. It was still trembling a little and she held tighter. "Although I do look forward to having someone curl up next to me in bed, it'll be someone without fleas and a lot less fur."

"Damn. Guess I better start shaving."

Matthew laughed, the tension releasing in his jaw and shoulders. "Don't pretend you haven't caught me checking out your legs." He touched her denim-covered knee, and she kicked herself for wearing jeans instead of a skirt. "Smooth and fucking perfect."

Desire darkened the blue in his eyes, and it took all her restraint not to climb into his lap.

Amber glanced at the clock, confirming that was out of the question. She'd be late to band practice if they didn't leave now, her heart fluttering with a rush of anxiety. Charlotte would understand, but Amber was *never* late when it came to band obligations.

Matthew's grip on the steering wheel had loosened, and his breathing was normal. Knowing she had a hand in calming him again gave her a little surge of pride.

"As much as I want to lunge at you right now," she said, "I need you to take me to Charlotte's."

He buckled his seatbelt and turned to her. "Even though I want you to lunge at me like I want my next breath, I will *never* get between you and your band obligations."

Amber touched the back of his neck as he pulled out of the parking lot, her fingers skating over his skin and dragging through the hair at his nape. She was grateful he respected and understood her priorities. If she wanted to make this work, he needed to be high on that list too. Even as her career took off like a California wildfire, she had to remember the lessons learned from her breakup with Marco and not let Matthew drop to last place. With their friendship as a strong foundation, this relationship could be everything she'd ever wanted and more.

All they had to do was keep from fucking it up.

19

Amber

When Matthew and Amber walked into Charlotte and Tyler's studio, Charlotte was perched on a stool with a guitar. The second she noticed them holding hands, her jaw dropped.

She set her guitar in its stand. "What is this?" she asked, gesturing at their hands.

"We stopped being idiots." Amber pecked her on the cheek. Tiny beads of sweat clung to her skin, so she must've been playing for a while.

Charlotte's foot darted out, tapping Matthew's leg. "About damn time."

"Amber told me the good news about your warrior spawn." Matthew gently poked Charlotte's belly, making her laugh. "I'm buying that little badass their first tattoo, mark my words."

"Sure thing, Uncle Matty." Charlotte touched her stomach with a wide grin. It was nice to see her smiling again. "Did you pick up the tuxes?"

He lifted an eyebrow. "Don't worry about my list, lady. I got my shit handled."

"And I'll grab the bridesmaid dresses tomorrow, so no worries there either." Amber moved to the lounge area, and they followed. Her dress was gorgeous and hugged her curves perfectly after the alterations. She was grateful her friend would never pick some tulle and taffeta bullshit like a lot of brides do. "Use the next two weeks to rest up for that honeymoon. You and Ty can put all those bachelorette party gifts to good use."

Amber flopped onto the massive couch, and Matthew sat beside her.

"Nope," he said. "There will be no talk about my brother's sex life while my ears are in the room."

"We'll behave." Charlotte sat on Amber's other side, her chocolate brown eyes darting between them. "So, give me details. How did this start, and how was the kiss?"

Amber shrieked and covered her face. "You're not supposed to ask when he's sitting right next to me, weirdo. That level of girl talk's reserved for late-night phone calls and bar bathrooms."

"Then we'll save the second half of my question until this knucklehead isn't around." Charlotte aimed a thumb at Matthew, who just laughed. Their sibling dynamic was sweet and often entertaining. "So, how did this start?"

Amber tucked her hair behind her ear. "He came to my house, which was still very penis-y from last night, met all my sisters except Tara, and we fessed up to our feelings. And he brought me chunky peanut butter. I'll explain why that was sweet during our girl talk session."

Matthew shook his head. "Totally not uncomfortable you ladies are going to talk about my personal life. On an unrelated note, you got any rum?"

Charlotte scoffed. "After last night, you should kick back on the booze for a while, my friend. Although, your drunken blab-fest was what sparked this new relationship, so it wasn't all bad."

Matthew leaned forward, his eyebrows knitted. "Blab-fest? What are you talking about?"

Charlotte's gaze slid to Amber and back to Matthew. "Sorry. I figured you knew."

Amber sighed. She might as well clear this up, even though he'd be embarrassed. "We were all in my living room when you left the message. Tara said maybe Denise was calling for a ride, so I played it—in front of everyone."

Charlotte touched his wrist, sympathy in her gaze. "It wasn't that bad. It was actually pretty sweet."

"So, *everyone* heard it?" Matthew ran his hands through his hair, tugging at the roots. "What the fuck did I say?"

"You said…" Amber chewed her thumbnail, not looking forward to his reaction. "You said you liked me. And wanted to… taste my peaches."

"*What*?" His cheeks flamed with crimson, and his eyes bugged out.

Amber gave his knee a reassuring squeeze. "Every woman in that room has said shit a thousand times more embarrassing after a few drinks, I promise."

"Yeah, it was weirdly romantic," Charlotte said. "This bitch does smell like peaches."

He leaned forward with his head in his hands and let out a deep groan, his elbows braced on his knees. "I'm never drinking again."

Amber touched his back. "Seriously, Matty. It was nice. If you hadn't left that message, I wouldn't have shown up at your house this morning, you wouldn't have met my sisters or kissed me, and you wouldn't be holding my hand."

His forehead wrinkled. "I'm not."

Amber took his hand, lacing their fingers together.

"Aww, you guys." Charlotte's head tilted as she smiled. "Ty's going to flip his shit. We've been hoping both of you would find someone worthy of your awesomeness, and this couldn't be more perfect."

The door opened, and Tyler strolled in.

"Hey, beautiful." He touched Charlotte's chin, tipping her head up and kissing her. "Did you get that chorus figured out?"

"Yep," she said. "The writer's block is officially over."

Tyler sat beside her, slinging an arm over her shoulders. "How's it going, Amber?" When his gaze slid to her hand in Matthew's, a knowing grin tugged at the corner of his mouth. "What did I miss?"

"This happened." Matthew lifted their connected hands. "Glad my drunken rambling about fruit didn't scare her off."

"Yeah, you said some super weird shit, bro." Tyler laughed, his jaw working as he chewed a wad of gum, probably laced with nicotine. "Things got a little out of hand after that second bottle of tequila."

Matthew clutched his stomach. "Don't fucking remind me. I'm *never* doing shots with Zack and Adam again."

"You said that last time," Charlotte pointed out. "When you guys whipped your shirts off and ran across the Burnside Bridge screaming 'O'Doyle Rules' at three in the morning. You're lucky you weren't arrested."

"Hold up." Matthew turned to his brother, his eyes narrowing. "How did *you* know I said weird shit? You said you didn't hear me."

"I talked to him outside your place this morning," Amber explained. "He saw me in my car and asked what was up."

Tyler shoved Matthew's knee with his boot. "She was crying, dick."

"Fuck, Amber." Matthew frowned, tiny lines framing his mouth. "I'm so sorry."

"Don't sweat it." She wasn't one to hold a grudge against a friend, and their first kiss quickly erased any sting of disappointment that remained. Now, she was only looking forward to the next one. "You can make it up to me later. Are you guys hanging in here while we work on these tracks?"

"No, they're not," Charlotte said. "I don't want Ty to hear them until they're finished."

Tyler stood, stretching his arms over his head. "That's our cue." He kicked Matthew's shoe.

"You ladies have fun." Matthew leaned over and kissed Amber on the mouth, lingering for a second. Every touch from him made her crave more. But it was time to switch gears from being Amber, the incredibly turned-on woman who wants to jump Matthew's bones, to Amber, the hard-working drummer of Killing Daisies who wants to jump Matthew's bones.

After the guys left, she grabbed a pair of drumsticks from a cabinet in the studio and made her way behind the massive kit Tyler bought for the space. She had a healthy savings account, but there was no way she could afford anything that nice. Being in a band with Charlotte had new perks.

Amber warmed up, loving how her sticks hit in the room's perfect acoustics. It beat the hell out of her garage.

Once her muscles came alive with help from the adrenaline boost she got from playing, she found her groove. She closed her eyes and focused on the sounds of Charlotte's guitar, seeking out the most complementary beats to lay behind them with a little trial and error. It was like working out a puzzle in her head, and she loved the challenge. Even when something sounded nearly perfect, she kept at it, changing a beat or a fill until a satisfied smile pulled across her face, and she knew she'd nailed it.

The studio door opened, and Sandra came in with a happy skip to her walk. She took a seat on a stool and listened, rubbing her chin. After they played the final notes, she clapped.

"Yes!" She punched the air with both hands. "You figured out the ending! That was fucking awesome."

"Grab an axe and jump in, slacker." Amber gestured to the dozens of guitars hanging on the wall.

"Luke's the slacker." Sandra walked to the guitars. "He's not here because of a wicked hangover. I'm late because I had to take Christa to the airport so she could visit her dad." She stopped at a black and red Mustang and removed it from the rack. "Now let's get to work so I'm distracted from missing the smell of her goddamn hair or whatever."

Charlotte chuckled. "Are you still going to try and convince us you aren't in love with her?"

Sandra held back a grin as she tuned her guitar. Finally, it broke through, and pink bloomed in her cheeks. "Fine. I love her. Happy now?"

"Yes!" Charlotte squealed. "I'm so fucking happy for you!"

"Yeah, now I'm happy as hell and terrified of losing it." Sandra waved her hands in the air. "Yay!"

"Pretty much sums it up," Charlotte said. "Amber's on her way to joining us."

"Excuse me?" Sandra's head whipped toward the drums. "Spill it, girl."

Amber twirled her sticks between her fingers, her body buzzing with frenetic energy. "Matthew and I..."

Sandra gasped. "Get the fuck out of here! Seriously? Because of that message he left?"

Amber nodded. "As crazy as it is, that drunken confession set things in motion."

"It's going to be super weird seeing you guys kiss and stuff, but you'll be good for each other." Sandra pointed at Amber, loving concern etched in her expression. "Just be careful. That boy's fucking *awful* at relationships, and if things don't work out, you have to stay friends."

"I'm no master at them either." Amber set her sticks in her lap. "The last thing I want to do is mess up our tight circle."

"Sounds like Matty wants to get at your tight circle." Sandra laughed at Amber's raised middle finger. "Seriously, I'm happy for you guys."

"Thanks." Amber picked up her sticks, ready to work. "Now, saddle up, bitches. We have songs to finish."

⚫

After two hours of perfecting the new songs and running through the set for the release party, minus Luke, they decided to take a break. Charlotte grabbed three water bottles from the lounge fridge, and they sat on the couch to go over their schedules for the next few weeks.

As expected, free time between the album release events and the wedding would be almost nonexistent. At least their schedules were packed with good stuff, not funerals or dental appointments. Still, it would be nice to have more time to spend with Matthew. Aside from wanting to do a lot more kissing, she was eager to help with the stage area at the brewery.

Someone knocked softly on the door before it opened, and their manager, Eliza, walked in. She was dressed more casually than usual in black slacks and a flowy peasant blouse. Amber couldn't remember seeing her in anything but business clothes and heels.

"How's it going, Daisies?" Eliza's expression was tight, inscrutable.

"Great," Sandra said. "We made a lot of progress on the new tracks Charlotte wrote."

Charlotte sipped her water. "We'll be ready to test them during the tour."

They planned to sprinkle in the ones they were working on with songs from the new album and older fan favorites, switching up the setlist every night to keep things fresh. The last thing they wanted was to put on a predictable cookie-cutter performance.

Eliza sat on the edge of the couch, facing the women. "I have some not-so-great news to share."

Amber's stomach sank. Her first thought was Europe was canceled. Or something went wrong in the planning of their record release party in five days. Another possibility was that Rafael's brother had finally reached Eliza, and she was about to break the news. Amber held her breath, waiting.

"I spoke with your P.R. rep this morning. There's buzz around town that someone's working on a tabloid hit piece on your band. The last thing we need is negative press overshadowing the album release and tour."

Charlotte muttered a curse.

Unfortunately, she'd been through this before. A tabloid once used an innocent photo of Charlotte hugging then-married Tyler to claim they were having an affair. Beside it was a shot of him grabbing Amy by the wrists. He was stopping her from attacking Charlotte, but the article called him an abuser. The whole thing was framed as a twisted love triangle.

Those vultures had no interest in truth, only in what dirty headlines would sell copies of their useless rag. It was hard to gauge exactly how much the shadow of those lies impacted the band, but with a new album coming out, the threat of negative press made Amber queasy. Fortunately for her, drummers were usually left out of the tabloids while singers were targeted, but she'd kick anyone's ass who came after Charlotte or Sandra.

"Apparently," Eliza continued, "they've been fishing all over town for juicy gossip."

"What the motherfuck?" Sandra gritted out. "Who's writing it?"

"I don't know, but I'll find out. Trust me. In the meantime, be extra cautious about who you trust. Same rules as always: don't do or say anything in public you wouldn't want to be made even more public. These bottom feeders have eyes and ears all over."

"Here we go again," Charlotte mumbled. "Do you know who they've talked to?"

Eliza shook her head. "They tend to knock on the doors of jilted exes, former friends, estranged relatives. They'll approach a damn mailman if they think they have dirt."

Sandra huffed. "They can have at it. The worst my exes would say is I work too much and talk in my sleep."

"What if they find out I'm pregnant?" Charlotte asked, touching her stomach. "I don't want that public yet."

"Who have you told?" Eliza's perfectly manicured brows pinched.

"Just you and the band. Zack and Adam know. And obviously, my doctors and anyone who worked in the E.R. when I was in the hospital. And Jessica was there when I told Matthew."

"Jessica?" Eliza asked. "Who's that?"

"Matthew's ex," Sandra said.

"I'm not worried about her," Charlotte said. "She's not dumb enough to risk her job or face the wrath of these two." She aimed her thumbs at Amber and Sandra.

"Even so," Eliza said, "if Matthew's still out there with Tyler, please have him come in here. I'd like to ask a few questions."

Amber stood. "Yeah, I'll get him."

Was Jessica stupid enough to talk to the press? There were laws against nurses spilling patients' secrets, so hopefully that was enough to keep her mouth shut. If not, Amber would shut it for her.

She walked through the hallway, listening for voices to clue her into where the guys were. Roxy popped out of their bedroom and ran over, barking and bouncing with excitement.

"Hey, Rox." Amber leaned to scratch her ears. "I swear you get cuter every time I see you." The beagle ran off and returned with a squeaky soccer ball. Amber chucked it down the long hallway, and Roxy chased after it.

Amber found Tyler in the living room, alone.

"Where's your brother?" she asked. "Eliza wants to talk to him."

Roxy dropped the ball at her feet, tail wagging and mouth hanging open in anticipation. Amber picked it up and threw it down the hallway again.

Tyler took a lazy pull from the beer bottle in his hand and exhaled a long breath, as if delaying whatever he was about to say. "He's not here."

"Let me guess. Beer run?"

Tyler shook his head, and a look of sympathy washed over his expression that instantly made her nervous. "He went to Jessica's."

"*What*?" Amber's mouth went dry, her heart in her throat. "Why?"

Tyler gestured at the couch with the neck of his bottle, and she took a seat.

"It's not what you think," he said. "She called because a patient died, a kid. She sounded really upset. I don't think Jessica has people to lean on like we do, so she asked if he'd come over to talk."

Amber's eyes burned as she bit her wobbly bottom lip, refusing to let herself cry over this.

But it hurt. Just a few hours ago, they were kissing and laughing, and now she imagined him holding his ex-girlfriend and drying her tears.

Never let a man have your heart because he'll take it with him when he leaves.

She hadn't given him all of her heart, but enough for the words to echo through her mind like a scream in a cave.

"My brother would never hurt you on purpose, but he doesn't always think shit through." Tyler set his bottle on the coffee table. "Like I said earlier, he probably feels he owes her after how she helped him. How could he say no?"

"By saying *no*. Maybe I'm a cynical jerk, but since she was at his house this morning and now this, it's clear she's trying to get him back." Amber crossed her arms over her chest, fuming with anger and disappointment—in him and herself. She couldn't have these complications when she needed to focus on her band. "Why else would she call him? Doesn't she have coworkers who deal with death every day or parents she can cry to?"

Tyler shrugged.

Amber stood, forcing on her brave mask while trying to accept things with Matthew could be over when they'd barely even started. "The way I see it, he made a choice." She swiped at the one stubborn tear that wouldn't stay where it belonged. "Her. It's great he wants to help people who are hurting, but he should draw the goddamn line when it's someone he's slept with, especially right after starting things with me."

"Amber, I'm sorry." Tyler sighed. "I don't know what else to say."

"Don't apologize." Her hands curled into fists, buzzing with the urge to hit something. "You're just the messenger. Your brother's the asshole."

20

Matthew

Why is it so hard to know the right thing to do?

On the drive to Jessica's, Matthew couldn't shake the feeling he was making a huge mistake. He replayed every detail of the last ten minutes, mining the conversations for clues as to whether he was a nice, compassionate guy or king of the boneheads. Maybe he was both.

Tyler handed Matthew the phone.

"Sorry to call like this." Jessica let out a sob so raw, it tugged at his heart. "I got Tyler's number from Charlotte's chart. I need to talk to you."

"What's wrong?"

"I lost a patient. A little boy. I held his hand while he—" Her words cut off, and she was crying too hard to finish.

"Just breathe, Jess." He looked at Tyler. Along with the look of pity, there was a warning in his eyes. He might understand why Matthew hadn't hung up if he could hear how desperate she sounded. "What do you need?"

How many times had she dropped everything to help him through hard times? If she wanted someone to listen, he could do that.

"A hug. More tissues. And I need to get these thoughts out of my head. Can you please come over?" She was quiet for a moment. "I know we're not together anymore, but all my friends are either busy or not answering their phones, and I didn't know who else to call."

Matthew sighed with resignation. "Okay." He pulled his keys from his pocket, warring with his choices. She'd been there for him without hesitation whenever he was in distress. What kind of man would he be if he turned his back on her when she needed someone to listen while she processed her grief? "Where are you?"

"At home." She sniffed. "They said to take the rest of the day off."

He grabbed his jacket off the couch. "I'll be right over. It'll be okay, I promise."

Matthew hung up and put on his jacket while avoiding his brother's eyes, which would no doubt be filled with disapproval. "She lost a patient. A kid. I have to make sure she's okay."

Tyler touched his arm. "I'm sorry she's upset, but isn't there anyone else who can do that?"

"Her friends are selfish, superficial assholes, Ty." Finally, Matthew looked at him. "She was always there for me, and I can't say no when she needs my help."

Tyler nodded, disapproval written all over his face, as expected. "What about Amber?"

Matthew considered the question. She wouldn't like this. He couldn't predict exactly how she'd react, but it was a safe bet she'd be even madder if he said nothing and ran off to see his ex.

"I'll tell her. She'll understand." Matthew's shoulders sagged. "I hope."

He walked the hallway toward the studio. When he cracked the door, Amber's steady beats thumped behind the guitars.

Before stepping inside, he hesitated. She never pursued relationships because her band was her priority. Matthew understood and respected that. If he went in to tell her he was going to Jessica's, she'd be upset. Even worse, distracted. This practice was too important to derail with something so meaningless.

Then, he thought about how crushed she was when she came to his house to confess her feelings, only to spend the next couple of hours thinking he was back with Jessica. Wouldn't this stir up those feelings of rejection and doubt?

He shut the door.

Fifteen minutes. That's all it would take to let Jessica talk out her feelings and hand her tissues while she cried. It would take another ten to drive back to Tyler's. The women would be practicing for hours, so he could get back before they even knew he'd left.

He didn't want to start their relationship with dishonesty, but it seemed like the option least likely to hurt Amber and derail her work. He returned to his brother in the living room.

"I'll be back in forty minutes or less." Matthew grabbed a box of tissues off the coffee table and tucked it into the crook of his arm.

"All right." Tyler's head moved in a slow nod like he was trying to give Matthew a few more seconds to change his mind. "I hope she's okay."

Replaying everything that came before his drive to Jessica's didn't clarify things as he'd hoped. Matthew was ready never to see her again, but he'd never said no to someone in need. He wouldn't start now just because the circumstances weren't ideal.

Whether it was the right choice or not, he stood at her door, ready to listen.

After he rang the doorbell, Jessica answered with red, swollen eyes and tissues wadded in her fist. He handed her the box of tissues he'd taken from Tyler's.

"Hi," she croaked, taking the box. "Thanks for coming."

He followed as she walked into her living room and curled up against the arm of her white loveseat.

"Want some water or tea?" Matthew took the pink, fuzzy throw blanket from the back of the recliner and covered her with it. "Or a glass of wine?"

"No." She wiped her nose with the wad of tissues. "Thanks, though."

He sat beside her feet. "Want to tell me what happened?"

Jessica grabbed a fresh tissue and blew her nose. "He was seven. Ricky. Brought in with severe stomach pain. When I lifted his shirt, there were bruises *everywhere.*" Tears trailed her cheeks as she spoke. "Internal bleeding was too extensive. I held his hand as he slipped away." Her shoulders quaked with sobs. "His parents—fucking monsters—were arrested."

Matthew touched her back, feeling helpless to ease her misery. "At least he wasn't alone. You gave him comfort in the end. It sounds like he didn't get it much in his life."

She turned to him, tears dotting her lashes. "Do you know what Dr. Betts said when he saw how upset I was? 'These things happen. It's sad, but it's part of life and our jobs.'"

Matthew frowned at the heartless words. "That's cold. I'm sorry."

"No, *I'm* sorry. I get it now. Why what I said to Charlotte was awful. Just because something's part of life doesn't mean it isn't painful to accept." She wiped her nose. "Please tell her I'm sorry."

"It's behind them now." He took the used tissues from her hand and tossed them in the trash before handing her fresh ones. "The baby's okay, and they are too. So, what can I do to help?"

"Coming over and listening is enough." She dabbed her eyes before continuing to talk about her day, describing how difficult her job can be and expressing her fears about losing patients when she becomes a doctor.

Matthew listened, letting her cry and vent until it was all out.

"I don't know how I ended up with so many people in my life who can't be bothered when I need some support. But you..." She nudged his hip with her toe. "You're such a nice guy. I should've been a better girlfriend to you."

Matthew shook his head, unwilling to go down that road. "Let's not get into that."

Jessica sniffed. "I'll still go to your brother's wedding with you if you need a date." She grabbed a fresh tissue, wiping away the last of her tears. "As friends, of course, if that's what you want. I know you looked forward to going together. And I already bought that dress you liked."

He'd been looking forward to having her beside him at the wedding, but that image left his mind when they broke up four days ago. Now, when he envisioned Tyler's big day, he was slow dancing with Amber and kissing her under the stars. The only feelings he had left for Jessica were gratitude and now, sympathy for what she was going through.

"I appreciate that," he said, "but no." The urge to return to Amber suddenly made him feel twitchy and uncomfortable. Jessica had stopped crying and seemed calm enough to handle things on her own, so it felt like a good time to go. "Speaking of which, I have some best man duties to take care of with Tyler."

Jessica's bottom lip quivered. "You're leaving?"

He got to his feet. "Yeah, sorry, I have stuff to do. Can I get you anything before I go?"

"No," she snapped. "You've obviously washed your hands of me, so I wouldn't want to inconvenience you any longer with my fucking feelings."

He stared at her for a moment, frustrated and confused. And angry—she was being rude after he'd gone out of his way to help her. "Why did you even want me? You made it clear I'm not good enough as I am, so what made you even bother?"

"Matthew…" She shook her head like she couldn't believe he'd asked the question. "You're *real*. I've never met someone like you. I went to fancy private schools and a fancy college, and never met a single person who wasn't a product of their parents molding them into a perfect doctor or lawyer because nothing else was acceptable. My parents were embarrassed I wanted to be a nurse until I told them it was a stepping stone to med school."

Matthew bit back a scoff. She'd tried molding him into what she wanted. How could she be so oblivious she was just like them?

"And you're different," she continued. "You built your own business and forged your own path doing something you love. You're kind and have a sense of humor, unlike all the stuffy, uptight med students and doctors I dated before you."

"And I let you take care of me."

He'd suspected for a while she liked having him rely on her—maybe a little too much. She provided the crutch that got him through his hardest days, but a crutch is supposed to be temporary. Something to lean on while you regain lost strength. But he didn't feel stronger with her. He felt inadequate and small. And stupid for letting the weight of her expectations push him to be someone he wasn't. Amber would never do that, and the urge to run back to her grew stronger every second.

"Yes." She grabbed his hand before he could step back. "And you let me take care of you. I felt needed and wanted, and that felt good."

Matthew's hand slipped from hers. "I'm grateful for all your help, but we both need to move on." He pulled his keys from his pocket, making it clear he was done. "Can I call one of your friends to come over?"

Her eyes narrowed into slits. "We *both* need to move on? Have you already done that?"

There was no use denying it. "Yes. I have." One reason he was terrible at breakups was he didn't hold back the reasons he wanted out. While he didn't want to inflict pain, he didn't like leaving anything ambiguous or unsaid. "We're not right for each other, Jess. You deserve someone who already has the qualities you're looking for. No matter how many button-up shirts you bought me or ugly, expensive furniture you pushed me to buy, I was never going to be enough for you. Find someone who is."

She crossed her arms and turned away. "I'd like you to leave now."

As Matthew walked to the door, she exhaled a loud, shuddering breath. Guilt hit like a fist, but he had to keep walking, away from the life that didn't work for him and toward one that felt right and honest.

Matthew drove back to Tyler's a few miles over the speed limit, too eager to see Amber to give a shit about risking a speeding ticket. He got the closure with Jessica he hadn't realized he needed. A thrilling new future was calling, daring him to go all in with the woman he was aching to feel in his arms.

When he let himself in, the house was silent. He shouted for his brother, but there was no answer. Matthew made his way to the studio, opening the door a crack. Sandra sang a melodic tune before shifting to her angry punk growl with Charlotte's guitar and Amber's signature drumbeats backing her. He recognized it as "Peace in Pieces," a song off their new album.

He peeked inside to avoid disturbing the women's creative process. Behind the glass, Sandra's fingers danced across the guitar strapped to her back, sweat glistening at her hairline. When he crept into the lounge space, he met

Charlotte's eye as she played. Her chin tipped up in acknowledgment without breaking her rhythm. He walked further into the room, sitting on one of the cushy black leather recliners to watch them work.

As always, Amber beat her drums like they owed her money. Her taut biceps flexed as she moved, evidence of the thousands of hours she'd dedicated to her craft. He marveled at her strength and how long she could maintain such a furious pace. Matthew got winded moving his coffee table a few feet to the left.

When Amber's gaze collided with his, her rhythm stumbled. She stopped playing and groaned, throwing a stick at the wall. "Fuck!"

"It's okay, babe," Sandra said, wiping her forehead. "That fill is fucking brutal, and you haven't played it in a while. You'll kill it after a few more runs."

"Let's take a quick break, yeah?" Charlotte opened a bottle of water and pounded half of it. "You guys need anything from the kitchen? I'm craving a cherry popsicle."

Sandra set her guitar on a wall rack. "If you have lime, I'm in. Amber?"

Amber shook her head. She put her other stick on the snare and stood while Charlotte and Sandra left for the kitchen.

"Hey." Matthew patted the recliner beside his. "Want to join me in being as lazy and comfortable as possible?"

Her lips pressed in a tight line as she stood a few feet away, her expression unreadable.

"What's wrong?" Anxiety prickled in his chest. "The bad note? You sounded great—"

"Stop!" Amber walked to a Christie Hynde poster on the wall and stabbed it with her finger. "Do you think she would've made it if she'd been distracted by a guy when her career was taking off?"

The question and the anger radiating off her had him dumbstruck.

"What?"

"The answer is no," she said, the volume of her voice raising. "Instead, she was sweating it out in the studio until her fucking fingers bled."

He was no closer to figuring out what set her off, but her rage was clearly aimed at him. "I don't understand."

"Understand this." Amber's finger left the poster and jabbed the center of his chest. "I've worked too damn hard to let stressing about a guy running to rescue his ex break my focus."

Fuck.

She knew he'd left.

On top of regretting going in the first place, he felt like an asshole for distracting her when she was working. And making her feel like he'd ditched her for Jessica. The situation wasn't so black-and-white, but his choice had hurt her.

"Let me explain." Matthew closed the distance between them before she took a few steps back. "Please."

"You don't owe me anything, Matthew." Her shoulders lifted in a shrug before sinking low.

"She lost a patient, a kid. His parents beat the shit out of him, and she had no one else to talk to. She helped me so much when I struggled, and I couldn't say no when she asked me to return the favor."

Amber blinked hard, her eyes shining when they opened. "You *left*." Her voice broke with emotion, and she shook it off, the tough mask she wore for strangers slipping on. "Eliza wanted to talk to you, and when I went out to find you, you were gone. With her. I'm not some pathetic, jealous weakling, but you made me feel like one."

"Amber, I'm sorry. I didn't want to disturb your practice because I know how important it is." He reached for her hand.

She yanked it away, wrapping her arm around herself like a shield. "We should go back to being friends and forget anything ever happened."

Her words triggered a crushing feeling in his chest.

"Is that really what you want?"

She said nothing, her gaze drifting to the carpet.

"Amber, you have *nothing* to be jealous of. Nothing to worry about."

"You could've talked to me first." She shook her head, her soft blonde waves falling over her shoulders. "But you just left."

He'd made the wrong choice. In trying to spare her feelings, he'd hurt her more than if he'd been honest at the start. Knowing what Amber's father did to her family, knowing how certain she was that all men leave, he should've known better than to disappear without an explanation.

"I'm done with Jessica," Matthew said, stepping closer, "I promise."

"You said the same thing this morning."

He'd never lied to her, but she had every right to doubt him in this case. Twice in one day, she'd had to worry he'd chosen someone else.

He had to set things right and never give her reason to doubt him again.

"You're right," he said. "I meant it, but I can see how my choices hurt you, and I'm so sorry. If you give me another chance, I'll do my best not to let it happen again."

If Matthew wanted this relationship to work, he had to learn to think before reacting, give her the respect she deserved, and communicate before doing something that could hurt her.

Amber chewed her bottom lip, still staring at the floor. She was probably trying to decide if she could forgive this and if he was worth the trouble.

Please don't give up on me.

Matthew held his breath.

"You'll never see her again?" she asked. "Even if her kitchen sink is clogged or some crazy blonde bitch stabs holes into her fucking tires?"

"Please don't do that." He laughed, and she got close, her lips twitching. "I'll never see her again."

Her chin lifted, but she stayed quiet.

"Like I told you before, I'm shit at relationships." He took a chance and reached for her hand again. This time, she let him take it. "But I want to make this work."

She nodded slowly. "I guess being too nice for your own good is better than being a cold-hearted asshole." Her fingers toyed with the ends of her hair as she studied his face. "You sure I'm the one you want?"

Matthew used her hand to draw her closer. "Completely. Do you have any idea how long I've wanted to be with you?" He brushed the backs of his knuckles against her cheek. "The day we met, your fucking adorable dimple winked at me, and I almost busted in my goddamn jeans."

Amber huffed a laugh, a soft but cautious grin lighting her eyes. "Over a dimple? Interesting kink."

"You looked so tough in your leather jacket and boots, but that dimple and the beautiful smile that came with it couldn't have been sweeter. I knew right then there was a lot more to the story than what you let most people see." He touched her chin, his thumb stroking the spot on her cheek where the dimple was hiding. "And I wanted to find out what else was beneath that outer layer of sexy badass."

Her gaze slid to his mouth. "Sexy, huh?"

He leaned in, his lips brushing hers. "Every single fucking thing about you is sexy." His tongue darted out, skimming her bottom lip. "This mouth I haven't been able to stop thinking about since that first kiss." His fingers slipped from her face, drifting down her arms. "These muscles you earned by playing your heart out." He rested his forehead against hers. "Those gorgeous blue eyes that look as hungry as mine." His hands slid into the back pockets of her jeans, pulling her flush against him. "I want this, Amber. I want *you*. And I'm looking forward to getting you alone to show you how much."

When their lips pressed together, a gentle whimper rose from her throat. Her head tilted, and her tongue parted his lips, plunging into his mouth as her wild heartbeats pattered against his chest.

"Fuck, I want you too." She jumped, and her legs wrapped around his waist. It was impossible not to imagine her doing that while they were naked. With one upward thrust of his hips, he'd be buried deep inside her. He gripped her ass, the feeling of her pressed against his hardening cock making his legs weak.

"See what you do to me?" He bucked his hips, and she gasped, her legs squeezing his waist even tighter.

She nipped his bottom lip before sucking it into her mouth, slowly dragging her teeth along his flesh as she pulled away. "We could lock the door and tell them to fuck off when they start knocking."

"Tempting." He walked backward until the backs of his knees hit the recliner. As he sat down, he held her close to straddle his lap.

She slipped a hand behind his neck and pulled his face to hers. Their lips met and the kiss quickly turned ravenous, their tongues tangling as his hands moved from her ass to slide up the back of her shirt. Her skin was damp with sweat, and just thinking of her pounding the drums made him harder.

He desperately wanted to peel her clothes off, piece by piece, before sinking into her tight heat.

Someone cleared their throat behind them, and they broke the kiss.

Charlotte held a popsicle stick with one inch of red left on it. Her lips, curled into a coy little smirk, were stained the same color.

"I can relate to your enthusiasm over finally hooking up," she said, "but please don't fuck on our brand-new recliner." She bit her popsicle around her widening grin.

Sandra came in next, her lips stained green. Her eyebrows shot up when she saw Amber in his lap. "I guess you forgave him. Now, can you please stop riding Matthew and get your ass behind those drums?"

21

Amber

Green and blue spotlights danced across the stage, lighting up the ecstatic faces in the crowd. As Amber hammered away at the drums, sweat stung her eyes and slid down the back of her neck, pooling between her shoulder blades. Throughout the set, she'd fed off the crowd's energy, the electricity in the room sizzling in every cell of her body. Every time she glanced at her bandmates, it was clear they felt it, too.

This was the best performance they'd ever given.

It was their first time playing the new album for an audience and judging by the roaring applause after every song, it was the best album they'd ever made.

When the last song kicked off, Charlotte's head tipped back as she grinned, her fingers flying over her strings as she played the solo she'd dedicated countless hours to perfecting. Sandra gripped the microphone in her fist as she sang and growled, her guitar swinging from its strap in front of her chest. Luke was in his zone. He bounced around the stage on the balls of his feet, beaming at the crowd as his thumping basslines echoed from the floor to the rafters.

When the final notes were played, the crowd exploded. Amber closed her eyes as she caught her breath, a wave of pride crashing over her. She joined her bandmates front and center, their arms dangling over each other's sweat-drenched shoulders as they took a bow.

Their manager, Eliza, jogged to the center stage microphone. "Thanks for coming, everyone! Give it up one more time for Killing Daisies!"

Amber would never get tired of hearing her band's name shouted into a microphone. They wanted a name that conveyed beauty and brutality, naughty and nice. And it looked cool as hell on a T-shirt.

Another roar of cheers and applause rolled in from the hundreds of fans, record execs, and other industry bigwigs invited to celebrate the release of *Razor Smile*, the album poised to propel the band to a level of success most musicians only dream of. They'd worked damn hard to get there, and Amber was enjoying every second of the ride.

"Get home safely!" Eliza waved to the crowd as she left the stage with the band.

After long daily rehearsals squeezed between photo shoots, meetings to discuss possible endorsement deals, and interviews with radio, print, and TV, the week of non-stop work and chaos was finally over.

They'd done it.

They'd pulled it off.

"Well, ladies," Eliza said, "And Luke, I hope you're incredibly proud of yourselves for what you did out there. I knew you guys would kill it, but this was above and beyond."

Amber was incredibly proud and grateful for the day three and a half years ago when Charlotte and Sandra walked into the café where she worked. They became regulars, and one day, she overheard them talking about drama in a band Charlotte was in. Amber struck up a conversation while refilling their coffees, and they clicked. They bonded over bands they loved and went to shows together. A few months later, Amy booted Charlotte from Scarlet Love Letter, and Charlotte and Sandra started their own band. They invited Amber to try out, and Killing Daisies was born.

From garages to Satyricon to stages all around the world. And hopefully soon, to platinum-selling status.

But no matter how high they climbed, they'd never forget their roots.

"I'm not going to be able to sleep for a week." Sandra looked wired, her pupils wide like she'd guzzled a pot of coffee.

"Once the buzz wears off," Amber said, "I'll probably do nothing but sleep for a week."

With the hectic schedule, she only got a few hours of rest every night. To compensate, she'd been living on caffeine and adrenaline. When it came, the inevitable crash would hit like a boxer on steroids.

She'd squeezed in sister time and as much Matthew time as she could, but it wasn't nearly enough. They still hadn't been able to do anything beyond making out and dry-humping like horny teenagers, and the sexual tension was driving her insane.

"How are you doing, babe?" Sandra grabbed a bottle of water and passed it to Charlotte.

"My big dumb grin didn't clue you in?" Charlotte laughed. "One of the best nights of my life. Thanks for bringing your A games, everyone."

Luke peeled off his shirt and used it to wipe sweat from his face. "I'm so glad a film crew was here to capture that. I can't wait to see it again."

Eliza's cheeks flushed, and she averted her eyes. "There are towels back here for that, Luke."

"Oh. Sorry. I'm not used to so many females backstage who *don't* want to see me without a shirt." He slipped it back over his head.

"We're all super impressed with your pecs, bud." Sandra smacked his sweaty chest before it was covered, and he playfully shoved her shoulder. "Is our ride here?"

Eliza nodded. "'s waiting outside. But so is a wild pack of fans who'll do all they can to find a crack in our security. If we didn't need the photo op for the press, I'd sneak you all out the back. There are metal barriers to keep you safe and several bodyguards to help you to the car, but keep your heads up and eyes open."

Matthew and Tyler jogged up the stairs with backstage laminates around their necks.

Tyler hooked a hand around Charlotte's waist and kissed her hard. "Baby, you were amazing. That solo on 'Weakness' blew my goddamn mind."

Matthew grabbed a towel from the pile and patted Amber's forehead. "I'm speechless, so give me a second."

"If you won't be using your lips for talking…" She pressed her mouth to his, the high from the show and the taste of him making her body buzz. It was fun when Matthew came backstage as a friend, but this was better.

"You were unbelievable," he said. "Your sisters were behind me, and my ears are still ringing from their screaming. They said to tell you they loved the show, and they'll see you at home."

"It's been a hell of a lot of fun," Tyler said, "but I need to get this rock goddess to bed. It's been a long fucking week."

Eliza set up the event so all the meet-and-greets and mingling happened before the show, knowing they'd all want to bail afterward to get some much-needed rest. She hugged everyone and said her goodbyes. Everyone else headed to the dressing room to meet the bodyguards assigned to escort them to the car.

"This is weird," Amber said. "We've never needed this much security before. Should we be worried?"

"Yes," Tyler said without skipping a beat. "This is what it'll be like from now on. While most of the ride will be as exhilarating as you feel now after that show, some of it is fucking terrifying." He pulled Charlotte tight against his side.

Amber's heart was already pounding, and Tyler's ominous words made it stutter in her chest. It was all part of the ride, but she didn't want strangers' hands grabbing at her body or screaming in her face. "Thanks for that, Ty. Now I can't breathe."

"Hey." Matthew brushed damp hair off her face and kissed her. "I've got you." His arm wrapped around her shoulders and held her close.

She knew it was true. Even though he still didn't feel as strong and self-assured as he did before the attack, Matthew would never let someone hurt her or anyone else he cared about.

A massive tank of a man with *Security* printed across his shirt entered the room. "All right, everyone. Stay close to my guys; we'll get you out safely. Ready?"

"Hell yeah, dude." Luke bounced on his toes, as restless with pent-up energy as everyone else. "You hear those screams? Let's get out there and say hi."

Amber and Matthew took the lead, flanked by two bodyguards. As they walked through the mostly empty areas of the club, the din of the crowd outside grew louder. Matthew's fingers slipped between hers. He probably caught the nervousness making her hands shake.

When they reached the front of the club, Amber took a deep breath.

The doors burst open.

The excited screams tripled in volume. A parted sea of bodies squeezed together like sardines in a can, everyone fighting for a spot against the metal rails.

"Holy fuck." She knew no one could hear it, but it was exactly how she felt. It was exhilarating and petrifying, like leaping out of an airplane or bungee jumping off a bridge.

She held Matthew's hand tighter as the bodyguards stayed at their sides, ushering them forward. Her eyes roamed over the faces in the crowd. Some people waved pens and band photos, and some held CDs, but everyone looked thrilled to see them in the flesh.

"Amber!" The high-pitched shout rose from the crowd.

To her right, she spotted a girl about twelve or thirteen jumping up for a better view. Their young fans were the best. It was gratifying to help inspire the next generation of girls to pick up an instrument and let it rip. She released Matthew's hand and took the Sharpie and band photo the girl was waving in the air.

One of the bodyguards leaned close to Amber's ear. "Miss Jamison, you have to get to the car."

She put up her index finger so he'd give her a second. "What's your name, beautiful?"

"Oh, my god!" The girl squealed with joy, her eyes wide and glassy with shock. "It's really you! I play drums, too, and you're my favorite. I'm Shauna."

Amber grinned, remembering the thrill of meeting her hero, Sandy West of The Runaways, at a record shop in Portland when she was fourteen. It was surreal to think this kid might hold onto their shared moment as tightly.

Amber signed the photo and handed it back. "Keep rocking those sticks, kid."

Shauna screamed and showed the photo to a woman beside her, probably her mom.

"You're amazing," Matthew's lips grazed the shell of Amber's ear, sending a tingling shiver up her spine.

Behind them, a male voice yelled, "Stay the fuck back!"

Someone bumped her from behind.

Amber was about to turn and see what happened, but a pair of strong arms shielded her from the chaos.

She turned her head.

Matthew.

"Everything's okay," he said against her ear. "Just keep walking."

She'd been so excited she hadn't considered how he might feel in such a high-stress situation. The arms around her were steady, and with his chest to her back, she could feel the rhythm of his breathing—also steady. She glanced at him over her shoulder, and he smiled back as they pushed their way to the car.

People shouted her name, but she kept moving.

A hand reached out from the sea of people and grabbed the back of her shirt. Before she could react, Matthew smacked it away like a pesky fly. He guided her closer to the center of the path and took off his jacket to cover her, the warm fabric settling on her shoulders.

He gripped her waist as they reached the black limousine idling at the curb.

"Amber!"

The booming male voice cut through the chaos, stopping her feet from moving.

"Amber! Over here!"

She turned, her stomach dropping.

"*Dad?*"

At the center of the crowd, staring at her with an expression she couldn't decipher, stood Bryan Fucking Jamison. Her runaway father. He looked mostly the same as she remembered, but his face was a little fuller, and his hair was now streaked with grey.

The word snagged Matthew's attention, and his head snapped to the left.

"What are you...?" she whispered to herself. She was too stunned to finish the question, but plenty of others spun through her brain.

What are you doing here?

Why aren't you at your new home with your new family?

Why did you leave us and never look back?

Then she noticed his hand on someone's shoulder. The person was a foot shorter than her father, and the only other detail she could make out was a head of short, sandy brown hair.

Amber drew in a sharp breath as she realized who it was. "Oh, my god."

People in the crowd blocked the person's face, but it had to be him—the precious son her father had always wanted. The boy who wrote the letter sitting unopened in the top drawer of her dresser.

She was curious about what he had to say, but even more, she was afraid something in that letter would reopen old wounds that would bleed all over the life she'd built.

This kid replaced her, replaced her sisters. He got all the time with their father they'd lost. His mother fucked a married man, and together, they shattered Amber's mother's heart into so many pieces it still hadn't recovered. What could the product of that betrayal possibly say she'd want to hear?

Someone stepped on Amber's toes, the pain making her flinch and hiss through her teeth.

Matthew's warm breath on her neck yanked her back to reality. "Sweetheart, we have to go."

She glanced back at her dad, watching him fade into the crowd as it surged.

Matthew helped her into the backseat and slid in beside her, shutting and locking the door.

"Don't lock it," she said, still dazed. Did she imagine her father standing there or was it real? It seemed so impossible. "Sandra's right behind us."

"I'll watch and open it when she's closer. I've been to enough of Tyler's events to know how rabid fans get and how quickly they can get past security." His knuckle tucked under her chin, his eyes roaming her face. "Are you okay?"

Amber nodded, though she wasn't sure it was true. It was one of the biggest nights of her life, and the high from moments before had been obliterated.

"That was your dad?"

The backs of his fingers stroked her cheek. She imagined the shock that must be on her face, and he knew exactly how to soothe it.

She nodded. "I think his son was with him."

"Seriously?" His fingers stilled. "What the fuck were they doing here?"

"I have no clue. Maybe my dad read a blurb about the event, but I don't know why he'd want to see me after all this time." Her mind raced in a million directions. "I wonder if my sisters saw him or if—"

"Hey." He pressed his forehead to hers, demanding her focus as her thoughts spiraled. "This is a *huge* night for you. Did you see the stunned faces in that crowd? They couldn't fucking believe what they were seeing. It's a story they'll tell their damn grandkids. I was there the night Killing Daisies blew the roof off Satyricon." He mimicked an old man's voice at the end, making her laugh, though it was halfhearted.

Heat flooded her cheeks. "How dare he show up here!" Her emotions were all over the place, and it was anger's turn at bat. "What gives him the fucking right to come here with his kid on one of the biggest nights of my career?"

Matthew frowned, a muscle ticking in his jaw. "He's a fucking asshole and should've stayed away. I'm sorry he upset you."

Her mind spun in yet another direction. Part of her still missed her dad and hoped he'd changed. Maybe he was finally ready to apologize for his mistakes and forge a new relationship with his daughters. This could be the first step.

"What if he wants to make amends?" Amber gnawed her thumbnail. What he did felt unforgivable. But it was easier to say she'd never speak to him again when that was the only option. "Do I let him or tell him to fuck off?"

"Why don't we save those questions for tomorrow? Savor the moment because you worked incredibly hard and earned it. Speaking of savoring..." He pulled her legs onto his lap, cupping the back of her head as he moved in closer. "All night, I've been dying to kiss the drummer of my favorite band."

His lips touched hers, and she surrendered to the kiss. Matthew was right. The big, serious stuff could wait if she chose to even think about it. For now, she let herself enjoy the slide of his warm tongue against hers and the soft, low growl of desire rising from his chest.

Thank god for tinted windows.

Her hands slipped under his shirt, craving the comforting warmth of his skin beneath her fingertips.

A knock at the window startled them.

Sandra stood outside, flanked by two beefy bodyguards cloaked in dark blazers, their faces tense. Knowing her, she'd been hugging fans and shaking hands while they fought to keep her from getting mauled. It was safe to say the guys earned every cent of their paycheck.

Matthew unlocked the door before sliding over with Amber to make room.

Sandra gave one last wave to the crowd and blew a few kisses before diving into the car.

"The others are right behind me." With a loud exhale, Sandra sank into her seat and closed the door. "Fuck, you guys! That crowd was wilder than a pack of Chihuahuas on speed."

Through the window, Amber spotted Charlotte. She was signing an autograph with an ear-to-ear grin while tucked under Tyler's arm. Two more members of security shielded them from the sea of outstretched hands, desperate for even a fleeting brush with the band they'd all come to see. Tyler didn't look happy as he guided Charlotte to the car, opened the door, and climbed in behind her.

He frowned, his worried gaze skittering over Charlotte's face. "Are you okay? That fucker almost tripped you." He pulled a bottle of water from the pocket of his green army jacket and passed it to her.

"You're definitely brothers," Amber said, nudging Matthew's knee. It was sweet how protective they were. In fact, it was one of her favorite things about the man beside her. As expected, when hands in the crowd grabbed at her, he kept her safe. Matthew doubted his strength, but she didn't.

"I swear, I'll never get used to this shit," Tyler said. "And it's a whole different experience when people are screaming and grabbing at my pregnant fiancée. I was seconds away from ripping a few throats out."

"I'm not made of glass, Ty." Charlotte snuggled against his chest. "And I love you too."

His arms wrapped around her, pulling her as close as their seatbelts would allow. "Ladies, that was hands-down the best show you've ever done. Sandra's vocals were like a sweet gut punch, my girl's riffs were next fucking level, and Amber... How the hell are your arms not broken? You slammed those drums like a beast."

Sandra's lips quirked. "Thanks, Ty. Now maybe assholes will stop saying we're only touring with you because Charlotte fucked us to the top."

The article was in a tabloid delivered to mailboxes and newsstands nationwide that morning. It painted Charlotte as a manipulative starfucker using Tyler to boost her fame. They all guessed it was the article Eliza warned them was imminent. It could've been worse. No one who mattered would ever believe such an insulting load of bullshit.

"Stop!" Charlotte covered her ears. "I *never* want to hear that again. We did kick ass and take fucking names tonight. I'll admit, I doubted whether we'd earned the co-headline spot with this rock behemoth right here, but tonight convinced me. We left sweat and blood on that stage." She pointed at the venue, still swarmed with screeching fans and paparazzi.

"Open it for Luke," Sandra said.

Tyler opened the door, and Luke climbed in, taking the open seat beside the minibar.

"Have I told you lately how grateful I am you let me in your band?" Luke was coated in a fresh layer of sweat, and he peeled his damp shirt away from his chest before it stuck right back to it when he let go.

"And we're grateful you aren't a flakey shitbox like those who came before you." Sandra buckled in as the car lurched forward.

Luke inspected the contents of the minibar, the bottles and crystal glasses tinkling together. "Who wants a drink? We've got vodka, gin, rum..." He opened a small cabinet beneath the glasses to reveal at least a dozen more bottles of water and booze. "Fucking everything, basically."

"I could use ice and more water," Charlotte said, waving her empty bottle.

"You got it, mama." Luke plinked a few ice cubes into a glass and passed it along with a fresh water bottle to Charlotte. "Anyone else?"

After Luke took their orders and whipped up drinks for everyone, a soothing silence fell over the car. A glance at her watch told Amber it was nearly three in the morning. It'd been a very long night.

Coming down from hours of adrenaline high, the limo's gentle rocking and the lulling effects of two glasses of champagne made her eyelids heavy. She rested her cheek on Matthew's chest, and he pressed a lingering kiss to the top of her head. A chill from the sweat drying on her skin made her shiver, but as she snuggled closer, the warmth of his body soaked into hers.

Earlier, he'd used the word *savor*, and that's exactly what she did. The feeling of his bare arm against the nape of her neck. His fingertips gently brushing back the rogue hairs that fell across her cheek. No one had ever made her feel so treasured before. Like her sharp, rough edges had been smoothed, and it was finally safe to be soft and vulnerable.

As she savored his scent and touch, she realized how easy it would be to fall for Matthew Hall. The thought was a little scary, but mostly, she was excited about the possibility of building a future together.

The car passed through the gates of Tyler and Charlotte's house.

"Wake up, baby," Tyler said, gently nudging Charlotte as she slept on his shoulder. "We're home."

Her head lifted, and her sleepy eyes opened halfway before she settled back against his shoulder and closed them.

"You have to carry her, dude," Matthew said with a chuckle.

Charlotte sat up, lightly slapping her cheeks. "No, I'm up. Thanks for tonight, everybody."

Tyler opened the door as the car came to a stop. "See you at my wedding, party people."

Everyone in the car whooped at that, the sleepy vibe conquered by a burst of excited cheer.

The next stop was Luke's, then Sandra's, and finally, Amber and Matthew were the only ones left. He wrapped both arms around her and held her close.

"Do you want to come back to my place?" His deep, sexy baritone rumbled beneath her ear.

She lifted her head to look at him. It was a question she'd answered plenty of times, usually with an enthusiastic "Hell yes!" For some reason, the question from him made her heart gallop in her chest.

His eyes squeezed shut. "I just realized how that sounded. I'm not expecting anything, and there's no pressure to... Anyway, I figured you're exhausted, and your sisters will probably be up, and you might not want to tell them about seeing your dad in case they didn't and—"

"Okay."

"Okay?"

She smiled up at his handsome, bewildered face. "I want to go home with you."

"Well..." He nodded, his Adam's apple jumping as he swallowed. "Okay."

Amber chuckled at his sudden nervousness. It was pretty damn cute.

"Matthew," she said, sitting straighter. Something needed to be established before he said or did something that made her shred his clothes off and fuck him senseless. Because as he looked at her with those ocean-blue eyes, that was exactly what she wanted to do. "Sex can't happen tonight. After the week I've had, I'm spent. And we've both been drinking. I want us to remember every detail of our first time together."

He was quiet, studying her.

There was an almost imperceptible nod before he pinched her chin and leaned closer. "Amber, you don't have to explain. I'll wait as long as you need." His warm exhales grazed her mouth before he brushed his lips against hers and kissed her softly. "And I promise you..."

The air between them shifted, crackling with electricity.

"When I'm inside you for the first time..." Their eye contact and closeness held. Her pulse ticked in her neck, the anticipation stalling the flow of air into her lungs. "You sure as fuck won't forget it."

She sucked in a sharp breath as his words sent warm tingles through her body that moved south, settling between her thighs.

They were quiet for a moment, long enough for a surge of self-doubt to wriggle in.

After a week of foreplay, was it unfair to take sex off the table? She'd been accused more than once of being a cock tease—was that what she was doing? Was it stupid to just sleep at his place and go home in the morning? When had a guy ever wanted to just *sleep*?

"Hey." A crease formed between his brows. "What's wrong?"

"Do you still want me to stay?" she asked, inwardly cringing at the lilt of insecurity in her voice.

The crease deepened, and the corners of his mouth pulled down. "I didn't invite you over just for sex, Amber." The hurt on his face instantly made her feel like an asshole. She knew him better than that, but the question just popped out. "Maybe I shouldn't have said that. I promise I'm not trying to pressure you, and I don't expect anything you aren't ready for. I'll take the couch or the spare room if you're more comfortable. I guess I just..." He blew out a quick rush of air that ruffled the hair framing her face. "I'm not ready to say goodbye. I like the idea of waking up, and you're there. Is that stupid? Maybe it's too soon to say that."

Once again, he'd said what she needed to hear before she even knew she needed to hear it.

Amber pulled his face to hers and kissed him.

After only five days together, maybe it was too soon to dread goodbyes, but she didn't care. Kissing him on the cool leather seats of a limousine on the way to his house, his bed, felt good and right.

"I'm not ready to say goodbye either," she said.

Their goodbyes would come too soon, regardless. Europe was only nine months away, and he couldn't join them for the whole tour. Before that, there would be more press and joint promotional events with Tomorrow Mourning and a whirlwind of activity and obligations that would keep them apart.

So, for now, she was determined to savor every second before the next goodbye.

22

Matthew

After unlocking his front door, Matthew held it open for Amber. He couldn't resist a few moments of checking out her ass as she walked in. Her black leather pants looked painted on, every taut muscle flexing as she walked. Did she have a dimple on one of those cheeks, too?

"Want something to drink or eat or anything?" he asked, hoping she'd decline so her mouth would be unoccupied. He'd nearly fallen asleep in the limo with her resting in his arms, but seeing her in his space was like a double shot of espresso. And knowing that his sheets would smell like her for days made him desperate to kiss her again.

"I'm good, thanks."

She looked around, taking in the changes he'd made since she'd last been there. He'd put a few candles on the coffee table to make the place smell nice, set up his DVD collection in the new entertainment center, and tacked a few band posters above the couch. She moved to the spot between the living room and kitchen where he'd put framed photographs and memorabilia on the wall. When one of them caught her eye, a smile woke up the dimple on her cheek.

"You saved the flyer from our first headlining gig?" Her fingernail tapped the glass covering the crinkled paper. "I always look so pissed off in promo shots." She laughed. "It's sweet that you saved it."

"I had to steal it back from Ty. It was too priceless to stay in his dresser drawer."

When she turned to him, something in her eyes made him forget to breathe. They sparkled in the light as she slowly moved closer. "Why is it priceless to you?"

"Because I'm so proud of my friends and how far you've come. That night, you accomplished something massive. It wasn't my victory, but I was honored to be there." A corner of his mouth twitched, a pleasant memory charging in. "I couldn't keep my eyes off you. You were so happy and filled with pride, you glowed. It was beautiful."

Amber wet her lips before gripping the front of his shirt with both hands and kissing him hard. She tasted like expensive champagne as she melted in his arms, her fists pressed to his chest.

She drew back an inch. "I said no sex, but..." Her eyes looked drugged as her hot breaths ghosted over his lips. "I want you to touch me."

Her words were only a whisper, but their weight hovered in the space between them. Matthew froze while his pulse pounded in his ears, giving her the chance to take it back.

Finally, he sealed his mouth over hers and she groaned, the sound low and edged with need.

Matthew wrapped an arm around her waist and took three broad steps forward, stopping when her back pressed to the wall beside the couch. As the kiss deepened, he seized her wrists, trapping them above her head.

Amber's breath caught in her throat, and she broke the kiss, scrutinizing his expression. He watched as her pupils blew wide, crowding out the soft blue pools surrounding them.

"To be clear..." His gaze locked with hers. "I agree we need to wait to go all the way."

The lust darkening her eyes made him wonder if she'd changed her mind, but he'd never do anything she wasn't ready for. She'd already said no. Period. But she'd given him the green light to touch her, and there was no harm in exploring a bit.

He trailed slow kisses across her jawline and down the side of her neck, his tongue swirling over her pulse point. Her soft whimper in his ear made his cock throb in his jeans. Now that they were finally alone, he was eager to hear the sounds she made when she was unrestrained.

Or, maybe a *little* restrained.

"Is this okay?" he asked.

She struggled halfheartedly against his hold before she stilled. With all the lean muscle in her arms and strength in her wrists, he knew damn well she could break free and break his nose before he could blink if she wanted to.

"Yes," she whispered. "Please don't stop." Her muscles relaxed, surrendering to his hold. Feeling such a fierce, powerful woman let go and trust him was intoxicating.

The tip of his nose grazed her earlobe, and he inhaled. She smelled like peaches and summer sun, a welcome change from the cold, harsh winter he'd lived in since the attack.

"If I go too far..." He tugged her earlobe with his teeth, sucking the soft bit of flesh gently before releasing it. "Just tell me to stop."

Her mouth crashed into his, and her tongue slipped between his lips. She moaned into his mouth, her wrists fighting him a bit before settling back against the wall. "Let go so I can touch you."

Matthew pulled back an inch, his brow arched. "Are you sure that's what you want?" He gripped her wrists tighter, squeezing until her breath hitched. "I think you like giving up control." He pressed the front of his body against hers, pinning her to the wall. Her hooded lids and pulse hammering in her neck gave her away. "Or is your body lying to me?"

He'd suspected Amber would appreciate a firmer touch, and this confirmed it. While he wouldn't take it any further that night, he filed it away for a time when there were no more boundaries between them.

"Holy fuck." Her head tipped back, giving him better access to the column of her throat. He peppered it with kisses before sinking his teeth into her flesh like a starving vampire. He was definitely hungry, but not for blood.

"The bedroom." Her throat moved beneath his teeth as she swallowed. "*Please*. This is fucking torture."

"This is the opposite of torture, beautiful." He released her wrists, and she watched with widening eyes as he sank to his knees. His fingertips slipped beneath the waistband of her pants, stroking the smooth skin of her belly. "Can I taste you?"

A soft whimper escaped her lips, pink, kiss-swollen, and more tempting than ever. "I will never say no to that question."

They both grinned as her fingers dragged through his hair, pulling at the roots until his scalp burned. He slid her pants down her legs, inch by inch, revealing soft, pale skin he'd never seen, touched, or tasted. The three drinks he'd had would do nothing to dull the memory of this first.

After tossing her pants aside, Amber stood before him in nothing but silky black panties and her black tank top. The sexy sight and anticipation of what came next had him rock hard, his cock aching for release. But first, he wanted to make her feel good.

With his eyes on hers, Matthew dipped his head forward, slowly running the flat of his tongue up the center of the black silk. He left behind a dark, wet line that he traced again as the grip on his hair tightened.

"*Please*." Amber's eyes fluttered shut and found him again.

He answered her plea by closing his mouth over her mound, his tongue flicking at her clit through the fabric. When he pulled back, it was dampened with saliva and a bit lower, the unmistakable wetness of her pussy. He slipped a finger under the fabric, dipping inside her tight hole to the first knuckle. She was so slick, there was no resistance as he pushed a little deeper. A soft moan escaped her lips.

"Mmm... So fucking wet for me." He withdrew his finger, sucking it clean as she watched with hooded eyes that looked drugged with need. She did taste like fucking peaches, and it made the head of his cock ache, begging to join in. "I bet you'll taste even sweeter when this pretty pussy is clenching around my tongue."

A shudder ran through her. "Fucking hell."

Amber slipped her shirt over her head. His movements halted as his mind blanked.

Her breasts peeked out from behind more black silk, begging to be touched and teased.

"Did I tell you to stop?" Her brow arched, and a corner of her mouth rose in a devilish, lopsided grin.

While he was still dumbstruck, she used the grip on his hair to press his face against the damp silk between her legs. He sucked hard, drawing the tiny bead of her clit between his lips. They groaned in unison, his scalp burning as she held tighter. The teasing hint of her taste on his tongue wasn't enough.

"I hope this isn't your favorite pair." Matthew sat back on his heels, grabbing the tiny straps on her hips and tearing them from her body. He tossed the ruined fabric aside. His mouth watered as he stared at the beautiful, petal-like folds between her legs. The lips glistened with her arousal, and he couldn't wait another second to taste her without that damn fabric in the way.

He touched the tip of his tongue to her clit, circling the tiny bead before moving lower and slowly tracing her slit. When he reached her entrance, he plunged deep, greedily collecting every drop of her wetness and swallowing it down. The taste and scent of her overwhelmed his senses, stoking his building hunger as his cock grew almost painfully hard against his zipper.

"*Fuck*, you're good at that." The back of her head knocked against the wall behind her. "I knew that mouth of yours would drive me fucking crazy."

He ran two fingers along her slick folds, wetting them. "What about my fingers?" He slid them inside, exploring the front wall before settling on the slightly rough patch of her G-spot. He stroked with a firm touch, and a sharp inhale caught in her throat. "Do you like them too?"

She was tight, but his fingers moved easily, coated with his saliva and her arousal.

"Only if they keep doing that." Her hips thrust forward, and as his tongue circled her clit, her breath quickened. "Fuck, Matthew."

He locked away the sound of his name on Amber's lips, the word husky and low, colored with desire. "Just wait until it's my cock sliding into this greedy hole." He slowed the strokes of his fingers, and her knees wobbled. "It won't be tonight, but when we're ready, and I thrust deep inside..." Taking his time, he dragged his fingers out and slid back in with a corkscrew turn that made her cry out and grip his shoulders for support. "Every inch of this gorgeous body will feel it."

Her fingernails scraped the wall, and he prayed paint was underneath them. Every time he walked by the spot, he'd see a permanent reminder of that moment.

He took her clit between his lips, gently sucking as he fucked her with his fingers, bringing her right to the edge before pulling back, letting her craving for release build. She growled in protest.

"Please," she breathed. "Don't stop. I need—"

"Shh." Matthew kissed up her stomach, tugging her belly button ring with his teeth. "Patience, baby. I know what you need."

He dipped lower, sucking her clit a little harder while the pads of his fingers massaged her G-spot. The small patch of honey-blonde hair tickled the tip of his nose, and he breathed in her sweet scent as he tugged her closer to the edge. When he sped up his movements, she tipped back her head and let out a gravelly moan that shot straight to his cock.

"Oh, fuck," she squeaked out between panted breaths. "Just like that. I'm gonna come."

He hummed again, focusing the vibration on her clit, his tongue tracing the sensitive bud beneath the hood in a steady rhythm.

Amber bucked her hips forward with a sharp cry, and he gripped the flesh of her ass, sealing his mouth over her mound as she hit her peak. He was right again. As her body tensed and her inner muscles squeezed and pulsed around his tongue, she tasted sweeter than anything else on earth. Her wetness coated his chin, lips, and cheeks, and he couldn't get enough.

When she went limp, her body sagged against the wall before she slid to join him on the carpet. A look of shock on her face morphed into a wide, beaming smile that made him want to do it all over again.

She reached behind her back, unlatching her bra and tossing it to the floor. Matthew's eyes rounded as they took in all her beautiful bare flesh. As he reached for her breasts, she slapped his hands away. His brow furrowed, and he worried he'd done something wrong.

Amber set her hands on his shoulders and pushed him to the ground, straddling his waist from above.

"You were right," she said. "I do like giving up control."

She slid his shirt over his head and down his arms, trapping his wrists behind him. For a split second, his pulse kicked up, and panic threatened to intrude. But the sight of her naked body on top of his squashed anything but desire and the need to be at her mercy.

"I also like to take it." She dipped forward, tracing his lips with her tongue. "Especially from a big, strong man who could break me in half if he wanted to."

Matthew suppressed a grin. It was a bit of a stretch. He had decent muscle tone and at least eight inches of height on her, but he was no pro wrestler or lumberjack. If it was part of a fantasy she had, he wasn't about to interrupt it with reality.

"Don't you dare break out of this." Her nipples grazed his chest as she made sure his hands were secure. His mouth ached to suck them until they were wet and marked with pretty shades of pink and purple. "You got to play with my body and make me feel good." Her hands drifted to his belt, the metal clanking together ramping up his anticipation. "Now it's my turn."

She unbuttoned his jeans and lowered the zipper with a slow, torturous drag. "When we were alone in that limo, I wanted to sink to the floor between your knees and suck your cock until you spilled down my throat."

All his blood rushed south at her filthy words and the image they conjured. Her hands fisted the waistband of his boxers and the front of his unbuttoned jeans.

"Can I taste you?" She arched an eyebrow, obviously pleased with herself for throwing his line from earlier back at him.

He couldn't resist doing the same. "I will never say no to that question."

They laughed together, but it quickly died when she slid his jeans down his hips.

His heart raced as she took her time. *This* was torture. The most delicious torture that was on its way to replacing the meaning of the word in his vocabulary.

Finally, his cock sprung free, hard as concrete, and so ready for her mouth it ached.

"Mmm…" She dipped forward and pressed a soft kiss to the tip. "I'm a lucky girl."

He was hypnotized by the sight of her lips on his cock. "No, baby." It took all his restraint not to thrust his hips. "I'm the lucky one."

A corner of Amber's mouth hitched up. She crawled backward to kneel at his feet before removing his shoes, socks, and everything else that'd been a barrier between them.

This was a step they'd never be able to reverse, and he hoped like hell she'd never want to.

"I didn't expect you to say such filthy things to me." She crawled up the center of his body, her legs and hands beside him like the bars of a cage he'd never want to escape. "And I certainly didn't expect you to pin me to a wall and make me come in your mouth."

Her perfect tits swung as she moved further up his body before hovering above his torso. "How can I return the favor?" With her knees, she spread his legs wider and settled between them, sitting back on her heels. Her head dipped, and the flat of her warm, wet tongue glided over the underside of his cock in a long, slow line.

He groaned at the rush of sensation, his fists clenching beneath him.

A dot of precum glistened at the tip, and she lapped it up with a slow, swirling lick.

Matthew's fists squeezed tighter, his hands itching to break free and touch her. "Fuck, you're killing me here."

She chuckled softly before painting a few more broad strokes along the sides of his cock. It twitched when she pulled her mouth away, beckoning her to come back for more. "You don't get to use your hands, but I do." Her fingers wrapped around his length, pumping once, twice before the swollen crown disappeared between her lips. She released it with a loud, wet pop. "I bet you wish you could grab my tits, pinch my nipples? We'll see if you can earn it by being a good boy."

He didn't know what that entailed, but he hoped like fuck he was doing it.

Amber's hand went between her legs, and her fingers slid over her pussy before dipping inside. He watched in rapt attention as she rubbed her arousal over his erection. She used it as lube to slide her fist over the aching flesh.

"You kept going on about how sweet I am," she said. "Maybe I should find out for myself."

He barely breathed as she slowly licked him from root to tip. Her tongue settled on the sensitive underside of the head, swirling and flicking without breaking eye contact.

"Fuck, Amber. You're... I can't..."

"What's wrong, baby?" Her head tipped to the side, a few strands of blonde hair drifting over her forehead. "Forget how to finish sentences?"

He was panting as she continued the assault with her tongue. "Please..."

"Please, what? Please do this?" She took his length to the back of her throat. He banged his head on the floor as it fell backward in bliss, agony, or both.

"Please kiss me," he begged. He didn't want this to stop, but he couldn't pass up the chance to taste her again, this time on her tongue. Watching her clean her wetness off his cock was one of the hottest fucking things he'd ever seen.

"Hmm. Another thing I wasn't expecting. You're a man of many surprises, Matthew Hall."

Her bare breasts slid along his belly and chest as she slowly made her way to his mouth. His arms were numb, and he wanted to come so badly, it hurt, but this was what he craved above everything else.

When his tongue swept past her lips, he groaned, the sound deep and desperate. Had he ever made that noise before? Ever craved someone as much? He could already tell Amber would ruin him for anyone else, but if he had his way, there would never be anyone else.

He devoured her mouth, licking and nipping her lips and flicking his tongue along the corners. Her tongue mashed against his with a passion that assured him she was as far gone as he was. Her sweetness mingled with the salt of his precum, their tastes mingling on his tongue.

She gave his bottom lip one last lick. "Begging for a kiss was a very good boy thing to do. Ready for your reward?"

"Fuck, yes." Beads of sweat tickled his forehead, but he couldn't wipe them away. A very small price to pay for whatever reward she had in mind. "I'll take anything you want to give me."

She reached beneath him and yanked his shirt loose.

He shook out his freed hands to get the blood flowing again. "Please say I can touch you."

She intertwined their fingers and brought them to her breasts. "I'd rather show you."

Amber's fingers fell away, and he cradled her breasts in his hands, kneading and pinching the pebbling dark pink nipples. He could feel a trail of wetness on his belly as she straddled his waist, grinding her pelvis against him.

He raised up on an elbow to bring a nipple to his mouth, sucking and nipping at the tip until she cried out. She pulled back, returning to the space between his legs.

"I miss your cock already." She pumped it with her fist, squeezing her index finger and thumb in a tight "O" as she made quick circles around the head. "I bet I *will* feel it in every inch of my body when you finally fuck me. It'll take some stretching to fit, but I'll gladly accept any pain it takes to earn the pleasure of taking you deep."

Matthew's panted breaths and the image she painted made him lightheaded. Or maybe it was the sensation of being so close to the edge that another slide inside her warm mouth would send him tumbling over.

"But now," she said, her voice husky with need, "I want to swallow every drop you give me."

Amber's lips wrapped around the head of his cock, sliding down his shaft until he hit the back of her throat. Her cheeks hollowed out as she withdrew and repeated the motion. This time, she swallowed around the head, and he muttered a string of curses that made her grin around his flesh, her eyes sparkling with wicked satisfaction. When she pulled back, she focused her mouth on the sensitive crown while her fist jerked along his shaft in quick, tight pulses.

This woman knew exactly what she was doing.

Matthew's fingers tangled in her hair as she brought him closer, closer, and in seconds, a low, guttural groan broke in his chest as he was shoved over the edge, falling without a single worry about where or if he'd land.

Her sapphire eyes stayed on his as his seed flooded her throat. The muscles in his arms and hips went rigid as he fucked her mouth with quick thrusts until he had nothing left. Her jaw flexed around him as she took him deep and swallowed hard.

"Fucking hell, Amber." His hands slipped from her hair, and his shoulders fell to the floor with a thud. The muscles in his hips twitched and relaxed as he came down. That was, without a doubt, the best goddamn blowjob he'd ever had. If she wasn't so exhausted from her show, he'd be thanking her with a few more orgasms.

She wiped the corners of her mouth before grinning like he was the best dessert she'd ever tasted. It was a look he knew he'd never forget.

"Want to take a shower with me?" she asked, her tone sweet and calm.

He slapped a hand on his chest as it rapidly rose and fell. "Let me catch my breath first, Rockstar." He patted the carpet beside him, and she curled up at his side.

"I know I said it before, but seriously..." Her head lifted to meet his eyes. "You are *not* what I expected."

He snickered. "What did you think? I was a plain vanilla lame ass who can't find a G-spot without a map?"

"No." Amber playfully smacked his arm, laughing. "I just thought you'd be gentle and take your time. Someone who'd whisper sweet nothings in my ear or whatever. Not that that's bad."

"I like gentle too." Matthew slipped an arm behind her back, holding her closer. "But after a week of foreplay and the way you looked at me when I pinned your wrists against the wall... This didn't feel like a sweet and gentle kind of night."

As comfortable as he was lying beside her on the plush carpet, a shower and a bed sounded better. He took Amber's hand and helped her to her feet. She followed him into the bathroom, and he set two fresh towels on the rack before getting the water to the perfect temperature.

When the steam fogged his glasses, he set them on the bathroom counter.

"As tempted as you may be to maul me again," he said, "we need to sleep. You must be beat from your show." He gestured to the floor of the shower. "Be careful because I didn't get the non-slip thingies yet."

He offered his hand, and she took it as she stepped into the shower and under the water. When they were clean, he wrapped her in a towel and tied one around his waist. He dug a spare toothbrush from a drawer, and they brushed their teeth, standing shoulder to shoulder over his sink. It felt oddly domestic watching her spit out toothpaste and rinse her mouth.

Matthew was glad she seemed comfortable in his space. While he was unpacking boxes that morning, he couldn't help imagining all the faults Jessica would find in every room as more of his familiar things filled the empty spaces. Not having to hide any part of himself was a welcome relief.

Amber picked up his glasses and slipped them onto her face. "Ooh, we could play sexy librarian with these."

Why was seeing her in his glasses so fucking hot?

Matthew chuckled, a corner of his mouth tipping up. "I think you just want to get spanked with a hardcover."

He swatted her ass over the towel and took his glasses back. When they'd finished at the sink, he led Amber by the wrist down the hallway and into his bedroom. He was glad all the new furniture was delivered, so they weren't stuck with an air mattress. Tonight, they'd be sleeping in his brand-new king-sized bed with the cherry wood headboard.

Amber would be the first woman to sleep over in his new place in his new bed, which was a fitting way to end a night of other thrilling firsts.

Matthew walked to the matching dresser in the corner and pulled out clean boxers and a black and purple Jimi Hendrix T-shirt.

"If you feel more comfortable sleeping in clothes." He held them out to her.

She dropped her towel, pulled back the sheets and blankets, and climbed into his bed.

"Even better." He blindly chucked the clothes behind him.

Amber laughed and lifted his side of the covers.

Before getting in, he stopped.

The joy on his face collapsed.

"What's wrong?" Her forehead creased with worry, her hand falling to the bed.

"Fuck, this is going to sound stupid, but..." His heart rate climbed as he struggled to figure out how to say this without sounding as pathetic as he felt. "I sleep with a nightlight. I have since the attack." His eyes fell to the floor, shame heating his face. "I was locked in that trunk and then the dark basement, and I—"

"Matty, look at me."

After a deep breath, he met her gaze.

The corners of her mouth curled down. "You don't have to explain anything. If you're worried it'll bother me, it won't. I promise." She lifted the covers for him again as he flipped on the nightlight and turned off the brighter bulb overhead.

This time, he slid in beside her. The smooth, cool sheets against his bare skin were soothing, but the embarrassing confession had deflated his spirits a bit.

"Want to share a joint before bed?" she asked. "I have one in my purse."

"I'll grab a lighter." He watched as her naked body moved through his bedroom. He forgot all about the lighter or even what the word meant.

Amber returned with a joint in her hand, and he stopped ogling her long enough to grab a lighter and an ashtray off his nightstand.

"Can I tell you about something I'm afraid of?" She sat cross-legged on the bed, took the lighter, and lit the joint, taking a deep drag before passing it. He set the ashtray between them.

Intrigued, he nodded and tried like hell not to let his gaze drop between her legs so he could pay attention. He hit the joint and passed it back.

"Water." She picked a piece of leaf off her tongue and flicked it away. "Specifically, water more than a few steps beyond the shoreline. When I was eight, my family rented a boat on Lake Crescent, so my dad could fish. I was nuts about swimming, so I jumped off the back when my parents weren't looking. The water was so cold it shocked my system. I panicked, and it was hard to breathe or move. I remember that feeling of helplessness. Water flooding my nose and mouth as I started to sink. Kate heard me screaming, jumped in, and saved my life."

"Oh, my god." He took her hand. "You must've been scared out of your mind."

She nodded and hit the joint, her face glowing as the ember flared. "I haven't been able to get on a boat since. It sucks because I loved going out on the water. Normal people are afraid of spiders or snakes, but I can't even look at a lake or the ocean without wanting to crawl out of my skin."

"That's awful, Amber."

She bit her bottom lip as she held the joint, the smoke curling around her face. "I've never told anyone that story before."

Matthew appreciated that she'd shared something so personal to make him feel better about his embarrassing admission. He squeezed her hand.

After they reached the bottom of the paper, she stamped out the roach in the ashtray and set it on the nightstand.

As the tranquilizing effects of the marijuana took hold, one side of his mouth drew up. "I'm really glad you're here."

"Me too." Amber smiled, her gaze sleepy and soft. "Can I ask a favor?"

"Anything."

"Can you hold me until I fall asleep? I can't remember the last time someone did, but I remember it was nice. With you..."

She didn't need to finish the thought. The request and the softness in her tired voice warmed his chest. It was so different from the tough punk rocker in leather pants, banging away on her drums hours before. He liked all sides of her and looked forward to digging even deeper into the complex layers of who she was.

Matthew laid on his back and pulled her into his arms. Her warm breaths fluttered against his neck, and he held her closer, his thumb lazily stroking her collarbone.

Every muscle in his body relaxed, his mind blissfully calm and quiet.

He couldn't remember the last time he'd been like this with someone either.

23

Amber

"**N**o!"

Matthew's scream beside her ear made Amber shoot upright in bed. She looked around and saw nothing. His eyes were screwed shut, his fists clenched above the blankets.

"Get the fuck away from me!"

She slid back, giving him space in case he swung an arm or kicked in his sleep. She tried to remember whether it was better to wake someone having a nightmare or let them ride it out.

The agony on his face made her desperate to save him from whatever horrors played out in his mind.

"Matthew?" She gently shook his arm, but he didn't respond. She got up and turned on the overhead light. "Matty, it's me. Wake up." She shook him again, and he launched forward to sit, gasping for air and clawing at his throat.

Tears clouded her vision. "You're okay." She set a hand on his knee, squeezing. "Hey, look at me."

His wide, petrified eyes flitted around the room before landing on her.

"Amber," he whispered, his voice shaky.

"I'm here. Lay back down with me." She slid under the covers, her heart still racing as his scream echoed in her mind. "It's okay."

"Did I hurt you?"

"No, of course not." She held open her arms. "Come here."

He slid back under the blankets, hooking a hand around her waist to pull her close. Her arms wrapped around him while he fought to catch his breath. Should she offer to get his pills? If he got worse, she would, but it would be better if he could calm down without them. With their promise of quick relief, it would be very easy to become dependent.

Amber raised her chin and planted a soft kiss on his cheek. Sweat drenched his forehead, and she used her palm to wipe it away. "I like this tattoo." She stroked the mountain on his chest, hoping the touch and talking about something normal might help him settle. "Hood is my favorite place to hike and play in the snow. We should go together sometime."

Matthew was shaking like he was already in the middle of a snowstorm. She rubbed his arms and tucked the blankets around him more snugly.

"Want me to turn up the heat or turn the overhead light back off?"

"No," he answered too quickly. "I'm not cold; it's just what happens. It'll stop."

She curled further into his side, her face nuzzled into the crook of his neck. "Want to talk about it?"

"No." That one was quicker and sharper than the first. "Sorry, I don't mean to snap at you. Talking about it never seemed to help, so I've been trying to let them fade away."

Amber didn't want to judge his coping methods, but holding things in wasn't healthy. She didn't want to push and risk making things worse, so she kept it to herself for now. Maybe more distractions would help.

She touched the black ink on his bicep. "What does this one mean?"

His throat jumped as he swallowed. "Celtic symbol for brotherhood. Got it in Vegas with Ty when I turned eighteen." He exhaled slowly. "He has one too."

She traced the lines forming a triangle with entwined rings in the center. "I should get a matching tattoo with my sisters. Maybe a bird or a butterfly. But I'd slip the artist an extra hundred to make Beth's a donkey."

Matthew's chest jumped as he laughed, and Amber smiled at the little victory.

"Sorry I woke you up," he said.

"You have nothing to be sorry for." Her fingertips skated over his cheekbones and raked through his hair. "I'm glad I was here." She was relieved when he let out a soft sigh, and his body finally stopped shaking.

"Are you still tired?" he asked. "I won't be able to sleep again, but you can stay in here as long as you want."

The clock on the wall said it was eight a.m. They'd had maybe three hours of sleep, but after the shock of waking up to his screaming, it would be tough to settle again.

"No, I'm fine as long as you have coffee." She pressed a kiss to his neck, then another for good measure. "But I hope you aren't planning on moving soon because I like this. Feel free to flick me off like a pesky insect if I'm smothering you."

He kissed the crown of her head. "Not a chance."

After a long stretch of lying in each other's arms, Matthew slipped away and put on a pair of plaid pajama pants before hitting the bathroom down the hall. Soon after, his feet padded across the tile floor in the kitchen before cupboard doors shut, and the scent of coffee wafted in.

The tinkling of mugs and the promise of a hot caffeine boost drew Amber out of his nice, warm bed. She put on the boxers he'd offered the night before and snatched a High Notes shirt from the top of his laundry basket. It smelled like hops and spicy aftershave—a sexy combination she'd be craving after she left.

"I'm in love with your sheets," she said, hopping up to sit on the kitchen counter. "Are they like a zillion thread count?"

"Gift from Tyler, so probably. A perk of having a super-rich brother who'll never stop thinking he needs to take care of me." Matthew filled a mug with coffee and set it beside her. "I appreciate that he cares so much, but it can be annoying."

She picked up the mug and held it in the air. "I'll see your one generous brother and raise you four meddling sisters."

"Not much of a gambler. And having four nosy women give unsolicited opinions on your life sounds like hell."

Amber sipped her coffee, the backs of her heels lightly tapping against the cabinets below. "Maybe I exaggerate. I love them, I do. But like you're saying with Tyler, they'll always think they need to take care of me if I stay there. I have to pull the trigger and move out, sink or swim."

Matthew held his mug in one hand and parted her knees with the other. "With those strong arms, you could swim to fucking Mexico and back." He moved into the space between her thighs, and her pulse fluttered in her neck. "Seriously, with your drive to succeed and that fierce heart of yours..." He touched her chest, his hand warm from his mug. "There's no way you'd ever sink."

She brushed her lips against his and kissed him. "Thanks, Matty."

It was refreshing to be with someone who believed in her strengths and appreciated her ambitions. Most of her hookups checked out her tits, yapped about themselves, and asked shallow questions to pretend to be interested in more than a blowjob. While Matthew made no secret about appreciating her body and all the fun things it could do with his, it was clear that wasn't what had pulled them together.

"I hate to kill the mood," he said, "but how are you feeling about seeing your dad?"

That did kill the mood, but she knew he'd ask eventually. Seeing her father after thirteen years of silence was a hell of a shock, and she hadn't had a chance to process it yet.

"I have no idea." Her shoulders sank with a sigh. "If he wants to talk, he knows where to find me. I just don't know if I want to hear him out."

"Maybe he wants to know you again." Matthew stroked her cheek with the backs of his fingers. "If he doesn't, he's a fucking idiot. But leaving you all like that... Maybe he doesn't deserve your forgiveness." Matthew blew on his coffee and took a sip. "Then again, I'd give anything for one more day with my dad. I know it's not the same, but we both have that hole in our hearts. You might have a chance to mend yours. Someday, you might regret it if you don't try."

She nodded along as he spoke. "Maybe. I'll think about it. And I'll call my mom. She should know I saw him."

Matthew pressed a quick kiss to her lips and set his mug on the counter.

"You hungry?" he asked. "I'm not much of a cook, but I make a mean bowl of cereal."

"Fucking bachelor pads." She shook her head. "Never any real food and more dirty socks than a locker room."

"Hey, lady. I dare you to try to find a dirty sock in this place. I do my laundry twice a week. And I do have *some* real food. Pickles and hot dogs count, right?"

"Jesus Christ." She hopped off the counter and rifled through his cabinets. "Liar! It's not bad in here at all. Triscuits, Raisin Bran… I was expecting stale Froot Loops and Doritos." She pulled a package of bagels from the back of the pantry and checked the date—good for another week. "I hope you like bagels."

He smirked, his eyes glittering with amusement. "They're in my kitchen, so it's a pretty safe bet."

She smacked her forehead. "You finger-fucked the brains right out of me, Matthew." That and her brain needed at least three more hours of sleep and two more cups of coffee to function. She threw the package at his chest, and he caught it, laughing. "Toast these, smartass. And I'll grab the cream cheese if you have it."

He split two bagels and set them in the toaster.

"You have grapes!" She stared at the contents of his fridge. "Your sad bachelor card is officially revoked."

After eating their bagels with two more cups of coffee, they brushed their teeth together at his bathroom sink. She felt at home in his space. And it was weirdly thrilling to get ready for the day at his side. Maybe because it was one more thing making the shift from friends to something more impossible to miss.

Amber splashed cold water on her face and patted her skin dry. She didn't care that she didn't have her trusty face cream, a hairbrush, or makeup. With Matthew, she felt beautiful just as she was.

While he got dressed, she put on her clothes from the night before. They smelled like sweat, beer, and stale cigarette smoke from the show, but she couldn't go home in boxers and an oversized T-shirt. She'd just shower again before getting a few more hours of shuteye.

She followed Matthew into the living room and stepped into her shoes.

"Where's your phone book?" she asked. "I need to call a cab."

He shook his head and took her hand, pulling her into his arms. "I'll take you home. My Corolla isn't nearly as fly as a black limo, but it gets the job done."

Amber glanced at the front door and frowned. Since walking in after her show, they'd had a lot of fun together. She wasn't ready for it to end. And his terrified scream hadn't left her mind. She imagined the flashes from the nightmare that must still be haunting him and wanted to be there if he needed support.

Matthew grabbed his keys, his cheerful expression dimming. Maybe he felt the same about their goodbye. "Will I see you again before the wedding?"

She ran through her upcoming schedule of band obligations and bridesmaid tasks in her head, looking for an open timeslot and having no luck. The previous night was incredible, and she wanted to take it to the next level, but it looked impossible until at least the following week.

"Other than when I'm asleep, I'm fully booked until Tuesday."

"You're only free when you're asleep." He nodded slowly like he was working a math problem out in his head. "Would it be crazy if I invited you to sleep here again?"

She bit her bottom lip, considering the invitation. After last night, it would be hard to only sleep if she stayed over, impossible even. That weak argument warred with the memory of how perfect it felt to fall asleep in his arms.

"Never mind." He waved a dismissive hand. "I can't guarantee I won't wake you up like that again, and you need solid rest. But I'd love to take you to dinner when things settle down."

"I hope that doesn't mean you're withdrawing your invitation. I'd love to sleep over again." She held up a finger. "With one condition, that won't be fun for either of us."

His brows pinched. "What condition?"

"No. Sex." She shrugged. "You're right. I need solid sleep, and you do too. I'll have about seven or eight free hours to work with at the end of my days, so there's not much wiggle room to find time to get funky."

He laughed. "Get funky? Okay. Go on."

"Just like I want our first time to be sober, I don't want it rushed either. So, if you can resist the urge to merge, so can I."

"You're full of euphemisms this morning." He set his palm on her cheek and kissed her gently. "I accept your terms and look forward to having you in my bed again. It'll be fun building up the sexual tension until I can finally plow your wheat fields."

Amber was relieved he accepted the downside of her busy schedule so easily. It was further confirmation that he wasn't only in it for sex, though she already knew that. And it gave her hope the demands of her career wouldn't chase him away.

She laughed, shoving his shoulder. "At least my euphemisms didn't involve farming."

◆○◆

Amber closed her front door as quietly as possible and held her breath as she tiptoed toward her bedroom. After a few steps, two pairs of hands started clapping. She turned to find Beth and Tara wearing shit-eating grins at the kitchen table. She muttered a curse and walked over to join them.

"Nice walk of shame, sis." Tara shoved a piece of bacon into her mouth. "You know you can't sneak past all the eyes and ears in this house."

"Obviously," Amber mumbled.

"So, tell us." Beth moved her hands together and apart like she was asking someone the size of a fish they caught.

Amber picked a piece of bacon off her plate and bit off half of it. "Fuck off, Beth. He's a nice guy." She couldn't stop the grin from stretching her face when she thought about the not-so-nice things he said. Dirty things that got her so wet she probably stained his carpet.

"That smile says it's big." Beth raised her forkful of eggs in the air. "Good for you, babe. I bet he's a freak in the sheets like his brother."

Amber threw the other half of the piece of bacon back onto her sister's plate. "How the hell would you know how Tyler is in bed? Your disgusting dreams don't count."

"I read an interview in the *National Tattler* with one of the chicks he hooked up with before Amy." Beth fanned herself. "Apparently, that mouth can do a lot more than sing."

Amber rolled her eyes with a groan. "It's bad enough that you read that tabloid shit, but you actually believe it? What about what they're saying about my band? That we're only getting more attention now because we fucked our way to the top? Do you believe that, too?"

Beth frowned at the accusation, and Amber wished she could take it back. Still, buying and reading that trash encouraged the intrusive vultures to keep churning it out.

"Of course not. You made it because of your hard work and nothing else. Screw anyone who says otherwise."

"Judging by her messed-up hair," Tara said. "I think our girl's done enough screwing for a while."

Amber grumbled. "I should've ignored your asses and kept on walking to my bed."

She thought back to seeing her dad after the show, wrestling with the choice to tell them now or keep it to herself until she could find out what he wanted. She was usually open and honest with her sisters about what went on in her life, but this would upset them. Still, he was their dad, too, and it seemed like an unfair secret to keep.

She pulled out a chair and sat between her sisters. "I have to tell you guys something."

Beth gasped. "Oh, my god, you're three hours pregnant!"

Amber kicked her under the table. "Stop! This is serious."

"What's up?" Tara asked.

"I saw Dad last night."

She studied their faces, a mixture of shock and disbelief washing over them.

"What do you mean you saw Dad?" Tara pushed her plate away, leaning forward on her elbows. "Where?"

"On the street after my show. He was in the crowd yelling my name. He looked a little older and grayer, but it was him." Amber fiddled with the tiny volcano saltshaker Denise bought in Hawaii. "If you're thinking I was mistaken, stop. He had the *exact* same color eyes as Dad and the same bump on his nose from when he slipped on the ice and faceplanted on the porch."

Amber couldn't remember the last time they'd talked about him. After their mom moved out, it was as if discussing memories involving their dad had been banned, even the good ones. It was easier to pretend he didn't exist, but his popping up unannounced made that impossible.

"Why the hell would he show up now?" Tara left the table, pacing across the living room floor. "There's no way it took him thirteen years to realize how badly he fucked us over."

"Why wouldn't he come *here*?" Beth asked. "We're in the same house he left behind, so he knows where to find us. Why wait for Amber outside her show?"

Tara stopped pacing and crossed her arms. "She always was his favorite."

When Amber was little, she felt like his favorite, but around seventh grade, that ended. It felt like a distance had grown between them when she started looking less like a little girl and more like a young woman. Like she made him uncomfortable, and he no longer knew how to talk to her. They'd been close her entire childhood, so the sudden rejection over something she couldn't change was like a knife to the heart.

The worst part was when he stopped taking her to the clubs where he played on weekends. He worked in construction five days a week—a job he loathed that left him grumpy and exhausted at the end of the day. But when he was on stage, he glowed. Nothing could wipe the joy from his face when he held those sticks. Amber missed sitting backstage, watching how his wrists flicked when they struck the drumheads, and his feet bounced right before the kick drum boomed in her chest. He said she couldn't go anymore because guys at the club would get "sinful ideas," but he'd never explain what that meant.

It was the first time he'd broken her heart, but not the last.

Was she willing to risk it happening again?

"He must've seen it in the paper," Tara said, "or on MTV News or something and took a chance."

"Can you seriously picture Dad watching MTV News?" Beth's nose wrinkled. "Now that I think about it, he kind of looks like a hairier Kurt Loder."

"Stick to the fucking topic for once, Beth!" Amber gripped her hair at the roots, wishing it was her sister's hair she was pulling. "What if he wants to make amends? How would you guys feel about that?"

Amber couldn't even answer that for herself. Forgiving him seemed impossible, but Matthew had a point that she might regret it someday if she didn't give him a second chance.

Tara raised her middle finger. "This is how I feel about that. I'd tell him to shove his stupid apologies straight up his ass."

She had more reasons than anyone to feel that way. The first time Tara brought a girlfriend home, their dad disappeared for two days. When he returned, their parents spent the next hour arguing in their bedroom. Words like "sinner" and "disgusting" were the only ones that made it past the thick wood of their door, but the message was clear to everyone in the house—his love was conditional. And he was far from being the hero they saw when they were too young to recognize what a cruel piece of shit he was.

Amber would love to believe he'd changed and become more accepting, but there was no way to know without meeting with him.

"Calm down. Let's think about this." Beth tapped her chin. "Maybe his wife left him. Maybe he cheated on her too. What if that life fell apart, so he wants to try to weasel back into ours?"

"What if he's broke?" Tara put their plates in the sink. "He sees his rockstar daughter on the news and comes looking for a handout."

"If that's the case," Amber said, "Wait until he hears Kate's a lawyer and you sell fancy real estate. He'll be sticking his hands in all our pockets."

"Why don't we wait and see what he says?" Beth brushed crumbs from the table into her hand and dropped them into the trash. "If he even comes around again. All this speculating's giving me a headache."

Amber had to tell them about the boy that was with him—their brother, regardless of the shitty circumstances that brought him into the world. It was another subject they never spoke of, but beneath the resentment, she'd wondered what he was like. Was he happy? Did he know about his sisters? Until the letter came, she didn't think so. She'd assumed their father thoroughly cleaned the slate with his new family, pretending like none of them existed. But if that was the case, why did they show up the night before?

"There's more," Amber said. "I think his son was with him."

Beth gasped. "How fucking *dare* he bring his golden boy here."

Tara shook her head, her fingers bending to claws at her sides. "If he thinks he can parade his perfect family around town after what he did—"

"Okay, enough." Amber rubbed her eyes, the lack of sleep making them itch. "I can't talk about this anymore, but you deserved to know. I'm going to shower and catch a few more z's before my drumming lesson."

Amber left the table and shuffled toward her bedroom. More than ever, she wanted to rip open the letter and read whatever was inside. It had to hold a piece of the puzzle of why their dad was in town, but as exhausted as she was, it would wait a little longer.

"Matthew kept you up all night?" Beth asked. "That kind of stamina's sexy. Lucky girl."

Amber offered her sister a middle finger as she turned down the hallway.

24

Matthew

Crumpled balls of notebook paper littered Matthew's kitchen floor as he sat at his table, trying to wrangle the right words into his best man speech. It should be easy. He loved and respected his big brother more than anyone else in his life. One discarded page on the floor declared that Matthew was Tyler's biggest fan, but he hadn't even finished the sentence before he ripped the page out and tossed it, cringing at how stupid it was.

He couldn't be happier that Charlotte and Tyler fell in love and decided to get married despite all the evidence around them that, more often than not, marriages crashed and burned like an airplane on fire. Zack was the only one in their group with long-married parents. The fact that he was a skirt-chasing horndog didn't lend much credence to the notion that two committed parents give their kids something to aspire to. Instead, Zack probably saw what a drag it was and wanted the opposite.

But nothing about Tyler and Charlotte's relationship seemed like a drag. It was something worth aspiring to. How could he put that in his speech? With Matthew's pathetic dating history, what could he possibly say about committing your time and attention to someone for life? Forever was a long fucking time to smell someone else's rank farts and listen to the same obnoxious chewing noises three times a day until one of you croaked. That sentiment wasn't speech-worthy. He guessed that if you find the right person, it must be easier to overlook the bad and focus on the good. Otherwise, all long-term relationships would fail.

Was Amber the right person? Already, Matthew could see a future with her. Since she went home that morning, he'd been looking forward to seeing her again. He'd never felt that pull with Jessica or anyone else.

He tapped his pen against the paper as a slideshow of his exes flickered through his mind. He'd met some of them in pubs he visited for research before opening the brewery. And at the video store, shamelessly flirting as they read the back cover of the same movie. A few he met at early Killing Daisies shows. The women got so worked up from all the high-energy music and sweaty friction in the mosh pit that they dragged him into the bathroom for a quick pressure release.

Many of his one-and-done encounters were with groupies he met backstage at his brother's shows. They had no chance of getting Tyler, so they settled for what they viewed as the next best thing. He knew because two of them said it—one before the sex and one right after. At the time, Matthew was barely an adult and didn't give two shits if they wanted him because he had teeth and hair.

Now, the memories turned his stomach.

His standards had always been low, but he never bothered to think about why. Feeling overshadowed by Tyler was part of it. Matthew would never be as handsome, talented, or cool, so he took what he could get when it came to women. Even before the attack, his confidence was lacking. He was too thin, too tall, too immature, too dorky in his glasses to attract the women he wanted to attract—women like Amber.

Even with Jessica, his standards were low. It wasn't easy to see at the time because she was so impressive on paper. She wanted him to become a better version of himself. That was the phrase she liked to use, and now, that turned his stomach too. Sure, there were things he wanted to change, but not what she wanted him to.

But he had to admit, once his stuff was in the new condo, he was glad he'd taken that leap. Why was he working so damn hard to come home to a water heater that only worked when it felt like it and carpet soaked with five years' worth of spilled beer and bong water? He'd earned the step-up in his living conditions. And it was pretty sweet to move a pot from the stove to the countertop without leaving a brown burn stain behind. Score one for granite.

His relationship with Amber felt like an important part of this new beginning. It was a chance to recognize and appreciate his good qualities instead of focusing so much on what was wrong with him. A chance to build a connection with a quality partner instead of feeling resigned to settling for less than he wanted. He sensed she could even help him start to heal from his trauma. She helped calm him when Rafael's brother showed up and again that morning. After his nightmare, her affectionate touch, gentle words, and soothing distractions were exactly what he needed. Maybe she was the missing link that would help make him strong again.

Matthew scratched his chin with the pen cap, his thoughts returning to the speech. What could he say that would inspire a few hundred glasses of champagne to raise in the air?

Here's to not ending up like Mom and shacking up with an endless string of losers!

Here's to Tyler not forgiving his cheating cunt ex-wife and ending up penniless or dead!

Those sentiments would inspire nothing but a barrage of dinner rolls and lobster tails chucked at his head.

He tapped the paper with the tip of his pen, making a series of dots that eventually turned into the five points of a star. Then, he doodled a crescent moon. An angry muffin with teeth came along next to devour them both.

Rip. Crumple. Toss.

Fuck.

The phone rang beside him, and he grabbed it halfway through the first ring. "Hello?"

"Was your hand hovering over the phone, willing someone to call?"

Matthew grinned. "Hey, Rockstar. Your sisters give you shit about coming in so late?"

"You know them so well already. They applauded my walk of shame and inquired about your dick size. Let the house hunt begin."

Matthew chuckled, shaking his head. "What did you tell them?"

"That animal control will probably arrest you for smuggling an anaconda in your pants."

He burst out laughing, and his glasses slipped halfway down the bridge of his nose. "Such a flattering description."

"I told them no dirty details. I don't kiss and tell. Or suck and tell, for that matter."

His cock twitched at hearing her say the word *suck*. "Good to know. And for the record, neither do I. Our friends will never know you whimper and buck your hips right before you come."

"Are we venturing into phone sex?" Amber's tone was low, husky, and sexy as fuck. "If so, I need to lock my door and put on music so my perv sisters don't taunt me later."

He smiled, pushing his glasses back in place. "As fun as it sounds, no. I'm still trying to write my speech and coming up empty. I discovered I'm a hell of a doodler, though, so there's that."

"Ugh. I'm so glad Charlotte and Sandra handle the lyrics. I appreciate the power of words but have no clue how to harness it. I'd rather be impressed and entertained by people who can."

Matthew doodled a drum set. "What can I possibly say about marriage? I'm a twenty-four-year-old dude who makes beer, and my longest relationship didn't last three months."

"Sure, but no one knows the happy couple better than you. Focus on that. And maybe think about how you felt on the best days of your past relationships. Did you ever get the warm fuzzies and you didn't want to leave the bed because you felt so comfortable and safe beside them? Or you stole their T-shirt because you knew you'd miss their smell and wanted to be able to get a fix later?"

She'd basically described that morning. Since their goodbye at her front door, he'd been looking forward to having her back in his bed. Luckily, it was only a few hours away.

A corner of his mouth tipped up. "Is that why I can't find my High Notes shirt? Your purse looked a little fuller when you left."

He tossed it into his laundry basket before bed, but it'd mysteriously disappeared. There were plenty more at work, and he liked that she took home something to remember him by.

"Good luck proving it."

He could hear her smile through the phone as he laughed.

"I do miss your smell," she said, "and the rest of you. I'm glad we're doing this, Matty."

Matthew stilled, replaying her words as his pulse kicked up. "Me too."

She was quiet for a moment. "This has been fun, but I have errands to run before I meet the girls to get manicures for the wedding. Imagine the look on the poor lady's face when I put my busted-up drummer nails and calloused hands in front of her. It'll take a miracle to make them look pretty."

He drew a smiling stick figure with long hair behind the drums before setting down his pen. "I've seen every inch of you now, and trust me, every part is pretty."

Amber's end of the line was quiet again. "See you tonight." Again, her voice took on a husky edge, lacing the words with a dark and naughty promise.

They ended the call, and Matthew blew out a long, slow exhale to help get his mind back on his task. He flipped to the next page in his notebook and picked up the pen, a surge of determination making him sit up straighter to get down to business.

What had Amber said? Warm fuzzies, comfortable beds, and stolen T-shirts. Could he work with that? How could he use that feeling in his speech? He searched his brain for the words Tyler used to describe that feeling when he first fell for Charlotte.

Finally, it hit him. Matthew wrote it on the top line of his page in big, bold letters.

Sparks.

Tyler said the first day they met, he felt sparks between them—an electric charge drawing them together. And when they surrendered to the pull, there was no going back. It was the start of their forever.

Even Matthew saw those sparks the first time he met Charlotte backstage after a Tomorrow Mourning show. He thought she was hot and planned to make a move, but the way she looked at Tyler, and the way he looked back said anyone else had an ice cube's chance in Hades of hooking up with that girl.

In the end, he was happy with how everything turned out. Tyler and Charlotte complemented each other perfectly, and aside from his brother, she was the best friend Matthew had ever had—something he needed and valued way more than a quick bang in a dressing room.

And in the nearly three years since he met Amber, there'd been moments of undeniable sparks igniting between them, too. She'd catch his eye while she played on stage, her tongue poking out the side of her mouth as she concentrated. She'd twist her face into a weird expression to make him laugh—a private joke created in front of thousands of sweaty strangers. Or she'd lean her elbow on his knee when she was stoned, and she'd be so close he'd catch a whiff of her hair. Those sparks hadn't faded with time. In fact, they'd grown stronger since that first perfect kiss in her bedroom.

Their sparks ignited a bonfire the night before; they just had to feed it to keep it burning.

His mind drifted back to Tyler and Charlotte, and his pen moved across the page as if possessed. The words poured out, and none of the lines tempted him to tear it up and start over.

He'd been putting too much pressure on himself to make the speech perfect, but life wasn't perfect. Love wasn't perfect. His words just needed to honor the connection that would bring everyone they loved to one place, raising their glasses for a couple who deserved to have the rest of their days filled with love, laughter, and all the beautiful memories they created together.

When Matthew reached the bottom of the page, he put down his pen, sat back in his chair, and gave himself a high-five. Amber's words had inspired him, and it felt good to finish the task he'd stressed about for weeks.

He'd be showing his gratitude later.

25

Amber

Matthew greeted Amber at his front door with a handful of sunflowers. How he knew they were her favorite and how he found them in October in Oregon was beyond her. The sweet gesture made her feel even worse about something that'd been bothering her since leaving the nail salon with Sandra and Charlotte.

During their manicures, someone dropped a heavy box behind them that slammed against the floor. Charlotte jumped from her chair, facing the sound with fisted hands, ready to fight.

When they were alone, she explained how loud, unexpected sounds even remotely resembling gunshots would set her off. She didn't leave the attack with PTSD like Matthew did, but certain things triggered those memories, the same potent rush of fear flooding her system.

Amber needed to talk with Matthew about what happened the night before and apologize for her thoughtlessness.

"Thank you." She took the flowers, offering a smile of gratitude before kissing his cheek. "They're beautiful."

"I ordered the fliers for the Halloween party. And the equipment was delivered to High Notes today, so we can—" His words died as he scrutinized her expression, his brows pinched. "Are you okay?"

"I know guys dread these three words, but can we talk?"

He sighed, his shoulders slumping. "We dread them for a reason. Have a seat."

They settled on the couch in the same spots as the last movie night. So much had changed in the eleven days since that it seemed like ages ago. The cellophane wrapping on the flowers crinkled as she set them on the coffee table.

"I want to apologize for some things I did and said last night. I know what you went through with Rafael, and I wasn't thinking when I bound your hands behind your back. And I used the word *torture* to describe something that was anything but. I shouldn't have said it. And—"

"Amber, stop." He scooted closer. "Is that what you're worried about? That you stirred up bad memories?"

She nodded, her gaze dropping to her lap. "It's probably why you had a nightmare. Charlotte would get them when something would trigger her trauma with the stalker, so it makes sense."

He shook his head. "I'll admit, there was an uncomfortable second when my hands were behind me, but it went away. I think you actually helped me by replacing that terrible memory with a fucking amazing one."

"Really?" Her chin lifted.

"Really. And I could've broken loose if I wanted to. It wasn't the same thing at all, and I'm okay. I promise you didn't cause my nightmare. They just happen. I'm sorry it messed up your sleep."

"So, we're both sorry for shit we don't need to be sorry about?"

Matthew's chest jumped with a laugh. "That about covers it." He used her hand to pull her onto his lap so they faced each other. Her short black skirt hiked up nearly to her hips. "I'm glad you're here. I missed you."

Butterflies fluttered low in her belly at their closeness and his words. "I missed you too." She pushed the hair out of his face with both hands and fused her mouth to his. Their tongues tangled, and she felt his erection through his jeans, growing long and thick between their bodies. All that separated their naughty bits were denim, cotton, and obscenely expensive red lace. Knowing he'd almost certainly see her in her underwear, she wore something nicer tonight. She'd just tell him not to be so rip happy this time.

His fingertips slipped underneath her shirt and skated up her spine. It was a gentle, slow touch that got the butterflies all riled up again.

"You smell good," she said.

Fuck, did he ever. Earthy hops, spice, and man—like the shirt she stole the last time she was there. Amber's lips moved against his, but she kept it sweet. She was still a bit gun-shy about not considering his triggers the day before, but that wasn't holding her back.

After worrying about her dad's intentions and the tabloid bullshit, she needed something more comforting and tender. He made no moves in a rougher direction, so maybe they both needed something less intense this time.

"So do you." His strong fingers raked through the hair at her nape, lightly massaging her scalp. It was so soothing, her eyes closed. "I could kiss you all night. I'm really kicking my younger self for not going for it in that janitor's closet in Phoenix."

Her head jerked back. "Why didn't you? I wanted it, and my poker face sucks, so you had to know."

His thumb traced her bottom lip. "Because I was lucky enough to be your friend and wasn't about to risk losing that. And I knew I couldn't be the man you deserve."

"So you settled for the chick with fake eyelashes and even faker tits that you banged in the backseat of her Jeep?" Her eyebrow cocked. "If you think that's what you deserve, you're delusional." She held his gaze. "Why can't you see what you're worth like I can?"

"I don't know. But maybe a blowjob would clear it up."

She hit him with a couch pillow while he laughed. It would've pissed her off from anyone else, but she knew he diffused discomfort with humor, so he got a pass.

"I see my worth more clearly than I did then," he said. "I'm still basically the same guy, but now I'm financially secure, own my own place, and I stopped being such a lazy fucking bonehead all the time." Something darkened in his eyes, like a cloud passing over the full moon. "But the things about the attack that still haunt me make me feel weak. You don't deserve someone weak."

"You are *not* weak, Matthew Hall." Amber tapped his chin when he tried breaking eye contact, and he found her eyes again. "I can't imagine going through what you went through. Only a strong person would survive that. And only a strong person would try therapy and reach out for help instead of holding it all inside until it stole the best parts of you." She took his face in her hands. There was still a lot he held inside, but hopefully, time would make it easier for him to open up. "One day, it'll stop haunting you. You'll wake up without nightmares, able to do all the things it's kept you from. I'll help you get there in any way I can."

He pulled her to his chest, and they held each other. She buried her face in the crook of his neck, peppering soft kisses on his skin.

Something he'd said earlier scratched at the back of her brain—she'd helped him by replacing a bad memory with a good one.

What if that could work again?

"Do you trust me?" she whispered into his ear.

He held her tighter, and she felt his nod.

"What if I can help you do something you haven't been able to do since the attack? By replacing another bad memory with a good one."

He drew back, studying her face. "What are you talking about?"

Explaining her plan might make him overly anxious before it could even begin, making him more likely to call it quits prematurely. She was optimistic it could work if he let her take the lead. Hopefully, the whole thing didn't blow up in her face.

"It'll work better if I don't tell you, but show you. I don't want to do anything that'll make it worse, so if it's too much, we leave. No need to explain; it'll just end."

She took his hand, his pulse racing in his wrist. Her plan involved easing his anxiety through distraction, so this was an excellent opportunity to test its efficacy.

"While you decide," she said, "I want to make you feel good."

She slipped his shirt over his head, biting her bottom lip at the sight of his tattooed muscles. Her fingers dragged over his chest and up the sides of his neck in a calming, whisper-light touch. She removed her shirt next but left on her bra, well aware of how red lace against her pale skin drove men insane. Having double-D tits behind it didn't hurt either.

She pressed a slow, teasing trail of kisses across his collarbone and chin. Matthew hummed with pleasure as his hands gripped her ass, grinding her lace-covered pussy against his growing erection.

"Fuck, you're perfect." He sucked the exposed swell of her breasts and moved to the lace covering her nipples. They were still sensitive from the night before, and as he sucked one and then the other through the fabric, her head tipped back with a needy whimper. His mouth moved to her ear, his hot breath making her shiver. "I'll do anything you want. I trust you."

Her lips curved into a grateful smile. Those three words meant the world to her, and she'd make sure he didn't regret them.

Amber grabbed her shirt and slipped it back on.

"Hey, we were just getting started," he protested with a frown.

"Put your shirt and shoes back on." She kissed the tip of his nose and left his lap. They'd miss out on decent sleep again, but if this worked, it would be worth it. "We're going for a drive."

26

Matthew

As Amber drove them over the Fremont Bridge, it was impossible not to worry about where they were going and why. Matthew did trust her. He didn't trust himself not to lose his shit and never be able to look her in the eye again without feeling ashamed.

What she witnessed in High Notes when Rafael's brother came in was bad enough. What if he broke down crying or pissed himself? Okay, he wouldn't do *that,* but he wasn't the biggest fan of unknowns, and this was that with a capital "U." He didn't want to feel weak around her.

And it felt risky. Amber had good intentions, but she wasn't a psychiatrist. Would she know how to help without pushing him too far? What if things went awry, and it made him worse?

She pulled against the curb outside a Greek restaurant with a giant smiling falafel in the window. He and Evan sometimes got takeout from there to eat at the brewery, which was a few blocks away.

"Have a craving for feta cheese?" he joked, trying to lighten the mood.

She smiled, but it was muted and didn't touch her eyes. "I know this might make you uncomfortable, but please give it a chance." She pulled a scarf from her purse and held it out. "Put this over your eyes."

He took the scrap of fabric and stared at it in his palm. "You want me... blindfolded?" The thought made his stomach lurch. Rafael and Amy never blindfolded him, but it meant darkness. He wasn't sure he could handle that.

"It won't be for long, I promise. I can put on music you like, and you can hold my hand if it makes you more comfortable."

"Amber…" The fabric shook in his hand, anxiety prickling in his chest.

Her hand settled on his knee, and he focused on the contact to help stave off the panic threatening to break through.

"I know you can do this, Matty." She leaned over the center console and pressed a kiss to his cheek. "I'm sorry to ask you to do something uncomfortable, but it's an important part of it. I promise it'll be quick."

With shaking hands, he slipped the fabric over his eyes and tied it behind his head. He took deep, steadying breaths, but his heart still thundered in his chest.

A few minutes later, the car stopped, and the engine went quiet.

"We're here," she said. "Keep your blindfold on for now. I'll come around and guide you."

Her car door shut, and shortly after, the cold night wind rushed against his side when his door opened. She guided him about twenty steps before stopping. "Focus on your breathing, and when I take off your blindfold, keep your eyes on me. Understand?"

Matthew nodded, his knees threatening to buckle.

She kissed him softly. "Remember, eyes on me." Her fingers brushed the back of his head as she slipped off the blindfold.

His gaze darted to the left, and he choked on a gasped breath.

They were in the High Notes parking lot. He was about two steps from where Rafael grabbed him and tossed him into a trunk.

"Eyes on me." She took Matthew's face in her hands, her firm hold demanding his attention. "You're okay."

"Amber, I can't do this." His bottom lip quivered, and he clamped onto it with his teeth.

"Give it a chance." She pulled his lip free and kissed him again. "Please."

His muscles were rigid and trembling.

He couldn't reach for her or even move.

His mind screamed *RUN* in an endless loop.

"Focus on my touch," she whispered against his lips. Her hands slid up the back of his shirt, her fingers drifting up his ribcage to his shoulder blades and back again.

It felt good, but words of protest still burned on his tongue.

He wanted to be back home behind a locked door, hidden from the people and places that reminded him how broken he was.

But he'd tried that. It didn't make anything better; it only reinforced his weakness.

This, he hadn't tried—letting someone he trusted walk with him through the darkness.

If he ever wanted to feel strong again, he had to fight for it.

So, he did as she instructed, concentrating on the sensations she was giving him instead of the flashes of memories threatening to reduce him to a boneless puddle on the concrete.

"Focus on the feeling of my tongue sliding against yours." Her tongue slipped inside his mouth, and after a few moments, the softness of her lips and caress of her warm skin crowded out his thoughts.

Her body demanded his to respond, and as her fingers slipped under his waistband and her nails bit into his hips, he couldn't resist deepening the kiss. She hummed with pleasure, and his cock swelled in his jeans.

"That's it, baby." She grinned against his mouth as she pulled his hips flush with hers. "Get hard for me."

Her fingertips grazed his stomach before she started unbuckling his belt.

"Amber..." His breathing changed for a new reason.

He wanted her. Of course, he did. But here? Now? When he was still shaking and on the verge of bolting and running the three miles home.

"Trust me." The metal clinking against metal echoed in the empty parking lot as she slid the leather strap loose from the buckle. "You know as well as I do the stores on this block all close by eight. Even if someone were on the sidewalk, we're hidden by trees, and that dumpster that smells like old lettuce."

He laughed, which seemed to surprise her as much as it did him.

"It's just us here," she said.

With his belt and buttons undone, she sank to her knees.

It was a beautiful sight, but he worried about the concrete scraping her skin. "Put my shirt underneath you." He went to take it off, but she stopped him. "You'll get dirty."

She pulled his cock loose from his boxers and teased the tip with her tongue. "That's the whole idea."

With her gaze locked with his, she took every inch of him into her mouth. He gasped when her hands slipped to his balls, gently cupping them while she sucked him hard.

"Fuck, Amber." He fell against the white brick wall behind him for support.

She chuckled low and wicked around his length. "Whose back's against the wall now?"

Matthew grinned at that. The roles had reversed, and this time, he was at her mercy. For the first time since they'd arrived, he could breathe freely without the invisible hands squeezing his throat.

Her mouth dipped lower, and her tongue massaged his balls before taking each into her mouth and gently sucking.

"Fucking hell." His hands fisted in her hair, and she moaned, the vibrations shooting spikes of pleasure all the way to his toes. She returned her attention to his cock, her tongue lapping at the veins underneath before she took him to the back of her throat again.

She released him and rose to her feet. While holding his gaze, she stepped out of her panties and tucked them into his pocket. "I'll want those back later."

He laughed softly, looking forward to whatever came next.

"Put your hand under my knee and lift it," she said.

His laughter died. He didn't know what she had in mind, but whatever it was, he wanted it badly. He did as she said, positioning her bare pussy so close to his cock he could feel the damp heat radiating off her core. In the golden glow of a nearby streetlight, he could see how slick it was.

His mouth watered, remembering how fucking sweet she tasted when she came on his tongue.

"We're going to play by the rules and not fuck," she said, "but I remember the look in your eyes last night when I tasted myself." She pressed her slit to the base of his erection and moved to her tiptoes, sliding it up to the throbbing head. "You feel how wet it made me to fuck you with my mouth?"

She repeated the motion, and his spine stiffened against the wall.

One slight push would be all it took to be inside her. To finally feel her pussy stretch and let him in. Matthew's eyes shut, and his head fell back against the bricks, overwhelmed with the thought and every delicious sensation she gave him.

Amber went back onto her knees and snapped her fingers. "Eyes on me."

He obeyed.

In that moment, he would've cut off his right hand if she asked him to.

The wetness she left behind glistened in the light, and he watched as she slowly licked it off with long, languid strokes and quick flicks of her tongue.

"Holy fuck." He cupped her chin. "I'm not gonna last much longer."

Amber pulled her shirt over her head and handed it to him. "Hold this."

"Why—"

She took him back into her mouth as her hand jerked in a quick, smooth rhythm over the base of the shaft. When the muscles in his hips twitched, she pulled her head away and used only her hand. From root to tip, she tugged him closer, closer until he blew.

Matthew bit back a groan.

She aimed his cock at her chest, streams and drips of white painting her skin. He collapsed against the wall, out of breath, and spent. While he watched, she licked the last drops off the almost too-sensitive tip before rubbing his seed over her tits and up the column of her throat.

He'd never seen anything more sensual and filthy, like a fantasy he didn't know he had just came to life.

"Are you real?" he asked, his knees still weak.

Her lips curled at the edges. "Lucky for you, I'm as real as the moon above our heads."

He looked up.

A bright, brilliant full moon glowed above them. The dim light wasn't from a streetlight, after all. He'd been so stuck in his panic and then distracted by her he'd failed to notice.

How could he have missed something so beautiful?

Matthew offered her his hand, and she took it, rising to her feet.

He kissed her long and slow, greedily devouring her taste that lingered on her tongue.

"I have another trick up my sleeve," she said with an arched brow and mischievous grin. "Er, down my boot." She dug into her boot and pulled out a black Sharpie. "I snatched it from your junk drawer."

"First my shirt, now my marker?" He slid his finger through the wet pool between her breasts. "You're a dirty little thief." He pressed his finger to her lips and pushed it inside. She hummed in her chest, sucking his finger clean.

Amber took the cap off the marker. "Turn around."

Matthew turned, facing the wall. She put the marker to the brick and started writing. When she finished, she stood back and admired her handiwork.

He barked a laugh. "For a good time, call Janus? Nice one."

"Your turn." She put the marker in his hand. "You said you were a master doodler, so have at it."

"Stealing and defacing public property." His tongue clucked against his teeth. "Someone needs to spank the criminal out of you."

Her cheeks pinked, telling him all he needed to know.

When they got back to his place, her other cheeks would be red before he was done with her.

He put the tip to the wall, drawing a full moon over two stick figures—a man and a woman. Really, the only difference was in the hair length, proving he was far from being a doodle master.

"You drew us?"

Matthew turned to look at her, and her smile made the dimple pop in her cheek. He brushed her hair back and kissed the spot. "Now, whenever I take out the trash or walk to my car, you'll be there."

She pressed her lips to his, lingering for a breath. "For a man who just jizzed all over my tits, you're very sweet, Matthew Hall."

He laughed, the sound muffled against her mouth.

"Is that why you brought the marker?" he asked. "To trigger the good memory whenever I see it?"

Amber nodded, their lips and the tips of their noses brushing with the movement. "And now you're standing here for the first time in months." She touched his neck above his pulse point. "Your heart isn't racing, and you're breathing fine." She kissed him again, longer this time. "I'm so fucking proud of you, Matthew."

And right then, his pulse kicked up.

A strange, unfamiliar feeling washed over him that scared him a little, but it was unlike the fear from before. This fear was one he didn't want to run from because, deep down, he knew something amazing waited on the other side.

27

Amber

After signing at least two hundred CDs, vinyls, and posters at Center of the Road Records, Amber's hand was cramping up. She could hold drumsticks for hours, but something about pinching a Sharpie and repeatedly writing her name pissed her fingers off. Even so, she loved meeting their fans face-to-face. Without them, the band would still be playing to stoned college kids in dive bars every night instead of gearing up for a massive European tour.

The new album had only been out for three days and already sold what the last album did its first month. Nowhere near platinum, but they got closer every minute.

Sandra sat beside her, shaking hands, giving hugs, and eating up all the attention. Given her mad skills as a guitarist and frontwoman, she'd earned it.

"Hi," Amber said, taking the record from the next in line—a twenty-something woman with bright green hair and a pierced lip. "What's your name?" She held the marker tip to the album, waiting.

"Jane. And yeah, I know I totally don't look like one."

Amber laughed. "Nothing plain about you, sweetie. Love the hair." She signed the album and handed it back. "Thanks for listening."

A female fan shrieked Luke's name at the end of the table, and Amber turned to find Charlotte smiling and shaking her head beside him as she signed a poster.

Next in Amber's line was a young boy with a mop of light brown hair past his ears. He looked twelve, maybe thirteen, and clutched a copy of their latest CD in his shaking hands. It was sweet when their young fans were starstruck.

As she looked him over, there was something vaguely familiar she couldn't place.

With Jane out of the way, there was a wide gap between the boy and the table, but his feet wouldn't move.

"Don't be shy," Amber said, beckoning him over. "What's your name?"

He stared, his expression slack. "Uh, Nick." He took a few steps forward.

"Come on up here, Nick. I don't bite, but Sandra might. She skipped lunch."

Sandra's head turned, eyeing him. "I'd rather have a burger. Are we famous enough to make people fetch us food?"

Amber held out her hand, but he just stared, clinging to his CD like a lifeline. He was a bit young to be a creep or stalker. Maybe he was nervous. The first time Amber saw Joan Jett backstage at a festival, she couldn't speak either. Not that she was nearly as awesome or famous as Joan. At least, not yet.

"We're getting pizza right after this," she said to Sandra. "You'll survive." Amber turned back to the boy. "Want me to sign it?" When he still didn't budge, her eyebrows pinched as she studied his features. The longer she looked, the more familiar he seemed. "Do I know you?"

Finally, he handed her the CD. "Sort of."

"What does that mean?" She signed the insert right underneath her photo.

"You're my sister."

Amber dropped the Sharpie and her head shot up, her skin going cold. "What did you say?"

Sandra's gaze swung between them. "Holy shit. You have the same eyes. Freaky."

Amber took a closer look, confirming Sandra's observation. His eyes were the same almond shape and exact shade of blue as hers—like her sisters and their shithead father. He also had their dad's sharp jawline and broad nose, leaving no doubt he was telling the truth. But why was he here? And where was their dad?

A hand touched Amber's shoulder, and she tore her gaze away from the boy. Eliza bent beside her ear. "Everything okay?"

Amber struggled to swallow past the lump in her throat. "I need a minute."

Eliza gestured to the line. "Can it wait fifteen? We're almost done here."

The boy, Nick, shuffled his feet, looking uncomfortable. "I can go."

"No!" Amber took a deep inhale and whooshed it out. If he left, she might never get this chance again. She dragged a folding chair beside her. "Hang here, and we'll talk when I'm done. Cool?"

He nodded, taking the seat.

Amber's heart was pounding so fast she was lightheaded as she signed the rest of the autographs in a blur. How did he find her? What did he want?

She felt like an asshole for not reading his letter. Maybe it held all the answers, and she'd been too stuck in old resentments to bother reading it.

Eliza returned with a can of cola and a bag of potato chips, setting them in front of Nick.

"Thanks," he said with a forced half-smile.

Amber stole glances at him between autographs. The kid looked miserable. The corners of his mouth were downturned, his shoulders hunched. He still looked nervous, but also deeply unhappy.

What happened to you?

Was he bullied? Did a girl break his heart?

Maybe something in Nick's home life put that tortured look in his eyes. Was her father's mistress a terrible mother? Was their dad as absent and selfish with the son he wanted so badly as he was to Amber and her sisters when they were no longer fun and little?

As Nick sipped his soda with downcast eyes, he looked like he could burst into tears at any moment.

"We're grabbing pizza after this," Amber said to him. She signed a poster and handed it back to the guy with a foot-high purple mohawk. "If you aren't in a rush, you can join us."

Somehow, Nick looked even sadder. "No rush. Dad doesn't care what I do."

A burning knot squeezed in Amber's chest as she fought to keep her tone neutral. "Do you like video games?"

His face brightened a little. "Yeah."

Amber took a vinyl from the next fan, signed it, and passed it back. "The place we're going has an arcade. If you can kick my ass at *Street Fighter*, I'll buy you a milkshake bigger than your head."

His chin lifted as he smiled. "Cool."

When the line was gone, Eliza returned to her office, and Luke left to grab a drink with his shrieking fan. Sandra and Charlotte chatted with the store owner, Jake, who'd easily take first place in a David Crosby look-alike contest. Eliza tried convincing the band to move the signing to a bigger shop, but Sandra said they owed him one and insisted.

"You guys ready?" Amber flexed her tired hand as Nick followed her to the door.

Sandra and Charlotte said goodbye to the owner and headed over.

"Who's this?" Charlotte asked, tipping her head toward Nick. She must've been too far away to hear their exchange over the fan chatter.

"My brother, apparently."

Charlotte shot Amber a look of surprise, her eyebrows raised. "Wow. Okay."

"Yeah," Amber said. "Nick and I have some talking to do later, after pizza."

Besides the occasional, brief interactions with young fans, she was never around kids and didn't know how to talk to them. It would be better to speak with him alone first, but she wasn't ready. She needed her friends' support while she adjusted to the situation.

Charlotte held out her fist, and he bumped it. "Nice to meet you, Nick." She turned to Amber. "Matty and Ty are meeting us there."

Amber had been looking forward to seeing Matthew all day. Her cheeks heated as a flash from their naughty parking lot adventure the night before rolled in, but her awareness of the teenage boy beside her quickly squashed it. They walked two doors down to Napoli, home of the best slices in Portland.

As they entered the restaurant, a bell jingled above their heads and they were hit by the scents of garlic and tomato sauce. Matthew sat at a booth in the back, and when he caught Amber's eye, a rush of warmth fluttered in her belly. She wasn't used to feeling so affected by a guy, and it was a nice change from not giving a shit. Tyler sat across from him wearing his usual out-in-public ball cap and hoodie, and both men held full pints of beer.

When Tyler spotted them, he waved them over. "How'd it go?"

"Great." Charlotte slid into the booth, and he put his arm around her. "Jake says hi."

"Hey, Rockstar." Matthew smiled up at Amber, patting the seat beside him. His shoulders were loose, and there was light in his eyes. He looked like any other twenty-four-year-old guy, relaxing with his friends and a cold beer, not someone haunted by nightmares and trauma. Whether it had something to do with her unconventional parking lot therapy or came from something else, she was grateful. His gaze slid to Nick, and his brows pulled together. "Oh. Hello."

"Guys, this is Nick," Amber said. "My brother from Chicago."

Matthew's mouth fell open before snapping shut. Like everyone else at the table, he knew what that meant. This boy came from her father's affair—a faceless product of his betrayal who was now here, face and all.

Amber introduced her friends and sat beside Matthew. Nick stood at the end of the booth, looking awkward and uncomfortable again. "Sit here." She scooted closer to Matthew's side, and Nick took the open space.

"So," Sandra said from across the table. "We have a super important subject to discuss, folks." She pointed at Nick. "Favorite pizza toppings. Go!"

His smile was shaky at the corners but seemed genuine. "Olives, mushrooms, and sausage."

"Hell yeah," Matthew said, high-fiving Nick over Amber's head. "I'm with him."

Amber knew Matthew hated olives. She set her hand on his knee, more grateful than ever for the cool, considerate guy he was. If Nick became part of her life, there was no doubt her friends would welcome him into the fold with open arms and affectionate fist-bumps.

But if Nick were in her life, their father would be too.

It was a lot to process.

Sandra stuck out her tongue. "For those of us who despise fungus, we'll get a cheese and garlic. My girlfriend's out of town, so stinky breath be damned."

Nick sat straighter. "You have a girlfriend?"

Sandra grinned. "Christa. She's rad. How about you? I bet you drive the Windy City ladies crazy."

His smile slipped as he shook his head. Amber and Sandra exchanged a quick look of concern.

"You'll get there, bud," Tyler said. "I was a lonely band geek with zits, and now, I'm marrying the prettiest girl in Portland." He kissed Charlotte's cheek as she smiled.

"Only five more days," she said, waggling her engagement ring.

Nick's face flamed with crimson. Guys often reacted to Charlotte like that, and it was cute he wasn't immune to her charms.

The waitress came by, and they ordered two large pizzas and a pitcher of root beer for the table.

Amber's brain kicked into overdrive while everyone chatted. *Where's Dad right now? Why did he bring Nick to Portland?* She needed a minute alone with her friends to regroup before interrogating her brother.

She fished several quarters out of her purse. "Want to play a few games before the food gets here?" she asked, handing Nick the coins. "I'll be there in a sec."

"Thanks." He slid out of the booth and headed for the arcade on the other side of the restaurant.

Matthew touched her shoulder. "What happened?"

"He came to the signing." She shrugged. "Saw it advertised in yesterday's paper and snuck away from their hotel while my dad was gone. I haven't had a chance to get more details."

"Seems like a nice kid," Charlotte said. "What are you going to do?"

Amber shrugged again. "No idea. Get to know him, I guess."

"Maybe he'll want to meet your sisters while he's in town." Matthew sipped his beer and licked foam from his lip.

Amber hadn't thought of that. Would *they* want to meet *him*? They knew he existed because of their gossipy grandmother but never voiced interest in ever seeing their half-brother on the other side of the country. Instead, they called him "the golden boy," usually with a tone dripping in sarcasm and resentment. It was easy to resent him all those years, but it wasn't Nick's fault their family fractured. Messy, complicated emotions made that easy to forget.

"I'll be back." Amber squeezed Matthew's knee and left the table.

She waded through the maze of computerized music, robotic beeps, and flashing lights before finding Nick at the Frogger machine. He was staring at the screen, his face slack, eyes vacant. A surge of emotion tightened her throat and pricked her eyes. Someone that young and innocent had no business looking so wounded and lost. She needed to find out what or who had caused it.

Nick snapped out of his sad trance when he noticed her beside him.

"Nice choice." She slipped two coins into the slot, and the game came to life.

"Is that your boyfriend?" he asked, nodding toward their table.

Amber glanced at Matthew over the sea of vinyl-covered booths and noisy pinball machines and smiled. "Yeah. He is. We've been friends a long time and just started dating."

She watched Nick's frog hop halfway across the street, darting backward before getting smashed by a truck.

"Shit!" He winced the second the word was out. "Sorry."

"For cursing?" Amber laughed. "I'm a drummer in a punk band. If you only knew half the shit that comes out of my mouth."

That earned her a laugh, and the small victory eased the tightness in her throat.

"You're a drummer like Dad?"

Amber's smile collapsed. "Yeah. Like Dad." It wasn't easy to suppress her feelings toward her father, but she wouldn't badmouth him to Nick. "Do you play?"

He frowned, shaking his head. "I'm learning guitar."

"Got something against drums?" She crossed her arms and leaned against the side of the machine.

Nick's mouth tipped down further, and his frog fell off a lily pad and drowned. "They're the reason Dad's never home."

Amber's eyes stung again, pieces of the puzzle connecting. The fucking asshole never learned from his mistakes. This poor kid was stuck with the same part-time parent she had before he was nothing at all. No wonder Nick was miserable.

"You avoid drums for taking him away," she said, "and I used them to pull him closer."

Nick looked away from his game to meet her gaze. "Sorry it didn't work." He returned to his game. "Trust me, you aren't missing much."

His words scratched at a wound deep in her chest. For thirteen years, she'd mourned the loss of her father in her life. Missing his baritone laugh, the way his beard hairs ticked her cheek when he hugged her, listening to The Who at full blast when he picked her up from school in his truck. But he was also the man who broke his daughters' hearts over and over. Destroyed her mother.

What if all this time... they'd been better off without him?

"Hey." Amber touched Nick's arm, but he stared at the machine. "Are you okay? You don't really know me yet, but—"

"No." When he finally looked at her, his eyes shined with tears. "He's never around and treats my mom like shit when he is. She forced him to bring me because she doesn't know what to do with me either." He sniffed. "Dad was supposed to show me where he grew up, but he's been weird this whole trip, disappearing a lot." He stopped to breathe, the words rushing out like they'd been logjammed for years and finally broke loose. "He was fun when I was little but doesn't care anymore. And he hates me because I—" His mouth clamped shut, and he returned to his game. "Never mind."

Amber didn't need another reason to be angry with her dad, but here it was. "He was like that with us too—fun until we were old enough to call him on his shit. I'd hoped you got a better version than we did." She nudged his elbow as he concentrated on his game. Or at least pretended to. "But I'm sure he doesn't hate you. He always wanted a son."

Nick shook his head, his knuckles going white as they gripped the controls. "Trust me, I'm not the son he wanted." His lip quivered before his teeth sank into it.

Amber didn't know how to make him feel better—hug him, make a joke, give him money? She was slowly figuring out how to help Matthew with his issues, but what could she do for a teenage boy she'd just met? She needed more information to work with.

"What do you mean?" she asked.

His frog died, and he let go of the machine, turning to face her. "What are they like? Your sisters?"

Amber grinned as the faces of four beautiful, sometimes aggravating women flashed in her mind. "*Our* sisters are amazing." As she described them, he listened with a soft smile that grew with every word. Matthew was right—Nick wanted to meet them.

"They sound cool. I hate being an only child."

"Guess what?" She tapped his shoe with hers. "You're not anymore."

Since the record release party, the mystery of why he was in town with their father has been poking at her. She needed it settled.

"Did Dad bring you to Portland to meet us?"

He shook his head. "He said he had business to take care of. He's on the phone a lot and keeps leaving me alone while he meets with people. I don't know why. He didn't even tell me why we were outside your show."

Business? As far as she knew from her grandmother, he was still in construction, but failing to hold a steady job because he was lazy. What business could a deadbeat from Chicago have in Portland?

Tyler walked over and held out his closed fist in front of Nick. "Open your hand."

Nick blushed again, averting his eyes as he held out his palm.

Tyler's fist opened, and at least two dozen quarters spilled out. Some fell to the floor, and Amber picked them up and added them to the pile.

"Thanks." Nick gave him a bashful grin, his cheeks redder than before.

Holy shit.

More pieces of the puzzle locked into place.

Nick wasn't crushing on Charlotte back at the table after all.

When Tyler returned to their friends, Amber moved closer to Nick so no one else could hear their conversation.

"When you said Dad hates you because of something…" Amber's hands balled up at her sides, knowing if her suspicion was correct, what was coming would make her angrier at her father than she ever thought possible. "What were you going to say?"

Nick stuffed the quarters in his pocket, his eyes downcast. "Doesn't matter."

"Of course it does." Amber touched his chin, raising it. "Nick… Are you gay?" she whispered.

His panicked eyes darted around the room, and he looked like he might puke or bolt for the exit.

"It's okay if you are." Amber set a comforting hand on his shoulder as he struggled with whatever was going on inside his head. "You can trust me."

He nodded so slightly that she almost missed it. His cheeks flamed red for a different reason—one she knew well.

He was ashamed.

Amber's hand dropped from his face. "And that's why Dad—"

"Treats me like a fucking disappointment?" Nick's voice was small and shaky, her heart cracking at the sound. "Yeah."

Amber threw her arms around him, squeezing him to her chest so tightly he squeaked. He didn't move to hug her back, but he didn't fight it. Hot tears slid to her chin, soaking into his T-shirt as she held him close.

She couldn't fall apart in a pizza parlor, especially when Nick needed *someone* stable and supportive in his life. Clearly, their father had failed him, but she wouldn't. Amber wasn't used to being anyone's rock, but she'd proven she could be that for Matthew. Now, Nick needed her to step up and protect him before it was too late.

"I'm so fucking sorry, Nick." Their bastard father should be the one apologizing and feeling ashamed. In all those years since rejecting Tara for the same reason, he hadn't changed. "I'm glad you found me, little brother." She wiped her damp cheeks and let him go.

"You..." His chin wobbled, his eyes red and rimmed with tears. "You don't think I'm a freak?"

"Oh, Nick." She laughed and hugged him again. "I don't know you well enough to say for sure, but I hope so. And if you are, welcome to the fucking club."

This time, he squeezed her back, leaning into the hug like he was starving for it. Her heart cracked even wider. How long had it been since someone held him like this, offering acceptance and comfort without conditions?

"What about your mom?" she asked, stepping back. "Does she feel the same way as Dad?"

Nick roughly wiped tears from his cheeks as he nodded. "She makes me go to Bible study at some weird church, hoping it fixes me."

Amber shook with anger and grief for this boy she barely knew who'd already claimed a place in her heart. And for the little girl inside her who felt like something was wrong with her, too, because of their father's judgment. She'd do anything to save him from all the terrible things that could grow from that pain.

Nick huffed a humorless laugh. "She should go herself for sleeping with her boss."

"What, what?" Amber froze as his words sunk in. "Seriously?"

"I caught them making out in his car once when he dropped her off after work."

Amber bit back a grin. Finally, the kid had good news to share. It buoyed her spirits to know her dad was getting the swift kick of karma he deserved. He didn't deserve a sweet kid like Nick, and Amber intended to do something about it.

"Ready for pizza?" she asked, letting the suppressed grin break through.

Amber hooked an arm behind his neck, and they returned to their seats.

She sensed Matthew watching her. Her eyes were probably red from crying, and she widened her grin so he wouldn't worry.

"Whenever we tour in Chicago," Amber said, "we'll get this kid in the front row."

Unless he's out of Chicago and away from those assholes before then.

Nick's eyes brightened. "I've never been to a punk show."

Sandra gasped dramatically, clutching her chest. "We *have* to fix that. We'll bring you backstage and everything."

Amber poured root beer into two cups and put one in front of Nick. "He wants to learn guitar."

"Badass, dude." Tyler raised his beer. "Charlotte and I both play. We could show you a few riffs sometime. How long are you in town?"

Nick swirled his straw around his soda, the joy on his face crumbling. "I leave in the morning. Dad's staying longer, but I have to get back to school."

Amber didn't like the idea of her father lurking around her city with some secret agenda, but even more, she didn't want Nick returning to a mother who was as shitty and cruel as her husband.

Everyone grabbed a slice, and Amber watched as her friends made Nick feel comfortable enough to open up about school and his life back in Chicago. He and Matthew bonded over a shared love of skateboarding, and Matthew promised to take him to his favorite skatepark next time he was in town. Tyler and Charlotte suggested guitars for beginners. Sandra made him laugh by being Sandra.

Amber wished they had more time and that he'd be returning home to people as warm and accepting as her friends, but at least he'd be going home with some nice new memories.

After saying goodbye to everyone, Amber took Nick back to the hotel where he was staying with their dad. The paint was peeling, the pool was empty, and the bushes leading to the lobby were brown and wilted. The place looked like it'd been a one-and-a-half-star hotel thirty years ago and was lucky if it held onto the half. She wanted to take him back to her house but knew she didn't have the right.

"I'm here if you ever need to talk or need anything." She pulled a pen from her glovebox, scribbled her number on a show flyer, and handed it to him. "Anything at all. Any time, okay?"

He nodded, staring at the paper before folding it and stuffing it into his pocket. "Did you get my letter?"

Fuck. Her mind scrambled for an excuse that wouldn't hurt him—he'd been through enough. But he deserved her honesty.

"Nick, I'm sorry." Amber sighed, her words laden with regret. "I didn't read it. I have a lot of anger over Dad's choices and how badly he hurt my family. That has nothing to do with you, and none of it was your fault, but I wasn't strong enough to hear what you had to say." She managed a weak smile and ran a hand over his hair. "I am now, I promise."

He stared out the windshield where three rusted, abandoned shopping carts sat on a patch of dead grass. "It's okay you didn't read it. You can throw it away because now you know everything. I didn't have anyone to talk to, and I saw your address on some of Dad's old mail in the garage. Your name's the only one I knew because you're the only one he's ever talked about. He likes that you're famous."

That surprised her as much as it pissed her off. Every one of her sisters was incredible and didn't deserve to be treated like they didn't exist.

"Besides Mom and Dad," he said, "I've never had family. Grandma and our aunts turned on Dad for what he did to your family, and Mom's family lives in Texas and never visits."

"Hey." She squeezed his shoulder as he met her gaze. "I'm your family, too."

He smiled, but it was brittle at the edges. The weight on his shoulders made him seem older than his thirteen years. It was so unfair that instead of a carefree childhood spent in a loving home, he had to return to a life where he'd be unappreciated and shamed for who he was. Amber's childhood was far from carefree, but at least she had plenty of happy memories to hold onto. And even after her dad left, she still had a loving home to return to at the end of every day. Every kid deserved that.

"Thanks for today." Nick glanced at the hotel and turned back to her. "Bye, Amber."

Tears stung her eyes. She never thought she'd meet him or even wanted to. Now that she had, she wasn't ready to say goodbye. "Later, little brother."

He left the car, disappearing inside the room beside the vending machine.

Amber stared at the weathered door to room sixty-three. Anger and a fierce need to protect the sweet, lost little brother she never knew she wanted burned like fire in her blood.

Fuck this.

She left her car and knocked on his door. If her dad answered, it would take all the restraint she could muster not to break his fucking jaw.

Nick opened it, looking understandably confused. "What's up?"

She peeked inside the room, and it looked even more rundown than the outside. The bedding was a hideous baby puke green, and the wallpaper behind the twin beds was wrinkled and torn at the corners.

"Let's go."

"Huh?" He squinted, studying her face. "Where?"

If there was anyone who could help her solve this problem, it was her sisters. But if given the choice, they wouldn't want to meet him. The same pain and resentments that kept Amber from opening Nick's letter were embedded too deeply in their hearts to look past them. So she wouldn't give them the choice. They'd always been there for each other; now, Nick needed them. First, he needed to get the fuck away from this roach motel and the roach who dragged him into it.

"To meet our sisters."

28

Amber

While Amber's sisters sat around the living room waiting for an explanation for why she'd called a family meeting, she fidgeted with the hem of her black T-shirt.

"We haven't had a family meeting since Mom lived here," Beth grumbled. "I have a date in an hour, so this better be important."

"I met our brother." Her sisters stared, wide-eyed shock on all of their faces. "He came to my signing. Alone. His name's Nick, he's fucking awesome, and he needs us."

"Slow down." Kate put a hand up. "What do you mean he needs us? Needs us for what?"

"We're fresh out of dads for him to steal," Denise joked.

"Not funny." Amber scowled when Denise rolled her eyes. "He didn't steal anyone. Dad leaving wasn't Nick's fault."

"So where is this golden boy?" Beth asked. "And what does he need from a bunch of women he's never met?"

Amber exhaled a frustrated sigh. "Stop calling him that. Dad's never around for him either and treats his mom like garbage. Sound familiar? And now, they're rejecting him for being... different than they'd hoped."

It didn't feel right to reveal his sexuality without his permission. If he wanted to share that, it was up to him.

"He must be around thirteen now," Tara said. "That's about the age we stopped being fun for Dad too. Poor kid."

Amber was encouraged by that. They had to stop linking him to the affair and abandonment so they could see Nick for who he really was.

"Where is he?" Kate asked.

"In my car, listening to music."

Beth's jaw fell open. "He's *here*?"

Amber nodded. "Give him a chance. He's a scared, lonely kid with no family except the assholes who made him. We've always supported each other, and regardless of how he got here, he's our brother."

The room fell silent, a rare occurrence in that house. She imagined each of them shuffling through layers of anger, rejection, and pain to determine whether they could handle this.

"Okay," Kate said, smoothing the front of her blouse and sitting up straighter. "Bring him in."

The other women nodded, and Amber's tense shoulders sank in relief. She'd expected them to require a lot more convincing and was grateful for their trust. She went out to the driveway, turned off her car, and led Nick inside the house. Her sisters still sat around the living room, trying to look casual and not as uncomfortable as they must've been.

"Hi, Nick." Kate left her seat, extending her hand while her eyes roamed his face. "I'm Kate, the oldest and wisest sister."

He hesitated before shaking her hand. "Hi."

Tara came up beside them. "Holy damn. You look just like him."

Nick's gaze dropped to his shoes.

"Nope," Beth said, cupping his face and lifting it. "This kid's way more handsome than Dad."

Amber gestured to the living room. "Stop crowding him, and let's sit. I'll raid Beth's candy stash because we'll need a lot of sugar for this."

Once Nick relaxed a little, he told the sisters about his life back in Chicago. They asked questions but stuck to safe topics, like school, his friends, skateboarding, and bands he liked. The women took turns telling him about their careers, and Kate even brought out a photo album to share memories of their lives throughout the years. Beth looked triumphant when she got him to laugh at one of her stupid jokes, and Denise appreciated that he was a fellow neat freak.

"How are things at home?" Kate asked.

With that, the upbeat energy in the room fizzled out.

"Bad," Nick said, popping a few Skittles. "My parents always fight, Dad's always gone, and he found something out about me that made everything worse."

Amber sat beside him and wrapped an arm around his shoulders. "It's okay. You're safe here, I promise."

Nick's chin dropped to his chest, his hands shaking as he clutched the bag of candy. "I passed a note to a boy at school, and he showed it to everyone in class." Tears welled in his eyes, and Amber hugged him with both arms. "The teacher took it and told my parents."

Kate's gaze flicked to Amber before turning her attention back to Nick. "What was in the note?"

Nick sniffed, wiping his nose on his sleeve. "That I liked him. I thought he was like me, but he just laughed about it with his friends."

"You're gay?" Tara asked.

His head turned to her, and he silently nodded.

"Cool," she said. "Me too."

Amber caught his barely-there gasp. The tightness in his shoulders loosened beneath her arm.

"Really?" he asked, his chin raising.

"Sure." Tara shrugged, tearing open a chocolate bar and taking a bite. She probably looked unaffected to an outsider, but Amber recognized the fire his admission ignited in her eyes. Looking around the room, they all had it. "Dad didn't like it when I told him, but I wouldn't let him shove me back into the closet. If he tries to do it to you, he'll have five angry women to answer to."

Nick laughed even as tears trailed his cheeks. Tara left her seat and hugged him from the front while Amber held on from the side. Soon, Denise and Beth joined in. Amber could hardly breathe as the huddle tightened, but her love for her sisters and now, her little brother, swelled in her chest.

They let him go and returned to their seats, all eyes in the room glossed with tears.

"So," Kate said in a voice that was all business despite her quivering chin. "You're too young for emancipation, but if you want out, we can discuss other options. Just be sure it's what you—"

"Yes," he said. "That's what I want."

"Okay then." Kate clapped her hands together. "It'll take time and work, so you'll go back for now, but I promise we'll do all we can to get you out."

Amber and Kate drove Nick back to the hotel where he was staying and sent him off with a bag full of candy and a photo of all the sisters to take back to Chicago. They all got his phone number and promised to keep in touch.

Hopefully, he'd feel a little less alone now.

She worried about his future, but Amber was grateful she didn't have to figure out how to help him on her own. Once the sisters joined forces, nothing could get in their way—least of all a common enemy with the same deep blue eyes but a cold, callous heart.

29

Matthew

"Are you guys ready?" Zack scratched his neck underneath the black bow tie. "I can't wait to get this damn thing off."

"Are you crazy?" Adam asked. "The four of us look like James Fucking Bond, and I'm gonna be raking in the pussy after the ceremony. Did you see the trio of hotties we passed in the lobby?"

The seven-story-tall Fairy Falls Inn and the twenty acres surrounding it were reserved for Tyler and Charlotte's wedding and reception, with security posted at every entrance. The women were getting ready in a large dressing room on the other side of the inn from the one set up for the men. The inn's expansive lobby was at the center, where guests could check in, grab coffee and pastries, and, if they were pretty and female, get gawked at by Adam and Zack.

Tyler smacked Adam on the back of the head before Matthew had the chance. "Those are Charlotte's cousins you're talking about, asshole."

"Was one of them the cousin I'm walking up the aisle with?" Adam asked.

"No." Tyler attached his cufflinks. "That's Kyla. She's running late."

"Is she as hot as the others?" Adam stepped out of striking distance when he asked.

Tyler's gaze narrowed. "Don't even think about it."

"What?" Adam asked, his hands up as if he could ever be innocent. "Just curious. She might get lonely later and want a few hours in the middle of a Zack and Adam man-wich."

Tyler smacked him again, and Matthew laughed.

"Don't you guys want something better than a quick, sweaty bang in a coat closet for a change?" Tyler asked. "Something real?"

"That waitress I hooked up with last night felt pretty damn real," Zack said.

"Yeah, except for her massive balloon tits," Adam chimed in. "I swear I could smell the silicone."

Matthew tried tuning out the nonsense while running through his best man speech in his head. No matter how much he practiced, he was sure he'd flub it by stuttering or knocking over a wine glass. Amber stayed at his house the last few nights, and he rehearsed it a few times with her as the audience. It was easy to get through it when a beautiful naked woman was watching, but a crowd of hundreds of friends, family, and strangers was a different story.

He was really looking forward to taking her back to his suite after the reception. When she stayed at his house, they had so little time and energy by the end of the day he still hadn't plowed her wheat fields. It was getting harder to resist with every dry hump, hand job, and all the mind-blowing oral he couldn't stop thinking about.

Now, they had a couple of days before she had more band duties, and Evan was covering him at the brewery all weekend. With the usual obstacles out of the way, they could finally take that step that would deepen their already intense connection.

Zack checked his hair in the mirror, smoothing the sides with his palms. "You're just jealous because you had a date with your right hand and a bottle of lotion."

Tyler groaned. "I love you guys, but could you please shut the fuck up so I can enjoy the fact that I'm about to marry the most amazing woman on the planet?"

Zack clapped Tyler on the shoulder. "You're so damn lucky, Ty."

"Seriously, man," Adam said. "Charlotte's the best. All the chicks I meet just want to steal my wallet while they blow me."

Zack buttoned the vest beneath his black tuxedo jacket. "Maybe that scientist cloning sheep can clone girls like Charlotte instead. Then they can outnumber the wallet-stealers."

"You're a genius, dude." Adam picked up a glass of champagne from a catering tray and raised it high. "To science!"

Tyler shoved his shoulder, spilling half the champagne onto the floor. "When you idiots give your toasts, I hope you have better material than that."

Zack gave a reassuring thumbs-up. "We got you, dude."

Matthew grabbed a glass of champagne and drained half in one gulp. He was confident in his speech, but public speaking freaked him the hell out. How his friends and brother could go on stage in front of thousands of people for a living was beyond him.

The door opened, and Sandra walked in, her hands over her eyes. "Is this a penis-free zone?"

Tyler laughed. "We still have them, but they're all covered up. Come on in, Sandra."

Her hands dropped, and her face lit up with a beaming smile. "Look at you studs! I've only ever seen you guys in band shirts and jeans. I had no idea you'd clean up so well."

"Look who's talking," Tyler said as he hugged her. "You look amazing."

Sandra's fiery red curls were swept up in a loose bun surrounded by tiny white and blue flowers. She wore an elegant gray silk gown, the hemline falling right above her knees with a plunging neckline and open back showing a lot of skin. Matthew said a silent prayer to the gods of geeky stoners that Amber was wearing the same dress. The mental image alone made his cock stir.

"I do, don't I?" she said with a twirl. "Christa's already tried tearing this dress off me—twice."

"I don't doubt it." Tyler grabbed a glass of champagne and sipped it. "Please don't tell me you're here because Charlotte has cold feet."

"Hell no! That girl's feet are as hot as the rest of her. Wait until you see her in that dress." Sandra fanned herself dramatically.

"Champagne?" Matthew held up the tray.

"No, thanks. I wanted to talk to you and Ty alone for a minute, if that's cool."

Adam tossed back the rest of his drink. "Sure thing. Come on, Zacky. Let's go scope out the lady situation outside."

"Easy on the champagne," Tyler said to their backs. "I'll kick your asses if you get wasted at my wedding and pull any stupid shit."

Adam shot him a thumbs-up and left the room with Zack, shutting the double doors behind them.

"Don't worry, I'll keep an eye on Beavis and Sluthead." Sandra looked up at Tyler and grinned. "I don't often get sappy, but I want to thank you. For making our Charlotte so damn happy and always being good to her. I'm sure you know exactly how lucky you are."

"Yes," Tyler said. "I do."

"Save that last bit for Charlotte." Sandra winked. "There's no one more deserving of her, and coming from me, you won't find a higher compliment."

"I know." Tyler hugged her again. "That means a lot."

"And we have Matthew." She turned to him. "You're about to be part of Charlotte's family on paper, but you've always been like a brother to her. And me." She pulled him in for a hug and whispered in his ear. "If you hurt Amber, I'll gut you like a fucking trout."

Matthew laughed and whispered back, "I don't doubt it."

The doors opened, and Tyler and Matthew's mom walked in, her eyes shining when she saw them.

"Look at my handsome boys." Her voice shook with emotion.

"Hey, Mom." Tyler hugged her, and she sniffed as a tear slipped from the corner of her eye.

Matthew hugged her next. "You look beautiful."

She wore a pale green dress, and her blonde hair was swept up in a twist dotted with tiny white flowers. The diamond earrings they'd given her last Mother's Day sparkled in the lights.

"I'll give you guys a minute," Sandra said. "See you out there, you lucky motherfucker." She patted Tyler's arm on her way out.

"I'm so proud of you, son." Their mother smiled at Tyler as she touched his cheek. "Charlotte's wonderful, and I know you'll be as happy as I was with your dad."

The rare and beautiful connection their parents had was evident in the way they held each other's hands and stole kisses when they thought no one was watching. The way they looked at each other made it clear they knew exactly how lucky they were. It was the kind of love both brothers had been chasing all their lives. Tyler had found it. Maybe now, it was Matthew's turn.

"He would be proud, too," she said.

"Thanks, Mom." Tyler's eyes shined with tears as he hugged her again.

Tyler and their mother had come a long way in mending their strained relationship, and it was he obvious that he appreciated having her there on the most important day of his life.

She turned to Matthew. "And I chatted with Amber while the ladies got ready. Such a sweet girl. She even put the flowers in my hair." She touched a tiny white bud beside her temple. "I hope you hold onto that one, son."

Matthew intended to, knowing exactly how lucky he was.

"He will," Tyler said. "We've both finally got it right."

As a swell of emotion rolled in, Matthew pulled him in for a hug.

Tyler's arms wrapped around him. "I love you so much, Matty."

Tears stung Matthew's eyes, and he held on tight. As if he'd be losing a part of himself once he let go. "I love you too, big brother."

"Okay, boys." Their mom wiped her eyes. "Enough blubbering. Let's get you hitched."

Tyler and Matthew each hooked an arm through hers, and they walked together toward the sound of water tumbling over rocks. When they reached the front of the aisle, she kissed them both on the cheek before sitting in the front row beside an empty chair holding a framed photo of their father.

The sight of it made fresh tears burn in Matthew's eyes, and he blinked hard to clear them.

Tyler shook hands with Zack's father, Gary, a minister of a small nondenominational church in Portland. Tyler had known the family since high school, and Gary looked thrilled to be officiating.

Molly waved at Tyler as she walked to the front of the audience carrying a twelve-string acoustic guitar. She sat in an empty chair with her instrument in her lap, waiting for her cue.

Matthew tapped Tyler's shoulder. "You ready for this?"

Tyler grinned. "Abso-fucking-lutely."

Gary cleared his throat.

"Sorry, Gary." Tyler laughed. "But I can't be held liable for whatever comes out of my mouth today. I'm so damn happy, I can't see straight."

Matthew went to meet up with the rest of the wedding party in the staging room off the lobby. Inside, people were lined up in two groups, like they'd practiced that morning.

He spotted Amber at the front of the line and his heart stuttered in his chest. Her beautiful golden locks were curled and dotted with tiny flowers, and her gray silk dress clung to every soft, sensual curve of her body. The only place it would look better was on the floor of his suite.

She was talking to Zack and hadn't noticed Matthew, so he snuck up behind her.

"You look incredible in that dress," he breathed into her ear.

Amber shivered, flashing him a coy smile over her shoulder. "Hey, you."

"Ty freaking out?" Adam asked. He was the only one standing alone, so Charlotte's cousin must not have arrived yet.

"Nope." Matthew kissed the curve of Amber's neck. "Cool as a fucking cucumber."

Charlotte stood at the back of the line, talking with her dad. Smiling in her white dress, she looked beautiful and excited to get the show on the road.

"See you up there, gorgeous." Matthew was walking with Sandra, so he let go of Amber and moved beside the maid of honor, offering his elbow with a sarcastic flourish.

Sandra laughed at the gesture. "I know you too well, Matty." She hooked her arm through his. "You can't fool me into thinking you're a gentleman."

"Kyla!" The resounding baritone of Charlotte's dad, Mickey, rose above the chatter, and Matthew turned to see him hugging a young dark-haired woman who looked a lot like Charlotte. Sandra and Amber greeted her, too. When Mickey let go, Charlotte led Kyla to stand beside Adam with a look that said she regretted pairing them together. Her lips were pursed, the edges of her mouth curling down.

"That's Char's cousin," Sandra explained. "She's cool as hell."

"Get to your places, please," the wedding planner called out.

She propped open the doors, and the sounds of Molly's guitar filled the air. It was something light and breezy that Matthew didn't recognize. With all her talent, she probably wrote it for the occasion.

"That's our cue," the wedding planner said, gesturing for Sandra and Matthew to go out first. They slowly made their way down the aisle, where Tyler and the minister waited.

When they reached the front, he parted with Sandra to stand beside his brother. Behind them was the pebbled path from the Fairy Falls Inn to the cascading waterfall that began hundreds of feet above them before crashing onto the rocks below.

Matthew looked around as he waited.

Dozens of chairs were set up in rows on each side of the makeshift aisle, filled with friends and family of the bride and groom. The trees were dressed up in autumn shades of red and gold, and snow-capped Mount Hood provided a breathtaking backdrop for the ceremony.

Amber slowly made her way down the center aisle with a bouquet of tulips in her hand, wiping a tear from the corner of her eye when she reached the end. She met Matthew's gaze, a knowing grin tugging at her lips. She must've recognized the lust that was no doubt written all over his face.

Amber took her place across from the groomsmen. Again, her eyes slid to meet his, and she wet her pink, begging-to-be-kissed lips with her tongue. He mouthed *You're beautiful*, earning the sweet, dimpled smile he'd hoped for.

Next, Charlotte's cousin Kyla came out with Adam. She held a similar bouquet, and every inch of her face lit up with a wide, beaming grin as she walked. At the end of the aisle, she stood beside Amber before everyone's attention turned to the inn's doorway.

When Gary gave a nod, Molly began playing an instrumental version of Led Zeppelin's "Thank You"—a favorite of Charlotte's mother. Like his dad's photo, the song was a way to honor the people they loved who'd passed far too soon.

Molly paused before the second verse, and everyone rose to their feet.

When Charlotte took her first step out of the doors, Tyler gasped. Matthew watched his brother's eyes fill with happy tears as she approached.

Charlotte's deep chestnut hair cascaded in waves down her back and over her shoulders beneath a crown of wildflowers. She wore a sleek but simple white dress, the hem brushing against the pebbles as she approached with a gentle smile on her lips and love in her eyes. Her elbow was hooked through her father's, his broad smile brimming with pride and joy.

As the music played, Matthew tried to remember the lyrics of the next verse. Something about inspiration. As Tyler and Charlotte prepared to promise each other forever, Matthew was inspired by the fearlessness it took to give yourself to someone else and accept them in return, the good and bad, for better or worse.

He wanted that with Amber. It was too soon to promise forever, but he wanted to reach the day when every fear that held them back from fully letting someone in was obliterated. He wanted all of her and to offer all of himself in return.

When Charlotte reached Tyler, she wiped a tear from her cheek. They joined hands.

"You're so beautiful, baby." Tyler lifted her fingers to his lips and kissed them.

She gave him a warm, sweet smile in return.

Gary recited the typical words sealing a marriage as legally binding, but nothing about the moment felt typical. It was remarkable, magical, and un-forgettable, but not typical. They were becoming a family, making promises of forever. It was fitting their tough little offspring was part of the moment. That baby was a sign their future would be filled with hope and thrilling new beginnings. And a shitload of diapers.

After Tyler and Charlotte said, "I do," Gary pronounced them husband and wife, and they were in each other's arms before the word *kiss* was spoken.

Everyone got to their feet and cheered as Tyler dipped his bride backward, pressing his lips to hers as the new chapter of all their lives began. Matthew looked over at Amber again, and she was watching the happy couple, batting at a few more tears while smiling and cheering.

Seeing her love for their friends and how touched she was by their joy made him fall a little harder.

Tyler and Charlotte went up the aisle together, and the wedding party followed. They gathered by the entrance to the ballroom as guests scattered in all directions. A waiter came by with a tray of champagne flutes and sparkling cider.

When everyone had a drink in their hand, Matthew raised his glass. "To Tyler and Charlotte."

They all repeated it in unison before their glasses clinked and emptied.

Music thumped through the walls of the ballroom, turning their heads.

"That's what I'm talking about." Zack's head bobbed to the beat as he loosened his tie and walked with Adam toward the music. "Let's start the fucking party!"

"I want a few minutes alone with my wife," Tyler said, the backs of his fingers sliding along Charlotte's cheek as she gazed up at him, her brown eyes sparkling like the diamonds on her finger. "We'll see you guys inside."

Christa wrapped her arm around Sandra's waist, dragging her toward the reception.

Matthew and Amber stood there for a moment before he held out his hand. "Will you dance with me? I'm not any good, but I promise to try my best not to fuck up your shoes."

"I trust you." She brushed a golden curl off her forehead before taking his hand. "They're Beth's anyway."

They laughed together as they walked, and he laced his fingers through hers. They made their way to the dance floor as the opening bassline of "Another One Bites the Dust" kicked off, making the glasses on the tables vibrate and buzz.

Amber set her hands on his chest as her hips popped and swayed in time to the music. His fingertips slid down her bare arm, and he watched goosebumps rise in their wake.

She took a small step back before giving him a slow, thorough perusal. "I like you all dressed up."

He grabbed her waist, pulling her closer. As her chest grazed his, the faint hint of peaches and flowers hit his nose. He still didn't know if that scent was her shampoo or her, but it was intoxicating. And addictive.

"I'll have to take you somewhere fancy so you can see it again." He moved his mouth to Amber's ear to be heard above the music. "And I'd eat broken glass if it meant you'd wear this sexy fucking dress again. I want to peel it off you with my teeth." He nipped her earlobe and felt her sharp inhale against his cheek.

The song ended, but they stayed like that for a while—touching each other in places appropriate on a public dance floor, but the contact still made his palms sweat. The sexual tension building for weeks was stretched to its limits, and his control was about to snap.

"I'm pretty sure it's a crime to say something that hot without kissing me."

A corner of his mouth kicked up. "Then let's fix that."

Matthew's eyes locked on hers as he tucked a loose lock of hair behind her ear and kissed her softly. She tasted like champagne—sweet and worth taking the time to savor.

The next song started, and Matthew's pulse raced as their bodies moved together. Tiny beads of sweat glistened at her hairline while the house lights danced on her skin.

Zack and Adam sidled up to them, each holding out a full glass of champagne while draining their own.

"Drink up, my friends." Zack looked Amber over, letting out a slow whistle. "You look fucking hot in that dress, Amber."

"Seriously, woman," Adam said. "God damn."

"Thanks, guys." She turned to face them and grabbed one of the glasses.

Matthew resisted the urge to kick them, grudgingly dropping his hands from her hips to take the other glass. "Don't forget what Ty said about not getting wasted today."

"Don't sweat it." Adam snatched a bottle of champagne off the nearest table and refilled his glass. "We'll stop after a little champagne. We won't be stupid."

"You can't guarantee that," Zack said. "But if we are, it won't be because of alcohol."

Amber laughed, pointing her glass at them. "You both owe me a dance later."

"Find us before we sneak off with one of these hotties, and you're on." Zack kissed her cheek before dragging Adam to a table of pretty women doing shots.

"Cheers, gorgeous." Matthew clinked his glass against hers and took a drink. He let the bubbles fizzle and dance on his tongue before swallowing. "Do you want to find our seats or hit the buffet?"

A slow song started, and bodies around them connected and swayed to the music.

Amber shook her head. "I'm fine right here." She drained her glass, setting it on a nearby table and he did the same.

Her hands slid behind his neck, her hips gently moving to the beat. The hemline of her dress brushed the tops of her knees, and he couldn't help imagining slipping it over her head.

"You look beautiful in that dress. Have I said that yet?" As her cheek brushed his, he felt her grin.

"Once or twice."

Matthew chuckled softly. "I'll try to keep the ogling to a minimum, but it won't be easy." He slipped his hands behind her and touched the exposed skin at the small of her back, his thumb gently stroking as they danced.

"The wedding was nice," Amber said against his cheek. "Not what I want, but I'm glad Charlotte has her perfect day."

Matthew was quiet for a moment. Should he ask the question her words stirred up or keep it inside to avoid possibly spoiling the moment? As the song changed, he decided to go for it.

"You don't want to get married someday?" Matthew shifted his feet along with hers as the tempo picked up. His clunky shoes made a few close calls with her toes, but so far, no injuries.

"I do. I just don't want the traditional stuff. I hate wearing white, and there's no dad to walk me down the aisle. Plus, I'd rather drop a load of cash on an amazing adventure for a honeymoon than a few hours of dancing and an open bar."

"What do you want?" Matthew's feet slowed as he waited.

"My sisters would kill me, but I like the idea of running off to Vegas for the trashiest wedding possible." She laughed, her warm breath tickling his neck. "Fake Elvis, dress covered in hideous sequins, hooker heels, the whole nine. Hell, maybe even do it at a drive-through chapel."

Matthew chuckled at the mental image of her hanging out of a car window in that very un-Amberlike outfit while Elvis conducted the ceremony with a curled lip and occasional pelvic thrusts. It was impossible not to imagine himself in the driver's seat, yelling his vows like he was ordering a number three with a side of onion rings.

"Sounds cool."

It felt ridiculous and inadequate to say, but that's all he had. A fancy wedding wasn't important to him either. If Matthew was lucky enough to fall for someone so hard he couldn't wait to promise them forever, those details didn't matter.

As he held his sweet, stunning goddess of a girlfriend in his arms, it seemed more possible than ever. And he wanted it more than ever.

"You're not a bad dancer, after all." Her lips curved in an appreciative smile as she gazed up at him. Even after two weeks together, it was surreal to have someone so beautiful look at him like he was the only man in the room.

Before he could say more, the music stopped, and a loud male voice echoed in the space.

"All right, everyone!" The emcee adjusted the microphone, turning everyone's head except Matthew's. He couldn't tear his eyes from Amber if a grenade went off at the cake table. "Let's hear it for the bride and groom! Please welcome to the dance floor, Mr. and Mrs. Hall!"

That got his attention. Matthew clapped and cheered, turning toward his brother and new sister-in-law, making their way to the front of the room.

"Time for their first dance as a married couple." The emcee raised a glass, and many hands in the crowd followed suit. Amber handed Matthew his refilled champagne, and they did the same. "Congratulations, you two."

The floor cleared out, and Tyler and Charlotte danced, their eyes (and occasionally lips) glued to each other. Love like that was so rare and beautiful that it'd always seemed out of reach for Matthew... but maybe it wasn't.

Matthew and Amber sipped their champagne side-by-side, their shoulders bumping as they swayed to the music. She leaned close to his ear. "This champagne is going straight to my head. I need to eat something."

He placed his hand on the small of her back to guide her toward the buffet and, knowing his speech was due soon, a lot more champagne.

After everyone ate their fill of steak and lobster and all the plates were cleared, the emcee handed Matthew a cordless microphone. He could already feel all the eyes in the room on him, and his palms started sweating.

Amber squeezed his knee and whispered, "You got this."

He took a deep breath and stood while the lobster in his stomach did backflips. "Hey, everyone." The microphone let out a high-pitched squeal, and he winced. "Thanks for celebrating this incredible day with our family as we welcome one more."

Matthew thought *two more* in his head, but most of the people there didn't know about the baby, so he kept it to himself.

"When I first met Charlotte, I thought she was a knockout. In fact, I planned to ask her out as soon as my dumbass brother left the room." Everyone laughed. "But before I could, I saw the way she looked at him. And how he looked at her. They'd only met once before, but they had an unmistakable connection. You could almost see the sparks."

He paused to take another steadying breath and let it out. "Their journey wasn't easy and didn't run in a clean, straight line. But everything that came before—good and bad—brought them to this day. That part of their journey is over, and a new one begins today. One filled with endless love, an even deeper connection, and eventually, little dark-haired, music prodigy rugrats."

There was a sprinkling of laughter from the crowd, and when he looked at Tyler and Charlotte, they both had tears in their eyes.

Matthew lifted his glass. "Here's to my big brother and my new sister-in-law." He swallowed the swell of emotion rising in his throat. "I love you both so much."

Tears pricked his eyes as he smiled at the blissed-out couple. He couldn't be happier for them, but it felt like an ending for him too.

No more long, carefree nights of laughter and music. Tyler and Charlotte's lives would revolve around each other more than ever, and in a few months, they'd spend most of their time taking care of their baby. That might mean the end to movie nights and the brothers' weekly pub hang to catch up over beers. A distance would grow as their lives followed different paths.

Matthew would miss a lot about how things used to be, but seeing how happy two of his favorite people were... he wouldn't trade it for anything.

He returned to his seat and received a round of applause for the speech thankfully behind him. Someone tapped their fork against a glass, and Charlotte grabbed Tyler's face, kissing him hard. There was a chorus of wolf whistles and *aww*'s throughout the room.

Matthew was startled as Amber's soft, warm hand slipped into his.

"That was a great speech, Matty." She rested her head on his shoulder. "Maybe later you can tell me why it made you sad."

With that, he fell a little harder. The fact that she recognized his pain even as he smiled meant more to him than she'd ever know.

At that moment, Matthew realized all the endings he'd been dreading would be easier to bear because of this thrilling new beginning with Amber. And that not all changes were to be avoided and feared. Without change, they wouldn't have gone from strangers to friends to this incredible new reality where he could kiss and hold her, their future full of endless possibilities.

They'd only been together two weeks, and there was already so much to look forward to—exploring Europe together, cutting the ribbon on the music space she was helping him create at the brewery, and of course, the long stretch of alone time they'd soon have in his suite. There'd also be dates, movie nights, concerts, and long talks in bed, growing their connection and becoming even closer. He couldn't wait to see where it would all lead.

And maybe someday, if he played his cards right, it would lead them to a fake Elvis in a Vegas drive-through.

30

Amber

"I can't get this fucking shoe *off*." Amber fiddled with the buckle of her heel, the alcohol making her fingers as useless as they were blurry.

Matthew looked at her shoe with half-closed eyes before bending forward and effortlessly slipping it off her foot.

"My hero." She laughed, wiggling her toes after freeing them from their stiletto prison.

The guests had mostly cleared out, and Tyler and Charlotte left for their mini honeymoon in a Mount Hood cabin over an hour before. It was time for Amber to get out of her fancy outfit and under the cool, silky sheets in her suite upstairs—or Matthew's suite—whichever was nicer.

Matthew had an adorable perma-grin from all the champagne, and it widened a few inches. "Anything else you want me to take off?"

Fuck. Yes.

Amber's teeth clamped onto her bottom lip. Even with her tipsy brain, she knew that night wouldn't, couldn't be *the* night. She was more than ready, but they were both wasted on champagne, stuffed from too much cake, and exhausted from several rounds on the dance floor. For one more day, she had to put her libido on pause.

"Your room or mine?" she asked. "I have a jacuzzi tub on my balcony."

"I have a view of Mount Hood *and* a jacuzzi tub."

Amber was an Oregon girl through and through, and Hood was her favorite mountain in the world. "Ding, ding, we have a winner!" *Fucking champagne.* It always made her a little goofy.

Matthew draped his tuxedo coat over her shoulders and slid a hand behind her back to help her stand.

She grabbed her shoes and they dangled from her fingertips by their buckles. "What's your room number?"

"Five-six-three. Or six-five-three." He shrugged as she breathed in his scent that lingered on his coat. It did not help to tamp down her libido. "We'll try both."

She snickered, and he supported her weight as her knees wobbled. "I can't remember mine either, but I think the door's green. Hell, I'm lucky I remembered my sister's shoes."

They laughed as they made it to the elevator, huddling together against the wall as it climbed to the fifth floor. Luckily, his key worked on the first door they tried. Amber stumbled in on her bare feet and faceplanted on the bed, loving the feel of the cool fabric against her cheeks and forehead.

"Matty," she mumbled against the blankets, "I think I'm drunk."

He chuckled. "I can see that, sweetheart. But you're not alone." He faceplanted beside her. "I'm pretty fucking drunk too."

"I'm not *wake up with my head in the toilet* drunk, though." She turned to face him. He was blurry, and his hair was a mess, but he was handsome as always. "I'm *I want to get naked and fall asleep on you* drunk."

"What a coincidence!" His laughter shook the bed. "So am I."

"Then let's get to it." Amber didn't move. "I'm afraid the room will start spinning if I get up."

"I got you." Matthew stood, swaying on his feet. "Arms in the air, hot stuff." He slipped the dress up her body, tickling her armpits when he got there.

She let out a cackling laugh and fell onto the floor, her head bouncing on the thick carpet. "Ow. Do you have any idea how many people die in tickling accidents every year?" She blew a lock of hair off her face with a loud huff.

"Are you okay?" He got on his hands and knees, his body hovering over hers.

"Getting better every second." She dragged her fingertips in a slow, teasing line down the center of her body, and his eyes followed the trail. "Take off your shirt."

Eager to obey, Matthew rose to his knees, fiddling with the buttons on his black tuxedo vest. "Fuck. Booze and buttons don't mix."

Amber sat up, spreading her legs to wrap around him. "Let me help." She wasn't much better at it in her state, but she managed to get them all undone. The collared shirt and its cuffs took longer, and when she got it opened, she growled with frustration at the white T-shirt underneath. "Another layer? You're killing me here."

He laughed as he tugged off both shirts and tossed them across the room.

"Mmm…" She ran her fingers over his bare chest. "That's better." His inked skin was warm, his muscles firm beneath her fingers. "Fuck, you look good without a shirt on."

"Look who's talking." He kissed the rounded tops of her breasts and down her stomach. "Let's get rid of your extra layer, shall we?"

"Shall we?" She giggled—another thing that only happened under the influence of champagne. "Are we in medieval England?"

He unhooked her bra and tossed it behind him. "Don't mock the man who's about to ravage you with his tongue."

A low moan came through the wall beside the bed, followed by a high-pitched cry of bliss.

"Sounds like someone's getting ravaged next door," she said, arching a brow.

"Fucking Adam." Matthew shook his head. "I knew I should've switched rooms."

"Ooh, he was checking out Charlotte's cousin all night. I bet it's her." Amber propped herself up on her elbows, and the room shifted. When she laid back down, she slapped a hand over her eyes as the walls swirled and the ceiling went fuzzy. "Uh oh."

"What's wrong?"

"Spinning room. Not good."

"Do you need to hurl, or should I get you into bed?"

"Bed, please."

He slipped his arms under her knees and behind her head, lifting her off the floor. "Don't drop her. Don't drop her. Don't drop her."

"No!" she shrieked. "Don't drop her!"

"Was I saying that out loud?"

Amber opened her eyes a crack to find him smirking. She slapped his chest. "Dick."

He laughed, gently setting her on the bed with a pillow under her head.

Her arms dropped heavily to her sides. "Would you judge me if I'm disgusting and don't brush my teeth or wash my face and just pass out?"

Matthew kissed her forehead. "Baby, you couldn't be disgusting if you were dipped in sewage." He removed the rest of his clothes, turned off the light, and flopped beside her on the bed. "We'll be disgusting together because I can't guarantee I won't puke if I move around too much."

"Then don't move." Amber pulled the blanket over them and settled on his chest. "I like you right where you are."

They were quiet for a while. She listened to the crickets chirping in the garden beds beneath the window, and her eyelids grew heavier.

"Hey, Matty?"

"Yeah?"

"You turned out the light."

They were quiet again.

His heartbeat beneath her ear didn't change its rhythm.

He held her closer. "I guess I'm not scared anymore."

31

Matthew

Amber stirred in Matthew's arms, letting out a big yawn.

"Fucking hell." When his eyes opened, the first pangs of a headache hit as the morning sunlight filtered through the curtains. "Does the sun have to be that bright?"

"Seriously, what's it trying to prove?" Amber slid out of bed despite his grumble of protest. "I'll take coffee duty, so feel free to veg until it's ready."

She was bare aside from the pink lace panties they were too wasted to remove the night before.

"Perfect." Matthew slid on his glasses and turned onto his side, away from the light and facing her nearly naked body. "I'll just enjoy the view."

A corner of Amber's mouth lifted as she dug into the mini-fridge. "Drink this," she said, putting a bottle of water in his hand. He stared at it for a moment before twisting off the cap. Everything he'd been avoiding and hiding from was easier to face when she was around.

"Thank you." He propped himself on an elbow, chugging half the water in three gulps.

Amber set up the coffeemaker and went to the bathroom while it brewed. A few minutes later, she came out with her hair in a ponytail and a toothbrush in her mouth.

"Brushing before coffee?" He drank the rest of the water and tossed the empty bottle in the trash.

She popped the toothbrush out. "My mouth tasted like stale ass, so yeah." After grabbing something from her purse, she returned to the bathroom.

The glorious scent of coffee filled the air, and the brewing light was off when he looked at the machine. Before he could get up, Amber came out and filled two mugs.

"You're my favorite," Matthew said, taking his mug.

The corners of her mouth curled up, and she returned to the bed with her coffee, sliding under the covers with her back against the headboard.

It was the truth. They hadn't been together long, but seeing Amber was the part of his day he looked forward to most. Not only because their sexual chemistry was off the charts but because she made him feel seen, safe, and understood. She'd helped him start to heal from his trauma in ways he didn't think were possible.

And Matthew was in love with her.

He'd never felt it before, but there was no doubt this was it. He'd watched Tyler and Charlotte fell in love, so he knew what it looked like when it grew and bloomed. He saw his parents' love—a glimpse into what it could become after years of strengthening that connection.

Something inside him came alive when Amber was in his arms, and that feeling grew stronger every day.

He loved her.

And once their hangovers eased and the time was right, he would tell her.

"I hope Ty and Charlotte are having fun at the cabin." Amber blew on her steaming mug.

"I don't doubt it. Hell, they probably won't even leave it all weekend."

"Hey." She tapped his knee. "What made you sad after your speech?"

Matthew swallowed a mouthful of coffee and sighed. "A lot hit me at once, I guess. Things are changing. My friendship with Charlotte isn't what it was because we both have different shit going on in our lives. Ty's about to be busy with dad duties, so our weekly Beer and Bitching pub visits are probably out. And they might want to hang together after shows instead of with the group.

Hell, I bet they'll leave right afterward once the kid's here." He winced. "Fuck, I sound so selfish."

"It's not selfish." She touched his shoulder, stroking his bare skin with her fingertips. "When you love how things were in the past, it's understandable to wish you could hold onto that feeling forever." Something changed in her eyes, like a light went out.

"Now you're the one who looks sad."

Amber's eyes were downcast as she circled the rim of her cup with her finger. "I hate my dad for what he did to us and my brother, but I have good memories too. How he'd hold the drumsticks in my hands to teach me how to keep a beat. The way he'd put on a record and grab my mom by the waist when she was washing dishes to dance with her. How he'd take me out for ice cream after my soccer games." She shrugged a shoulder. "I know most of the good times were an illusion, but I wish my family could've stayed like that forever."

"Can you forgive him?"

"After what he's done to Nick, I don't see how." Her head raised, meeting his eyes. "He's such a sweet kid. I hope we can get him out before more damage is done."

"He's lucky to have you and your sisters. I'm sure you'll find a way to help."

They sipped the rest of their coffee in a comfortable silence.

"Want to go for a walk around the property?" Matthew's hangover was lifting along with the lingering gloom from the conversation. He was excited to see what the day would bring. "Ty said there's another waterfall half a mile up the trail."

"How do you feel?"

"Great, actually. The water, coffee, and beautiful company killed the hangover. And I'd forgotten how recharging a full night's sleep is."

Matthew hadn't had a nightmare since the first night Amber slept over. And he still couldn't believe he'd slept in a pitch-black room without even a hint of anxiety. He knew it had nothing to do with the champagne. It was her.

"I'm glad to hear that." She leaned forward, pressing a gentle kiss to his lips. "And I'm glad we have this break together. The last few weeks have been amazing but hectic. We finally have a day to do whatever we want."

Matthew grinned as the possibilities swirled in his head. He didn't want to waste a single minute. He'd wasted enough time by not chasing what he wanted, not fighting for what he needed, and pining for a beautiful, unreachable girl instead of making his feelings known. Now, everything he'd dreamed of was within reach.

As he looked at Amber, reflecting on all the best moments of their three years of friendship and the two incredible weeks since their first kiss, he almost blurted out the three words getting harder to hold back.

"Ready to hike?" he asked.

She got up and slipped on her bridesmaid dress. It was wrinkled from spending the night on the floor, but the way it hugged her curves still made his cock stir. "Let's stop by my room first, and you're on."

She changed into much more hiking-appropriate attire in her suite: jeans, a black sweatshirt, and sneakers. After a quick breakfast in the inn's dining room, they headed down the trail toward the waterfall. A dense forest of evergreens and ferns surrounded them as they walked, and mossy rocks of varying shapes and sizes lined the trail. The sky was grey, but like all true Oregonians, they'd never let the threat of rain keep them from an adventure.

About a half mile in, they were greeted by the unmistakable sound of water rushing over rocks. They quickened their pace, chasing the unique natural high that comes from witnessing something wild and pure in the great outdoors.

Around a bend in the trail, there it was. The falls began at least a hundred feet up, sending torrents of water crashing onto the rocks before churning and mixing with the river below.

Amber closed her eyes and inhaled, a gentle smile touching her lips. Matthew watched her, the mist coating his skin as he breathed in the fresh scents of Oregon forest and wet earth.

A rush of tingling warmth filled his chest, everything he'd ever felt for her striking all at once—admiration, a sense of comfort, desire, protectiveness, and so much love it almost hurt.

It was overwhelming and a little frightening, but he surrendered to the sensation, letting it take him.

Matthew took her hand. "Amber?"

Her head turned, and her beautiful blue eyes met his. "Yeah?"

He took a deep breath, but it did nothing to calm his racing heart.

"I love you."

She looked startled, her eyes popping wide.

"What did you say?" she whispered.

He took her damp face into his hands and kissed her. She was rigid at first, but soon, she returned the kiss, fisting the front of his hoodie and pulling him closer.

"I love you," he said again, his thumb caressing the soft skin of her cheek. "I love waking up to you and kissing you. I love that you introduced me to your sisters and let me into your life. And I love that you didn't just accept my broken parts—you helped me start to fix them."

"Matthew, I..." Her chin wobbled, and tears glistened in her eyes. "I don't know what to say."

"You don't have to say anything." He was a little disappointed she didn't say it back, but it was okay she wasn't there yet. When and if she said it, he wanted it to be real, not done out of a feeling of obligation or pressure. She had to be certain; he knew it might be a while before she could get there. "You look so beautiful standing by the water, and I couldn't hold it in anymore. I've never been in love before, but I know damn well what this is."

Her hand covered the one still cradling her cheek. "I'm sorry I'm not there yet."

"You have *nothing* to be sorry for."

"Just listen." She touched her fingertips to his lips. "I've never had feelings this strong either. I want you to know that." Her hands fell to her side. "But I need some time."

Matthew didn't doubt her feelings for him. The most important man in her life broke her heart, so it wouldn't be easy to let herself fall. He'd wait as long as it took for her to trust he would catch her.

"Take all the time you need." He brushed the hair off her forehead, dampened by the mist. "I'm not going anywhere."

He pulled her to his chest and kissed her with everything he had. The way she relaxed in his arms said those words meant even more to her than *I love you*.

She broke the kiss, desire blazing in her eyes. "Take me back to the room."

Matthew had never walked so fast in his life as they made their way back to the inn.

The room key shook in his hand as he opened the door and pulled her inside.

His hoodie and T-shirt were off before the door even closed. As soon as it clicked shut, her sweatshirt joined his clothes on the floor. She slid his jeans and boxers to his ankles, and he kicked them away. He peeled off the rest of her clothes like an excited kid digging into the wrapping on the biggest box under the Christmas tree.

When they were both naked, their bodies collided.

Matthew walked them to the bed, and they tumbled onto the covers with her lying beneath him.

"Fuck, I've never wanted anyone this badly," she said, her voice a husky rasp edged with need.

Amber's fingernails bit into his hips as he kissed her again, their tongues plunging and desperate. He slid his cock along the seam of her pussy, groaning at how slick she was. There would be no resistance if he slid inside her in one push.

"I'll grab a condom from my jeans."

She shook her head. "I have an IUD and got tested after my last... experience. If you know you're good too, I'm okay without one."

"I've always used condoms and got tested after my ex."

A corner of her mouth tipped up. "Then what the hell are you waiting for?"

Matthew grinned, kissing the curve of her neck and working his way to her mouth. He moved his hips forward, sliding the underside of his cock along her wetness a few more times before letting the tip drop lower, nudging at her entrance.

With his eyes on hers, he gently, slowly rocked his hips forward, and she gasped as he stretched the walls of her pussy and sank deeper, inch by inch. When he was all the way in, she sighed in a way that made him kiss her again.

If that sigh meant *finally*, he felt the same.

"I love you, Amber." He wanted the words bound with her memories of their first time in a way that could never be undone. No matter what their future held, she deserved to know what she meant to him as they took this major leap together. How special and appreciated she was. He planted soft kisses on her eyelids and cheeks as he withdrew and slid back inside. She felt warm and slick and so damn tight it almost hurt.

Her fingernails dragged up his back, but it was gentle. The frenzied energy when they ripped their clothes off had shifted. This was sweet and slow—the kind of rare, overwhelmingly beautiful experience you never forget for as long as you live. Like witnessing the flashing colors of the Northern Lights dancing in the sky.

Matthew pulled out and surged forward in one smooth slide. When he repeated the motion, Amber breathed his name. He quickened his pace, and her legs wrapped around him. She thrust upward, matching his rhythm, and he wet his fingers to play with her clit. His hand slipped between their bodies, and her teeth sank into his shoulder when he reached the sensitive bundle of nerves.

"Holy fuck, Matthew. How do you know?"

"Know what?" He didn't slow his movements as she spoke.

"How to make me feel so good I want to cry, scream, or both."

Matthew huffed a laugh, ruffling the hair at her temple. "Quite a compliment, and the feeling's mutual, Rockstar."

His fingers kneaded and circled her clit. When her thighs squeezed his hips, and she whimpered, he knew she was close. He wouldn't be far behind.

"I've never done this bare before," he said. "You feel so fucking good, I'm almost there."

Amber's fingers raked through his hair. "I'm glad you waited for me on both counts."

He smiled, something he'd been doing so much lately his cheeks were actually sore.

When Matthew picked up his pace, her breaths grew quick and shallow, and their eyes locked. He angled his hips to rub her G-spot, and after a few strokes, she let out an almost-pained groan as she hit her peak. He'd never forget that sound or the overwhelming sensation of her inner walls gripping and pulsing around him. He watched as a pale pink blush painted her cheeks, her eyes going hazy with the endorphin rush.

"Fuck, you're beautiful when you come." Matthew captured her lips with his, giving her clit one final stroke.

She relaxed in his arms as her peak receded, and he sped up his thrusts, chasing his. In seconds, tingling sparks of pleasure spread through his core, and he pushed deeper, his release spilling inside her as her lips muffled his groan.

Amber brushed damp hair off his forehead. "So are you."

After catching his breath, he kissed her again. She said she didn't love him yet, but he felt something like it in the way she kissed him back.

As he held her to his chest, their bodies still connected, a switch he'd been fumbling for finally flipped somewhere inside him, changing him into someone ready to leave the darkness behind for good.

After months of pain and struggle, Amber had become his light. Their connection had done more to heal his wounds than therapy ever did.

With her legs still hooked around his waist, Matthew lifted her and walked them into the bathroom. Without a word, he washed her from head to toe, and she returned the favor. When they were clean, they held each other under the rush of the steaming, soothing water.

Every barrier between them had fallen, every doubt gone. It was a feeling he'd been chasing all his life.

And she'd been worth the wait.

32

Amber

With the phone in her hand, Amber took a long drag off her joint and blew the smoke out her bedroom window. Her mom would want to know her loser ex-husband was in Portland for reasons Amber still hadn't learned. If he was even around anymore.

Unfortunately, that topic wouldn't be the only one ensuring this conversation wouldn't be easy or pleasant.

Amber was still riding the high of her perfect first time with Matthew the day before. The sexual tension sparked from their first kiss before had been building every day, making the experience more intense and satisfying than anything she'd felt before. From the second their bodies connected, it became about so much more than pleasure and physical release.

She could still feel the warm glow that bloomed in her chest as he eased inside her and took his time. Like he was gathering every detail and tucking it away in his mind just as she was. When their eyes locked, that warmth flared and spread, melting away her protective layers to reveal every last part of the woman beneath. It was terrifying and liberating all at once to let go of the fears that kept her safe but lonely for so long.

The experience left her feeling bare, changed in a way she still couldn't quite grasp.

And Matthew told her he loved her.

Despite his wounds and fears, he'd let her in. Amber felt that love in every brush of his lips and gentle touch of his hands. And he trusted her. In return, she let herself trust that after claiming a permanent place in her heart, he'd never break it.

For the first time in her life, she was almost ready to fully let someone in.

She wanted to tell her mother all about Matthew, but there'd be no joy or congratulations. A part of her held onto hope her mom would someday get over her instant distrust of anyone with a Y chromosome, but if today wasn't that day, Amber's joy would inevitably be dimmed. But it was news worthy of sharing, so she braced herself.

After four rings, she almost hung up, but finally, her mom answered.

"Hello?"

"Hey, Mom."

"Amber? Is everything okay?"

"Everything's fine."

"Oh. Good. You sound... odd."

There was no point in beating around the bush. "Dad's in town."

Silence.

"Mom?"

"I heard you. What the hell does he want?"

Amber gnawed her thumbnail. "No idea. He was yelling my name outside the club after my record release party. The crowd was crazy, so I couldn't stop to talk."

"You dodged a bullet, sweetie. Avoid that spineless fucking coward, and if he finds you again, kick him in the balls for me. Hard."

"I'm not kicking Dad in the balls." A corner of Amber's lips lifted in a weak half-smile. It was no mystery who she'd inherited her filthy mouth from. And while there wouldn't be kicking, she'd be tempted to at least slap him. "Do you have any guesses about what he wants after all this time?"

Her mother's sigh crackled in her ear. "Forgiveness, money, who knows? He's probably going mad with jealousy. I've seen a few articles in the paper about your band. If they're talking about you in Alaska, I can only imagine what press you're getting in a big city like Chicago. Maybe he wants to leech onto your fame because he failed to get it himself."

"Mom..."

"I'm serious. In college, that man played shitty bars every weekend, swearing he'd be the next Keith Moon. He drank and did enough drugs in those days to rival ol' Keith in that department."

"Why didn't he make it?" She'd never asked but always wondered. He played clubs all the time, sometimes backing major acts when they rolled into town, but success eluded him.

"If you asked him, he'd say I wasn't supportive enough. That means I didn't let him drag us all to Chicago so he could chase his dream by backing local blues bands, praying for the day some producer recognized his 'genius' and gave him a record deal. In the meantime, we would've been at home, broke, wondering when he was coming home." She scoffed. "That's how it went anyway, except he wasn't mooching off us while chasing an impossible dream. Well, impossible for assholes with swollen egos who are only in it for the groupies, cash, and fame."

Amber didn't know how to respond. It was a side of him she'd never seen, but she believed her mother.

She relit her joint and puffed with her hand over the receiver. "I hate these questions hanging over my head. I want to know what he wants, but I also want to tell him to fuck off back to the life he chose over us."

Hearing about Amber and her sisters meeting Nick would hurt her mother even more, so she kept that to herself.

"If you want to hear his reasons to put your nagging mystery to bed, have at it. But you'll probably regret it." Her mom cleared her throat. "What else has been going on in your life? How are your sisters?"

"They're fine." Amber ashed the joint. "The record's doing really well. Our manager thinks we'll hit platinum before Europe."

"That's great, honey! I listened to it yesterday, and though punk rock isn't my cup of tea, I liked it."

Even if she said it to be nice, Amber appreciated the support.

While the conversation's vibes were positive, it seemed like a good time to talk about Matthew. She was nervous, but her mom deserved to know about Amber's life beyond her band.

"I'm seeing someone. Matthew. He's already met Beth, Denise, and Kate and got their seal of approval. I think you'd like him too."

The line went quiet, and Amber took a long drag, waiting, hoping her mom could just be happy for her this time.

"Keep your eyes open, Amber."

The smoke rushed from her lungs in a loud exhale. "Please don't start with the 'all men are shit' lecture." She'd heard it so much, she knew it by heart.

"I want you to protect yourself, honey. So you don't end up like I did. Maybe it's all roses and sunshine now, but there will come a day when he gets tired of doing the work it takes to keep a relationship alive. They all do."

It hurt that instead of asking what Matthew was like, her mom defaulted to assuming he was just another asshole. Matthew was nothing like her father. If anything, Amber would be the one off chasing her dreams while he held things together back home.

"Mom..."

"That's all I'm going to say. I'm meeting your Aunt Rita for coffee, so I have to go. I love you. Hug your sisters for me."

They said their goodbyes, and Amber tried to shake off her mom's usual words of warning. She meant well and had valid reasons to feel the way she did, but it wasn't easy to hear how cynical and closed-off she still was to the idea not all men are heartless bastards who inevitably run away.

When Amber's dad left, her mom had a complete nervous breakdown. That was followed by months of depression that made her unable to function. Raising five headstrong daughters on a receptionist's salary while nursing a shattered heart was impossible. It broke her. Amber and her sisters did their best to take care of her and each other, but it was terrible seeing their once-happy mother too distraught to leave the bed in her darkened bedroom. She tried different medications, but they all made her feel like a zombie, so she'd stop taking them a few days in.

They would've lost their house if it hadn't been for Amber's grandmother paying it off. It quickly became clear a major thing holding their mother back from healing was that the house, and even the city, held too many memories. Even the good ones had soured in her mind, tainted by how everything turned out.

One day, Kate called a meeting with all the sisters. They knew their mother would never get better if she stayed, so they agreed to work together to keep the house up and take care of each other. A month later, their mom left for Anchorage to live with their Aunt Rita, focusing on her mental health and mending her broken heart. The move was supposed to be temporary, but she fell in love with Alaska. There, she found herself again, and her depression lifted. The sisters didn't want to risk setting back her progress, so they told her to stay.

Her mom had every right to feel the way she did about Amber possibly reconnecting with her dad. How could someone who put his family at risk of being on the streets and rejected his children ever deserve forgiveness?

That question would have to wait. She didn't know if he'd come around again and had no interest in returning to the rat hole motel to track him down. Hell, he might be back in Chicago, chasing an impossible dream and leaving his wife and kid home alone while he chased it.

The conversation with her mom poked at the fears that kept Amber lonely for so long. Would Matthew get tired of sleeping alone while she was on tour? Would he pull away when she was working herself so hard, there wasn't much time and energy left for him? As tempting as it was to let herself fully trust him, the fear her mother's warnings would prove true someday might never fully leave her.

But it was useless to worry about things out of her control, and the strong marijuana made that easy. Amber finished the joint, curled up on her bed, and closed her eyes. Soon, all her muscles relaxed, and she let a warm, soothing wave of calm pull her under.

33

Matthew

Matthew sat across from Tyler in a back corner booth at Mac's, a dimly lit downtown pub that smelled like stale beer, cigarette smoke, and French fry grease. Peanut shells littered the floor, and a group of college-aged guys and their girlfriends occupied the two pool tables near the bar. The Rolling Stones played on the jukebox, punctuated by the occasional crack of the cue ball hitting its target.

Tyler was in one of his usual baseball caps pulled low with his hair tucked underneath. So far, only a handful of their Beer and Bitching sessions had been spoiled by a fan recognizing him. It usually began with a loud gasp or a high-pitched squeal that meant fun time was over, and they had to bail.

So far, no one had noticed except possibly the bartender, whose gaze lingered a bit too long before a brief shake of her head.

"I'm glad you could make it this week, Ty."

Tyler was too busy with wedding preparations and band business to make it to their weekly pub hang the last two weeks. They'd seen each other at the record release party and spent some time together at the reception at least. Matthew was busy with Amber, so he couldn't complain.

The quick honeymoon was over so Charlotte could get back for another round of promotional events for their new album. It was the perfect opportunity to catch up over a few beers.

"Let's see if you still feel that way after I tell you what I'm about to tell you."

"Seriously?" Matthew frowned, disappointed this wasn't going to be the laidback quality time with his brother he was hoping for. "We finally get to go out for drinks, and you're going to toss heavy shit at me?"

"Finish your beer." Tyler made eye contact with the nearest server and held up two fingers.

She nodded, heading to the bar to grab them another round.

Matthew chugged the rest of his Imperial IPA, swallowing past the tightness as anxiety crept in.

The server put their empty glasses on a tray and set two fresh beers onto their coasters. When she glanced at Tyler, she did a double take. "Oh, my god. Are you—"

"Nope," Tyler said, shaking his head, "But I get that a lot."

She didn't seem satisfied, but let it drop. When she was gone, Tyler leaned across the table on his elbows.

"I talked to Eliza a few weeks ago. After you told me about Rafael's brother surprising you. She met with his family to hear them out and to see if she sensed any bad intentions."

"And?" Matthew wrapped his hands around his glass. That wasn't what he was expecting to hear, and it was the last thing he wanted to think about while things were finally going in the right direction for him. Now, he was even more frustrated by the loss of the stress-free night out.

"She said they seem like normal people grieving a loss and trying to make sense of it. She did a background check, and so did I. Rafael's the only one in their family who's had trouble with the law."

Matthew pulled the bottle of pills from his pocket and dropped two onto his tongue. There were at least seventy left from Dr. Vega's final refill. He hadn't needed them in weeks, but he could already tell things would go badly if he didn't block the panic before it could take hold.

He grabbed his beer and took a swig, struggling to swallow past the lump in his throat. Even if he could think of a response to what Tyler said, the words would be stuck anyway.

Tyler's brows pinched. "I thought you couldn't mix those with alcohol."

Matthew ignored him. "Are we supposed to go to their house for fucking tea and cookies or... what? This is ridiculous." Suddenly feeling lightheaded, he rested his head in his hands.

"You don't have to do it, but Charlotte thinks it'll help. It's up to you."

"So now Charlotte knows. And she's in? How the fuck can she want to shake hands with these people? And how can you trust they don't want to hurt her? That they won't look at her and see a killer who took away someone they love?"

"Watch it." Tyler's tone was low and edged with warning. "And keep your fucking voice down. I know you're upset, and I understand what you're saying, but I really don't think that's what this is. I was against it, too, before Eliza met with them. She's a great judge of character and wouldn't risk Charlotte's safety either." Tyler sipped his beer. "And we agreed on conditions."

"What conditions?" Blood rushed in Matthew's ears while he waited for the pills to take hold.

Tyler pulled a pack of nicotine gum from his pocket and shoved two pieces into his mouth.

They both had their vices.

"We're meeting in a neutral location we choose. They sign a non-disclosure agreement to ensure nothing said in that room leaves that room or we sue them blind. A bodyguard will be there we hire, and he'll check for recording devices as an extra precaution. That's especially important with tabloid rats sniffing around." His lungs deflated in a sigh. "And the bodyguard checks them for weapons."

Matthew's knee bounced under the table as the details sank in. "You're worried enough to check for weapons and hire a bodyguard, but you're still letting Charlotte be in that room?"

Tyler's nostrils flared, his mouth pressed in a tense, tight line. "Do you think for a *second* I wouldn't do everything possible to keep her safe? And *let her*?" He glared at Matthew across the table, clearly angry but trying to keep his cool. "Have you fucking met my wife? She doesn't require or ask for my permission to do a goddamn thing. She wants to help these people, so I'm doing everything in my power to eliminate the risks."

Matthew ran a trembling hand through his hair. "I still can't believe you're agreeing to this."

Tyler gave a weak shrug. "I'm going to be there for Charlotte and for you if you decide to go."

"When?"

"In a week. The twenty-fourth at noon." Tyler's gum popped and snapped between his teeth, grating Matthew's frayed nerves. "I can see Charlotte needs to do this. Maybe we all do. Like you couldn't say no to Jessica needing help after losing that patient, Charlotte can't say no to another mother in pain."

Matthew nodded slowly, thinking. Should he do this? Would revisiting that night to help a couple of strangers help him too, or would it set back his progress?

There was no way to know for sure until he was in the room with his attacker's family staring him in the face, and it was too late to back out.

The thought made him want to dig into the pill bottle in his pocket to pop another one.

"I'll think about it."

Tyler reached across the table, setting a reassuring hand on his wrist. "No pressure, but I hope you come." He sat back in his seat, his jaw working as he chewed his gum. "Fucking hell, I need a cigarette."

"So do I and I don't even smoke." Matthew didn't know how much more stressful talk he could handle and was grateful for the subject change. "What you need is to watch your kid grow up by not dying of lung cancer."

Tyler met his eye, sadness overtaking his expression. He must be thinking the same thing—how nice it would've been to have their dad alive when they were growing up. Tyler could've been a kid instead of a substitute parent. Matthew would've had a strong, capable guide to teach him how to be a man who could survive anything and come out swinging. He might've been better at relationships if he'd had more time to watch how his parents kept their connection strong. And he and Tyler wouldn't have a permanent hole in their hearts nothing could ever completely fill.

"Thanks, Matty. I needed to hear that." Tyler sank lower in his seat. "With all the major things happening in my life, I've been thinking about Dad a lot lately. I hate that he missed my wedding and that he'll never hold his first grandkid."

The warm, soothing pull from the pills and alcohol began to set in, and Matthew leaned in hard to the chemical relief. "He would've loved Charlotte."

"Yeah." Tyler smiled, but it didn't touch his eyes. "He would've loved Amber too. Dad thought drummers were the coolest part of a band. Or he just said that to mess with me because he knew I loved guitars."

They laughed together, the somber mood lifting. Matthew appreciated it whenever Tyler shared memories of their dad. From stories Matthew heard from family and what he'd seen in the photo albums he'd flipped through, Jude Anthony Hall crammed a lot of living in the thirty years before a motorcycle accident took his life.

There were so many things about him Matthew was too young to understand or remember, but he was grateful for the things his mind held onto. Like the way their dad's aftershave smelled or how it sounded when he laughed—that deep, joyful sound echoing through their cozy little house. Tyler knew him longer and was older when their dad passed, so his memories were stronger of the man they lost far too soon. That was impossible not to envy.

"So…" Tyler spit his gum into a napkin and wadded it up. "Speaking of Amber, what's up with you guys?"

"I told her I love her."

Tyler's eyebrows shot to the ceiling. "I'm glad I spit out my gum because I'd probably be choking on it. That's huge, man."

Matthew sipped his beer and held it in his hands, the cool condensation dampening his fingertips. "The night of your wedding, I slept in the dark for the first time since the attack. She made me feel so safe and comfortable, I didn't even realize I'd turned out the light until she mentioned it. And she helped me get over my fear of the parking lot at work. And fucking water bottles. Hell, I haven't even had a nightmare since the first night she slept over." He turned his glass, watching the tiny bubbles pop in the foam at the top of his hoppy, golden ale. "I've spent months under the control of my trauma, hiding, avoiding my triggers to avoid pain. With her... I finally feel like I'm strong enough to face them."

"Damn, Matty." The broad grin stretching Tyler's face eased the last threads of anxiety tightening Matthew's chest. "I can't tell you how happy I am to hear that."

"Thanks, brother."

"Keep in mind mistakes you've made in past relationships, and don't repeat them. *Learn* from them. That's something Dad drilled into my head. I wouldn't have had what it took to get Charlotte back after we broke up if I didn't learn from all the fuck-ups that led to it."

Matthew nodded along, appreciating the words of wisdom.

Tyler had made a lot of mistakes in his life, but once he let go of Amy, his destructive vices, and the guilt and grief he held from their dad's death, he became like a new person.

He was stronger than ever.

Matthew couldn't think of a better source of inspiration for making the changes he needed to become stronger too.

34

Amber

Beth's scream startled Amber awake.

She was supposed to sleep over at Matthew's, but after the stressful talk with her mother and the strong weed that accompanied it, she fell asleep on her bed and zonked out for hours.

The scream sent her running through the house.

Tara was hugging Beth beside the open front door, telling her everything was going to be okay. Beth clutched a magazine in her fist and threw it across the room. Amber moved out of the way to dodge it.

"What the fuck, Beth?"

"Sorry, sweetie." Beth left the hug, moving toward Amber with slow, cautious steps. Her demeanor and the fact that she'd used a nice nickname instead of making a smartass dig made Amber even more nervous. "I didn't see you there. Did you sleep okay?"

"Yeah, until you screamed like someone was running at you with a fucking axe." Amber rubbed the sleep from her eyes. "What's going on?"

Tara glanced at Beth. "Grab a bottle of the good wine Kate keeps stashed above the fridge and three glasses."

"Wine? It's..." Amber glanced at the clock on the VCR. "Six thirty in the morning."

"Trust me." Beth sighed heavily. "You're gonna want wine for this."

The opened bottle of Cabernet sat on the coffee table in front of the three women seated on the couch, full glasses in their hands. Amber chewed her thumbnail as she waited for Beth to spill whatever was on her mind. Tara got up, rifling through the scattered pages of the magazine on the ground before grabbing one between pinched fingers like it was diseased.

She set the paper in Amber's lap.

The headline on the front made her want to throw up.

Wild Rocker's Dad Tells All

Right below it was a picture of Amber when she was twelve. Her dad's arm was around her shoulder like someone who loved his daughter. Like someone who wouldn't leave without a word a year later.

"What the fuck is this?" Her hand shook, and Beth took her glass and set it on the table.

"There's stuff about the other members of your band too," Beth said. "But the stuff about you is the worst."

She shushed her sister, skimming the body of the article.

Certain words and phrases burrowed underneath her skin, crawling around like bugs: *spoiled, promiscuous, taught her everything she knows about the drums*

Tears blurred the tiny black words, but they remained clear enough to tell her exactly what her father really thought about her—she was an obnoxious, uncontrollable inconvenience who wasn't worthy of his love.

"The motherfucker takes credit for your success!" Tara said through gritted teeth. "He taught you how to hold the sticks and bailed. Everything you have and everything you know came from hard work and dedication—two things he's never bothered with in his miserable fucking life."

Amber kept reading. "He basically calls me a slut."

Beth rubbed her back. "You're not alone in this, sis. There's also a nice little dig about his other 'wild, unruly' daughters and their 'cold, vindictive' witch of a mother. Like we all chased him away."

Tara scoffed, setting down her glass. "I guess we magically took away his access to phones and birthday cards for the past thirteen years too. Fucking dickwad."

Amber grabbed her wineglass, chugged half of its contents, and read aloud. "As the baby of the family, Amber was a spoiled, moody child and nothing was ever good enough. As her teenage years began, she became so out of control with boys and drugs that I felt like I lost her." Her voice trembled as tears flooded her eyes. "Like she'd killed the little girl who'd sit in my lap when I played drums and clapped with pride as she watched from backstage when I'd gig on the weekends. From the sidelines, she was dazzled by the life of a musician, and clearly, it drove her to be who she is today." She swallowed hard to shove back the bile rising in her throat. "I only hope she's stopped succumbing to destructive temptations."

Deep down, Amber was convinced his leaving was her fault.

Now, she was staring at the proof.

In the weeks after he left, Amber would lie awake in bed, reflecting on all the times he'd been disappointed by her grades, frustrated by her bickering with her sisters, or angry with her for forgetting to drag the garbage cans to the street. Once, he caught her in the backyard smoking pot with a girl from her soccer team, and after a screaming lecture, he ignored her for days. She was convinced his catching her making out with Derek Russell on their couch was the final straw.

After threatening Derek and kicking him out, her dad loomed over her with a red, twisted face. His expression reeked of something more hurtful than disappointment or shock—he looked disgusted.

"No boy will ever love or respect you if you look and act like a *slut*. Go wash the damn makeup off your face and change your clothes."

Four days later, he was gone.

His look of revulsion never left her. It was one thing when the idiots at school called her names, but when her own father did it—the man she loved and respected the most—she felt like the word *slut* was branded on her skin for everyone to see. He left because the little girl who sat on his lap while he played drums had grown into something dirty and shameful. Even when Amber learned about the affair, she remained convinced that if she'd been the good girl he'd wanted her to be, he wouldn't have left.

Nothing in her life had ever hurt worse.

The rebel she was doubled down—her skirts got shorter, her makeup thicker. She was hungry for attention and got plenty of it. But not from the person she needed it from most.

Amber shook her head to clear the memory.

It wasn't my fault.

Mostly, she knew that. But it was hard to fully believe it as the shock and pain from the words in the article consumed her.

"If I ever see that miserable asshole again," Beth growled, "I'll strangle him with my bare hands."

Tara set a comforting hand on Amber's knee. "It's all lies. You know that, right?"

It was almost that funny he claimed she was a boy-crazy druggie when her slutty stoner years came after he left. Like some twisted part of her was trying to prove him right.

Amber kept reading.

There were recent photographs of her father, looking exactly like when she'd seen him outside the club. In one, he stood outside her old elementary school. In another, he stood on the stage where she'd played her first Killing Daisies gig three years ago. How did he even know where it was? He sure as hell never asked her.

When he left Nick alone at the motel, he must've been giving this shithead reporter the grand tour of Amber's life.

The last photo made her bolt to the bathroom, barely making it before she stuck her head over the toilet and threw up.

A gentle hand held back her hair as she wretched over the bowl. From the shoes, she knew it was Beth. "I know, honey. I'm so sorry."

"He was in front of our fucking house, Beth!" Amber yanked off a few squares of toilet paper and wiped her mouth. "He brought a goddamn photographer here, stood in front of the house full of women he abandoned for a fucking *photo op*! Smiling!"

"There weren't any cars in the driveway, so we must've all been at work," Tara said from the doorway. "He probably waited for it, knowing we'd expose his bullshit to the reporter if we saw him out there."

Tears streamed down Amber's cheeks, and she buried her face in her hands and sobbed.

The betrayal was almost worse than when he'd first left. They'd had time for the wound to heal enough to be manageable, and this yanked it wide open and poured in the salt.

"I hate him." Amber's voice was muffled behind her hands.

The problem was, even after this, it wasn't true.

She didn't know what to do with all the feelings overwhelming her: regret, anger, betrayal, confusion, rejection, and so much pain as they all churned together in her gut.

"What am I supposed to do about this?" Amber looked up at her sisters, her gaze flickering between them.

"Nothing, babe." Tara brushed Amber's hair off her face, her mouth downturned in a frown laced with pity. "We already knew he was a useless, selfish asshole. This kind of shit is part of the career you've chosen, as fucked up as it is."

Beth scoffed. "I've read articles about Tyler being a wife abuser and that he has a foot fetish. Another said he's secretly gay, for fuck's sake! The opinions of people who believe this shit don't matter. And before you can say it, yes, I'm canceling my subscription."

"Damn right, you are." Tara helped Amber off the bathroom floor. "Now, let's go finish that bottle of wine, and draw devil horns and Hitler moustaches on Dad's photos."

Amber huffed a weak laugh. "Go get me a fucking pen."

35

Matthew

"S*leep well?"*

Matthew's eyes opened just as the flashlight clicked off.

Rafael kicked his knee in the dark.

Matthew groaned as fiery spikes of pain bloomed at the spot and radiated down his calf.

He could hear breathing and sense the mass of the figure looming over him, but the darkness made it impossible to make out any details.

Not knowing was always worse.

His mind ran wild, imagining Rafael raising a knife or pointing a gun at Matthew's head. He'd already been threatened with a gun, so it was around there somewhere. It ensured he went along with whatever they wanted him to do.

Drink this.

Swallow this pill.

Stay quiet or I'll go shoot your brother in the head.

A crinkling noise snapped his head to the right. It sounded as if it were descending the steps along with a series of soft, steady taps.

"Hey, Matthew."

Amy.

His pulse spiked, and acid churned in the empty pit of his stomach.

Just the sound of that taunting fucking voice had Matthew's bound, aching hands curling into fists. They hadn't taken all the fight out of him yet, but they'd sure as hell tried.

"Remember how I said we'd punish you if you tried to escape?" Amy's voice grew closer along with the crinkling, and Matthew's heart thrashed wildly in his chest. "The duct tape on your ankles was torn." Her tongue clucked against her teeth. "Big mistake."

Panic seized his throat, his racing heartbeat thundering in his ears.

He'd kicked and twisted his legs for hours before the thick layers of tape finally gave. It felt like a victory until Rafael discovered what he'd done. Matthew was surprised when there hadn't been a consequence, but now... here it was.

"You boys have fun," she said.

The crinkling grew louder for a second before the tapping went back up the steps.

The overhead light flicked on, illuminating the cramped space that was stacked with random junk and cardboard boxes covered in black patches of mold.

Rafael stood over him holding a plastic bag.

Ice water flooded Matthew's veins at the sight of the blank, dead-eyed face staring down at him.

Without a word, he slipped the bag over Matthew's head.

Rafael squeezed the opening tightly around his neck, and after a few panicked breaths, all the air was sucked out. Matthew helplessly kicked and flopped on the cold concrete floor like a fish out of water, but the fucking monster only held tighter. The bag clung to Matthew's mouth and nose, his brain screaming for oxygen.

This is it.

Blackness bled into the edges of his vision, his chest burning with the desperate, primal need for air. Images of his brother, his friends, his father flickered through his mind.

Finally, Rafael released his hold and tossed the bag aside.

Matthew gasped and choked, hideous wheezing and gagging echoing in the space.

"Try it again and I won't be so nice next time."

Rafael stomped back up the stairs, darkness once again filling the room when he reached the switch at the top.

Matthew bolted upright in his bed, gasping for air.

When his eyes opened, he was greeted by the same blackness from his nightmare.

He reached for Amber but felt nothing but cold sheets.

A strangled cry cracked in his chest, and he groped for the switch on the bedside lamp. The violent tremors in his hands knocked the base, sending it crashing to the floor.

He tried to stand to turn on the overhead light, but his knees buckled and he collapsed beside the bed, sharp jolts of pain spiking in his wrists as they broke the fall.

"Fuck!"

You're safe. It was only a dream.

The darkness made it impossible to believe. Stinging sweat dripped into his eyes, merging with the tears of frustration and panic, but he was still too trapped in the nightmare to bother wiping it away.

He crawled on his hands and knees, groping blindly for any familiar objects that would lead him to the light switch on the wall.

When he reached the switch and flipped it on, the relief he'd hoped for didn't come.

He could see his bed, his dresser, and every other detail telling his brain he was out of that basement and safe.

But it refused to accept it.

Matthew's lungs burned just as they did when he was suffocating on that plastic bag, certain it was the end.

Sometimes, the nightmares felt so real, so visceral, he was convinced Rafael's vengeful ghost was to blame, torturing him with the only weapon he had left—Matthew's own mind.

This was one of those nightmares. And the worst by far since they'd begun.

They'll never stop. You're too broken to ever have a normal life again.

He dropped back down onto the cold, hardwood floor and hugged his knees to his chest, his body wracked with uncontrollable sobs.

He was angry at his brother for telling him about the meeting with Rafael's family. Since their talk the day before, an ominous feeling of dread had set in, digging its claws so deeply he was certain it'd triggered this.

But this wasn't Tyler's fault. It was Matthew's stupid fucking brain, poisoned by the aftereffects of the trauma that refused to let him go.

He crawled to his nightstand and retrieved the bottle of pills from the top drawer. He popped three and swallowed them dry, bitter powder coating his tongue as they started dissolving before hitting their mark.

He wanted to call Amber. To beg her to come over so he could hold her to his chest until he could breathe again. But she couldn't see him like this—so pathetically broken and weak.

Who could ever love someone they constantly had to take care of?

And how could she ever count on him for anything if he couldn't even peel himself off the floor after a bad dream?

The clock on the wall said it was nearly seven in the morning. All the normal, sane people were still safe in their beds. The thought of going back to sleep and risking another nightmare was out of the question. He'd call Evan in an hour to say he couldn't make it to work. Fortunately, it was Thursday and there wasn't much to do until Monday besides watch the temperature on the tanks and serve people who came into the tasting room. The electrician was finishing up the wiring for the stage set-up, but all Evan had to do was let him in. Knowing he wasn't leaving his friend with a massive burden made Matthew feel a little less guilty.

Around quarter to eight, he finally stopped shivering. He tested his legs and was able to make it to the living room. He turned on every light in the house and sank into the couch.

Exhaustion threatened to pull him under, and he slapped his cheeks, fighting it. Matthew made a full pot of coffee and sucked down the whole thing in minutes, scalding his throat, but the jolt of energy from the caffeine racing through his blood felt good. He was still miserable, but at least he wouldn't be sleeping anytime soon.

It was tempting to smoke some pot to help him relax, but he was afraid it would cancel out the caffeine and make him tired again.

Matthew spent the next few hours zoning out in front of the television, not really watching but clinging to the distraction like a lifeline. He called Evan, lying about having a sore throat and headache to avoid the kind words of concern that would only worsen the guilt. Evan told him to take care of himself and that he'd handle things at the brewery over the weekend. Said he'd see him Monday. Doubtful.

At around eleven, Matthew's phone rang. The noise startled him before he flipped the channel to some Spanish soap opera and let the machine pick up.

"Matty, it's me."

Amber's voice streaming in from the kitchen made him turn up the volume on the TV to drown her out. Everything hurt too much already, and the ache to see her, touch her, smell her sweet, comforting scent made him feel even worse.

He'd get two words out before she knew something was wrong and rush over.

Matthew was in holey sweatpants, stubble darkened his face, and he still reeked of sweat and adrenaline from the nightmare. He couldn't stomach the thought of her seeing him like that. She'd already witnessed more than enough of his damage, and she'd done more than anyone else to help him get better. He thought he was, but clearly, it was all an illusion.

How would Amber feel to see the progress she'd helped him make erased? And she had more important things in her life that required her time and attention. It would be unfair to expect her to drop everything to babysit Matthew while he fell apart at the seams.

Fresh tears soaked the cushion pressed against his cheek.

This was worse than falling apart. It was like sinking into a cold, black pit with nothing to grab hold of. If Amber wasn't ready for the biggest tour of her career because he dragged her down with him, he'd never forgive himself, and neither would she.

Pain ripped through his chest at the thought of losing her, but after this, he had to let her go. To save her from a life she didn't deserve—a life wasted on trying to fix the unfixable.

Amber deserved someone who could wake up without screaming and sleep beside her in the dark without losing their shit. Someone who wasn't cursed with relentless demons that would eventually claim her too, if she made the mistake of falling in love with him.

Now, Matthew was grateful she hadn't. Because as hard as it was to accept, the only way to save her was to set her free.

36

Amber

After the machine picked up at Matthew's for the fourth time, Amber slammed the phone, frustration heating her face. He'd be getting ready for work, so why wasn't he picking up? She needed to hear his voice and ask if he'd seen the tabloid. It was strange he hadn't called the night before when she hadn't shown up as planned.

Your life's too messy.

He's done with you.

She knew Matthew wouldn't bail on her so easily, but it didn't stop the intrusive thoughts from creeping in. She was about to drive over to see if he was home when the phone rang.

"Hello?"

"Hey, it's Charlotte." She was silent for a few beats. "I read the article. I wanted to check on you before the band stuff later. You okay?"

"Fuck no." Amber sat cross-legged on her bed, the phone tucked beneath her ear. "I don't know how you and Tyler have been putting up with this shit for so long and stayed sane."

"Sane is debatable." She huffed a laugh. "People will whisper behind your back for a while, the real dickheads will say shit to your face, and then it'll pass. I promise."

"I guess I need to develop a thicker skin if this is what it's like in the big leagues." Amber gnawed her thumbnail, a nasty nervous habit that'd reduced it to a jagged stump. "I'd hoped since I hide at the back of the stage, I'd get a pass."

"No such luck. Ask Adam. When they toured Australia, someone snapped a shot of him swimming naked in the ocean. Of course, it only boosted his reputation as a sexy bad boy. Can you imagine the headlines if it were one of us?"

"Punk Slut Has a Splashing Good Time?"

Charlotte went quiet. "You can't see me, but I cringed hard at that word. He had no right to imply that's what you were. Your own father!"

Amber tore his photo from her wall and shoved it into the trashcan. "Fuck him. I hope I never see his stupid Kurt Loder-looking ass again." She returned to gnawing on her thumbnail, pent-up frustration buzzing in her veins.

"I thought he looked familiar. Anyway, fuck him is right. You should've heard the things Tyler wanted to do to your dad after he read it. The most violent horror movie scripts aren't that graphic."

"That's sweet in a sick kind of way." Her nail cracked between her teeth, and she flinched. A dot of blood rose from the break as it throbbed. "Have you heard from Matthew?"

"No, why?"

"I keep calling and getting nothing. I was supposed to sleep over last night, but I crashed out early at my place. I hope he's not upset about that."

"Matty? Not a chance. If he's mad, he tells you. Maybe he went to work early."

"Maybe. I'll try there in a few. Thanks for checking on me. See you at rehearsal."

"Wait!" Charlotte sighed. "One last thing, and this one's a little selfish. *Please* try to kick your dad's bullshit out of your head. Seriously. We have a *huge* tour starting in a few months, and we all need to focus. And the haters who say we don't deserve this boost or that we earned it in any way except hard work and ass-kicking will eat their fucking words."

"I know." Amber held a tissue over her bloody nail. "The best revenge is success and all that."

"Exactly. See you later, babe."

Amber flopped backward on her bed, so emotionally wrung out, her body ached. Someone knocked softly on her door.

"You awake?"

"Yeah, Kate." Amber waved her in as the door cracked open. She hadn't had a chance to talk about the article with her oldest sister and wasn't looking forward to rehashing the details. "Come on in."

Kate climbed onto the bed, lying beside Amber. "Hey, sis."

When Amber was sick or broke up with a boy and needed comfort, Kate would lie with her like his. She'd stroke her hair and tell her everything would be okay. Amber wasn't in the mood to hear that this time because the pain was still too new and raw for *okay* to feel like a possibility.

"Did you know," Kate said, "that I was Dad's favorite before Tara came along?"

Amber gave a weak shake of her head.

"She was the favorite until Denise was born. Then, it was Beth. Then, your tiny blonde self came along with that million-watt smile and dimpled cheek, and we were all chopped liver."

"Wow," Amber deadpanned. "Way to cheer me up."

"When we were little, we didn't see his flaws. He got to be the fun dad who spun us around in the air and carried us to bed tucked against his chest if we fell asleep in the car. We didn't notice Mom was doing all the hard stuff. She made sure our teeth were brushed and our clothes were clean while he was off playing make-believe rockstar."

Amber turned to face her sister. "What's your point?"

"My point is, his betrayal and rejection say a lot more about him than it does about any of us. Instead of loving his kids unconditionally and being a good husband, he played favorites, breaking our hearts one by one. Instead of changing into a good man, he's still a selfish, backstabbing prick who sold his family out for a payday. He exploited his successful daughter, probably because he was jealous you made it while he became more of a sad has-been that never was. His opinion means shit."

"He called me a slut, Kate."

"I'm not defending him, but he didn't say that *exactly*."

"Not in the article. Right before he left. He came home from work early and caught me making out on the couch with Derek Russell. Clothes on, hands nowhere inappropriate, by the way. He kicked Derek out, scowled at me like I was trash, and said no boy would ever love or respect me if I kept looking and acting like a slut."

Kate frowned, sympathy in her eyes. "Oh, Amber."

"He left four days later. When I thought of the disgusted look on his face when he caught us…" She shrugged, her chin wobbling at the memory. "How could I not blame myself?"

Kate's eyes grew wet with unshed tears. "Honey, it wasn't your fault."

"I know that now." There were still times she doubted it, but mostly, she knew she wasn't to blame. "But it doesn't change the fact that thousands of people woke up this morning and read that my own father thinks I'm a worthless slut."

"Listen to me." Kate pressed her forehead to Amber's. "You are not and have never been a slut. Dad started abandoning us long before he packed that suitcase. When we were grumpy teenagers with acne and synced-up periods, we weren't so fun anymore, and he pulled away. That left you vulnerable with a hole in your heart. So, you sought out male affection and connection because you didn't get it at home. It was his fault, not yours."

Amber had never thought of it that way before. She didn't know exactly what drove her into the arms of random guys, but she'd felt a desperate need inside her to feel wanted nothing seemed to satisfy.

Until Matthew came along.

"Matthew told me he loves me."

Kate grinned. "That's wonderful, sweetie. I like him a lot. I think he's good for you."

"I feel something stronger than I've ever felt before, but I don't know if it's love. What if I don't have it in me to ever love him back? What if he quits on me because I can't let go of my fear of him quitting on me?" She had let it go when they were together at the inn, but the talk with her mom nudged it back into her mind and heart. His not answering her calls pushed it further.

"Oh, honey." Kate stroked Amber's hair and her eyes slid closed at the comforting sensation. "You're overthinking it. Turn down the volume on that busy brain of yours and focus on how you feel. If he's the right guy for you, he'll wait until you're ready to love him back."

As usual, Kate was right—Amber's brain was on overdrive, buzzing so loudly with doubts and insecurities she couldn't hear whatever her heart had to say. Or maybe, she wasn't ready to listen to it.

Kate took Amber's hand, weaving their fingers together. "I'm so proud of you, little sister. In a few months, you'll be on the biggest adventure of your life. If you ever doubt yourself, remember how far you've come and all you survived to get there."

Amber blinked back tears as Kate got to her feet. She bent at the waist to kiss Amber's forehead. "I'm going to make you one of my famous grilled cheese sandwiches with a side of tater tots, and we're going to gorge on comfort food until I meet with a new client at two."

"Thanks, Kate."

"Anytime, butterfly."

Amber smiled at the nickname she hadn't heard in years.

Kate used to call her that because Amber would spend hours outside, standing by the bush in the backyard that overflowed with pink flowers every spring. Tiny yellow and black butterflies would land on the petals, and she'd carefully cup them inside her hands. It was thrilling to feel their little wings beat against her fingers before she opened her hands and watched them fly away.

Letting go was the best part.

She got out of bed and put on jeans and the T-shirt she'd stolen from Matthew. It still faintly smelled like him, which made it a little easier to wash her face, run a brush through her hair, and start the day.

After having lunch with Kate, Amber called High Notes. Evan answered, saying Matthew was home sick. He seemed fine when he dropped her off after returning from the wedding. Maybe he caught something then. There were at least two hundred guests, and it was autumn, so germs were everywhere.

He still hadn't answered his home phone, so she grabbed a few cans of soup from the pantry, along with tea bags and cough drops, before driving to Matthew's. His car was in the driveway, and his lights were on.

Amber knocked on his door, softly at first in case he was asleep.

Nothing.

She knocked a little louder—still nothing.

After about ten minutes and a few more knocking attempts, she left the stuff she'd brought to help him feel better on the porch and drove to Charlotte's to rehearse for the upcoming tour.

She couldn't help feeling a sting of rejection.

Why hadn't he reached out?

Of course, it'd only been a day since they talked. She'd thought her schedule would keep them apart, but so far, they'd made it work. Still, just because they'd seen each other nearly every day since getting together didn't mean it would always be that way. He had a life too. Was she being too clingy and needy?

The band worked through the night, and she drove past Matthew's on her way home. His porch and living room lights were off, so she kept driving.

Her mind raced in the silent car, drifting down the same dark avenues they did anytime she started to care about someone, and she feared they were pulling away.

He's bored with you.

Your baggage is too much for him to handle.

When he said he loved you, he didn't mean it.

No man could ever really love you.

Tears flooded her cheeks, blurring the road ahead.

Did Matthew read the article? Maybe that's why he was keeping his distance. Now that the media frenzy he'd dealt with after his attack had finally died down, why would he want to risk getting tangled up in Amber's mess?

When she reached her driveway and shut off her car, she slumped against the steering wheel and cried until her eyes hurt. The autumn chill crept into the car, making her shiver. Cold and exhausted, she shuffled inside the house before crawling into bed and crying some more. When the sun brightened the pale gray curtains on her window, she pulled the covers over her head before finally drifting off to sleep.

Angry shouting in another room jolted Amber awake. She rubbed her tender eyes and shuffled down the hallway, her feet bare and cold on the hardwood.

"You're not welcome here!" Kate's volume and the rage in her tone made Amber jog toward the living room to see what was going on.

When she rounded the corner, her heart jumped to her throat. "Dad?"

Bryan Jamison, their asshole father, stood with his hands braced in the doorway while Kate tried to shove him back outside. The man was still built like a linebacker, and her five-foot-seven frame wasn't getting anywhere.

His head whipped to the right. "Amber! Please tell your sister to let me in. I just want to talk."

"You had thirteen years to explain yourself," Kate gritted out. "We sure as shit don't want to hear your excuses for selling out your own daughter. Get out!" She screamed it in his face, her cheeks as red as the streaks in her hair.

Amber wouldn't be surprised if the neighbors called the cops. She moved behind her sister. "It's okay, Kate. I got this."

"Good," he said, a smirk tugging at the corners of his mouth beneath the thick, salt-and-pepper mustache. "At least one of my daughters is willing to hear me out."

"Amber, no!" Kate's shoulders tensed. "After what he did to you?"

"Let's go to the sidewalk." Amber gestured at the front yard. "We'll give Kate a break."

While he walked down the driveway with his back turned, Amber grabbed the garden hose and cranked it on full blast. She aimed the nozzle at the back of his head, squeezing the metal trigger to increase the pressure.

Her dad turned around, sputtering as water blasted him in the face. "Amber, what the—" He ducked behind his car to avoid the spray.

"You have some fucking nerve coming here!" She aimed the nozzle at his opened car window and soaked the interior. "You called me names, sold my fucking story to the wolves, and tried to take credit for my success! Over a decade after you fucking *left us*!"

"Amber, turn the goddamn water off and listen!" He frantically tried to get in his car, presumably to close his window, but he kept dropping his keys through slippery, frantic fingers.

"No, *you* fucking listen!" She held the hose steady as the stream flooded his car, water gushing out the cracks beneath the doors. "You left mom all alone to take care of five daughters, a house, and a mountain of your debts. She had a nervous fucking breakdown because you piled so much bullshit on her shoulders. You never called or even sent a damn Christmas card. Then, we find out from Grandma you started a whole new family. Like it was so easy to replace us with newer, shinier versions. Now you've failed them too!"

Confusion flashed in his expression before falling away. "Amber, stop!" He managed to get the window up, and she tossed the hose to the ground. "This isn't who you are!"

She stomped to where he hid behind his car, shoving his shoulders so hard he stumbled back a step. "How the *fuck* would you know who I am? Everything I am is because of Mom, my sisters, and my hard work. Something you know nothing about. I made it without you, and I sure as hell don't need anything from you now, so do what you do best. Walk away and don't look back."

"I'm sorry," he said, throwing up his dripping hands. "For all of it. I can explain if you let me. That's why I went to your show. To explain and apologize."

She wasn't interested in hearing his excuses or apologies. As soon as Nick told her how their dad rejected him, she was resigned to the fact he could never be forgiven. The article cemented it further.

Now, she wanted him gone for good.

Sirens squealed from up the street, and Amber rolled her eyes. "Fucking perfect."

A police car with flashing lights stopped in front of the house.

Kate slung an arm around Amber's shoulders. She must've been watching and enjoying the show. "Nice job, sis. I've got plenty of lawyer friends and bail money if you need it."

As he exited his squad car, the officer's eyes roamed over the very wet domestic dispute. "Can someone explain what's going on here?"

Amber's dad opened his mouth, but she cut him off.

"This is our dad, a loser deadbeat who bailed on us years ago and sold me out to a tabloid. He was just leaving."

"Okaaay." The cop's eyebrows lifted as he peeked inside the soaked car. "What's with all the water?"

"My daughter and I had a disagreement, sir." Their dad squeezed water out of his shirt. "Everything she said is correct, and I'm not pressing charges."

Kate scoffed. "We should press charges for defamation, you miserable shit."

The officer held up a hand as if to say *cool it*. "No more screaming in the street or name-calling, please. How about everyone goes their separate ways, and dries off?" His lips twitched with amusement as he stared at their dad who stood dripping on the concrete, looking like a drowned rat.

"Works for us," Kate said. "Sorry you had to come out here for this, officer."

"Wait." His head cocked as he studied her face. "Are you Kate Jamison?"

"Yes, why?"

The officer nodded, recognition flashing in his eyes. "You helped my sister with her divorce after her husband left her for her best friend. Well, former best friend now, obviously. I remember you from the hearing." He grinned, clearly impressed. "You were a shark. Got her everything she asked for plus some."

Kate smiled back, her cheeks flushed pink. "That's what I do." She pointed at her dad. "And that's why I do it. I saw firsthand what abandonment does to families and made it my mission to stick it to assholes like him while getting women and children what they deserve."

Their dad nodded his stupid wet head. "So, both of you have me to thank for your success?"

Kate's eyes narrowed in a glare. "Amber, hand me the hose."

The cop stepped closer. "Come on, now. No more of that." He turned to their dad as he shook out his drenched hair like a bulldog climbing out of a swimming pool. "These ladies obviously don't want you at their home, so move along."

With his head shaking like he was the one who'd been wronged, their dad opened his door. Water streamed out from the floorboards and into the gutter, earning laughter from the three spectators on the sidewalk.

When the dripping car disappeared around the corner, the officer held out his hand to Kate and she shook it.

"I'm Officer Callen." He held on for a long moment before pulling his hand back. "You can call me Alan. And yes, I realize how ridiculous my name is, and I'm convinced my parents secretly hate me."

Kate laughed and touched her collarbone the way she did when she was about to flirt. That meant it was time for Amber's exit.

"Thanks for sending him off," Amber said to the cop. "See you inside, Kate."

"From now on, young lady," he said, "use your hose to water flowers, not human beings." His eyebrow lifted above his sunglasses. "Although, it sure sounded like he deserved it."

37

Matthew

The faces on the television vanished behind a dense white cloud of weed smoke.

After five days of experimenting, Matthew had figured out exactly how many pills and how many puffs were the perfect combination to keep him numb. While it made the pain manageable, the awareness that the fix was temporary was always there.

At last count, there were forty-two pills left—enough for one more week.

While focusing all his energy on getting through one day at a time, what came after sat on the horizon, a horrifying unknown.

Whenever Amber stopped by, Matthew peeked out at her from between the curtains, fighting every desperate urge to fling the door open and pull her inside. He looked around at the sea of potato chip bags, pizza boxes, empty beer bottles, and other evidence of how far he'd sunk and couldn't do it.

The soup and other things she left on his porch to make him feel better made him feel worse. There was the guilt over lying about being sick. And for being a heartless asshole who shut her out.

Evan believed his lie about having the flu and left medicine by his door, heaping more guilt onto the pile. Finishing the music space was put on hold. The Halloween party they'd planned at the brewery, canceled.

Tyler stopped by a few times too, and he didn't answer for him either.

Matthew couldn't believe he was back to this.

Square fucking one.

Hiding from the world and doing anything it took to avoid triggering his panic or remembering the things that haunted his sleep. He almost understood why Tyler had taken heroin after losing his friend and mentor, Jim. When you're trapped inside a mind that runs your worst memories in an endless loop, a desperation to escape claws at your insides every second you're awake.

If someone handed him a "get out of this pain free" card, he'd gladly take it.

Amber sounded more worried with every message she left. She'd called at least five times a day at the beginning of his isolation, but as of yesterday, it was down to three.

She was losing hope.

Knowing how cruel it was to push away someone whose biggest fear was abandonment ate away at him. He'd tried picking up the phone to reach out countless times, but his unsteady hand always set it back in its cradle.

Matthew was a coward.

A weak, pathetic worm who hurt anyone stupid enough to care about him.

The phone rang.

Machine picked up.

Again.

"Hey, Matthew." Amber's voice shook. He could tell she'd been crying, and regret hit like a brick to the chest. "I can take a hint. Charlotte told me about the meeting with Rafael's family in a couple days, and if I know you like I think I do... you're probably in a bad place over it."

She sucked in a stuttered breath. "Well, guess what? Things aren't so great for me either. I wish you'd let me in so we could be there for each other."

She paused, the air stalling in his lungs as he waited. "But if there's one thing I know well it's that I can't force someone to stick around, especially when things get tough. It was fun while it lasted."

A tear slipped down his cheek.

"And also..." She sniffed. "Fuck you."

The line went dead.

Along with his hopes of ever being truly happy again.

38

Matthew

The knob on Matthew's front door jiggled along with the faint clink of metal. He ran to latch the deadbolt, but before he reached it, the door opened.

Charlotte walked in.

He'd forgotten he'd given her and Tyler a spare key.

Her eyes widened as she took a long look at him and then his living room.

"Okay." She rolled up the sleeves of her black sweater. "Now I know what I'm working with. Do you have clean towels?"

He blinked. "I think so."

"Good. Use one to take a *very* long shower because I love you, but you stink. Shave and brush your teeth while you're at it. You'll feel better when you don't look and smell like Sasquatch."

Despite his unkempt state, Charlotte stepped closer and hugged him tight. After seven miserable days, the loving, comforting touch instantly made tears flood his eyes. Matthew hesitated for a second before wrapping his arms around her and holding on tight.

"It's going to be okay." Charlotte's voice cracked with emotion and when she pulled back, she swiped her fingertips over her damp cheeks. "Now, seriously, go shower. And put on your most comfortable and hopefully clean sweatpants because we're about to kick it old school, my friend. Pepperoni or sausage?"

His lips twitched, the first smile in days threatening to break free. "Both."

"I like your style." She nudged him toward the hallway. "Go!"

When Matthew was shaved, dressed, and smelled human again, Charlotte was in the living room stuffing a garbage bag with the trash scattered around his living room. The dishwasher and washing machine were running. All the empty junk food bags and beer bottles were gone, and she'd even lit the sandalwood-scented candles on his coffee table.

"You didn't have to do all this, Charlotte."

"You're welcome." She kissed him on the cheek and kept cleaning.

He grabbed the vacuum and ran it over the weed stems, chip crumbs, and popcorn kernels on the carpet in front of the couch. Since the start of his isolation, if it didn't go into a microwave or get delivered to his porch, he hadn't eaten it. He wrapped up the cord and tucked the vacuum back into the closet.

"Matty, do you remember what I said to you in the park last summer, after we didn't talk for four days?"

He nodded, knowing exactly where she was going with this. "No more secrets."

"Right. No more secrets." She set down the almost-full trash bag and took a seat on the couch, patting the cushion beside her. "Your brother said I should give you more time to process the whole thing with Rafael's family, but I think you've done enough processing."

"I don't want to talk about this, Charlotte." Matthew rubbed at his temples as the beginnings of a headache throbbed in his skull. "Not now, not ever."

"Tough shit." Her mouth was set in a tight, determined line. "I'm not as easy to scrape off your shoe as your brother and Amber, and before I leave here, you're going to fucking talk to me."

He stayed quiet.

"Fine. I guess I'll get comfortable." Charlotte slipped off her shoes and set her feet on his coffee table, tucking her hands behind her head. "If you think you can out-stubborn me, you're sadly mistaken."

As they sat in silence, something fractured inside him.

With the weed, pills, and avoidance, Matthew had built a glass cage around his pain to keep it contained. Now, it was starting to break.

He trapped his bottom lip between his teeth as it trembled. Charlotte's feet dropped from the table, and she took his hand into hers.

Tears clouded Matthew's vision as flashes from his worst nightmare returned. "I thought he was going to kill me, Charlotte. Rafael put a fucking plastic bag over my head. Started suffocating me."

She whimpered and moved closer, wrapping an arm around his back as his limbs shook.

"I've never been so fucking scared in my life. I couldn't move, couldn't breathe, couldn't scream." He let the tears stream down his cheeks, soaking the front of his T-shirt. "Then he took the bag off and locked me in the darkness again."

Matthew raised his head. Charlotte was crying too, her eyes rimmed with red.

"You never told me that," she whispered.

He'd only told her details about his time in the basement he thought she could handle—the drugged water, duct tape, and darkness. She knew they threatened her and Tyler to keep Matthew compliant. He stuck to basic things that would fill in the gaps for her when he was missing for three days but wouldn't give her more reasons to worry.

"I never even told Dr. Vega that." He wiped his eyes with his sleeve. "That's the real reason I stopped going. We reached a point where there was too much I couldn't bear to say out loud. Whatever I talked about ended up in my nightmares. Like I'd woken them back up again. She wanted me to write them down, but I just wanted to forget. Then, when I dreamed about the bag the other night, I realized no matter what I do, I'll *always* be haunted by this shit." His voice broke. "I thought after more time passed, they'd stop. But they won't. I tried therapy, medications, even fucking yoga classes Jessica took me to. I keep trying to get better and put it all behind me, but I *can't*. This is who I am now, and I can't fucking stand the thought of living like this forever."

"This is all temporary, I promise you." She hugged him tightly and his eyes squeezed shut. "You've taken some of the right steps but haven't done everything it'll take to heal from something like that. Until you do, nothing will change, and probably, it'll keep getting worse."

"I'm obviously fucking clueless, Charlotte." He pulled away, meeting her watery gaze. "What are the right steps? How do I stop this?"

"I know it sounds impossible, but you need to meet with his family. You need closure. Then, give therapy another chance. I remember how hard it was to open up when I started. Trusting a stranger with your deepest fears and secrets isn't easy. But I couldn't live like I was, so I did everything Dr. Vega told me to. Eventually, I felt stronger. My fears weren't in charge anymore. I was. You push through when it's uncomfortable and work even harder. Or this will continue to haunt you and change you."

She was right. Meeting with Rafael's family sounded impossible. Matthew was more willing to try therapy again because he had to do *something*, but the thought of being in a room with that monster's family churned his stomach.

"I can't do it, Charlotte." He sniffed, exhaling a ragged breath. "When I looked at his brother, all I saw was the man who trapped me, drugged me, and made me think I was going to die. The man who almost killed you and Tyler."

"But it's *not him*. That's my point. I think if you face this fear head-on, you'll be able to move past it." She nudged his knee. "Do you remember that quote on Dr. Vega's wall about avoidance?"

How could he forget? The words stared him in the face at every session. He figured she'd purposely placed the framed poster at her patients' eye level to help the message sink in.

"Avoiding problems you need to face is avoiding the life you should be living."

"Exactly," she said. "You've been avoiding your friends, your family, and numbing yourself out to avoid thinking about the terrible shit you went through instead of facing it head-on. You're letting the fear win. I know it's tough, but Matty... you're tougher. You can heal from this, I promise."

"What if I can't?" As much as he wanted to believe her, he still couldn't see a way out that would actually stick.

"Do you remember the other quote on Vega's wall? Depression lies to you. It says you're not enough, you're weak, and things will never change. And they won't if you keep hiding and shoving your feelings aside. Maybe you need to get off the fucking pills, stop smoking weed for a while, and let your head clear."

The thought of letting the chemicals fade and waiting for the pain to rush back in was too overwhelming.

"Matty?" She frowned. "You haven't thought about…"

"What?"

"Hurting yourself?"

He'd reached a very dark place, but not that dark. He wanted to be numb and alive, not dead and buried. The rational part of his brain that was holding on by its fingertips assured him the pain wouldn't always be this bad.

"No," he said. "Never. I swear."

"Good. But if you ever do, you *need* to reach out." She hugged his arm, her chin resting on his shoulder. "I love you, Matthew Hall. Your brother loves you. Your friends love you. We know you can get back to the happy, sweet, strong guy you really are. Stop giving up and fight for it. You've come too damn far to let the bastards win."

She made it look and sound so easy. Charlotte once said that shooting Amy and Rafael helped heal her PTSD from the stalking. They'd made her scared and vulnerable, and she took the power back. Still, it was strange she seemed so unaffected by something so terrible.

"Do you ever think about that night?" he asked.

Charlotte nodded. "Of course. But before it digs its claws in, I picture Amy in her prison cell with a big, scary bunkmate. Having to shit and shower in front of other criminals. Eating lumpy mashed potatoes and salty commissary ramen in her ugly orange jumpsuit."

Matthew couldn't help smiling at the image.

"I fought for my life in that room," she said, "and I'll be damned if they get to spoil another second of it."

A knock on the door startled him.

"I don't want to see anyone like this." He pressed his palms into his raw, swollen eyes.

"Don't worry. It's probably the pizza." She peeked through the peephole and opened the door. The delivery guy handed over the pizza box, and she locked the door behind him.

Matthew shifted in his seat, and three DVDs spilled out of her purse. He picked them up, another weak almost-smile making his mouth twitch.

She set the pizza box on the coffee table and opened it, the scent of cheese, oregano, and salty meat filling the room. "Which one are we watching?"

"*Friday* will make me want to smoke more weed, so my vote's *Billy Madison*."

"I figured." She laughed, grabbing a slice and taking a bite. "You'd never pass up a movie with Farley in it." She put the DVD in the player and sat back down with the remote. Her familiar, calming presence made some of the misery he'd been stewing in finally lift.

"How's Amber?"

The mention of Chris Farley made him think of the movie night they shared. He was so at ease as they sat together and watched rain tap at the skylight above their heads. Why couldn't things have stayed that easy and uncomplicated? Over the past week, he kept wondering what she was doing and how she was handling his silence. Would she ever forgive him? How quickly would she move on and put him in her past? He couldn't stand the idea of her with someone else, but her happiness was all that mattered in the end.

"Does she hate me?" he asked.

"She could never hate you." Charlotte set the remote on her knee. "She's hurt that instead of opening up to her, you shut her out. A lot's happened with her, too, while you've been holed up in here. Maybe the timing's bad, and you both need to sort out your messes before trying again."

"What happened?" The corners of his mouth tipped down. "Is she okay?"

Charlotte hesitated before giving a nod. "She will be. It's just a temporary annoyance that comes with our job."

"Stop being vague. What's going on?"

Her mouth opened and quickly shut again. "I shouldn't have said anything. I promise it isn't that bad." She offered a sympathetic smile. "I know how much you love her. We've got her back, Matty. Just focus on what you need to do."

He hated that Amber was hurting but felt powerless to help when he couldn't even help himself. If it was something serious, Charlotte would've spilled without hesitation. Whatever it was, her friends and sisters could give her the support he couldn't.

"I'll see her at practice tomorrow. I'll talk to her. Everything you told me stays in this room, but I'll try to help her understand why you pulled back."

Matthew scrubbed his hands over his face, frustration heating his blood. "Fuck, things were going so well. But I took five steps forward, mostly with her help, and then a hundred steps back. She deserves better than the person I am now."

"Your stubborn brother used to say the same thing to me. That he was too broken to be the partner I deserved. When he finally faced his problems and changed..." She shook her head, a smile curving her lips. "He became the man he was meant to be. The man he knew I deserved. It took struggle and pain to get there, but he did it. And you can do the same." She picked up the remote and started the DVD.

As the movie played, Matthew thought about everything she'd said.

If he met with Rafael's family, he wouldn't be facing them alone. He'd have the support of two people who loved him. They'd have his back if he fell apart.

And if he didn't fall apart, maybe it really would help to put the trauma behind him for good. Maybe this was exactly what he needed to take his power back.

"I'll do it."

Charlotte's head snapped to him. "Really?"

Matthew nodded, still not fully convinced, but willing to give it a shot. "But I reserve the right to run the fuck out of there if it's too much."

"Of course." She tried to hide her satisfied grin as she turned to the movie, laughing at the giant penguin on the screen.

"Hey." Matthew nudged her elbow. "Thanks for... everything."

She set her pizza slice on the lid of the box. "Do you know how many times you came over when I was scared to leave my house? I thought my life would never be good again, and you pulled me out of the dark." She rested her head on his shoulder. "Glad I can return the favor."

39

Amber

The vibe in Charlotte and Tyler's studio was as disjointed and murky as Amber felt.

"Damn, ladies." Luke pinched the bridge of his nose with a head shake. "We suck today."

Charlotte had just returned from throwing up for the second time and nodded in agreement. "Sorry I keep running to the bathroom. I swear I'll be ready for the tour, I just—"

"Nope." Sandra cut her off. "No apologizing for shit you can't control. Or puke you can't control."

"It's my fault," Amber said, wiping sweat from her hairline with her wrist. It was obvious by all the concerned glances thrown her way when she stumbled or missed a beat that they all knew it, but they'd never say it. "My head's somewhere else, and I'm throwing Luke off."

The rhythm section needed to be tight to support everyone else, and Amber wasn't holding up her end. She swore she'd never let a guy affect this part of her life, but all she could think about was the shit with Matthew. Along with not trusting a man to stick around, it was another self-imposed rule she'd broken that left her with nothing to show for it but frustration and a broken heart.

"Are we calling it?" Luke asked. "Think it over while I take a piss."

Sandra's nose wrinkled as she slung her guitar to her back on its strap. They were still getting used to having a dude in the band and the delightful phrases and habits that went along with it. At least this time, he hadn't belched or scratched his balls.

Once he left, Charlotte faced the drums.

"Amber, we need to talk." She crunched a saltine and chased it with ginger ale. "When Luke leaves, you girls should hang back."

"If it's a Matthew thing," Amber said. "I'm not in the fucking mood. He made his choice."

Not being in the mood was an understatement. Now, she wanted to forget. Her head was filled with happy memories from their friendship and brief time together, making it more painful to let him go.

Scratch that.

He'd let *her* go.

She was the one being forced to accept it and move on.

"It's not that simple," Charlotte said.

"Sure it is." Amber set her sticks in her lap. "I'm not going to sit around anymore wondering if I did something wrong, if telling me he loved me scared him off, or if he's yet another guy to get what he wanted out of me and bail."

Her mother was right—all men leave. Amber had hoped like hell Matthew would've proven that wrong, but he only reinforced it. Whether they got bored, grew tired of her complications, or only wanted one thing, they always fucking left.

Charlotte frowned, an angry line forming between her brows. "You know him better than that."

"Do I?" Amber huffed. "Because I sure as shit never saw this coming. I'm halfway tempted to attack Luke just to fuck Matthew out of my head."

Of course, as she said it, Luke walked back into the studio.

"You're gorgeous, and I'm flattered, but—"

"I wasn't serious. I'm just upset. Sorry. But if I wasn't already in love—" Amber slapped a hand over her big, stupid mouth. It was the first time she'd said it out loud. While she'd give anything for it not to be true, everyone in that room knew better. "Pretend I didn't say that."

"No take back-sies." Sandra crossed her arms over the guitar strap on her chest. "I fucking knew by the way you looked at him when you danced together at the wedding. You need to tell him."

"Are you insane?" Amber's mouth fell open and snapped shut. "Hey, Matthew, I know you stopped talking to me and won't return my calls, but I love you." Her tone dripped with sarcasm.

"Exactly," Sandra said with a shrug.

"I'm not some puppy he can kick, and I'll crawl back with my head down, hoping he doesn't do it again."

"Luke," Charlotte said. "Let's call it a day. Sorry it was a waste."

Amber's face heated. She hated letting her emotions get away from her. And she knew better than to talk about him like that in front of Luke, a relative newcomer to the group. It felt disloyal and shitty, which paired well with the grief and confusion already driving her crazy.

Luke shook his head. "Not a total waste. I got to watch your face turn a pretty shade of green and hear that Amber thinks I'm fuckable." He dodged the stick Amber tossed at his head.

When he was packed and gone, Charlotte moved to the couch in the lounge with Sandra. Amber trailed behind, dreading whatever she was about to hear. She sat on the end beside Charlotte.

"Matty's not okay." Tears instantly welled in Charlotte's eyes when the words were out. "He needs us all more than ever, and you have to let go of your anger so when he's ready, you can hear him out."

"Where was he when *I* needed *him*?" Amber struggled to keep her voice calm as the anger she damn well wasn't ready to let go of burned in her throat. "I get that you're saying this because you have his back, but who has *my* fucking back? He's the one who stopped calling me. He's the one who told me he was in love with me and then shut me out. He ignored my calls and all the times I knocked on his goddamn door. He knew how much all of that would fucking hurt me, and did it anyway."

"Sweetie..." Sandra leaned forward in her seat.

"Don't *sweetie*, me, Sandra." Hot tears filled Amber's eyes. "I've spent the last week crying and confused, wondering what I did to make him feel like he couldn't lean on me. He trusted me, and then he didn't. I helped him. He was getting better."

"And then he wasn't," Charlotte said. "He had a nightmare that scared the shit out of him. Worse than all the others. None of us know everything Rafael and Amy put him through, but he has to live with those memories every day. You helped him forget for a while, but those memories caught up with him. So, he did what he's always done when hurting and overwhelmed—hid from the world, refused to 'burden' us with his problems, trying to numb it out." She put *burden* in air quotes. He was better at helping others than asking for it for himself, not wanting to inconvenience someone else with his issues.

But that's not how relationships work. There has to be give and take. If you need help, you ask for it. If someone you love is in need, you help them.

What are you supposed to do when they won't let you?

How could she be with someone who refused to let her in when it mattered most?

"Poor Matty," Sandra sighed.

Charlotte nodded, her eyes still wet with tears. "I basically had to break into his house and force him to talk to me. He's depressed and ashamed, and he didn't want you to see him like that. I can understand because..." She wiped tears from her cheeks, her chin trembling. "He looked so broken. His place was a mess; he hadn't showered in days. The things he told me... I can understand why it sent his progress so far backward."

The first tears broke loose, and Amber let them slide to her chin. "Why didn't he call me before he let himself sink so far? Or answer any of the dozens of times when I did? Even if he didn't want me to see him like that, I could've talked him through it."

"Honey, it's not as simple as that. He thought you were better off without him." Charlotte touched Amber's shoulder, waiting until their eyes reconnected. "Depression lies to you, and he doesn't think he'd ever get strong again. But after we meet with Rafael's family, Matty gets back into therapy, and he ditches the meds that have become a crutch, he'll get there. I know he will."

"Depression?" The word echoed in Amber's mind, and she thought of her mom. How hard it was to get her to do the most basic human tasks like showering and putting on clean clothes. Her heart ached at the thought of Matthew locked in the same poisonous mental fog that, for a while, stole all the best parts of her mother. "What am I supposed to do with that? If he won't let me in, how do I help? And how am I supposed to forget he made me feel abandoned after we got closer than ever? After he told me he loved me?"

"Give him time," Charlotte said, sipping her ginger ale. "He doesn't want you to have to take care of him. He wants to be equals. You're strong as hell, and he wants to be strong again too."

"He will be," Sandra said, rubbing Charlotte's back with one hand and passing them both tissues with the other. "Our Matty's not a quitter, so don't quit on him. You guys were great together, and you will be again when he's ready."

The kneejerk response in Amber's head was *he quit on me*, but reacting without thinking never made things better. Was she supposed to camp out on his doorstep like Tyler did when he wanted Charlotte back after their breakup? Amber wasn't one to beg or surrender all the control in a situation to a man, no matter how much she loved him.

If she followed their advice and gave him time, would it become easier to forgive and forget the pain he'd caused? Or would she grow to resent that he held all the power to accept or reject her?

"You don't have to decide anything now," Charlotte said, as if reading her mind. "But think about what I said. He needs you. He needs all of us. Be patient until he's ready to let us all back in for good."

Even after all the pain he put her through, Amber still needed *him*. She ached to be back in his arms, surrounded by his scent and warmth. Her love for him was still there, but had nowhere to go. She was afraid her anger would smother it, but maybe that would make it easier to bear.

"And Amber," Sandra said, "you know damn well we have your back. Always have. Always will."

"Yeah." Amber nodded, regretting the unfair accusation. "Sorry I said that."

"No sweat, fellow drama queen." Sandra stood, stretching her arms so wide she probably tweaked a muscle.

Charlotte stood beside Sandra, her arms open just as wide.

Ready to put the stressful talk aside, Amber joined them. They huddled in a tight group hug, their warm bodies squishing together as they held each other up.

It was impossible to feel lost and alone with love like that. The comforting hug was something Amber hadn't realized she needed, but they knew.

These women—the best, truest friends she'd ever had—were good at that.

The feeling made her think of her brother and how unfair it was that he didn't have anyone around him to lean on.

When Amber got home, she locked herself in her bedroom and called him.

"Hello?"

She smiled for the first time that day at the sound of his voice. "Hey, little brother. What's up?"

On his end of the line, she heard muffled yelling in the background. A door closed, cutting off the sound.

"Mom's flipping out," he said with a sigh. "Dad won't be home for five more days, and she found a bill for another credit card he didn't tell her about."

Amber scowled, biting back the angry words burning in her throat. "Who's she yelling at?"

"No one. She's drunk and ranting, going through all his shit."

Her doing that while her son was home spoke volumes about the kind of mother he was cursed with.

"I'm almost relieved," he said. "Before she found the bill, she was screaming at me for ditching school."

"Why'd you ditch?"

He was quiet again.

"Nick?"

He exhaled a loud breath. "Yesterday, the boy I gave the note to threatened to kick my ass. And someone slipped a rotten egg in my backpack. His best friend slapped it so it would break in the hallway. Must've been him."

"Those stupid little motherfuckers! What did your Mom say?"

He scoffed. "She complained about the smell. Said I brought it on myself for having sinful thoughts."

Fucking hypocrite. "Kate and I are working on a way to get you out. Between her smart lawyer brain and my stubbornness, it'll happen. Hang in there, okay?"

"I miss you guys. Tell Tara thanks for the candy. And it was nice of you to send thirteen birthday cards. And a little crazy."

Amber laughed. "I missed all your birthdays. We have lost time to make up for when we get you back to Portland."

"Yeah." He sounded somber, maybe even unconvinced. She knew too well how easy it was to lose hope when you're trapped in a string of miserable days that feel endless. "How's Matthew? Thank him, too. He never gave me his number."

Her brows pinched. "Thank him for what?"

"He sent me a gift certificate to the skate shop up the street. It was in the mail a couple of days after I got back. I finally got the gear I've wanted for ages."

Matthew must've sent it when they were still together but never mentioned it. She didn't have the heart to tell Nick about the break-up.

"I'll thank him for you." Amber swiped a thumb beneath her lashes.

"I have to go. That twisted Bible study's in fifteen minutes, and I guess now, I'm walking."

"Sorry you have to do that bullshit." Amber's arms ached to hug him. She didn't have a maternal bone in her body, but she felt a unique protectiveness for Nick that made her want to take his pain away. "There's nothing wrong with you, okay?"

"Mmhm." Again, he didn't sound convinced, and she was disgusted by the people who made him feel that way.

"I love you, Nick." She'd never said it to him before, but she meant it. In the last few weeks, Amber proved herself capable of opening her heart in ways she never imagined. She loved her little brother, and she sensed he needed to hear it.

He sniffed. "Love you too, sis. Even if you can't get me out of here... I'm glad we can talk. I don't feel so alone anymore."

Amber smiled, her bedroom blurring behind fresh tears. They said goodbye, and despite her broken heart, she felt a little less alone, too.

40

Matthew

On the drive to meet Rafael's family, no one spoke. Tyler and Charlotte sat in the front seat, their hands joined in her lap. Matthew sat in the back alone, warring with the urge to pop a couple of Xanax or to power through without them. There were only ten left, so he had to make them count. He slid his hand into his pocket, the feel of the prescription bottle bringing as much comfort as anything could in such a shitty situation. If he needed them, they were there. Like the people in the front seat.

Tyler parked in front of a red brick building covered in trailing ivy. His head turned in every direction, most likely checking for any sneaky paparazzi that caught their trail and followed them. Having this meeting made public would ensure the wound remained open, which was the last thing any of them wanted.

He ran a hand over Charlotte's hair before kissing her forehead. "Are you sure you want to do this?"

Tyler's expression wasn't hard to read. This was the last fucking thing he wanted any of them to do. But he would do it for her.

"I'm sure," she said.

They exited the car, and Tyler slung an arm over Charlotte's shoulders, tucking her against his side. Matthew walked beside them until she suddenly stopped.

Her hand slid into Tyler's pocket, pulling out the taser he kept in his glove box.

"Tyler Hall! Put it away." She held it out, and he took it with a sigh that made his shoulders sink. "If you have anything else you shouldn't, put that in the car too."

Tyler stared at her for a few beats before pulling a folded knife from his pocket. "Fine." He opened the trunk and tossed the weapons inside. He cradled her face, their eyes locked. "But if he tries anything, I'll rip his fucking throat out with my bare hands."

Matthew wished he had one-tenth of the fire his brother had. Before the attack, he did. Nothing scared him, and he wouldn't think twice about jumping between someone he loved and someone posing a threat.

More than anything, he wanted that fire back.

Tyler opened the glass door for Charlotte and Matthew before returning to her side. Eliza stood by a dark wooden door along with a man the size of a refrigerator. He was solid muscle from head to toe, and it wasn't hard to figure out this was the bodyguard she promised to bring.

"Thanks for coming. I know it's not easy." Eliza gestured to the man beside her. "This is—"

"Walter!" Charlotte hugged the man. "I almost didn't recognize you without the badass Terminator sunglasses."

One side of his mouth lifted in a lopsided grin. "Good to see you again, Charlotte."

She turned to Tyler and Matthew. "Walter was the head of our security team for the Canadian tour. Taught me a few Krav Maga moves before I accidentally elbowed him in the crotch."

Walter's face reddened as he chuckled. "Hey, I should've been ready and blocked it."

"I'm Tyler, and this is my brother, Matthew." Tyler shook his hand. "Thanks for watching out for her, Walter. And I'm glad you're here for this."

Matthew stayed a few steps behind everyone, watching. It eased his worries a bit knowing this massive wall of muscle would be in the room, but it was doubtful he'd take a bullet for them if it came to that.

"I assure you," Eliza said, "we'll all be safe. Walter's here to give you an added sense of security. They'll pass through a metal detector, also purely for your reassurance."

Matthew wiped his sweaty palms on his jeans as the room began to spin.

"I can't do this." All heads turned to Matthew, making him want to run until his lungs gave out. "What if it's a trap? What if—"

"Matthew," Eliza said, her gaze soft, "they only want closure, not revenge. I've spoken with them at length, done thorough background checks, and I assure you, they're good people."

Charlotte left Tyler's side and took Matthew's hand. "You can do this. And you will because it's what you need to feel strong again." She spoke softly enough so only he could hear, her words making the backs of his eyes burn. "Rafael stole that from you. Don't let him keep it from you one more goddamn second."

His arms wrapped around her, hugging her close. "What if I break the second I see him? What if—"

"Shh..." She held him tighter, and a warm hand squeezed his shoulder. He knew without looking that it was his brother's. "If you break, we'll help put you back together, I promise. Like you always helped me. Hold your head high, and let's do this together."

Charlotte let him go but retook his hand and held tight. Her other hand curled into Tyler's. They all went through something awful together, but they'd survived it. Like Matthew had trusted Amber to walk with him in the dark and guide him past his fears, he trusted them to do the same.

And no matter how intense things got in that room, they would survive this, too.

Eliza held the door open, and Walter walked in first. The room was still empty, as promised. Four seats were arranged on both sides of a long table coated in black vinyl that looked like it'd been designed for business meetings, not whatever the hell this was. A fluorescent lighting fixture hovered above, illuminating the space while it hummed at a volume barely audible but loud enough to grate Matthew's already fried nerves.

"I'll wait in the lobby to greet them." Eliza checked her watch. "It shouldn't be long." She stepped out, closing the door behind her.

Everyone took a seat except Walter, who stood behind Charlotte with his arms crossed over his broad chest. In any other situation, his large, looming presence in Matthew's periphery would've reminded him of Rafael and sent him spinning into a panic attack. In this case, knowing he was on their side made it easier to handle.

Charlotte sat between Tyler and Matthew, their hands linked and resting on the table. He imagined what Rafael's family would think of the united front greeting them when they walked in. There wasn't much time to consider that before there was a soft knock at the door.

Everyone's head snapped toward the sound.

Matthew's heart thumped wildly in his chest, sweat beading on his forehead. Charlotte squeezed his hand. He forced himself to take a slow, deep breath and let it out as he stared at the door, waiting.

Walter left for a few minutes, presumably to check them for recording devices and weapons, as agreed. Matthew's head swam, and he slipped his free hand into his pocket to feel the bottle of pills.

The door opened.

Eliza entered first, followed by a short woman with dark hair streaked with silver. Rafael's brother came in next. The sight of him made Matthew forget to breathe, and Charlotte squeezed his hand again, her thumb gently sliding over his wrist. As they took their seats, Matthew focused on the comforting touch and the pill bottle in his hand.

The woman's gaze flicked between the three of them before landing on the bodyguard. "Is he really necessary? We were hoping to speak privately."

"He's here for us," Tyler said. "I'm sure you can understand why we'd feel on edge. He's signed the same non-disclosure agreement you did, so anything said in this room stays in this room. Pretend he isn't there."

Her eyes widened with *are you kidding*, probably because the idea of trying to ignore someone that size was ludicrous. He was literally like an elephant in the room. She shifted her attention to Charlotte.

"Hello, Charlotte." The woman's mouth slowly raised into a forced and shaky smile. "I'm Mona Bruce. And this is my son, Frank. Thank you for agreeing to meet with us."

Charlotte nodded. "I hope we can help each other. I know we can all use a bit of closure." She cleared her throat. "And I'm sorry for your loss."

Matthew's head jerked to her. "What—"

She turned to him, her head shaking. He shut his gaping mouth, listening.

Mona looked confused by his reaction, her gaze flickering between Matthew and Charlotte. "Thank you, Charlotte. Not many people have said that because of the... circumstances. There's nothing harder than losing a child, and I appreciate the sentiment." Her voice broke with emotion at the end, and she pulled tissues from her purse.

The realization of why Charlotte wanted to do this suddenly struck.

She almost lost her baby.

Knowing her, she'd sat and thought about how much more painful it would've been to raise that child, love them unconditionally for decades, only to have them closed in a coffin and buried six feet underground.

Charlotte wanted to help ease the pain of this woman—this fellow mother—in any way she could. He'd never doubted the depths of his friend's compassion and generosity, but this was above and beyond what she would've been capable of before the attack.

If she could grow past her pain and reclaim her strength, so could Matthew.

"And I'm sorry for what my son put you through." Mona sniffed. "All of you. He was such a good boy growing up. He got caught up with the wrong crowd in high school and strayed for a while, but I got him counseling, and things got better. Then, he met *that woman*." The words came out through clenched teeth. The visible proof she hated Amy made Matthew relax a little. He hadn't expected them to have something in common.

"What do you need from us to help you, Mona?" Charlotte asked.

Frank set his elbows on the table, leaning forward. "We want to know my brother's last words. And if he suffered."

Mona frowned, dabbing her eyes. "I can't tell you the horrible things my mind has conjured up about his last moments. Did he suffer before the ambulance arrived?" Her gaze bore into Charlotte's face—the face of her son's killer, regardless of the circumstances.

"No," Charlotte said, barely above a whisper. "He was unconscious. We thought he was... gone before the ambulance arrived. He didn't suffer."

Matthew knew as well as anyone else in the room that Charlotte couldn't know that for certain. But clearly, Mona needed to hear it to find peace, justifying the little white lie.

"We also wanted to meet to apologize," Frank said, "for what he put your family through. I love my brother. I miss him every day." He paused, blowing out a loud, drawn-out breath. "I can't wrap my head around what the media says happened. I want to hear it from the only witnesses. Other than the habitual fucking liar locked in a cell."

This was it—the time to be brave or to stuff it all down and hide.

Neither road was easy, but only one led to healing and strength. Matthew deserved what waited for him on the other side.

And he thought about Amber. If they ever had a chance at a future, first, he had to face the past.

He let go of the pills and pulled his hand from his pocket. "It started three days before the attack. I was leaving work one night. It was dark, lots of shadows in the parking lot. Rafael grabbed me from behind, trapping my arms. Amy slapped duct tape over my mouth so I couldn't scream."

Charlotte leaned her head on his shoulder.

He could feel his brother's eyes on him as he spoke, and knowing they were there made it easier to continue. "They taped my hands behind me, then my ankles together, and tossed me into a trunk."

Mona whimpered, covering her mouth with the tissues in her hand. When she noticed everyone's eyes on her, she gave a nod. "Please, go on."

Matthew described the horror of being locked in the darkness of the trunk, not knowing where they were going. Would they take him to the woods and shoot him? Or toss him into a lake to sink like a brick and drown? He told them about being trapped in a basement for days that felt endless, choking down the drugged water Rafael forced on him.

Some things, he left out for Mona's sake. She didn't need to hear about how her son mentally tortured him, slapping him and taunting him until he broke.

Tyler took over when Matthew got to the day Rafael and Amy brought him to Charlotte's.

Matthew listened as his brother recounted the events that nearly led to their deaths. The binding with zip ties, the gun held to their heads. Rafael revealing he was Charlotte's stalker, torturing her for months with the threatening notes that made her afraid to leave her house.

Then, he got to the moment when Amy revealed their plan to stage a murder-suicide.

Tyler described how they planned to frame Matthew as Charlotte and Tyler's killer. He talked about the secret photographs taken of Charlotte they'd planted at Matthew's apartment to make him look like her stalker. To make it appear that Matthew was secretly obsessed with her and wanted to kill them for getting together and breaking his heart.

Matthew's stomach roiled as he listened. As if it wasn't bad enough to take their lives, those sick fucks wanted everyone to believe *he* was the monster. He imagined the endless headlines and TV news reports with "murderer" stamped beneath his photo.

Would his mother believe it? His friends?

He shook it off as Tyler explained the silent plotting between him and Charlotte about the location of her gun and the bottle he'd used to strike Amy. Mona and Frank listened in rapt silence, their faces paling as the details about the end of their loved one neared.

Mona looked like she might vomit.

Matthew held his breath and listened. It was surreal hearing details he was too far gone to witness. Some bled into his nightmares, but others he'd never felt ready to ask for. It was hard picturing Charlotte and Tyler—loving, peaceful people—preparing to defend themselves with violence, not knowing whether they'd succeed or leave the room in body bags. He shuddered, imagining the degree of terror they must've felt.

"He's breathing, but out cold." Tyler scrubbed a hand over his face and shifted in his seat. "Those were Rafael's last words after he injected my brother with the heroin that almost killed him."

Matthew looked at his brother, and their teary eyes locked.

Like they'd done a million times since they were kids, they shared a look that silently communicated everything they felt—grief over how close they'd come to losing each other, gratitude that they'd survived, and the unconditional love that held the power to heal them.

Charlotte's head left Matthew's shoulder, and she whispered something in Tyler's ear. He pressed a kiss to her forehead and nodded. "We hold no grudge against you for the actions of your son." He gestured to Frank. "And brother."

"Is there anything else you want to know?" Charlotte asked.

Mona looked at her son and back across the table. "Are you all okay?" Her voice broke again, and she took a moment before continuing. "I realize it's a stupid question, but it's been eating at me. I worry about how my son's actions have affected your lives." She turned to Matthew. "Frank told me you were upset when he came to your place of business."

Matthew shook his head. "No." The word came out with so much force it stole his breath. "I haven't been okay in a *very* long time. I used to be strong without a care in the world, but now I'm a twenty-four-year-old man afraid of the dark. I have nightmares about your son and had a panic attack when I saw Frank because he looks so much like the man who tried to kill me and the people I love."

When Mona opened her mouth to speak, Matthew held up a hand. Her mouth closed, and she settled back in her seat.

"But I will be okay." He paused, letting the words soak into his bones. "I have work to do to get there, but honestly... I was against us doing this. I didn't think I could handle being in a room with you and talking about what happened to us. I didn't see what good could come from it. But now, I'm glad we did. I think I needed it, too. So I can move on."

Mona gave a weak smile. "I'm very glad to hear that, Matthew."

"So am I." Charlotte leaned over to hug his arm and whispered, "I'm proud of you."

"Sorry I spooked you at your job," Frank said. "We were frustrated we couldn't reach any of you, and I knew my mom needed this. I'd do anything to help her heal from this mess."

Matthew nodded, feeling lighter as his pulse slowed and the heavy sense of dread that'd burdened him for days—months, really—finally began to lift.

"We know the feeling," Charlotte said.

In the lobby, Charlotte and Mona hugged while everyone else shook hands before heading to the parking lot. When Matthew shut his door, the silence in the car didn't feel heavy like on the drive over. He figured they were processing everything too.

Charlotte turned her head toward Matthew.

"Told you so." She stuck her tongue out like the adorable brat she was, and the car filled with the sound of laughter.

Matthew couldn't argue with that.

Tyler looked in the rearview mirror, and their eyes met. "I'm proud of you, little brother."

"Thanks," Matthew said, a genuine smile curving his lips. "I'm proud of me too."

41

Amber

"A fucking *Christmas party*?" The way Zack said it, you'd think Amber invited him to a polka competition. He took a long pull off his joint and passed it to Adam. "We're rock musicians. Not boring ass lawyers or office workers or whatever."

The members of Killing Daisies and Tomorrow Mourning sat in a circle around the firepit in Tyler and Charlotte's backyard. Amber had called a joint meeting, and, of course, Adam and Zack misunderstood what she meant by that. So, they moved the meeting from the studio to outside so Charlotte wouldn't give herself or her baby a contact high.

Tyler tossed another log onto the fire, the glowing embers popping and crackling beneath it. A late October chill had set in, and everyone was bundled in puffy jackets, hooded sweatshirts, and beanies, looking like a bunch of rockstars on their way to a ski lodge.

Amber hugged a notebook to her chest filled with pages of party planning notes. The event was her idea, and so far, the girls and Tyler were into it. This was their first chance to discuss it with Luke, Zack, and Adam, but she was hopeful they'd get on board.

"My sister Kate's a boring ass lawyer, so watch it." She aimed her pen at Zack. "And it would be on the twenty-third, so no one misses Christmas with their family."

"Hey, a party's a party," Adam pointed out, smoke curling around the dark blonde spikes in his hair. "As long as there's booze and music, I'm in."

Zack backhanded his shoulder. "Ooh, maybe we can get some naughty girls to sit on our laps and tell us what they want from Santa."

Amber could already see them waltzing in wearing white beards and mistletoe belts.

Charlotte's eyebrow lifted. "How would my cousin Kyla feel about that?"

There was laughter around the circle as Adam slumped in his chair.

He pointed his beer at Zack. "He said it, not me."

"You're still seeing Kyla?" Luke asked. "I saw you kissing her the day after the wedding, but I figured it was a goodbye after a one-night thing."

Adam shrugged. "She's cool as shit. Just seeing how it goes."

Amber was shocked when Charlotte first told her. Not that Adam and Kyla hooked up after the reception—she'd heard them through the walls of Matthew's room—but that he'd called her every day since and even driven down to Corvallis to visit her. Seeing a girl for more than an hour was new for Adam, let alone for almost two weeks. Whether the shift was temporary or a sign he was truly reformed was anyone's guess.

"Anyway..." Charlotte's eyes rolled. "We figured this would be a good opportunity to let the crews of both bands mingle and get to know each other before we're all traveling together for two months."

"I'm in, but you're talking a couple hundred people." Luke took the joint from Adam before passing it to Amber. "Don't we need more than two months to pull off an event that size?"

Amber pulled the smoke into her lungs and let it drift from her lips as she spoke. "I've already called a few caterers to check availability, and the Cascade Suites downtown has the ballroom and top floors available to reserve for the twenty-third."

She didn't mention the three dozen places she called before that were already booked. Caterers' schedules were pretty full that close to Christmas, but she had two very strong maybes that should work out. If not, there were others. Hell, she'd make Kraft Mac and Cheese and hot dogs herself before she quit.

Amber was determined to make this party work. She needed to get lost in the distraction while she struggled to accept things were really over with Matthew. The Halloween party they'd planned together for the music space at the brewery was supposed to be in five days, but Evan called to say it was canceled—another disappointment to get over.

Every morning, she woke up missing Matthew, wondering if that would be the day he reached out. It never was. She missed his warm hugs, the sound of his laugh, the way he gently brushed her hair away from her face with his fingertips. She missed his friendship. How easy he was to talk to. Really, she missed everything about him, spending her days longing for something she never thought she'd have and may never have again.

"I'm making contact lists for everyone we'd invite from our side," Tyler said.

"And I'm doing the one for Daisies," Amber said.

"I can do that since you're already doing the other stuff." Sandra hit the joint and coughed before swigging her Zima.

"Or I can," Charlotte said. "You're already doing a lot, Amber."

"I need a fucking project, okay?" Amber's words came out in a rush, sounding harsher than she'd intended. A touch of crazy was in there, too, and she could feel the concerned looks aimed in her direction. "Sorry, guys."

Amber scrubbed her face, frustration buzzing beneath her skin. She wanted to ask how the meeting with Rafael's family went two days before, but it didn't feel like the right time or place. When the joint reached Zack, he sent it in reverse order, and everyone helped pass it back to Amber.

"You okay, babe?" Sandra asked.

"Mostly." Amber took a long drag, and the smoke left her lungs with a weary sigh. "One of my drumming students moved to California, and the other's mom pulled her because of my dad's article. Aside from rehearsing for the tour, I've had more free time than I like and want to stay busy. But yeah, if you want to do the contact list, Sandra, have at it." She took another hit before passing the joint to Luke.

"Is this a Matthew thing?" Luke asked. "Unless you don't want to talk about it."

"Yeah." Amber's bottom lip quivered, but she refused to break. "It's a Matthew thing. And I don't want to talk about it."

"That boy's looking good these days," Adam said. "Healthier and shit."

"Good for him." Amber pretended to scribble notes on her notepad. She was glad to hear that, but it still hurt like hell that he hadn't reached out to her. "What does everyone think about doing a few songs together at the party?"

"Ty and I hung out with him yesterday." Zack sucked the joint down to his fingers and tossed the nub into the fire. "He was smiling, joking around. Like he's getting back to who he was before psycho and her shit puppet fucked him up."

"Stop." Amber didn't care anymore if she sounded harsh because now, she was pissed. She really couldn't handle talking about Matthew when the pain was still so raw. "Can we go back to talking about the party, please?"

"Give him time, Amber." Tyler's tone was gentle, his expression etched with sympathy. "The meeting with Rafael's family went well. I can tell it helped him a lot."

Despite her hurt feelings over Matthew's rejection, that was great to hear. She wanted him to put those demons behind him for good and to feel strong again, even if she wasn't there to watch it.

"It helped all of us." Charlotte touched her husband's knee and they shared a smile.

"I'm glad it went well." Amber watched the flames lick the edges of the log, her eyes burning. She tried to convince herself it was from the smoke and not the memories of Matthew flashing through her mind.

At least she could still see him somewhere.

"What did his family want anyway?" Luke asked.

Everyone else had likely already heard about the details from the meeting, but all heads turned to Tyler anyway.

"Closure," Charlotte said. "Exactly what Matty needed too."

"I appreciate how good you've all been to him through this." Tyler's gaze moved around the circle before stopping on Amber. "Thanks for being there for my brother when he needed it most."

Amber gave a slight nod before her gaze returned to the fire, red and gold sparks popping off the center log. Even in her pain, she had few regrets about her relationship with Matthew. She was glad to be there when he needed support. It felt good helping him work past his fears and having the trust of someone who didn't give it away easily.

And he showed her she was capable of a more meaningful relationship than a shallow, casual hook-up. That trusting someone with her heart was still a risk, but one she could handle if it meant opening herself up to the possibility of real, lasting love.

She'd wanted that with him, but even if it weren't possible, maybe coming out of the relationship with that growth and the priceless new experiences was enough.

It had to be.

Because as the silence between them stretched on, it was all she had.

"Speaking of brothers," Sandra said. "What's up with Nick?"

One corner of Amber's mouth hitched up. She was grateful for something more positive to talk about. "He's hanging in there. Kate and I are working out how to help him, but I don't want to share the details until it's a sure thing. Ask me again after tomorrow."

Amber knew how easily it would be for the plan to be judged as foolish, but it was a family matter. While the people surrounding her were family in their own way, it was different than the bond with her siblings. No one else needed to understand her choices. Hopefully, everything went as well as expected in the morning, and she'd have good news to share.

<hr>

After another restless night, Amber began her day with a mission. She had someone else's problems to worry about for a change. So, she threw on jeans and the sweatshirt that still smelled like smoke from the firepit at Tyler and Charlotte's the night before, more than ready to get the bullshit task over with.

At the motel, the paint on the door of room sixty-three was peeling, revealing a strip of aged wood the color of rusted metal. Amber knocked with a tight fist that ached to make contact with the face she hoped was on the other side. Her other hand held her sister Kate's.

The door opened a crack, and half of their dad's head peeked out. His thick, dark brows furrowed. "Amber? Kate?" He eyed them as if checking for weapons. Or another hose.

"Good morning, shithead." Kate offered a fingertip wave.

"What are you—"

"Ten thousand dollars," Amber said, pushing her way inside the room with Kate beside her.

His head jerked back, and he stared, mouth gaping like a hungry bullfrog. "What are you talking about?"

"The reporter paid you to sell me out, but you're staying in this shithole. That tells me you're still buried in debt up to your stupid balding head. Am I right?"

He nodded his stupid balding head as he closed the door, looking confused but intrigued. "I was going to get evicted. I had no choice."

"Poor you." Kate's eyes rolled. "There's no excuse for what you did."

He scrubbed a hand over his face. "You're going to give me—"

"Ten thousand dollars," Amber said. "Yes."

"For what?"

Amber took in the dark circles under his eyes, empty beer bottles scattered around the room, and the stench of greasy takeout food. She was more certain than ever that this was the right thing to do. "For Nick. You terminate your parental rights and talk your wife into doing the same."

"And let me be his legal guardian," Kate added. "Then, the money's yours."

If Amber's career didn't involve frequent travel and late nights, she would've taken that responsibility. But there were endless reasons Kate was the better choice. She was the surrogate mother who encouraged Amber to pursue her passions. She was a stellar role model, showing her sisters the value of hard work and resilience. Amber had no doubt she'd be the same positive influence for

Nick, and nowhere would be better for him to grow up than in their house, full of the love, acceptance, and stability he needed.

Their dad sputtered. "You want my *son*? But you don't even know him!"

Amber and Kate exchanged a look, coy grins curving their lips.

"Your head's so far up your own dumb ass," Kate said, "it's ridiculous. We saw him when he was in town. So did your other daughters—remember them?"

"How?" He sank into the filthy chair beside the door, its upholstery ripped and stained. "Where?"

"He wrote to me," Amber said. "Then came to my record signing up the street." She didn't want to get Nick in trouble for contacting her, but there was no way around it. "You're always gone, rejected him for his sexuality like you did to Tara, treat him like a disappointment, and you almost lost your house. Your wife's just as useless, forcing him to join a group trying to pray the gay away. He deserves better."

Heat surged in Amber's chest as she remembered how miserable Nick looked when describing his home life and how desperate he was to get out.

Kate squeezed her hand, offering a calming anchor before Amber's temper got the best of her. "What would you have done if you didn't have Amber to exploit for cash? Make him live in a shelter? Mooched off relatives? Come begging for money from the daughters you abandoned?"

"I don't know," he said. "I was desperate enough to do anything."

Kate scoffed. "Anything but hold down a decent job and stop being a selfish prick. He's better off with me."

Amber's temper had cooled, but the urge to see him hurt won over. "And you won't have to worry about child support if we take him," she said. "But you will if your wife leaves you for her boss."

"*What*?" He shot out of his chair. "What the hell are you talking about?"

Kate raised a questioning eyebrow at Amber, but she just shrugged. She couldn't help herself.

"Nick has a big fucking mouth," he said, "and doesn't know what he's talking about."

Amber released Kate's hand, moving closer to him. When the scent of beer and body odor hit her, she stepped back. "You know you want to say yes. What will you do the first time he brings a boyfriend over for dinner?"

The lines framing his mouth deepened as he grimaced. "Over my dead body."

Amber's fists balled up at her sides. If she hit him, he'd sue. Even worse, it would jeopardize their plan, and she'd never do that to Nick.

Kate grinned and slow-clapped. "Father of the Year, ladies and gentlemen."

"Ten grand," Amber said. He obviously cared about money more than his kids, so he'd give in. "Think of how great it'll be to have that burden lifted. You can focus on your favorite hobbies—chasing fame and chasing tail." She hated calling Nick a burden, but she knew it was how her father saw him now that he wasn't a fun, naive little kid who worshipped his dad without question.

He sat back in the chair, the metal legs creaking beneath him. His gaze swung between the women. "Twenty."

Gotcha. Amber smiled even as anger and disgust raged in her gut. "Fifteen. Final offer." The five sisters would put in three grand each—a small price to pay for saving their brother. "And you never bother any of us again. Nick can reach out if he wants to, but you leave us alone. If you ever slander me in the press again, I'll sue you and take it back, plus whatever else you've managed to scrape together."

"Deal?" Kate asked.

After a moment, he held out his hand, and both women laughed. They weren't about to touch that shithead.

Amber didn't miss the irony that she'd spent years wishing he'd return, and now she couldn't wait to never see him again.

Kate pulled a business card from her pocket and stuck it in his palm. "This is the contact info for a colleague who will prepare the documents. Once your wife agrees, call the number and get things started. When everything's complete, you'll get your money."

He stared at the card before looking at Amber. "How can I trust you after... everything?"

That was the smartest thing he'd said so far. They couldn't put their agreement in writing, and nothing stopped them from waiting until the paperwork was complete and giving him the middle finger. It would be fun watching him sweat.

She shrugged. "Fair question. I guess you'll have to hope my word means more than yours."

42

Matthew

"I'm glad you decided to come back, Matthew." Dr. Vega smiled warmly. Her trusty notebook and pen sat in her lap. "I know I've said that at every session in the past seven weeks, but it's true. I see how hard you're working to heal from your trauma."

Matthew set his mug of green tea on the oak coffee table between their chairs. "It hasn't been easy, but I'm glad too." This time, he didn't hold anything back. He'd spent their fourteen sessions detailing everything from the moment he was kidnapped to waking up in the ambulance with his brother holding his hand. He described every nightmare, every trigger for his panic attacks. Even the doctor shed a few tears as he bared his soul without restraint.

At the end of every session, she gave him work to do at home to help the treatment along. He kept a journal, exercised every day, learned new breathing techniques for stress, and read about how trauma affects the body and mind. Now, he understood how foolish it was to ever think time would magically make him better.

"Are you still coping well without the Xanax?" she asked.

Matthew nodded, relieved he could still answer that question the same way as last week and the week before. "Yes. I haven't taken one in over a month."

"Good to hear. It can be a very useful medication, but as you learned, it can also become a misused crutch."

"I won't go back to that. I still smoke weed, but not when I'm stressed. It helps me sleep. And makes movies funnier."

Her lips twitched with amusement. "I can't condone the use of illicit drugs, but I appreciate that you can distinguish self-medication from recreation."

One of the exercises she'd given him as homework helped with that. He logged his feelings throughout the day in his journal, and if he wanted to smoke, he'd reflect on how he was feeling. If he was sad or stressed, he wouldn't do it. If he just wanted to calm his mind for sleep, he'd toke up. Pot was something he'd enjoyed for years and as long as it didn't set back his progress, he didn't see a reason to give it up.

"Have you thought more about reaching out to Amber?" Dr. Vega asked.

Since he'd started feeling more stable, it was all he thought about. "I'm afraid to see the pain on her face—pain I caused. But I need to apologize. I owe her that."

No words could express the depths of his regret over hurting Amber, but he had to try. If she hated him, he deserved it. If she never wanted to speak to him again, he deserved that too.

"You still love her." Dr. Vega pushed a box of tissues across the table in front of him.

Matthew was so lost in his thoughts he hadn't even realized he was crying. He grabbed a tissue and wiped his eyes. "Of course I do. I always will. But it doesn't change the fact that she probably hates me."

"Hate is a very strong word." Dr. Vega shook her head, thick black curls brushing her shoulders. "Given your history as close friends, I think it's safe to say she's never hated you. And the way you accepted and trusted each other, despite your personal wounds, speaks to the strength of your connection. Bonds like that aren't easily broken."

He hadn't shared anything about Amber's life other than her dad leaving. It felt necessary since it was the source of so much of Matthew's guilt over hurting her the same way.

"I don't doubt she'll be angry," the doctor continued, "but she deserves to be heard. She counted on you to be an equal partner, and you weren't prepared to fill that role. But now, Matthew, you are strong enough to be that partner if she's open to giving you another chance. If she's not, it will be difficult, but you're strong enough to accept it and move forward."

For the rest of the session, he read a few pages from his journal. He hadn't had a nightmare in four weeks, so he'd written about the half-finished music space at the brewery. The stage was built and wired, but the equipment sat in boxes in the storage room. It felt wrong to finish it without Amber. He'd imagined letting her plug in the last piece of equipment after everything was set up. Maybe she'd even get behind the drums to break them in. The space he'd envisioned as a fun way to bring people together had become another sad reminder of what he'd lost because of his mistakes.

Quitting therapy was his biggest mistake, but at least that one had been corrected.

Dr. Vega's gaze flickered to the clock, and she set her pen and notebook on the table. The page was blank—not even a grocery list.

"You shared a lot today." She gestured to the notebook. "As you can see, I was too engaged in listening to jot anything down." The corners of her mouth tipped up. "I'm incredibly pleased with your progress, Matthew."

"So am I." His face stretched in a wide grin. "I'll see you next week."

43

Amber

Amber scanned her "Day Before the Party" checklist and made a few more marks.

"When the caterers arrive, have them set up there." She pointed to the back wall of the ballroom to ensure the hotel rep, Nina, knew exactly what she meant. "The tables go to the left, and make sure to keep the dance floor clear in front of the stage."

Nina nodded, following along.

If Amber ever quit music, she could give party planning a shot.

But she'd never in a million fucking years quit music.

"When guests arrive, have them come in through those doors." She pointed again. "With the tree where it is, we don't want people blocking the path to the stage and tables."

It was nice feeling in control of something. For two months, she'd struggled with the fact that losing Matthew was out of her hands. The anger and hurt over his failure to reach out were nearly as sharp and raw as in the beginning. Most days, she just wanted to blast angry music, watch terrible, kissing-free horror movies, and eat brownie sundaes in bed. Directing her focus into making this party perfect for her friends, old and new, had been the distraction she needed.

Of course, distraction wasn't the only reason for the party. She'd hung out with some of Tomorrow Mourning's crew backstage at their shows and looked forward to getting to know them better. And seeing how they blended with her band's entourage. If everyone got along, it would make for a better tour experience.

"The sound guys get here at nine in the morning," Amber said, "so please have someone available for any questions as they set up."

Nina nodded along. "No problem. Anything else?"

Amber glanced at her checklist and exhaled. "Nope. That's all I've got. Thanks for your help."

Nina smiled warmly. "To be honest, Miss Jamison, I'm a big fan. That new album..." She mimed her head exploding, which was always a nice compliment. "I'm thrilled you chose our hotel for your party, and I'll make sure everything goes smoothly."

"Nice to hear. And call me Amber. You're welcome to pop in during our set."

Nina's shocked gasp made Amber laugh. "Wow, thank you! I'll see you tomorrow."

Now that her checklist was checked and her friends were on romantic dates with their significant others, Amber wanted to return to her room and crash out early. It'd been a long day of phone calls, decorating, and rehearsing the three songs they'd play with Tomorrow Mourning. It was a surprise for the guests—a collaboration in honor of the co-headlining tour just over six months away and creeping up fast.

They'd kick it off July eighth in London, then Rome and Paris. Matthew was supposed to join them, but no one seemed to know whether that was still happening.

By then, Charlotte would have a two-month-old, and she'd been fretting about how it would work. But mothers have kicked ass for centuries at balancing their home life and career, so if anyone could find that balance, Charlotte could.

Amber took the elevator to the twelfth floor, pulled her hotel key from her pocket, and stepped inside.

A sweet, floral scent hit her nose. *The housekeeper went a little heavy on the air freshener.* When she moved in further, every surface in the room was covered in roses. Splashes of red, pink, and white lay across the dresser and desk, petals scattered along the floor.

Then, she turned the corner toward the bed.

The sight nearly made her knees buckle.

And instantly pissed her off.

The bed was covered in roses, and the scene had come right out of the romance novel she'd described to Matthew right after their first kiss—complete with the man who wounded her looking apologetic and ready to beg for forgiveness standing beside it.

"Why are you here?" Her tone was cold and angry. Fitting because she felt cold and angry.

Why was he here after two months of nothing? No "Can we talk?" or "I miss you" or even "I still love you, but I need space." She would've accepted and appreciated any of the above. Hell, even a "Hi" would've beat the big fat nothing she got.

Amber stood as far from the bed as possible while holding eye contact. Matthew needed to see her face when she told him to get the fuck out of her room.

Her arms crossed over her chest, repeating it louder. "Why are you here?"

"I know how badly I fucked up. I understand if you never want to see me again, but I have to explain why I pulled back."

"*Pulled back*?" She scoffed, tears of rage stinging her eyes. "You told me you loved me one day then vanished for over two fucking months! I needed you, and you ignored me. You know what my dad did to me, and you did the same goddamn thing! I hate you!"

He flinched like she'd punched him in the face. "I know." His head sank forward, his shoulders slumping as he sat on the edge of the bed. "You helped me overcome my fears, and I abandoned you."

"You threw me away like I didn't fucking matter. You were supposed to be different."

He lifted his chin, his eyes burning into hers. "I'm so sorry, Amber."

She wiped away a tear, determined not to shed another for this man who didn't care enough to stick around. "I'm done crying over you. You shouldn't have come."

"I fell apart when Tyler told me about the meeting with Rafael's family. Even worse than right after the attack. Then, depression set in, and... I didn't recognize myself."

It was impossible not to sympathize with that, but nothing excused his behavior. He hadn't been afraid to show her his fears before and had to know she would've been nothing but supportive if he'd let her in.

"You could've called me."

"I know you, Amber. If I'd reached out, you would've shoved everything else in your life aside to focus on me, and I didn't want that. I'd never forgive myself if you canceled rehearsals and interviews when your band needed you to focus and prepare for the tour. That had to be your priority, not me and my problems."

"It's not up to you to decide my priorities."

He shook his head, the weight of his regrets reflected in his eyes. "It was my own damn fault things got so bad. I never should've quit therapy, and I shouldn't have relied on the fucking pills to numb me out. But I've been back in therapy twice a week for almost two months. I do everything she says and hold nothing back. Now... I haven't had a nightmare in over a month. I'm off the pills. I finally feel like the man who can give you everything you deserve." He stood, taking a cautious step toward her. "I don't regret a second of what we had, but I shouldn't have started something with you before I was strong enough to fight to get my life back. Now that I am, I want *you* back. If you'll have me."

"I won't." She blinked back tears, refusing to let them fall. "It's too late."

"I've missed you every single day we've been apart. I'm sorry—"

"How do you expect me to forgive you? By making me feel sorry for you?" Her voice broke. She felt like an asshole for saying it, but it was a fair question. How could she forgive being cast aside like she didn't matter?

"I never stopped loving you, Amber." He took another slow step forward. "I don't want you to feel sorry for me. I want you to understand how ashamed I was to show you the ugliest parts of me. I knew if you fell in love with me, they would've ruined everything, and you'd end up with a lot more pain than if I just faded away. I wanted to make it easier for you to let me go."

A sob caught in her throat. "I never let you go! I've missed you every single day, too. I miss waking up to you kissing my forehead and joking about my morning breath. I miss being in your arms. I miss feeling like I belong to someone and they belong to me. I miss everything about you. About *us*."

He took another step closer and froze. "None of that was past tense."

Matthew was nearly close enough to reach out and touch. But as badly as she ached to be wrapped in his arms, she couldn't move. His rejection, the weeks of silence, hurt too much.

"No," she said, "it wasn't. But it'll take a lot more than a ridiculous amount of roses or kissing my feet to fix what you broke between us." She swiped a knuckle beneath her lashes. "You had no problem letting Jessica help you but didn't trust me enough to let me in all the way so I could do the same. I don't want to be with someone who can't be real with me, no matter how ugly things get. I needed the same in return when my life got ugly, and you couldn't give me that either."

The edges of his mouth turned down. "I read the article with the shit about your dad. I'm sorry you went through that. I didn't know for weeks and should've been there for you."

"Yes, you should've. But you weren't."

His eyes shut with a long blink, shining with tears when they opened. "What can I do to make it right?"

Amber shook her head as the answer burned on her tongue.

She didn't want it to be true. But when someone hurts you by cutting you from their life like an infected limb, there's no going back.

"You can't."

44

Amber

The hotel's ballroom looked like Rudolph the Red-Nosed Reindeer had puked up his lunch.

The Christmas party was in full swing when Amber made it downstairs. She shook hands, kissed cheeks, and gave fist-bumps as she moved through the crowd.

In the corner, a Christmas tree taller than her house was decked out with red garland and glass snowflakes that sparkled in the light from the chandeliers overhead. The star on top nearly touched the ceiling and was lit up with lights that shifted from silver to gold and back again.

Guests chatted and laughed as they danced, ate, and made merry or whatever.

The caterer's tables were stocked with enough food to feed the entire block, complete with colorful Christmas cookies shaped like little trees and reindeer.

It was beautiful—all of it.

Everything looked exactly like she'd imagined.

But she was too miserable to enjoy it.

Amber did most of the planning, but now that it was time to enjoy the fruits of her labor, she didn't feel like celebrating. Charlotte and Sandra each stopped by her room to drag her out when the party started, but she gave them excuses about why she wasn't ready.

Her hair wasn't cooperating.

She had a headache and wanted it to pass before going out in the lights and noise.

Fifteen minutes before walking down, she held a cold washcloth to her eyes, waiting for them to stop looking so puffy and raw.

She'd told Matthew she hated him and that there was no way he could make things right. As usual, Amber had let her mouth run before her brain could catch up. Or her heart. Her heart never would've let those words leave her mouth if it had any say in it.

When she calmed down and got some sorely needed rest, she reflected on everything Matthew said. He was back in therapy, off the meds, and working through his issues. He felt ready to be the partner she deserved.

While forgiving him wouldn't be easy, it wouldn't be impossible. And she sure as shit didn't hate him. Her eyes wouldn't be swollen from hours of crying if she did. She hated herself for saying it.

"Hey, Amber." Adam held a beer in one hand, the other around the waist of Charlotte's cousin, Kyla. "Kick-ass party." He wore a Santa hat and a T-shirt that said *Drummers Hit It Harder*.

"Nice shirt," she said. "Good to see you again, Kyla."

"You too." Kyla gestured at the room. "Adam said you planned this yourself. I'm impressed."

Amber shrugged. "Gave me something to focus on besides worrying I'll fuck up the tour somehow."

"Don't sweat it," he said. "If you tell anyone I said this, I'll deny it 'til my death, but..." He looked around before leaning in. "You're a better drummer than I am. Trust me, you got this."

A surprising admission from a guy whose ego was bigger than the ballroom they stood in.

"Thanks, Adam. Even if you're full of shit to make me feel better, I'll take it."

"He meant it," Kyla said. "One of your songs came on the radio on the drive over, and he said the same thing. He's amazing, but I can't argue. You're better." She pecked Adam's cheek. "But you're still my favorite."

"Damn right, I am." Adam turned to Kyla and kissed her, her arms wrapping around the back of his neck.

"Enjoy the party," Amber said, heading for the other side of the room before they started groping each other.

She stopped beside the food table and found her gaze drifting across the crowd, trying to spot a tall, handsome guy with glasses and dark blond hair that felt great between her fingers. Did her angry rejection make him go back home? He looked so hurt; she wouldn't blame him.

Amber grabbed a cup of spiked eggnog and a reindeer Christmas cookie, biting off its chocolate antlers in one chomp.

Matthew said he still loved her.

Despite more than two months of heartache, she still loved him too.

Would she throw that away because he'd made a mistake? A mistake made while he was at war with his own mind. A mistake made not out of callousness, but to shield her from his damage.

No.

She wouldn't.

Hopefully, a few hours of drinks, music, and friends would give her stressed-out brain the break it needed to figure out what to do.

"Amber!" Charlotte kissed her cheek and wiped off the red lipstick print she must've left behind. "This party's amazing! People are mingling, the food's fantastic, and the decorations are gorgeous. Thanks for putting it all together."

"I'm glad you're having fun." Her gaze drifted back around the room.

"He's not here."

Amber's eyes slid back to Charlotte. "What?"

"Matthew. He's not here." She smoothed the front of her red sequined dress. It was loose around her waist, but when her hands ran over her belly, the small baby bump showed. "You okay?"

Amber shook it off with a nod. "Great." She bit off a reindeer paw. "Want to dance?"

"Raincheck. I promised Ty I'd eat something before our set." Her eyes rolled, but it was clear she appreciated his loving concern. "See you in a few."

Amber tossed the rest of her cookie into the trash and poured the rest of the nog down her throat. The cream tempered the bourbon, but it still lit a fiery trail to her stomach. It matched the regret burning in her chest whenever she thought of how Matthew looked when he said she hated him when all she wanted was to run into his arms and say the opposite. It looked like she wouldn't get the chance that night, but hopefully, the opportunity would come soon.

She knew there was no fixing the past.

But if you're willing to do whatever it takes to learn from your mistakes, you can build a future that wouldn't need so much fixing.

45

Matthew

"Are you sure you want to do this?" Charlotte asked, the red and green bells on her earrings jingling as she studied Matthew's face. "You look like you're going to puke."

He nodded, not sure at all that he wanted to do this.

Or that he wouldn't puke.

The blaring Christmas music and chatter from the party on the other side of the curtain threatened to give him a headache on top of it.

"Take a few sips of this." She handed him a can of ginger ale. "It helps with my morning, afternoon, and middle-of-the-night sickness."

"Pregnancy sounds awesome." He took a drink and handed it back.

"There are worse side effects to unprotected sex," Sandra said. "Like herpes blisters or green goo coming out of your junk because you caught gonorrhea."

Matthew cringed at the mental image. "That's not helping me fight the urge to puke."

Tyler joined them backstage. "She's here. You ready, man?"

"To make a fool of myself in front of hundreds of people?" Matthew clutched his churning stomach. "What do you think?"

"You'll do great, Matty," Charlotte said. "When I get pre-show jitters, I imagine your brother naked. Works every time."

Matthew glared at her while she laughed. "I'm not doing that, and thanks for making my nausea worse."

Tyler clapped him on the shoulder. "You got this, bro. If you feel nervous, look at me." He arched an eyebrow at his wife. "Fully clothed."

There was only one person he wanted to look at while he did something he never thought he'd be capable of without running from the room, screaming, and vomiting simultaneously.

"Let's do it before I chicken out." Matthew stole another swig of Charlotte's ginger ale. "I wish that had vodka in it."

"You'll be fine." Charlotte gave him a quick hug. "I'll be in the front row, rooting for you."

"Break a leg, dude." Sandra fist-bumped him. "If my crazy ass can do it, anyone can."

Matthew laughed, feeling a little tension ease.

It came right back when Tyler grabbed his guitar and guided Matthew to the split in the curtains separating backstage from the crowd's view. Tyler waved at a sound guy, and the Christmas music stopped.

In his head, Matthew repeated the mantra *please don't puke* while waiting for his cue from Tyler.

With a nod, Tyler pushed his way between the curtains, and Matthew followed. The crowd cheered and clapped as they sat on the two stools at the center of the stage. He tried to avoid looking at the sea of faces while adjusting to the insane situation, mostly succeeding.

Tyler leaned toward his microphone. "Merry Christmas, motherfuckers!" More cheers erupted, and he smiled, tweaking a tuning knob on his guitar and testing the string. "My brother has something special to share with you all, so I'll let him take the lead. Go for it, Matthew."

Please don't puke.

Please don't puke.

"Hi." Matthew cleared his throat, wincing as the sound echoed through the room. "Just to warn you guys, I got exactly zero percent of the talent in the family. I apologize if your ears start bleeding."

Everyone laughed, making him feel a little less like bolting for the nearest exit. "And I'm terrible at writing anything more than a grocery list, let alone song lyrics, so again, sorry."

"Shut up and sing!"

"Take your top off!"

Matthew squinted past the bright spotlight, making out the faces of Zack and Adam, laughing in the front row.

"Zack and Adam, ladies and gentlemen." Matthew gestured to where they stood. "Later tonight, you can probably find them passed out naked in the fountain outside the hotel."

Several female voices in the room whooped while everyone else laughed.

Matthew's gaze waded through the crowd.

And there she was.

Excited flutters in his chest made him forget to be nervous, and he focused on Amber's face as she stood beside the massive Christmas tree, looking very confused. And heart-crushingly beautiful. She wore a green velvet dress with a red ribbon tied around her waist. Her hair was curled and framed her face, making her look like an angel that belonged on the tree beside her.

But her beauty had nothing to do with what she wore or how she did her makeup. When she first woke up in the morning, natural and bare, she was more beautiful than ever.

"Here goes nothing." Matthew gave Tyler a nod, and his brother's fingers plucked and danced along the twelve-string acoustic guitar.

Matthew took a steadying breath and began singing the words he'd scribbled on a bar napkin after leaving Amber's hotel room the day before. Her eyebrows drew together as she watched.

"Underneath the moon that night,

your hair shined like gold.

Beside a dumpster full of lettuce

that smelled five days old."

The edges of Amber's mouth lifted, her eyes locked on his.

"We doodled on a wall.

Can you call stick figures art?

You stole my favorite T-shirt,

and then you stole my heart."

He watched as Amber's smile collapsed. Her chin trembled like she was suddenly fighting tears.

The crowd's *aww*'s threatened to break his concentration, but Tyler gave a nod of encouragement and kept playing.

Matthew's attention returned to Amber.

"Being without you for two months

has been such a fucking bummer,

I've missed the smile and dimpled cheek

of my favorite fucking drummer."

She laughed again.

His nerves disappeared as he focused on the face he'd missed so much it hurt.

"I never thought I'd meet someone

I didn't just want but *need*.

Someone to whom I can honestly say

'I love you more than weed.'"

Amber laughed with the crowd, her hands coming up to wipe tears trailing her cheeks.

"The phrase is trite and overused,

but I've never felt like this.

Something changed inside me

with that first, perfect kiss.

Then, I fucked it all up, and I'm sorry

for the stupid shit I've done.

If you want someone to share your life with,

I hope I'm the one."

Amber moved closer to the stage, her eyes locked on his as she wove through the crowd. She stopped at the front row.

"I love you so much, Amber.

Please give me a second chance.

If you're not ready to answer,

think it over while we dance."

As planned, Tyler ended the song and started playing "Fade into You" by Mazzy Star.

It was Amber's favorite slow song, and when the first chords played, her feet stopped moving, and her cheeks flooded with fresh tears. She raced to the steps leading onto the stage and stumbled on the last one, tripping over her feet. Matthew caught her before she hit the ground, and she jumped into his arms, kissing him hard.

The room exploded with applause and deafening cheers that nearly drowned out the music.

Amber's lips moved to his ear. "You sounded terrible. Like, your singing voice is *really bad*." She pulled back to look into his eyes. "But that was the sweetest, most fucking romantic thing I've ever seen."

"I'm no deckhand turned boat captain, but—"

She shut him up with another kiss. Tears of joy filled his eyes as he held her to his chest and breathed her in.

The crowd roared on, and although Matthew would never be a rockstar like his brother or their friends, he was glad he'd been brave enough to pretend just this once.

"I promise I'll never hurt you again," he said, taking her face into his hands.

"I know." She grinned. "Just dance with me."

Amber rested her chin on Matthew's shoulder, and they swayed to the music.

Some of the other guests joined in on the dance floor, but no one else existed in that room but him and the beautiful woman in his arms.

The woman he would never be foolish enough to let go of again.

46

Amber

Amber and Matthew left the party around four in the morning. After they made up, she got to enjoy it, dancing, mingling, and sampling all the amazing food with Matthew by her side. She couldn't get over how much healthier he looked—his arms were more muscled, his posture straighter. His eyes were brighter and free of the anxious flicker the crowded ballroom would've triggered a few months ago.

The dedication to therapy and self-improvement also showed itself in other ways. His old familiar smile was back in full force, as genuine and glowing as the day they met. As he mingled and laughed with their friends, she saw the fun, carefree guy they all knew and loved before the trauma.

All night, she'd been looking forward to make-up sex, but as soon as they got to her room and started making out, they were both yawning too much to go further.

She didn't realize how much she'd missed being wrapped in his warmth as she drifted off to sleep. As sunlight filtered through the curtains and her eyes opened, she was reminded how much she missed waking up beside him, too. Their limbs were tangled, and his slow, steady breaths fluttered against her neck. She stayed still, savoring the moment. Then, an idea struck too tempting to resist.

Amber slid underneath the covers and took Matthew's cock into her mouth. It was already at half-mast, maybe from morning wood or dreaming of how they'd make up for lost time. She swirled her tongue around the sensitive spot at the base of the plump head as it swelled in her mouth.

"Mmm..." His voice was deep and gravelly with sleep and now desire. The sexy sound made her thighs press together as she slid his thickening length to the back of her throat. "Fuck, Amber."

He threw the covers off, watching her with his sleepy, hooded gaze.

She slid her hand along the shaft that was now at its full, impressive length and girth—smooth velvet sliding over steel. In the faint sunlight bleeding through the cracks in the curtains, a thick dot of precum glistened over the slit, inches from her mouth. Her tongue swirled and flicked at the head, greedily lapping up the first taste of his arousal.

Matthew's hands raked through her messy hair, fisting at the roots. "Hell of a way to wake up on Christmas Eve." He used his grip to fuck her mouth with long, deep slides that made saliva drip to her chin. With a jerk of his hips, he hit the back of her throat, and she hummed around his cock, the intensity shooting sparks of need straight to her core.

She let him slip from her mouth and wiped her chin with her wrist.

"I need you inside me." Wetness spread to her thighs, her pussy aching to be filled. Two months was a long fucking time to go without fucking.

Since they'd been apart, she'd had opportunities to hook up with other guys but turned them all down. Matthew had wrecked her for everyone else. No one would ever make her feel so good in a way that went far beyond the physical.

"Climb on top of me, gorgeous."

Amber straddled his waist, and in one swift thrust, he buried himself inside her. They both groaned at the overwhelming sensation.

"Fuck, you feel amazing." Matthew's strong hands massaged her breasts, grasping and kneading the sensitive flesh. He pinched her left nipple, and she cried out as the sensation shot between her legs. "Mmm... I can feel you getting wetter."

She rocked forward and back, the flared base of the crown rubbing her G-spot and stoking the fire blazing low in her belly. "Only for you, Matthew. No one's ever made me feel this good." It was the truth, and she wanted to hold onto that feeling and to him as long as she could—maybe even forever.

His fingertips dug into the flesh of her ass, matching her rhythm while sinking himself deeper with every pull. With a flick of his wrist, he spanked her hard, and she gasped. Now, she felt herself getting wetter.

Matthew propped himself up on his elbows, his hooded gaze falling to where their bodies joined. He groaned at the sight before his thumb slid across her bottom lip and pushed it inside. Amber circled the tip with her tongue, her cheeks hollowing out as she sucked. He moved his wet finger to her clit, rubbing in slow, smooth circles that had her panting. She groaned his name when she hit her peak, and in seconds, he was thrusting deeper, filling her with his release.

"I fucking love you, Amber." He sat up and brushed the sweat-dampened hair off her face, their eyes locking. "I love you. I never stopped and I never will."

She bent forward and kissed him as a rush of emotion swept over her. "I love you too, Matthew Hall." She pressed her lips to his chest, right above his pounding heart. "Every beautiful, complicated, messy, amazing part of you."

Amber wouldn't hide any part of herself from him again and wanted every part of him in return—his joy, fears, weaknesses, strength, and everything else that made him the man he was.

The man who'd always been an incredible friend.

The man she'd fallen in love with.

His movements stilled, his eyes searching hers. "Say it again."

"I love you. I almost said it that day at the waterfall; I just wasn't ready to get the words out. But I felt it." She pulled his face to hers and kissed him. "I never stopped either."

※

When Amber left the shower, Matthew was lying in bed with the covers to his waist and... Were those *pastries* on his stomach?

"Hungry?" he asked.

She laughed. "Is this why you wanted to shower first? So you could order room service and serve it off your naked body?"

"Sandra made me do it. And she said to have you call me Pierre and pretend we're in Paris. Do I even want to know what that means?"

She plucked a piece of croissant off his stomach and let the buttery perfection melt on her tongue. "Our friends are fucking weirdoes, and I hope they never change."

He set the croissants on the nightstand, reached under his pillow, and handed her an envelope with sprigs of holly printed on the corners. "Merry Christmas."

"Matty, you didn't have to get me anything." She took another buttery bite and sat beside him on the bed. Her finger slid under the seal to open it, and he touched her hand, stopping her. "I know I need to work to earn back your trust, but I hope you'll trust me with this."

She cocked her head, intrigued. "Should I be worried?"

"You won't like what's in the envelope, but I need you to give it a chance."

She didn't like the sound of that, but she broke the seal and pulled out the pair of tickets inside. "Happy Holidays. You've been gifted one…" Her stomach tied in knots at the words that followed. "Winter boat ride along the beautiful Willamette River." The paper shook in her hands. "Matty, I can't."

He pulled her to lie beside him with her back to his chest. "Yes, you can. I'll be with you the whole time."

She kept reading the details on the ticket. It was set for that night before sunset. "What if I can't even step on the boat and make a fool of myself?"

"Besides the captain—who better not look like Fabio—we'll have the whole boat to ourselves. The dock's right outside the hotel." He pressed a lingering kiss to her shoulder. "Trust me. You can do this."

"I'll ruin it for you. You'll be too busy talking me down from losing my shit to enjoy yourself." She tried thinking of more excuses, hoping one would make him relent and cancel. When she glanced over her shoulder, his expression made it clear nothing would work. "Why do you want to do this?"

"Because I know how much fear can hold you back from enjoying life, and how incredible it feels on the other side. I've been able to use the parking lot at the brewery since you helped me overcome my fear. At first, I still felt anxious, but seeing our drawings and remembering how beautiful you looked in the moonlight brought me back to that moment, and the fear disappeared." He took the tickets from her hand and set them on the nightstand. "Let me replace your bad memory with a good one like you did for me."

It must have been the same boats Amber watched from her suite. She had to admit, she envied how happy the riders looked as they drifted along the river. No one had fallen overboard screaming or hit their head and bled to death on the deck—at least, not that she saw. With light snow in the forecast, it would undoubtedly be a beautiful ride.

This was one of those opportunities that don't come around every day. One she'd regret if she passed it up.

"Okay," she whispered. She would let him see her in a way no man ever had—afraid and at her most vulnerable. Matthew would never push her too far. And if she did fall apart, he'd know how to help her.

The closer it got to sunset, the more nervous she was. She couldn't even finish the delicious dinner at the hotel's restaurant, plated with swirls of red and green sauces to look like a festive and delicious work of art. Her hands shook as she poked the sauces with her fork, remembering the feeling of sinking with nothing to grab onto. How the cold water stole the air from her lungs.

Amber nearly pulled out a thousand times throughout the day. But Matthew bought the gift with thoughtful intentions, and she wouldn't disappoint either of them by backing out. If she could overcome her fear of water, it would open endless possibilities for adventures they could share—kayaking in the San Juan Islands, taking the ferry to Victoria, B.C., or cruising around Hawaii.

She didn't want fear holding them back from living their best, fullest lives.

"Dress warmly," he said. "Jacket, scarf, gloves, seal carcass."

With shaking fingers, she put on her warmest gear and put her gloved hand into his. "I'm ready. I trust you."

He pulled back the hood of her coat to press a kiss to her forehead. "Let's go."

On the walk to the river, something caught her eye in a shop window, and she made Matthew stay outside while she ran in to buy it. They walked toward the water with a small shopping bag swinging from her wrist.

At the dock, her feet froze in place.

"Want me to carry you on?" He arched an eyebrow, probably only half kidding.

Amber shook her head, determined to make them both proud. After a deep inhale of frigid air, she exhaled a cloud and took another step. She grabbed the railing while Matthew held her from behind.

Her heart pounded as the boat rocked. If she fell in, the water would be much colder than when she fell into the lake as a child. It would feel like a hundred blades slicing through her skin, shocking her system, and killing her in minutes.

"It's okay, love." His gentle voice shook her from the dark thoughts. "Just step up."

"Good evening." The captain grinned, offering a hand. "Lovely night for a cruise down the river." She took his hand, and he helped her onto the boat with one smooth pull.

"You made it." Matthew was right behind her, his warm breath tickling her ear. "I'm so proud of you."

He guided her to the heated cabin, and they sat on a cushioned bench. There was a bottle of champagne in a bucket of ice, a few blankets stacked beside it. He grabbed the one on top, wrapping it around her shoulders before kissing the half-frozen tip of her nose.

"Doing okay?" he asked.

Amber nodded, too overwhelmed to speak, but as the boat rocked, she breathed through the panic threatening to break through.

The engine rumbled, and she was startled when the tether to the dock was removed, and the boat lurched. She shut her eyes, telling the anxiety tightening her chest to fuck right off.

Knowing Matthew felt as distressed or worse when she removed his blindfold in the High Notes parking lot made her even more impressed by how well he'd handled it. And she was honored he'd trusted her to guide him through it without pushing him past his limits. Plus, she enjoyed using her body to keep him focused on something good instead of the terrible memories of that spot.

She couldn't imagine he'd try anything sexual while in full view of other boats and anyone with binoculars, but just sitting beside him was nice. The tension in her shoulders released. When her eyes opened, she saw the city lights drifting past them, and her pulse kicked up for a different reason.

"It's so beautiful," she said.

As the sun set, the sky was painted with pale shades of lavender, pink, and gold. They passed under a bridge with intricate sculptures carved into its arch and mosaic brickwork underneath. Homes were decked out with twinkling Christmas lights, their reflections dancing on the water like thousands of tiny candles.

Matthew poured two glasses of champagne and as she took her first sip, movement outside the window caught her eye. White snowflakes dotted the glass before melting and sliding down like thin streams of rain.

"Thank you for doing this," she said. "It was a very thoughtful gift, even though it almost gave me a coronary."

Matthew's knuckles brushed her cheek. "Thank you for trusting me with your heart again."

"That reminds me." Amber reached into the shopping bag beside her and took out the small box inside. She held it between them, and he took it.

He removed the lid, pulling out a glass ornament shaped like a heart, tiny silver snowflakes etched in the glass. "Amber, it's beautiful. Thank you."

"I need you to understand something." She touched the hand holding the ornament. "I'm strong, but my heart can be fragile like this glass. And I'm trusting you to be more careful with it. To never break it again."

"Never again. I promise." His eyes reflected the truth in his words before he pressed a kiss to her lips. When he pulled back, they picked up their champagne flutes.

"Okay then." Amber clinked her glass against his. "Cheers to love and trust and the best fucking Christmas I've ever had."

"In the words of Zack and Adam," he said, "I'll drink to that."

Epilogue

Matthew

Five Months Later

It was early May, but the brewery was decked out like late October—fake spiderwebs stretched across the tasting counter, purple and black string lights wrapped around the microphone stands, and ghosts dangled from the beams in the ceiling. Their original plan to kick off the new music space with a Halloween party was too good to ditch, and since Matthew and Evan made the rules in that place, they stuck with it.

"There," Amber said, plugging in the last piece of equipment—the microphone in the center of the small stage. "You're officially ready to rock."

Molly nodded from the stool she was perched on as she tuned the black and white acoustic guitar in her lap. "Thanks, babe."

She'd be the first musician to play in the new space. Molly was shopping a demo around town as a solo artist while holding firmly to her guitar tech gig for Killing Daisies. She'd been with them from the beginning, as loyal and dedicated as the rest of their friends.

Amber walked to Matthew's side, and they stood back to appreciate their accomplishment.

"We fucking did it," he said. "And it only took eight months."

Amber huffed a laugh. "Life got in the way, but better late than never."

What they originally planned to do in four weeks took so long because other things had to come first. Matthew prioritized therapy, gave Evan well-deserved time off, and six weeks ago, they focused on moving Amber's stuff into the house they bought together. His condo was nice, but it didn't suit them. He wasn't a beige guy, and they were far from a beige couple. He sold it so they could buy something that was a better fit.

Amber's realtor sister Tara helped them find a two-story farmhouse with green siding and grey trim on a two-acre lot just outside Portland city limits. It was surrounded by woods and had a massive garage for Amber's drums, space in the backyard to grow sunflowers, and a lot more personality than a cookie-cutter condo could ever have.

"Is Nick coming?" Matthew asked.

"Nope." Amber wrapped an arm around his waist. "His friends invited him to the arcade. We can't compete with that."

Finishing the music space was also delayed when they helped move Nick's things from Chicago to Portland. When Kate was granted guardianship in March, he took Amber's vacated room. He was thriving at his new school, making new friends, and even talked their sisters into adopting a shelter dog. The fact that Denise was willing to put up with dog hair to make him happy said a lot.

Matthew had grown close to all of Amber's siblings and appreciated having so many people in his life who loved her as much as he did.

Evan came out of the back office and took in the finished stage. "It looks fucking awesome, guys. Nice work." He high-fived Amber and Matt as the bell jingled above the door. "Hey, Molly."

Her eyes lifted from her guitar, and a blush crept into her cheeks. "Hey."

Amber squeezed Matthew's hip. She swore something was brewing between those two, and he was starting to see it, too.

A trio of college guys walked in and sat at the tasting counter.

"Welcome to High Notes!" Amber said, her tone all cheer and sunshine. "And Happy May-oween. What can I get you?"

Matthew laughed as she took their orders, filling pint glasses from the taps beneath the counter.

"Does she work here now?" Evan muttered, earning a jab in the rib from Matthew's elbow.

"My girl can do whatever the fuck she wants in here." Matthew gestured to the stage. "This was eighty percent her, so when all the extra wallets come in to hear music tonight, you'll be kissing her fucking boots." His voice lowered so only Evan could hear. "If your lips aren't busy with Molly's."

Evan shoved him, grabbing empty glasses off a nearby table while Matthew laughed.

The rest of the day went by as usual, but when the sky turned gold and violet outside the expansive windows, Matthew's gut twisted with nerves. Would everything go well? What if there was feedback in the mics or a fuse blew?

Even more terrifying, what if Amber said no to the question he'd been dying to ask since they moved in together?

Fifteen minutes before the party began, Amber strolled behind the tasting counter and kissed him while he filled two tasting mugs with lager. "I'm so fucking excited, I could scream!" She bounced on the balls of her feet as he laughed, her blonde hair leaping off her shoulders and settling back again. "I'll be right back."

She disappeared toward the back office before he could ask where she was going. He passed the mugs to the pair of thirtysomething guys seated at the counter.

"That your girl?" one of them asked—he was short and stocky with a dark buzzcut. "She looks familiar."

Matthew lifted a shoulder. "Maybe because of this." He reached beneath the counter and tossed the latest copy of *Rolling Stone* in front of Buzzcut. A slow grin stretched Matthew's face as two jaws dropped in unison.

He'd never get over the pride of seeing his girlfriend's gorgeous face on the cover of magazines. Aside from tabloids, of course. Those, they ignored. But on this cover, she stood beside the big, bold letters he'd re-read a million times: *Best Album of the Year: Killing Daisies is Killing It!*

Buzzcut's eyes darted in the direction Amber had gone. "Fuck, dude! That was Amber Jamison?!"

Amber was getting recognized a lot more in public since Killing Daisies' third album went platinum a month ago. The band was all over music magazines and MTV. She'd done interviews for a few drumming publications and was even named number three in *Drummer's World's* top ten players of 1995. Articles claiming her band earned their status through anything but hard work and talent were a thing of the past.

Matthew chuckled, wiping a few drops of beer off the counter. "Yeah, but don't bug her. Want to try our new ale?"

As he filled three tasting mugs with Platinum Amber Ale, the guys were too busy chattering about their celebrity sighting to notice three more famous musicians walking in.

Tyler's arm was wrapped around Charlotte's shoulders, her hand draped across her swollen middle. She was due in ten days but looked ready to burst. Tyler guided her into the most comfortable seat in the house—a black velvet couch by the window. Sandra came in behind them, waving at Matthew before heading for the stage to say hi to Molly.

Matthew set the beers on the counter and walked to greet his brother. "Thanks for coming, Ty."

"It looks fucking amazing in here, Matty." Tyler wore a wide grin as he looked around, clearly impressed. Matthew loved making his brother proud. "There's no way we'd miss your big day." A corner of his mouth tilted up in a knowing half-grin. Aside from Molly, he was the only one who knew about the tiny box in Matthew's pocket.

Matthew pointed at Charlotte. "If that baby pops out on my couch, I'm sending you the cleaning bill."

She smacked his arm. "Don't you dare put that out in the universe! I came to see music and watch people enjoy your beer." Her chin tipped down as she rubbed her belly. "You hear me in there? This is *not* your birthday. Enjoy the cocoon for a few more days."

"You made it!"

Matthew turned to find Amber jogging over. In a pirate costume. A *sexy* pirate costume. The same one she'd worn two years ago that made him unable to stand up for fifteen minutes because his dick refused to calm down.

Fuck the music.

Now, all he wanted to do was drag her into the back office like a brute and pillage her beneath the jagged hemline of the tight black skirt. He imagined ripping those fishnets off with his teeth to get at the warm, wet apex of her thighs.

Amber shot him a sly grin, probably clocking the lust he couldn't disguise. She leaned in, her lips brushing his ear. "When everyone leaves, we can break the stage in properly." Her teeth nipped his earlobe before she pulled away, not helping to calm the erection pressed painfully against his zipper. He was grateful for the long flannel shirt concealing it from all the eyes in the room.

"Damn, Amber," Sandra said, plopping into the seat beside Charlotte. "You give new meaning to the term 'land ho.'"

Amber flipped her off with a grin. "Cute. I was sure you'd go with 'Captain Hooker.'" She bent over to pick up a napkin someone had dropped. Unable to resist, Matthew snuck a few glances at her very grabbable heart-shaped ass.

Holy fuck, she's trying to kill me.

As more people trickled in, he forced himself back into work mode, greeting their guests and taking beer orders. When everyone was settled in their seats, he and Evan walked to the microphone beside Molly.

"Thanks for coming, everyone," Matthew said. "This project took longer than planned, but here we are." Public speaking still wasn't his forte, but he'd be getting plenty of practice introducing the performers.

"We couldn't have done it without Amber." Evan gestured to where she stood beside a giant skeleton. "And she's the one who made this place all spooky and shit, so please give it up for her."

Applause echoed against the walls as Amber waved at the crowd.

When the room quieted, Matthew returned to the mic. "Please welcome the very first artist to grace the High Notes stage, Miss Molly Mars."

Everyone clapped and cheered, and Molly began a song she'd written herself, the melody slow and hypnotic.

Matthew took Amber's hand, guiding her to the brown leather armchair in the back of the room. He sat down, pulling her onto his lap. Her softness and warmth, along with her sweet scent, enveloped him, helping to calm his nerves.

While she watched the show, he swept the hair off her neck. "I love you, Amber."

She turned to him, a soft smile curving her lips. "I love you too. And I'm so fucking proud of you for..." Her eyes searched his. "Everything."

They'd come so far since their first kiss seven months ago. But it wasn't far enough. With Amber, he always wanted more of, well... everything.

When the song finished, everyone clapped. Then, Molly played the opening notes of "Fade into You" by Mazzy Star.

Amber's eyes sparkled as she pressed her palm to his chest.

"I think this is officially our song," she whispered against his lips.

Matthew's heart knocked wildly against her hand. "I hope so."

A crease flashed between her brows. "Are you okay? Your heart's racing."

Everyone's eyes were on Molly, so no one saw the kiss he pressed to Amber's lips or his hand sliding into his pocket. "I'm more than okay, Rockstar."

His arms encircled her, and he opened the small velvet box with his hands hovering over her lap. Her breath hitched, her eyes glossing with tears as she stared at the box. A large pear-shaped diamond was set in the center of the ring. A pair of smaller diamonds sparkled on either side as they caught the light.

"Amber, you're the one I want to wake up to for the rest of my life. I want to build so many incredible memories together that there's no more room for bad ones. And I want us to stand in front of our weirdo friends and a fake Elvis, promising to work together every day to build the beautiful life we deserve." He took the ring out, holding it between two fingers as his heart battered his ribcage. "Will you marry me?"

Tears glistened on her lashes as she scrutinized his expression. "How can you be sure this is what you want? Forever is a long time. If I say yes, that's exactly what I'd need you to promise me."

He cupped her chin, kissing her softly. "You're all I thought about while I fought to find myself again. I couldn't wait for the day when I'd finally feel ready to beg you for forgiveness and a second chance." He kissed her again. "When I did, you said yes. And I want to spend the rest of my life proving I'm worthy of that. I *am* promising you forever."

"I'll never want kids." The words rushed out as the first tears slipped to her chin. "What if you change your mind and decide you want them, and I can't give that to you?"

"I won't change my mind." He shook his head, pinning her with his gaze so she could see the certainty in his eyes. "But I hope you'll help me spoil my nieces and nephews rotten. We can drop them back at Ty's when they're cranky after all the fun and candy." He swiped a knuckle along the track of her tear. "I don't want to push you if you're not ready. I just—"

"Yes," she said as another tear broke free. He forgot how to breathe as the word sunk in. "You understand my chaotic life, put up with my crazy sisters, and no one has ever loved me like you do. You already feel like family, so this would make it official."

He swallowed the lump in his throat as her face blurred through the sheen of his tears. "Yes?"

"Yes." She took his face in her hands and kissed him hard. "I'll marry you, Matthew. You make me laugh, you make me think, and you make me wet."

He laughed, wiping his eyes on the sleeve of his flannel.

"And you make me so fucking happy," she said, "that I want to want to share my life with you too."

Matthew slipped the ring onto her finger. As he leaned in for another kiss, someone's loud gasp stopped the music.

Tyler leaped to his feet. "Oh fuck, oh fuck, oh fuck."

"Ty, what's wrong?" Matthew nudged Amber off his lap and bolted toward his brother.

"Everything's fine, Matty," Charlotte said, her cheeks crimson. "My water just broke. On your couch. Sorry, but it's your fault for jinxing it."

"Clear the path to the door, fuckers!" Sandra called out. "Anyone who tries taking a picture can follow us to the hospital so they can remove the camera crammed up your ass."

An odd sound stuttered from Matthew's lips as his brain switched gears from *holy shit, I'm engaged* to *holy shit, I'm about to be an uncle.*

"Wow. Okay. It's fine." Matthew took one of Charlotte's hands, and Tyler took the other as they lifted her from the couch. He couldn't care less about the wet spot or the hundred or so eyes watching as they got Charlotte out of the building and into Tyler's passenger seat.

"I never thought I'd say these words to my best friend," Sandra said, "but keep your legs closed, bitch." She kissed Charlotte's cheek as everyone laughed. "See you at the hospital. I'll tell them you're coming."

Sandra ran to her car and drove off.

Charlotte turned to Matthew, frowning. "Sorry I fucked up your party."

Matthew laughed. "You're about to push a human out of your body, and you're worried about my party? Get to the hospital, dork. We'll be right behind you."

He shut the car door and looked at his brother. Tyler's eyes were saucers, his face as pale as the ghosts hanging from the brewery ceiling.

Matthew pulled him in for a hug, clapping him on the back. "You got this, big brother. Need anything from the house?"

Tyler shook his head. "I put our bags in the trunk last week, just in case." When he stepped back, his eyes grew even wider with panic. "I'm really fucking scared," he whispered.

Matthew hugged him again. "I know. It's *huge*, but it's going to be okay. I promise." Tyler was always the brave one, but this time, Matthew was happy to be the one offering comfort and reassurance. "You're already an amazing brother, friend, and husband, and you're going to be the best fucking dad in the world."

Tyler let out a long, slow exhale. "Thanks, Matty."

Matthew stood in the parking lot, waving as Tyler and Charlotte drove off. Everything was about to change, but it wasn't scary anymore. He owed all the best things in his life to change.

Amber moved to his side. "Evan said he'll close up." When she laughed, he followed her line of sight to the drawings they'd made the night she got him over his fear of the spot where they stood. She clucked her tongue. "Fucking vandals. They deserve a good spanking for drawing on your nice, clean wall."

He swatted her ass with his palm, the sharp sound cracking in the cold night air. She gasped at the sting of pain before aiming a wicked grin his way, the gold coins in her necklace glinting in the moonlight.

"After we meet that baby," she said, "we have lots of celebrating to do." She surprised him with a slap to his ass cheek that made his laughter echo in the parking lot. "And more of that, too."

Matthew grabbed their jackets, and they took off for the hospital.

"I can't wait to see that little face!" Amber gripped his knee as he drove. "I wonder what name they settled on."

"We're about to find out." He smiled, his head shaking in disbelief. "I can't fucking believe Tyler's about to be a dad."

"Poor guy looked terrified and thrilled at the same time."

"Kind of like when I held out that ring waiting for a 'yes' or a 'go fuck yourself.'" A raincloud exploded overhead, and he turned on the wipers full blast.

In the hospital, they followed signs to the maternity ward on quick feet, the damp soles of their shoes squeaking on the tile floor. Finally, they reached the nurses' station.

Matthew slapped his hands on the desk. "We're looking for Charlotte Ross...er, Hall's room. I'm her brother-in-law."

The nurse checked a chart and pointed left. "Room twelve."

They ran until they reached the door. Amber opened it a crack, peeking in before pushing it wide.

"You're about to be a mom!" Amber gently hugged Charlotte while she chomped ice chips.

The hair around Charlotte's face was damp with sweat, and Tyler gently brushed it back. Her expression was tense, a crease between her eyebrows hinting at how afraid she must be. People had babies every day, but anything could go wrong. And knowing you're in for the worst pain of your life can't be easy.

Matthew hugged her next. "Looking good, Warrior Woman." He glanced over her shoulder at Tyler. "Did you call Mom?"

"Yeah, she's coming from a work training thing in Spokane." Tyler looked more relaxed now. He was a pro at cool under pressure, especially when someone he loved required his focus.

"Need anything, sweetie?" Amber rubbed Charlotte's arm.

Charlotte gave a weak nod while her eyes squeezed shut and her hands gripped the blankets. "More ice chips, a fan, and a lot of fucking drugs."

Tyler frowned, refilling her cup with ice chips before fanning her with a pamphlet with a grinning, toothless baby on the front. "Is it that bad already?"

She nodded. "And this is only the beginning. Good thing I'm tough as fuck."

"Good thing." Tyler grinned, bending over to kiss her forehead. "Both my girls are fighters."

Charlotte smiled at that. "Your daughter must want to prove you right. She just elbowed me right in the kidney." She rubbed her side before her gaze dropped to Amber's left hand. Charlotte seized her wrist, gaping at the ring. "*Excuse me*?! When did this happen?" Her eyes flicked to Matthew.

"When Molly played the Mazzy Star song," Matthew explained. "She and Ty were the only ones who knew. I wanted to see your shocked face when you found out, and as always, you didn't disappoint."

The door flew open, and Sandra burst in. "Oh, my god! Charlotte! Sorry I'm late, but I had to pee so bad my eyes were floating." She squealed with joy on her way to hug her best friend right above the swell at her middle. Right after Charlotte released Amber's wrist, Sandra grabbed it. "Matthew Thelonius Hall!"

His eyebrows shot up. "Thelonius?"

"I forgot your middle name, so I improvised," Sandra said. "Congratulations, you guys! What a wild fucking day."

"*Fuck.*" Charlotte cursed through gritted teeth as she fisted the blankets in her lap.

Tyler sat beside her, taking her hand. "Breathe through it, baby."

He inhaled loudly and slowly before exhaling in a rush. Charlotte joined in when he did it again. After a few minutes, her body relaxed, her expression softening.

"Why don't we give you guys some space?" Matthew aimed his thumb at the door. "I'll grab you stuff in the cafeteria."

"I'm not hungry, but grab food and coffee for Ty." Charlotte wiped the sweat off her brow. "We might be here a while."

Matthew nodded, taking one last look at the nervous but excited couple whose lives were about to never be the same. He walked into the hallway, the women trailing behind.

"My vagina hurts just *thinking* about what's about to go down in there." Sandra winced. "I'm happy for them, and I'll be one fun-ass auntie, but there's no way in hell I'd sacrifice my body and disposable income for a crotch goblin who spends its first few years shitting itself and crying."

"Amen, sister." Amber grabbed Matthew's hand as they walked toward the elevators. "It's a shame Christa didn't feel the same."

"Yeah, sorry things didn't work out," Matthew said. "I really liked her."

Sandra shrugged. "It's for the best. Hopefully, she finds a woman who wants kids and a man willing to splooge into a cup so they can have one."

They took the elevator to the cafeteria, and when the doors opened, the scents of hamburgers and pepperoni pizza hit his nose. What better way to keep patients returning than to offer delicious, artery-clogging food by the truckload?

"I'm going to wash my hands real quick," Sandra said. "Grab me an iced tea and any cookie that's not oatmeal."

Matthew and Amber picked up trays and headed for the start of the food line.

"What sounds good, pirate lady?" He pressed a kiss to her cheek. "Besides ducking into a janitor's closet."

"Matthew?"

A female voice behind them turned their heads.

"Jessica." Matthew couldn't keep the spike of disappointment out of his tone. "Wow. How are you?"

"Great. I'm dating a doctor in geriatrics. And still plugging away at med school. You?"

"Also great."

Amber scratched her chin with the middle finger of her left hand, and Jessica's eyes flickered to the diamond ring beside it.

"I can see that. You're getting married." Jessica's face turned pink, and her eyes narrowed as they darted to Amber. "To her."

Amber grinned. "Yeah, he proposed like an hour ago. We're very happy, and I wouldn't change a thing." She emphasized the last five words, and Jessica's face went from pink to red. "Charlotte's having her baby, so we have to get back. Good luck with your doctor."

Jessica bolted for the elevator, disappearing behind the closing doors.

Matthew moved his lips to Amber's ear as she grabbed a few premade sandwiches and put them on her tray. "I thought you were going to piss on me to mark your territory."

"Whatever floats your boat." She snickered. "Sorry I was catty, but she's a fucking idiot for letting you get away." Amber reached for a boxed salad and added it to her tray, along with a chocolate chunk cookie and an iced tea.

"For the record..." He planted a kiss on her neck, and she shivered. "I wouldn't change a thing about you either, Rockstar."

They paid, and when Sandra left the bathroom, they headed back to Charlotte's room with the food and a few coffees to help keep everyone conscious if the baby took her time coming into the world. When they reached Charlotte's room, her dad was pacing the floor outside her door. Zack leaned against the wall, chatting up a candy striper while Adam yawned and rubbed his eyes. He must've had another late night with Charlotte's cousin, Kyla. It was still hard to believe Adam had an actual girlfriend. Apparently, no one was safe from the poke of Cupid's arrow, even shameless players.

"Looks like the gang's all here." Matthew fist-bumped Zack and Adam. "Hey, Mr. Ross. Why aren't you guys inside?"

Charlotte's dad sighed, looking nervous for his daughter. "Her contractions are a few minutes apart, so they're checking her out. And we're family now, son. Please call me Mickey."

Adam's gaze slid to Amber, and he laughed. "Why are you dressed like a fucking pirate?" He slapped his forehead when the realization hit. "Fuck, your brewery thing. Totally forgot it was tonight."

She playfully shoved his arm. "Catch up on sleep, Loverboy."

A petite, dark-haired woman in a lab coat came out of the room. "Not much time now. You'll be a grandpa before morning." She patted Mickey's arm, and his shoulders relaxed. "Tyler's doing an excellent job as her coach, so no need to worry about your girl."

"Can we go in?" Sandra asked.

The doctor shook her head. "Might want to give them some time. She's approaching the most uncomfortable stage and needs as few distractions as possible so she can focus on her breathing and, soon, pushing. I'll find you all in the waiting room when it's time." She smiled warmly and walked into the next room.

Mickey stopped pacing. "A grandpa. I can't fucking believe it." His gaze swung between Amber and Sandra. "Pardon my French, sweethearts."

"Don't sweat it, Mickey." Sandra hugged his arm, concealing his very intimidating tattoo of an eagle perched on a sword. "I can't fucking believe it either."

After they spent three hours in the waiting room, the doctor returned. Amber's head lifted off Matthew's shoulder, and Zack smacked Adam's forehead to wake him up. Mickey popped out of his chair, waiting for the doctor to speak.

"Charlotte and the baby are doing fine."

Matthew smiled as ecstatic tears flooded his eyes.

"Are you all ready to say hello?" she asked.

"Hell yes, we are!" Sandra swiped her knuckle beneath her watery eyes. Matthew had never seen her cry before, and it touched him how happy she was to meet his brand-new niece.

Matthew opened the door slowly, his heart clenching when he spotted the tiny pink bundle in his brother's arms. "Tyler…"

"Crazy, right?" Tyler looked exhausted, but a broad grin lit up his face. "Come meet your niece, Anna Jude."

"Jude?" Matthew's voice cracked with emotion. "You named her after dad?" He hadn't expected that.

"And my mom." Charlotte smiled at Mickey, and he joined everyone in the crybaby club.

Matthew wiped his tears before holding out his hands and cradling little Anna Jude in the crook of his arm. "Hey, little girl. You don't look so tough."

Everyone laughed, and he met Charlotte's eyes. She looked exhausted, too, but she glowed with happiness as if she'd just exited the stage after the performance of her life.

"You should've seen her throwing fists and screaming when she came out," Charlotte said. "She won't take any shit from anyone."

Matthew looked down at the baby in his arms—the tiny nose, long eyelashes, and dark shock of hair on top of her head that matched his brother's. Tears blurred the little face, and he blinked them away. "You don't know how lucky you are to be stuck with these two." He dipped his head and kissed the impossibly soft skin between her eyes. His chin lifted. "Who's next?"

Mickey stepped up, greeting his first grandchild with wet eyes and a wistful grin. "Nice to finally meet you, sweetheart."

Sandra leaned her head on Mickey's shoulder. "Have you ever seen anything so beautiful?"

His head lifted to look at his daughter. "Sure have." They shared a smile, and he kissed the baby's forehead. "But you're a very close second."

Mickey passed her to Amber, and she held the baby close to her chest. "Hey, little rockstar. Auntie Amber's going to teach you how to play drums someday."

Sandra took a turn before handing her off to a reluctant Zack, who was terrified of dropping her and ending up a wad of gunk on the bottom of Tyler's shoe. After a few seconds of standing as stiff as a post, staring at the baby like she might shit on his arm, he gave Adam a turn.

"She weighs like nothing," Adam said as he stared at little Anna.

Sandra chuckled. "I'm sure Charlotte's boobs will fix that."

Looking suddenly uncomfortable about a subject that'd always been his favorite, Adam passed the baby back to Charlotte.

"Kyla said to say congrats," he said. "She'll swing by tomorrow after work."

The transfer made the baby stir, a tiny pair of eyes sliding open.

"Hey, you." Charlotte kissed her forehead. "Your eyes are a beautiful blue like your daddy's."

Tyler sat beside her on the bed. "She has your nose. And that cute little dip in your top lip."

Their gazes stayed fixed on their daughter, their eyes sparkling with love and awe.

"We're all wiped, guys," Matthew said, fighting back another wave of tears. The massive shift that'd just taken place in all their lives was overwhelming, but he was so fucking happy for them. "And it looks like the three of you could use some rest, too."

"Yeah, we'll check in tomorrow." Amber hugged Charlotte and the baby all at once before making her way to Tyler and hugging him, too. "Congratulations, soon-to-be brother-in-law."

When they reached the parking garage, everyone said their goodbyes and drifted to their cars on tired, shuffling feet.

Before Matthew could turn the key in the ignition, Amber stopped him.

"It's sweet how much you already love that baby. And how happy you are for your brother and Charlotte."

He could hear the dip of a *but* in her tone and stayed quiet, waiting for her to continue.

"Have you changed your mind?" she asked. "About not wanting kids?"

Matthew shifted in his seat, angling his body to face Amber. "No. I promised you I wouldn't change my mind, and nothing that happened up there changed a thing." He took her hand, stroking the backs of her knuckles with his fingertips. "What about you?"

Her lips tipped up in a smile that made him fall even more in love with her, if it was possible. "Not even a little bit. She's adorable, and I can't wait to hold her again and watch her grow up, but no. I still don't want that for myself. Or for us. You're enough for me and always will be, Matthew Hall."

Sometimes, Matthew looked at Amber and wondered what miracles he'd performed in a past life that earned him this one. He had a beautiful fiancé, a business he loved, a family that just grew bigger by one, and friends he could trust with his life.

The nightmares were over, he felt stronger than ever, and his biggest, most impossible dreams had come true. The path he took getting there hadn't been easy, but it had been worth it.

And he wouldn't change a thing.

Acknowledgments

Thank you to my brilliant critique partners, Bella, Ellie, Samantha, Lisa, and Theresa. I couldn't have reached the finish line without your priceless feedback. You all challenged me to get to know my characters more deeply, gave high-fives when I needed them, and helped me decide which darlings to kill. It's been a joy reading your work in return, and I look forward to seeing what comes out of your fabulous brains next.

Thank you to my amazing editor, Misha, for your mad skills, guidance, and encouragement. Your questions challenged me to dig deeper and the wisdom you shared helped me to shape and polish this book into one that I'm incredibly proud of.

I also want to thank my wonderful husband, Jason, who'd never picked up a romance novel until I started writing them. That's love. Thank you for being my first eyes on everything I write and for being understanding when I lock myself away for hours. Thanks for answering my million musician-related questions and for (mostly) not complaining when dinner was frozen pizza again because I was busy tapping away at my keyboard. I appreciate your love and support more than you'll ever know. I can't wait for our next coffee talk.

Thank you to my boys for all the tech help and cheerleading. Someday I'll write something you can actually read.

Thank you to Melanie and Tracy for all your support and encouragement. You both helped to inspire this series centered around love, loyalty, resilience, and friendship. Thank you for all the laughter, tipsy talks in bar bathrooms, and for always having my back. And thank you for reading my stories and giving your honest, but always kind, feedback. I love you both like crazy! Bring on the sangria.

HUGE thank you to my amazing readers! I appreciate all your feedback, reviews, and support on this journey, and I hope you enjoyed reading Matthew and Amber's happily-ever-after as much as I enjoyed writing it. I can't wait to share what's coming up next!

About the Author

Stephanie Louise has been obsessed with books since *Charlotte's Web* broke her heart when she was seven. She wrote short stories and poetry growing up, and now writes spicy love stories that keep the pages turning.

Stephanie lives in the beautiful Pacific Northwest with her husband, two sons, and way too many crazy pets. She has a B.A. in English from Washington State University. When she's not writing, she's hiking in the rain, going to rock concerts, or cooking something loaded with garlic.

For updates, bonus content, and exclusive sneak peeks at upcoming releases, sign up for my monthly-ish newsletter on my website: http://www.stephanie-louise.com

Email: stephanielouisebooks@gmail.com

Instagram: http://instagram.com/authorstephanielouise

Facebook: http://facebook.com/authorstephanielouise

TikTok: @authorstephanielouise